CW01460875

MUMMIFIED
MOON

EARTHQUAKE WAR

MUMMIFIED
MOON
PC NOTTINGHAM

4 Horsemen
Publications, Inc.

Mummified Moon
Copyright © 2022 PC Nottingham. All rights reserved.

4 Horsemen
Publications, Inc.

4 Horsemen Publications, Inc.
1497 Main St. Suite 169
Dunedin, FL 34698
4horsemenpublications.com
info@4horsemenpublications.com

Cover and Typeset by S. Wilder
Editor Jen Paquette

All rights to the work within are reserved to the author and publisher. No part of this publication may be reproduced, stored in a retrieval system, or transmitted in any form or by any means, electronic, mechanical, photocopying, recording, scanning, or otherwise, except as permitted under Section 107 or 108 of the 1976 International Copyright Act, without prior written permission except in brief quotations embodied in critical articles and reviews. Please contact either the Publisher or Author to gain permission.

All characters, organizations, and events portrayed in this novel are either products of the author's imagination or are used fictitiously. All brands, quotes, and cited work respectfully belongs to the original rights holders and bear no affiliation to the authors or publisher.

Library of Congress Control Number: 2022945565

Print ISBN: 979-8-8232-0062-2
Hardcover ISBN: 979-8-8232-0140-7
Ebook ISBN: 979-8-8232-0061-5
Audio ISBN: 979-8-8232-0060-8

To my three greatest loves: C-Z-E

TABLE OF CONTENTS

ΛCKNOWLEDGMENTS

THERE ARE SO many people to thank. You, dear reader, for picking up this book in the first place. The amazing team at 4HP for taking a chance on me and guiding me through this process. The phenomenal narrator who brought these characters to life. I was also blessed with some amazing critique partners: N.C. Scrimgeour, Michael Clark, Jaci M. Lunera, D. Everett Thomas, Kaela C. Woodruff, Cole Layne, Sam Barclay, Cyra King, Jon Gerung, Peter Manesbridge, Loren Huxley, Billie Grey, Tiffany O'Haro, Tracy Nelson, Maia James, Lance Andrews, and the whole "Cru" at the Radio Freewrite podcast. All of you in some way helped get this manuscript better. Dear reader, they are all amazing creators and worth checking out.

ONE

Hen4 Moon, fifty years after the Eleva War armistice

NOTHING QUITE HELD a mix of adventure, possibility, and death like a museum. Ready to be part of life-changing educational experiences for patrons, Alize strutted toward the employee room but paused in front of her favorite exhibit—a crumbling stone tablet covered in glyphs. She had a few minutes before she'd be officially late.

The piece had also drawn a little girl's attention, and she was dragging her father by the wrist toward Alize. The little girl could've been Alize's younger sister, with the same bright wonder in those dark eyes. Dyed pink hair was the only missing ingredient. And years of poverty, most likely.

Alize brushed a rogue curl behind her ear and knelt, meeting the kid's eye. "Want to know what those glyphs mean?"

Sharing the kid's contagious smile, Alize pointed to the museum's least appreciated piece. This allowed her to set down the stimbrew cups she'd been holding, pushing the carrier out of the exhibit's spotlight. Hopefully, nobody caught a whiff of the steaming beverages.

Under the too-dim fluorescent light, the young girl nodded, eyes widening.

Rising, Alize pointed to the top line of the carving behind the duraglass. "We think the phrase is Au-OM-Ru-OH-Y B'aD, LaA." She pronounced each syllable with care, mouth respectfully contorting. Responding to the girl's puzzled expression, she simplified. "Om-b'dlah."

The little girl mimicked Alize's pronuncia-tion. "Ombla?"

The kid's dad cocked an eyebrow. "That an Arkouda dialect?"

"No, it's Chamayna. But that's a common assump-tion. This is from a much older language family. The species was lost to history, so we only know tiny fragments about their civilization. The reason why 'Chamayna' sounds like an Arkouda word is—"

Grimacing, he whispered, "Cause those imperialist bastards think they own everything?" He pointed at his gravity harness, glowing a faint blue. Hen4's artifi-cial gravity was tailored to the Arkouda, not Humans.

The kid tugged on Alize's pant leg. "Um, how can you read the words?"

The man thumbed the gravity harness around his neck. "She works here, honey. She probably has a doctorate. Professional archaeologist or something.

Congratulations, by the way. You're probably the first Human to get a degree like that."

Alize gulped—not lying if she stayed silent, right? And she'd *eventually* be Dr. Alize Oze. She'd only received an emphatic "no" from the university board, which wasn't a complete no. All the same, Alize casually sidestepped in front of the cups of aromatic stimbrew that she needed to bring to the breakroom.

"I've spent so much of my life in the museum. You pick things up eventually." There. Truth. No need to clarify. "If you study, you can learn these ancient languages, too."

"But what do those glips say in Human?"

Alize's correction was gentle, the way Pops taught her. "Glyphs. Well, the problem is the Chamayna disappeared before the Arkouda ascended. All we have are educated guesses."

Other museum patrons milled around behind them, examining the more popular exhibits from the Eleva War. Not as much traffic in the prehistory wing. The stimbrew she barely blocked wafted up, cutting through the fading scent of cleaners. *Bad sign. I'll hear it if this wing doesn't smell like Arkouda soap soon.*

Alize stole a quick glance at the timepiece on her gravity harness. It flickered to note her shift had started. At least Dr. Dikaio wouldn't berate her in front of patrons.

Grinning wide, Alize said, "I think this is telling us the location of a superweapon."

"A superweapon?" The kid's eyebrows disappeared beneath frizzy bangs.

"Yeah. A weapon so powerful, they feared its name. The middle glyph says 'unspeakable.' And those six repeated glyphs on the second and fourth line—" She pointed to them individually, letting parent and child follow her. Alize couldn't hide her smile. She was a professor with an enraptured class of two. "B'ad-RoEoA. Those all say the same thing: a weapon of unspeakable power." She indicated the center glyph. "And this says 'transmit.' So I think they wanted to send it somewhere."

Retreating a step, the man folded scrawny arms over his chest. "So why'd they disappear if they possessed this unspeakably powerful weapon? They should've been dominant instead of the Arkouda."

Alize's grin widened. "I thought you'd ask that." She turned her gaze to the kid. "Weapons are dangerous to the user if they're pointed in the wrong direction."

A snarling female voice broke her concentration. "Oze." She incorrectly pronounced her last name: one syllable, of course. "What'd I tell you about bothering patrons?" All three meters of Dr. Dikaio lumbered forward, speaking in Arkouda. "You're late. Again. And if the stimbrew's cold, you'll be sorry." She turned her furry white head, peering down at the man. Without changing tone or language, she asked, "Provincial, was the custodian bothering you?"

He stiffened, averting his gaze. In clumsy Arkouda, he responded, "N-no, madam. The worker was helpful."

The kid lacked her dad's etiquette, and in Human, said, "She told us about the superweapon!"

Dr. Dikaio placed a heavy white paw on Alize's shoulder. Probably appeared friendly, but the weight and pressure threatened shoulder dislocation. With Dr. Dikaio's three hundred kilograms, snapping Alize would be simple. No repercussions, of course.

Lowering her head and bringing her snout to Alize's ear, Dikaio growled, "Get your scrawny ass in the breakroom and clock in before I get a new beggar to dust the bots." Glancing at the parent and child, she said, "Our custodian will not bother you again. Please, enjoy your stay and don't forget to visit the gift shop."

Released from Dr. Dikaio's vice grip, Alize slumped toward the breakroom to deliver the pungent stim-brew. One exhibit after another, each full of awesomeness and knowledge, most of which she could recite to any patron willing to lend an ear, just like Pops. Not that most patrons cared to listen to Pops due to his ubiquitous custodial jumpsuit.

With her hip, she opened the "Employees Only" door, entering sideways, preserving the stimbrew carrier's stability. Earth help her if she dropped one again. The door, meant for Arkouda—like the rest of the museum's architecture—towered over her, and only the handle's automated assistance mechanism let her open it.

The breakroom, doubling as a cramped locker room, reeked of the night shift's takeout. They probably ordered from the place that overdid the *bachar* spices. Even if Alize emptied the trash on her scheduled rounds later, she'd get blamed for the stench. It didn't pair well with the permanent musty sweat, either.

"Hey, Oze," called a familiar growling voice—Filenada, the only Arkouda who pronounced Alize's last name correctly with both syllables. "Bring anything good?" She lumbered over, gently shaking the floor with each step, fastening her guard's armor over her torso. Fitting into her armor required a few extra huffs and wheezes.

"Talking in Human like a lowly Provincial? And yes, only the best." Alize joined Filenada's protocol breach. The monitors in Arkouda armor didn't perform as well with deciphering "new" languages like Human.

"Stim brew?" Clearly, they discussed matters of utmost secrecy. Fil whiffed and stuck out her tongue. "Too much cream, I bet. Mental note: don't go into the bathroom after any admins today."

"Stimbrew. One word, Fil. Don't breathe in between the syllables. Ugh, you're right. And I'll be stuck fixing those toilets."

Filenada scratched her white fur and cocked her head, a grin climbing up her muzzle. "So, you brought stimbrew... anything else?"

Alize winked and withdrew a bag from her jacket pocket. "Future archaeologists can find everything. Proudly presenting a recipe from prewar Earth."

"Protein butter?" Filenada's long tongue emerged, wafting day-old mead breath over Alize.

"Gross. Don't say that."

"Whatever." Filenada grabbed the bag from Alize. "Best thing Humans ever made."

The compressed peanut scent teased Alize's nostrils, reminding her of a simpler time. "Right." Alize placed the stimbrew on the center table and opened her locker.

"Present company excluded, of course."

"Wow. Who taught you that phrase?" Alize scanned her locker. Jumpsuit, toolbox, and a row of handmade paper flowers crafted from the university board's rejection letters.

With the addition of last week, almost enough for a bouquet. After a sigh, Alize glanced over her shoulder at her friend.

"Thanks. No clue what it means—heard it in a movie."

"You're watching Human movies?"

"Trying. They're all weird. Something explodes, and somebody walks away without watching it."

Alize gently scoffed and pulled on her grimy jumpsuit. The oil stains and stench resisted all attempts at removing them after this long. Still too big, but why bother giving her a fitting uniform if this one bore the right name? Years of dust and machine lubricant would've turned most noses, but the dirt and stench were from Pops' lifetime of hard work. All so she could study and follow her passion. Yet here she was, folding up another rejection slip.

Fil cleared her throat. "Hey, Leeze?"

"Yeah?"

"What's a plarbr? I heard a Human mutter it when I walked by."

"Huh?"

"Kinda looked like a dorky version of you. Kid with him."

Alize timed her grunt with her locker slamming. "He compared you to an extinct animal from Earth. It's a derogatory term Humans use for Arkouda sometimes."

"Plarbrs?" A yellow light on Fil's armor near her shoulder glowed, indicating tardiness.

"Polar bears. And I'm not calling you one; I'm clarifying."

Filenada casually closed the distance. "You wouldn't dare." With a light tap to her armor, a small compartment opened, and Fil pulled out a cube, which she unfolded into a rifle. She aimed her guard's weapon at Alize. "Oh, don't make that face. Brighten up. It's not loaded. I haven't accidentally shot anyone in weeks."

"It's *lighten up*, and watch where you point that. The barrel's longer than my legs. Only Arkouda think weapons are funny."

Fil gulped. "Sorrysorrysorry. I'm a good shot. Not like you with darts, but still." She glanced down the barrel. "And the safety's—" she quickly rotated the handle, "the safety's on, so nothing to worry about."

"Hey, nobody's near my dart skill. That's the one thing I'm allowed to brag about, and it's gotten us more free drinks than your arm wrestling. And you of all people shouldn't joke about guns. You wouldn't be stuck guarding a museum if—"

"Hey now. I'd rather guard a museum and get snacks with you than go on the front lines, risking my tail. See the news about that Human attack?"

Alize opened the back door for Filenada. They trudged through the hallway toward the maintenance room, passing motivational posters and an employee of the month board from which Human entries were distinctly absent.

"Please don't say 'a Human attack.' We don't all support them. And yes. My professor mentioned something in class. They hit an archaeological dig site on the other side of the galaxy."

Filenada twitched her round ears and winced. "Oof. Archaeology class?"

"Those are the only classes I take. So yes."

"Gimme a break. I'm still hungover." Fil's ears drooped. "So how awkward was that?"

"Well, everyone stared at me. Nice to be judged for two different reasons."

A passing Arkouda docent stared at them, and Fil clicked her tongue while nudging Alize gently to switch languages.

"One of the other students actually asked me why I haven't turned anyone from Earthquake in. Like, hello, do I have their tattoos or haircut?"

"You didn't tell them your best friend's Arkouda? I feel like that's an easy out."

"And hurt your image? Never. They wouldn't even let me explain how I don't share Earthquake's politics."

After a devious grin and wink, Fil asked, "Hey, who asked? An Arkouda or a Lo-sat?"

"That's not important. For all you know, there are other Humans in the class, too. Maybe other Provincial species."

Fil chuckled and returned to speaking Human. "So Lo-sat, then?"

"Fine. The person who asked the prejudicial question *happened* to be Lo-sat."

"Damn scalies."

"Fil!"

"What?"

"Look, I gotta get to the repair shop. Dr. Dikaio's on a warpath today, so avoid her bad side."

"Impossible when all her sides are bad." Clearing her throat, Fil hunched on her knees to get closer to eye level and changed her tone. "Don't take *skata* from Dikaio or any of your classmates, all right? I don't understand all your theories, but I know you're right. If you stand around, waiting for everyone else's approval, you'll never make it anywhere." The yellow late light on her armor intensified, signifying docked pay.

"Thanks, Fil. There's some peanut butter stuck on your lip."

"Always watching out. See ya, Leeze."

With their ceremonial fist-paw bump, they parted ways.

Alize entered her workshop, the dust of the interior matching the grime of her inherited jumpsuit. Today's repair and clean jobs cluttered the conveyor belt and walls. "Too expensive to have a bot do these, huh?" she muttered. She turned up her nose once the oil and chemical odors hit her. She never noticed it as a kid, but now it made her want to gag.

How could Pops find so much meaning in this work?

She studied the photographs of herself and Pops which decorated the wall, safely tucked above tools and cleaning implements. Starting a shift any other way would disrespect tradition. The pictures tracked Pops' so-called career in the museum and her childhood.

Helping in the workshop and playing on the conveyor belt was fun then, but now, doing this to pay bills? Awful. Roaming the exhibits in years past brought joy. Now? Only a race to dodge Dr. Dikaio, with the occasional chance to drop knowledge flowers on unsuspecting patrons. She opened the cleaner bot's hatch. Fine strands of Human hair clogged up gears.

She tsked. "You only like Arkouda fur and Lo-sat scales, dontcha?"

The machine didn't reply. Not like it would, anyway. Not for Provincials. A long strand of hair wrapped itself around the bot's gears. Sighing, she grabbed the tweezers.

At least she had tonight's date. One of Pops' friend's kids. Not like she could meet anyone on her own with her class schedule. He wasn't the charming prince promised by prehistoric myths and fairy tales, but he acted interested. Sparingly.

Better to have someone who's meh than nobody, right?

Fil insisted Alize could do better, and Pops didn't know the whole story.

Behind the conveyor belt, a new photograph poked through—Alize and Filenada at the Goddess Festival work party.

Fil had scrawled in shaky pawscript: "Always a raging!" Unlike their stuffy coworkers, they'd decided to have a few beforehand. Arguably a few too many.

"Rager," Alize corrected the phantom with a smile. Drunk Filenada was quite the sight to behold. Maybe they'd need to get a round, or seven, after tomorrow's dissertation presentation. It couldn't possibly go worse than the last one. That horrendous dressing-down made for quite the large paper flower.

Hours whittled by as Alize repaired and replaced the legions of thankless bots, each one's clogged hair and old oil stench slowly transforming to the chemical aroma of cleaners and fresh fluids. All these honeycomb-shaped maintenance bots would clean and maintain the museum floor, yet none would deign to tidy her workspace.

Programming one to clean for her would be simple enough, but then she'd have to deal with Dr. Dikaio or some other pompous clerk complaining about her hijacking the system.

She couldn't concentrate on mentally preparing her next presentation, so she turned on the news audiocast. Wasn't good. More of Earthquake's actions. "Harping on the dig site attack," she grumbled. "Of course."

The Collective's spins were always interesting, though. "These extremists hate our values and want to destroy our culture. Enlist today!"

Why those Earthquake chumps would attack archaeologists was anybody's guess, but they must have an actual reason. Rational people wouldn't go toe-to-paw with Arkouda in battle lightly, as Filenada proved in every bar after discovering Human arm wrestling. Alize clicked off the news and slogged through the rest of her shift, playfully responding to the occasional ping on her omni-tablet from Filenada's armor.

Leaving the workshop, she glanced at the message over the door Pops scrawled before his last shift. "This is a step to something better, Lee-Z. I love you."

That wall scrawling comprised the single topic Filenada never joked about—the sentimentality of manual writing crossed all cultures. One last message from her pinged: "Leeze, go slaughter on that date tonight. Break your dry spell!" The rest of the message wasn't appropriate for the workplace, but it garnered a smile and blush.

Alize chuckled. *I won't tell her it's "slay." Her way's better.* Her smile faded as the specter of tomorrow's dissertation presentation loomed. They told her this would be her last chance for approval.

A ping from Filenada chimed, and Alize glanced at her omni-tablet. The message read: "Earthquake attacked again. Lots of casualties, apparently."

TWO

BINARY PINK MOONS illuminated the planet's salty crystalline surface. Between a cracked mesa and a long-forgotten parched riverbed, a huddle of archaeologists' tents shuddered in the breeze. The gun-toting Humans between the tents enjoyed greater freedom of movement with their gravity harnesses switched off.

A sharp gust kicked up azure sand around Rick Crith at the front of his squadron and defeated target. Cold pistol in hand, Rick steadied his breathing. Pointing a loaded weapon at a civilian's head afforded no joy, even if the person in question was Arkouda. Threatening the unarmed wasn't his modus operandi, but neither was disobeying orders. *He doesn't need to know I'd rather let him live,* Rick thought.

Rick puffed his cheeks to get the correct Arkouda pronunciation. "Last chance." The hidden camera affixed to his breather mask would capture the confession and allow Rick to let this guy live.

Guy's a historian. Not government, not military. Dammit all.

Even though he'd incapacitated his captive with precise gunshots to the knees, a cornered Arkouda wasn't above swiping and biting. Rick didn't dare inch closer.

The civilian whimpered and eyed Rick's shoulder socket where his arm used to be. "Fine," he said, returning his gaze to Rick's eyes. "The Arkouda weren't the first to master interplanetary travel. Those were our findings. The Collective won't publish the information and plans to cut our funding. Please…"

"No. That's—that's not what we're here for." Maybe Monsieur Tecton would want that tidbit, but that'll have to get edited. "Admit what the Collective did to Humans."

The historian's expression changed. "Excuse me?"

"You erased our culture and our history. Destroyed the Mars colony. Passed laws to weaken us. Admit it."

The Arkouda snarled. "We only erased what didn't serve the Collective. We found you in squalor and rescued you. Humans owe us. Do you think anything I say will make more Provincial scum rally to your pitiful cause?"

Orders were orders. After a fractional hesitation, Rick sighed as he pulled the trigger.

Crack!

The plasma bullet ripped through the historian's dark eye, leaving him winking in death. Purple blood splattered on the corpse's white fur and on Rick's boots. *Now some damn fanatic will want to buy my boots.* Even though this mission failed, he'd earn some extra credits for killing an Arkouda per Earthquake's policy. He knew a homeless shelter which could use his bonus.

He stooped over the Arkouda's splattered brains and foraged for identification on the corpse. Upon discovering this guy's name, he memorized it and updated his list. *I'll find a way to give you a proper funeral.*

Rick holstered his pistol and waved to the rest of his crew. "He wouldn't comply. We'll get what we need, one way or another." Phantom pains from his missing left arm tingled, and he fought the instinct to scratch his absent tricep. Rick walked around a cowering Lo-sat historian whose verdant scales shimmered in the harsh sunlight, using his long tail and thin claws to cover his snout.

Amid billowing tents and blasted digging drones, the various recruits scattered throughout the dig site. Homemade rifles in hand, each loomed over cowering historians and technicians—most of which sported thin frames or noticeable paunches instead of soldiers' builds.

The aliens shuddered behind overturned tables and piles of excavated sand. One Lo-sat held a hand shovel with his tail, as if he could defend himself.

Rick grunted. "We're not getting anything here. Time to ship out!"

Moreno, Rick's second-in-command and fifteen years his junior, addressed the squad. "You heard him, Earthquake. Take your shots."

"What?" Rick's heart stopped. "Belay that—!"

Gunshots and cheers drowned out Rick's protest. His knees buckled watching the mass execution. Desperate final cries of murdered noncombatants rang out in between the cacophony.

As the bloodbath of fur and scales abated, the men and women of Earthquake high-fived and discussed how they'd spend their kill bounties. Images and sounds from earlier horrors threatened the edge of Rick's consciousness, but he clenched his teeth and banished them. *No time for nightmares today.*

Two different recruits squatted over an Arkouda corpse, pilfering what they could from pockets and personal effects.

When the caterwauling of murder celebration faded, Rick steeled himself. "Let's head out. The Collective fleet won't be far behind."

The two looters didn't budge.

"Now."

One glared at Rick, scoffed, and grumbled before leaving the corpse.

Unacceptable. They wouldn't enjoy tomorrow's training and drills.

THREE

AFTER HER SHIFT, Alize found herself in one of her worst nightmares, otherwise known as the place her date picked to eat, more grill than bar. Allze convinced herself Garott Rymon was the best she could do, dude-wise. Not many guys she met were interested beyond one drunken kiss, and those weren't satisfying anymore. And Garott was employed, which was technically an upgrade from her previous relationship. Calling him "boyfriend" was too much of a stretch considering he selected this Lo-sat meat house after she explained she was a vegan. Twice.

But Garott at least showed dim interest in a relationship. She wasn't allergic to the flowers he brought along with her repaired omni-tablet, which she thanked him for. And he almost paid attention, too. At least her tablet worked properly—it was sweet of him to fix it for her.

Even though he'd broken it.

"Ali, you gotta try the steak." Garott pounded the only Human liquor they had. Stench of marinated economic irresponsibility wafted amid the clinking of plates, clatter of silverware, and squeaks of certain menu items. Mostly Lo-sats and wealthier Humans feasted inside, oblivious to how meat overproduction on Earth fueled its prehistoric ecological collapse.

"I'll pass. Not much of an appetite. Lo-sats don't have vegan options." Nobody acted more clueless than a man hearing something for the second time.

"Your loss." His partially chewed unsustainable meal was on display between words. Pungent spices contaminated his breath.

Alize inhaled slowly and pushed a drooping curl behind her ear. "Rough week. The dissertation board rejected my latest proposal. Sorry."

"Why?" He managed to close his mouth while chewing, which was an improvement.

Genuine interest? "They didn't like the title, they said. But I think they don't care about prehistory out-side the Collective."

"Don't say prehistory. That's what they want us to do." He leaned in and glanced around, like anyone else would honestly care. "I bet it's 'cause you're Human. We're dirt to them." He released a derisive snort and leaned back, folding his arms.

Alize stiffened. "That's not it. Can't be."

"They treat us like second-class citizens. Us and the Makawe."

"It's pronounced Muh-ah-ka-way. And legally, we are. So what? If losers like Earthquake stop rioting, maybe we could get Citizen status."

He wiped blood-colored sauce from his lips. "Losers?" he whispered. "Try patriots. Earthquake knows what's up."

"They're murderers. Most Arkouda have no connection to official Collective policy, but Earthquake kills indiscriminately."

"Whatever. Just sayin' we shouldn't be pushed around." He pounded his drink and "ahh'd" long enough for his breath to carry. "You really think you found something? Like, archaeological stuff?"

Finally smiling, Alize said, "Think? I know." She withdrew her omni-tablet and opened the galactic map, highlighting a hazy region on settled space's edge. "I figured it out. We have this old inscription from the Chamayna in the museum, and I finally had a chance to analyze the stone it's etched on."

"She-meina?"

"Cha-may-na. The ones I've been studying? The main thing I've discussed?"

"Oh, right."

Alize sighed. "Only two moons in the former Chamayna sectors haven't been colonized or turned into mining centers." Talking research lightened her mood. "And I snagged a scan of one. Totally empty!"

"Uh, that's bad, isn't it?"

"Well, no, that means the tablet in my museum came from the other moon. Something big is there, waiting to be discovered."

A Lo-sat patron passed, her long, scaled tail only centimeters away from Garott's arm, and he shied away like a child fleeing an insect. He cleared his throat and adjusted his arm in a fake-macho way. "Like, valuable?"

Of course, this putz understands that.

"Yeah, the inscription in the museum is incomplete, but it describes a superweapon. Archaeological find of the millenia, and I figured out where it is. Or at least where it should be."

Garott swallowed and leaned closer.

He's finally listening? I'll be in trouble if he keeps looking at me like that.

"So when I propose my dissertation again, I'm going to show the board where it is. And if they accept, maybe I can lead an expedition."

His eyebrow arched. "They'd do that for a student?"

Good question. Painful one. "I'm hoping they'll instantly fall in love with the idea."

A trio of Lo-sat waiters passed, carrying a decorative terrarium of rodents to a table of other Lo-sats nearby. The creatures squeaked, likely unaware of their fate.

"How come nobody else read the inscription and researched this superweapon before? Seems like something the polar bears would want. I could definitely see a slimy Bowsit trying to pilfer a tomb for anything it could sell."

"If you think Lo-sat are slimy, maybe we shouldn't go to their restaurants. Only a few people spent the time to learn Chamayna. A few Lo-sat linguists, mostly.

There's not a ton of scholarly consensus, so I could be wrong of course."

He rolled his eyes and swallowed another bite.

Alize frowned and glared at him. "I'm not wrong. This moon has something. If the university doesn't fund a dig or an expedition or something, they're missing out."

"Hm." He shrugged, his gaze lightyears away.

Alize sipped her water. Her stomach attempted roaring. Another waft of Garott's damp overly spiced breath assaulted her nose, quieting her raging appetite. "Are you almost done?"

Garott raised his eyebrows. "So, you, uh, wanna get out of here?" He made a show of placing a crumpled napkin over the picked-clean bones on his plate.

Cringe or end the dry spell? "No, I'm feeling a little sick." She left alone, dignity intact.

FOUR

<SENDER ENCRYPTED>
<RECIPIENT ENCRYPTED>

RICK STARED INTO the screen, waiting for his connection to Monsieur Jacques Tecton to establish. The blank reflection forced him to see the mandatory Earthquake haircut. Lopsided. Jagged. What he'd give for a fresh buzz. And the mandatory tattoos weren't much better. The whole getup nixed plainclothes infiltration.

With a dull hum, Tecton's angular features materialized onscreen. Tecton called from his home, not mobile headquarters. The greenish tint of the almost-clean Earth sky peeked through the windows behind him.

Didn't listen to me about that, either. At least he's not in his Senate office. Rick nodded. "Good morning, sir."

"Crith." Jacques' acidic accent contrasted most Earthers. "Why am I seeing 'mission failure' on your report? It was a success." Tecton's thick brow creased across his forehead.

Rick straightened. "The archaeologist wouldn't say what we wanted. Even after threats and a show of force. Then my squad misunderstood an order and killed their whole team." Rick paused. "All civilian casualties. We didn't get anything valuable." *Because there's no mystical silver bullet out there or magic wand to end our war for you, and if there were, the Arkouda won't dig it up and hand it to us.*

"I have copies of the recording, Crith. You don't need to rehash it to me."

Rick clenched his jaw and let out a thin exhale through his nostrils, careful not to flare them or tense his facial expression. "So you can see it was in fact unsuccessful."

"Fifteen dead Collective Citizens. Ten of them damn polar bears. That makes for a successful mission."

"We're not terrorists, sir."

"Of course not, Crith." Tecton leaned into the camera, taunting Rick with his sensible haircut. "We're a political organization. Symbols matter."

"Sir, the policy of labeling any mission a success on the basis of dead bodies is poor strategy and misleading. Our objective—"

"Your objective, Crith? Follow orders. Disagreeing is poor strategy. Don't forget who accepted you after the Collective military abandoned you."

Rick's nostrils flared. "I'm sorry, sir. Won't happen again. Failed missions will be renamed."

"Don't sass me. The lead archaeologist—did he say anything else off the recording about how the Arkouda lost the space race?"

Four thousand years before Humans learned to forge steel? Who cares? Rick shook his head. "I left the recording on the entire time. Everything he said, you have."

"Shit." Tecton pushed his normal hair back with his left hand. "In your estimation, is it worth sending a team back there to dig up more information?"

Disobeying orders, an eyebrow cocked. "No, sir. The Collective fleet would crawl all over the area. They'll destroy or lock away whatever information those historians uncovered. Extracting information from an archives vault would be a poor use of resources and manpower. Too many casualties for us. Any information gained has a low likelihood of utility."

"Mm. Well, we can use your clip to embarrass the Arkouda. And he didn't say anything about who mastered interplanetary travel first? It couldn't have been the Lo-sat."

Rick shook his head. "And it couldn't be the Makawe, either. My guess is the Blekk, but that seems wrong."

"Of course it does. The Blekk are thugs and pirates. Any tech they have is stolen." Tecton let out a disdainful chuckle. "But you know that from your years with the enemy, don't you?"

Rick squinted enough to obscure his vision. "Yes, sir. The Blekk I fought were ruthless. I also met some lovely Blekk traders, too. And one musician."

"I'm sure." Tecton folded his arms over his chest. "The media wing has the next recruiting ad ready. I'll have them send it to you, so you're not shocked when you see it."

Rick's face obeyed orders and didn't wince. "Oh?"

"It's tasteful. You're shirtless, holding the bloody stump of an Arkouda head. Giant letters at the bottom say 'Human Independence Now.' It's very eye-catching. It'll draw more to the cause. They even airbrushed your wrinkles and touched up your grays."

"You don't have to lie about my age." Rick wondered if they'd put claw marks on his shoulder stump this time.

Tecton waved a hand. "Also, there's a new recruit joining your team. He has information. I'm trusting him to you. You'll get your mission after he's vetted. This could get you that promotion you've whined about, so get it done. My way."

"Yes, s—"

The transmission cut from the other end. Rick clenched his fist. If this recruit was garbage, there'd be hell to pay.

FIVE

Hen4 Moon, Balliol System, Collective space

WEARING HER ONE nice suit, Alize greeted the approval committee who hadn't approved her yet, in a stuffy room with stuffier academics, seated around a parabolic table.

What're the chances they've noticed I wear the same outfit each time?

Four Arkouda, two Lo-sats. All professors with more tenure than she had years alive, none of whom had done any real fieldwork in decades. They were all seated, yet they loomed over the standing Alize all the same.

Dr. Ioann, a shrill Arkouda who reeked of day-old stimbrew, began the proceeding. "Provincial Oze."

DAMMIT, IT'S TWO SYLLABLES NOT ONE! "Yes?" she asked in a quiet, decisive voice. The wall-to-wall bookshelves stuffed with artifacts absorbed more sound than they should have, weakening her voice further. The table meant for larger aliens made her appear even smaller.

"This is your final hearing. After your last presentation with your ridiculous teleportation hypothesis…" The voluminous professor adjusted the mono-goggle over his left eye, adding to his pompous air. "The board agreed you appear unwilling to make the requisite changes. Archaeology requires flexibility and adaptation. If you don't pass today, we won't hear another proposal until you've completed more coursework."

Adaptation and flexibility, huh? Then why're you stuffy pricks so stubborn? She knew her Chamayna teleportation theory sounded insane, but their artwork supported it.

Dr. Lon-Suon, an old Lo-sat, stroked the verdant scales under his chin and nodded. "Your theories and proposals must benefit the Collective. If it doesn't advance our culture, it won't be accepted. This is how research survives. We learn from the past to improve the present and future."

Alize nodded, inhaling whatever calm she could. "Thank you, professors. Well, the Chamayna, although officially classified as a failed civilization, will have much to offer us. We can learn from their mistakes." The Arkouda cracked their necks and the Lo-sat slapped their tails to the ground and clicked claws on the table.

Jerks. A room full of musty Human academics would've rolled their eyes. At least that's quiet.

Clearing her throat, she continued, "I examined a late-period Chamayna stone tablet. After sampling the mineral deposit on the inscription, and analyzing the carbon, cross-referencing galactic substrata, I found the potential location of a Chamayna tomb. I believe an artifact is located there. What I'll share today is the requisite equipment, crew, and budget for an expedition and preliminary dig."

Shouldn't have said potential.

Dr. Vo-Danh, the other Lo-sat, slightly extended his neck frills. "And how'd you sample the minerals from a Chamayna inscription?"

Uh-oh. "Great question, professor—"

Dr. Kaoutsuk, another Arkouda, leaned forward, small round ears flattening. "How'd you run those samples through a carbon analyzer?"

Bad. Bad. Very bad.

After a growl which would've scared a statue, Dr. Ioann rose, furry paws smacking the table. "Provincial Oze, did you break into the university museum?"

"She works there." Dr. Lon-Suon raised his tail, neck frills extending. "She could potentially have faked credentials to access artifacts directly."

Alize's plastered smile faltered. "That's not quite what happened, distinguished members of the board. You see—"

Dr. Kaoutsuk folded flabby arms over her embroidered tunic. "How many other artifacts have you tampered with?"

Dr. Vo-Danh's neck frills quivered. "And how much university equipment have you used without authorization?"

Alize met the room full of judgmental gazes. "Well, professors, I have found the location of something valuable. Priceless, actually."

Dr. Ioann waved a paw. "That's quite enough, Oze. We'll examine security footage and rule on your expulsion."

So that's a no, then?

"Don't—don't you want to hear where this moon is? And what's on it?"

Dr. Vo-Danh scoffed. "We're more interested in what else we could've been doing aside from humoring your reckless antics."

Reckless antics, huh? This is the discovery of a lifetime.

Alize dared to raise her voice more than a Provincial should. "What if I received proper authorization for the artifact and the university equipment?"

"Can Dr. Dikaio at the museum confirm this?"

Alize stared at her scuffed shoes.

Dr. Ioann sat and motioned for the others to join. "I thought so. Dismissed. You'll be notified of your expulsion status within the week. Until then, you may not attend classes."

And how long before Dr. Dikaio finds out?

"Report to Dr. Dikaio for whatever termination or suspension plans she has for you. We're calling her now."

Head hung low, Alize left. She knew Pops was in hospice, praying for her.

Sorry. Years of bragging about his daughter, a future archaeologist ... down the drain.

These university wing hallways were far too large. Designed with Arkouda in mind, the ceilings and doorways towered, and the doors weighed more than most people. Other students passed, mostly Arkouda with the occasional Lo-sat.

An elderly Human mopped a fresh stimbrew spill. Alize cringed as his weak arms rotated the handle. She approached him and grabbed the spilled cup on the floor. His eyes were bright, and his voice was hoarse. "Aw, you didn't have to do that."

Alize nodded. "You looked like you were having a rough day." She tossed the cup in the trash bag attached to his cart.

"Seeing a Human student here makes it a great day." He winked at her. "Makes me think of my son here one day, too."

"Yep." Alize turned on her heel and left, biting her cheek and blinking back a tear. She withdrew her omni-tablet and pinged Fil. *How does 97 beers sound?*

Ping. *Odd number, huh? Bad news?* Before Alize lifted a thumb to respond, another ping arrived. *First one to get hit on by a creepy guy picks up the tab.*

A smile returned to Alize before the crushing reality sank in.

SIX

On an unnamed asteroid in the Kuiper Belt, Human demilitarized zone

THE CLOSED OFFICE door must have been the universe's signal to send someone to interrupt Rick. Two knocks, a half-pause between them.

Amanda.

"Come in." Rick didn't use the formality the recruits received. The Earthquake insignia on the wall reminded him this wasn't a real military, and he didn't need to be so formal, but the recruits needed discipline. She didn't.

Amanda Martinez stepped inside, frizzy hair bobbing, resisting the mandatory lopsided hairstyle. Her blazer tastefully covered her tattoos.

"Got the new updates?" Rick asked.

"Of course." Her bright smile displayed immaculate teeth. "But I don't know why you bother with these. It's not like anything ever comes of these catches."

"Still. Every job in the pool is worth examining."

"Please take me with you when you're promoted, all right?"

Rick flashed a rare grin. "Naturally. I don't trust most goons tossed my way." She didn't need to know he'd take her anywhere. "Who do we have?"

"So, a small-time Lo-sat crook ripped off one of the smuggle fronts." Amanda waved her hand dismissively.

"Which one?"

"The meat shippers. He used them to smuggle a group of people off a settled moon and never paid the crew for the service."

"How much of a rip-off was this?"

Amanda glanced at her omni-tablet. "Wealthy marks, so we could've gotten a good amount for them."

"This Lo-sat thief have a name?" Rick shifted in his chair, and the uneven leg tapped the floor with a click.

Another glance at her omni-tablet. "Yeah. Tentrom Binh."

Rick clicked his tongue. "I hate to correct you, but your pronunciation needs work. Ten-trom. And that's his last name. Binh's a first name. Don't make the 'H' so hard. They don't like that. Their whole language is monosyllabic."

She raised a dark eyebrow. "Really?"

"Pronunciation matters. We want to be taken seriously, so we take them seriously."

Amanda pushed a stray lock of hair behind her ear. "So what's the plan? The bounty probably won't make up for the fuel we'd need to reach his last known location."

"No," Rick sighed. "If you can, get me the comm-link for the ship captain he screwed over. I think I know what type of guy this Binh character is. If he doesn't know we know, he'll pull this stunt again. I'll tell the captain what to do."

"So you want to split the bounty with him?"

"No. The whole bounty system's ridiculous, Amanda. We should help each other out in this organization because we have the same goal."

Amanda shook her head. "How will you ever get promoted and get me onto a planetary base with an attitude like that?"

"I'm fixing Earthquake. If you don't like it, plenty of other squad leaders need assistants." *Too harsh.* Rick cleared his throat. "You're a damn good employee. I'm sorry my methods skew unconventional. I'll make sure you're compensated if I get passed over for a promotion. And if you choose to leave, I'll write you a recommendation for whichever squad you want to join."

Amanda averted her eyes. "I was teasing. Besides, those other squad leaders might put something in their offices like decorations and pictures of their families."

"Good to know. I have my framed dishonorable discharge papers."

"That doesn't count." Amanda pursed her lips. "You never let anyone talk about it, so why bring it up with me?"

Rick met her eyes for a second longer than he should have and overcorrected, staring into the riveted metal walls that needed a scrub. "Put me through to that shipping captain."

SEVEN

Hen4 Moon, Balliol System, Collective space

A FEW DAYS passed and Alize's massive hangover almost did, too. Pops' bare and taciturn hospital room seemed more appropriate for someone joyless like Dr. Dikaio. Alize's daily cards and Filenada's weekly flowers brought some joy into the room, but they barely dissipated the sanitized ammonia stench permeating the wing.

A bed, table, a meager viewscreen, and a half-functioning nurse mech cluttered the cramped space. Filenada had told Alize some tricks to secure Pops a citizen's room, but those lacked proper equipment for an ailing Human, anyway. And those beds were too massive and stiff. Pops shouldn't have to army crawl to reach his water.

Alize opened the curtain with the back of her hand. "Pops?"

"I'm awake, sweetie." His rasp made him sound like a grandfather, not a dad.

A shell of his former self, Pops lay in bed, his personality and memories trapped in a decaying body. His gaunt smile greeted her. "Don't tell me—they loved your presentation." The brightness in his dark eyes contrasted his emaciated frame. "I knew they would."

"Not this time." Alize crept over and grabbed his cold hand, knuckles like loose marbles dotted with liver spots.

He grimaced and blinked hard. "What a bunch of hacks. You'll get 'em next time. They don't know what they're missing, Little Leezy."

A smile creased her face. "Thanks, Pops."

"How 'bout those scans you, uh—" he winked with effort, "didn't borrow my old custodian's keys to get?"

She returned the exaggerated wink. "Those keys I certainly didn't borrow and the rock I certainly didn't tamper with brought some hypothetically interesting results."

"I thought they might … not." He laughed, which devolved into a coughing fit. His coughs, practically convulsions, made him wince each time.

Alize signaled the nurse mech for some water. "Calm down. No more joking. I found it."

"Really?" His eyes brightened like when he'd checked her grades before the diagnosis.

"You seem awfully excited about a weapon for a draft dodger."

"Conscientious objector, excuse me." Another wink. "Honey, I don't care it's a weapon. I care that you've studied the inscription and all those Chamayna arti-facts since you could walk."

"Pops…" She rolled her eyes, but a smile sprouted.

"Leezy, I'm serious. Superweapon, superplunger, superwater, doesn't matter. You found something and stuck to your ideas. That's my girl."

She pulled in her bottom lip. "Thanks, Pops. You're the best." She hugged his bony body. How she missed the days when he hoisted her on his shoulder and wandered around the museum. Even after Mom left.

"So Alize…" his tone darkened.

"Don't say it."

"Honey, you can't leave this conversation again." He straightened, grunting with the effort. "Will you hear me out?"

She tensed her shoulders. *Don't drop this bomb on me, Pops. You're fine. Please.*

"Some Collective lawyers came by today. Nice ladies. Got my affairs in order."

"You've never had an affair in your life." Alize forced a grin. "So I know you're not hiding a secret family."

He slowly raised and lowered his eyebrows. "Heh. Well, I don't have much money to give to anybody. But what I have is going to you."

Sweat beaded on her lower neck. "Well, the guy who never had an affair only has one kid. Shocker."

"Alize."

Damn.

He blinked hard. "They gave me a month. Probably less. They'll move me to their dying ward soon."

"A month." *That's it, then.* "But…"

"No buts, dear. The doctors and nurse bots confirmed it. You need to accept it."

"Can we get a second opinion?"

His eyes darkened. "It's not a matter of opinion, Little Leezy."

"But—"

Pops grunted. "What'd I say about no buts?" Moisture appeared around his eyelids. "Don't make this harder. Hey, I wanted to give you something."

Alize gave a stiff nod. Pops needed her strong. She'd tell Fil, and they could cry later at the bar. "Yeah?" Her voice cracked. *Talking was a mistake.* Tears bulged, matching Pops'.

"It's not much but check out what the social worker gave me." He nodded toward the small table. A wristband, pulsing green light, sat between a card and a flower vase. Hoisting a bony arm, he pointed to an identical one on his wrist. "Put it on."

Alize nodded and complied. "So we can match? Your hospital gown isn't fashionable enough?"

A thin smile crept along his face. "If I could make that old jumpsuit look good, I can work this gown, too. This wristband isn't quite a fashion statement. It's a heart monitor. Super-long-distance reception. So we can stay connected." His lit and flashed the same green. "This way, we'll know our hearts are beating. When one of us gets nervous, it'll speed up—"

She gave a knowing nod, and a hospital PA system interrupted Pops, guttural Arkouda words rang in her ears, calling some doctor to prosthetics.

"—and we can say a little prayer for each other. I hate how I can't go and cheer you on for your research proposals."

"Pops, you'd punch one of my professors if they said anything negative."

He shook a weak fist. "You say punch, I say knock sense into. It's an act of mercy, not aggression." His tone softened. "Come here. The bands' range spans the galaxy. There's a little delay the farther you go, but the manual said it'll work across lightyears no problem. So if you found that moon, I want you to take the last bit of my money and get there. Whether the university or museum supports it or not."

"Pops, I'm not abandoning you. You only have a—"

Nope. Not saying it.

Pops turned his head toward his shoulder, hiding his face. A slight tremor in his lips told the whole story. "It's your time to shine. It's bad enough for you to see me like this. And I don't want my last thought to be how I kept you back. You earned this, baby girl. You deserve it."

If Alize chomped on her cheek any harder, she'd bleed. "If the university grants me an expedition and fast-tracks it, I could be there and back in a month."

"Don't worry about that. I already know you're right, Little Leezy. Now it's time for the galaxy to see. First Human archaeologist in the Collective." His shaking voice and trembling eyelids told the truth. "Maybe I'll see your Mom after I pass. I wonder if she'll give me a tongue-lashing for all that museum food I snuck you over the years."

Alize forced a smile. "You know it, Pops. I'll make you proud."

His shoulders slackened and his face brightened. "You do every day."

EIGHT

Earthquake internal messenger:
SENDER: Crith, Rodrick
RECIPIENT: Tecton, Jacques
SUBJECT: Potential allies

Sir,

My contact with the Makawe Freedom Coalition responded. They're clean. They weren't keen on revealing their upcoming attack plans, but they're open to future collaboration. I cannot overemphasize how important positive interaction would be. The Makawe have more people against the Collective than sympathizing with it, unlike Humans. If we cooperate with them, we gain a strategic advantage. We wouldn't need to fight side by side for the practical reasons of lodging and language, but if we coordinated, we could force the Collective military to fight on opposite ends of the galaxy. To accomplish this, we need to show the Makawe we're committed to Human independence only. They don't wish to trade one tyrant for another.

Sir, I hate to tell you, but they have legitimate concerns with some of the rhetoric associated with our organization. They didn't appreciate the comparison to extinct Earth crustaceans. Few of the other squad leaders seem to heed our mission of independence. The xenophobia hurts the cause, both politically, by making us less popular, and militarily, since some commanders appear more focused on killing than mission objectives. If we can cull that xenophobia and racism, more Humans inside Collective space would take us seriously, and we wouldn't have to solely rely on frontier settlements.

I also received a communique from a Blekk mercenary leader, a guy by the name of Sjorover—no surname. He's an important member of the Drowned Star pirates. He named his price for attacking Collective freighters inside Collective space. Decently reasonable— not much more than a month's operating costs per hit. Details attached. If we expend some resources working with the Drowned Star without formally allying with them, we could add another front to the war. We could make the war too expensive and bothersome for the Arkouda to continue fighting. On pre- historic Earth, smaller, weaker, less funded forces defeated larger and more organized foes this way.

Symbolic victories have their place, sir, but we need tactical victories. Without disrupting Collective shipping lines and interplanetary travel, we're closer to a plasmasipper bug than an actual threat. We'll never earn recog- nition as a political organization or an independent nation without a stra- tegic shift.

With your permission, I'll engage the Makawe Freedom Coalition. My Ma'ak is proficient enough that I can handle the delegations with the Makawe. But I'll need a translator who can speak Blekker. The mercenary isn't entirely proficient in Arkouda, and we've had a few language issues already. Tactically, that's unacceptable.

My assistant pulled files of the translators we have on retainer. Of the three who can speak Blekker, I'd like two of them. This guy labels himself a pirate king, and if I seem like an ambassador with a team of dignitaries, the better. If you're willing to risk detection, you could have a proxy impersonate you and get on the deliberations to stroke his ego.

These missions would be a more effective use of my squad's time than chasing artifacts. I've got an eye on an undefended shipping lane and will send a hijack team to commandeer and decommission a cargo vessel for squad use.

Thank you for the consideration.

Onward,
RC

-Earthquake moves the galaxy.

NINE

Hen4 Moon, Balliol System, Collective space

FIL DRUMMED HER empty jug against the bar and whistled for the Lo-sat bartender to bring another round. Alize ordered their only drink which wasn't toxic to Humans, a synthetic vegan mead. The fake Arkouda honey mimicked the freezeflower bee from Fil's homeworld, and the sweet aroma of the synth mead usually brightened her spirits.

Loud conversation and music assaulted all but the passed out Arkouda drooling on the bar. Old students and young museum employees stared into their expensive drinks, avoiding eye contact with their dates. One Lo-sat perched with long legs crossed, peacefully reading something on an omni-tablet. This bar lacked a dartboard, so Alize couldn't hustle anybody for a free drink. Nobody expected her to be skilled, especially when tipsy. From her periphery, Alize spied the bartender's viewscreen. The bottom crawl ticked by: "Earthquake attacks heritage monument: Palaios, Uperaygros System." A Lo-sat barback obscured the screen before she could read anymore.

Damn. Can't wait to hear about that in class. A new stinging realization bit through her buzz. She wasn't allowed back.

"So," she shouted to Fil, "when'll you tell me about the musician?" Shaking her head, Alize returned her gaze to Fil, who waved a hefty and dismissive paw.

"He's old news. Nothing special. Already forgot his name."

Alize covered her ear nearest the sound system. "Why'd you bring me here? You hate noise."

"Forget our bet?" Fil winked. "I didn't want you to pay."

Alize scanned the room. *The busboy is the only other Human.* "That's sweet."

"I know."

The bartender passed Alize's drink and struggled to lift the three-liter jug of nectar mead for Fil. Switching languages, Fil thanked the bartender. "The Arkouda guy at the table behind us said to put this on his tab."

The bartender placed his thin, scaled wrists on his hips, a small towel clutched in one clawed hand. He inclined an eyeridge, slightly jutting out neck frills. "Really?"

Fil pointed to the insignia on her shirt. Collective military. "Do you really want to argue?"

He turned on his heel and sauntered over to another patron, tail curled tight behind him.

Alize tsked. "You know that'll haunt you one day."

Mead jug in paw, Fil shrugged and switched back to her accented Human. "Security guards are still legally members of the Collective military. He doesn't need to know I was—" she grimaced. "—reassigned. That the right word?" Fil took a swig.

"That's what you're saying now? Yeah, you used the right word. So the musician's out. Any other prospects?" Exhaling and rolling her eyes, Alize glanced at her own wrist. Gently pulsing green. *Pops is all right.*

Filenada wiped the dripping mead from her muzzle. "Well, there's moneypaws behind us. But don't worry about it. Garott really hasn't pinged you?"

"Not since the board rejected me." Alize tugged at the label on her bottle. "I told him they wouldn't hear me out, and then, nothing all week. I guess I'm not interesting enough for him, especially since I wouldn't put out."

"Or he's a looser. He isn't worth it, anyway."

"*Loser.* But if losers don't want me, who will?"

Fil shook her head and growled playfully. "Ever try showing artwork to a cub? Think they can appreciate a masterpiece?"

A pod of Arkouda walked by, sneering at Fil after eyeing Alize. Fil bared her teeth and flattened her ears. The snobby guy held up his paws and retreated, sidestepping them and heading to the other end of the bar.

Running a hand through her hair, Alize sighed. "Fil, Pops pretty much told me he doesn't want me to watch him die. He even gave me money to travel to the stupid moon—"

Filenada slammed her jug with enough force to splash Alize. "Then what in the Nightmare are we waiting for?" A smile slithered across her muzzle. "Let's go."

"We can't. That moon isn't near any population centers. Not even a fuel depot on an asteroid."

"Cargo ships go everywhere. We stow away on one going in the general vicinity, right? We make our lovely exit at a closer spaceport and rent a short-ranger."

"Do you have any idea how we'd go about doing that?"

Fil scratched behind her ear. "We hire someone? Smuggler? Thief? All-around professional lowlife?"

"And how will we find one?"

"Promise treasure."

Glasses clinked to their left, and expensive mead aroma wafted over. Alize chuckled. "There would be treasure, yeah. Fine. We don't exactly have a ton of time to shop around and interview people, though."

Fil rolled her eyes. "Once we see someone slick enough, we'll know. Let's find a thief."

Scoffing, Alize gesticulated at the room full of pretentious patrons, cheering after the local hive-ball team scored a goal on the giant viewscreen. "You think there's a thief around here? The only thievery here's the drink prices."

Alize noticed her reactions slowing. *Tonight's lovely dumb idea is brought to you by excessive alcohol.* "Fil, get the bartender's attention. Tell him you feel like getting in a fight. When he freaks out, ask him where you could go to get in one."

Nodding slowly with inebriated overconfidence, Fil approached the bartender. Switching languages, she called, "Hey slim, I'm in the mood to smack someone."

He dropped his towel, held up both claws, and retreated.

"Naw, I wouldn't harm a scale on your sweet face. I wanna mess up a lowlife. Where could a girl go to let out some aggression on cave scum like that?"

Tail and shoulders relaxing, the bartender gave them an address.

"Thanks, love." Fil scribbled the tip on the bartender's omni-tablet. "Get something nice for yourself and put it on that guy's tab. On me."

Alize rolled her eyes, arranging autocab service.

TEN

On an unnamed asteroid in the Kuiper Belt, Human demilitarized zone

TWO EARTHQUAKE RECRUITS plodded down the dimly lit bunker corridors. They didn't seem to notice Rick behind them. Not that Rick minded—seeing how his recruits behaved while at ease gave him better insight into how to lead them.

Unlike the rest of the buildings in the galaxy, the bunker sported Human-sized doors, Human-sized rooms. And food that didn't require a pharmacy to digest. Even the artificial gravity was set to Human standards, unlike everywhere else, tailored to the Arkouda's preferences. Some squad members and staffers walked around without grav harnesses. The sterile scent of fading cleaners, untainted by metric tons of shedding Arkouda fur made this place feel like home for Rick. Far from perfect, but it was Human.

The older recruit nudged the other. "Nice ink. Get it here?"

The younger one nodded. "It's my first."

"Figured. Anyone mention you only get more if you survive a mission?" He rolled up his sleeve, displaying a series of Earth tattoos, each with a diagonal line through it. "That's the local leader's office. Don't mess with him."

"Who is it?"

"You ain't heard of Rick Crith? The man was a war hero."

"Everyone called him a traitor back home."

"Where you from?"

"Garott City, Cornwallis."

The older recruit's tone dropped. "Your name is Garott Rymon, and you're from Garott City?"

The younger recruit nodded. "Pretty cool, huh?"

"Is that a loyalist settlement?"

"Yeah, right in the middle of Collective space. Barely anyone understands Earthquake. Bunch of alien appeasers."

The older recruit scoffed. "Hey, you know what Earthquake says, 'we'll move the galaxy.' But Crith ain't a traitor. They must not've told the whole story." He stopped and pointed. "Oh, that's the ladies' bunk. Don't joke about going in unless you want an ass whooping and latrine duty."

Rymon snarled. "Figures I wouldn't get the whole truth back home. Only Collective propaganda."

"Crith was in the Collective military. One of the first Humans to lead a squad. Sounds like progress, right?"

"Probably a diversity hire or something."

"Maybe." He gestured to the left with a limp arm. "There's the mess hall down that corridor. Don't get the gravy unless you want a weekend getaway with the toilet. Seriously, it smells like the real deal, but it's made with imitation Earth ingredients. But anyway, check this, Rick got injured, and the Collective wouldn't fix him up. His injury wasn't related to his service, they said, so they left him to dry."

The two seemed oblivious to Rick's footsteps behind them.

"So what happened?"

"Rick's real hush-hush about it, but that's why he's missing an arm."

Rymon's voice went up. "No prosthetic?"

"Nah, he refused to buy one. He said the Collective owed him, and he'd get it from them. And now it's his whole thing. Symbolic and shit. Him joining Earthquake is a big deal. Shows how little the polar bears care about us, and how we don't need them. Walking, talking proof, and he's a badass. You should see him fight. Don't let his age or slim build fool you. He earned those gray hairs."

"But like, what happened to his arm, though?"

The older recruit leaned in. "The rumor is—"

Rick interrupted. "I wouldn't finish that sentence, Lamont."

The recruits turned to face Rick Crith, towering over them, and they both jumped back.

Lamont stuttered. "I'm sorry, M-mr. Crith."

"We're military. Act that way. If you can't hear me coming, hostiles will get the drop on you."

Lamont stiffened, and Rymon followed suit. "Apologies, sir."

Rick slanted a thin eyebrow. "That was a lackluster tour for the new recruit. If he gets lost, I'm blaming you. I recommend you give him a more thorough tour. Without the gossiping commentary."

Lamont gave a series of rapid perfunctory nods. "Yes-sir-thank-you-sir."

Rick lowered his gaze to meet Rymon's eye. He let the pause linger until he saw a twitch. "Ensign Garott Rymon?"

The young man gulped and nodded. "Y-yes. That's me." He certainly had the crisp accent of someone from Collective space—the only thing in common between the two of them.

"Your recruiting officer said you had some information."

Rymon took the cue and stammered a yes.

"About the location of an undisturbed Chamayna tomb?"

The youth's eyes lit up and he nodded.

"Come to my office after you get a proper tour." He glanced at both of them. "Dismissed." If Rick had been in better spirits, he would've confirmed the bit about latrine duty and the gravy.

ELEVEN

Hen4 Moon, Balliol System, Collective space

AFTER DOWNING THEIR liquid courage, Alize and Fil stumbled out of the hovering autocab for the dingy street as a distant police drone siren whirred. This part of town was isolated from the university district, unofficially marked with a stark decline in building material quality and dimmer streetlights. If Hen4's city were on a planet, there would've been nocturnal critters rummaging through the garbage. Instead, rusty collector drones fumbled between alleys, humming as they scooped trash, too slow to mitigate the odors wafting over.

After a cough, Alize said, "Ding."

"Huh?"

"If you wore your armor right now, it'd chime because of the lowered air quality."

"Well it's cleaner than what I wrote on the locker room wall yesterday."

Alize snorted and opened the bar's door for Fil; a cloud of stale beer vapors mingling with forgotten vomit trudged out.

They descended into a cesspool of dark music, half-working lights, and raucous shouting. Loud clacks of angleballs bounced off each other amid players bent over tables, lining their shots into the corner holes.

A particularly lanky Lo-sat man who could split the difference between Alize and Fil's height used his tail to tap a player's anglestick from behind. The unaware Arkouda lining up the shot missed. The Lo-sat sidled to the end of the table, faced the other player, and said something with a cocky grin. Thundering music muted the exchanged words, but the Arkouda player balled a paw into a fist and readied a punch.

A clawfight between two Lo-sats erupted on the far end of the bar. Among the various curses they shouted at each other, Alize caught the words "limp" and "tail" but not much else. After a swear and a slash between them, the grizzled Arkouda bartender growled until they parted ways, hissing at each other.

Alize nudged Fil. "We'll get killed."

"Maybe. But at least there are some Humans here, too."

Would Pops kill me for coming here or slap me on the back for surviving the trip? Fil better not make me drink anything here.

They marched to the bar, grabbing the open seats beside an older Human staring into his shot glass.

Like Mom on her bad days.

They waved at the bartender, who lumbered over while drying a glass.

Fil addressed him in Arkouda. "She's with me. We're hoping to hire someone."

Alize gulped and sat on her hands, unable to elbow jab Fil in public.

The bartender grumbled and lowered his scarred eyebrows. "Buy something. Information ain't free."

A whiff of salty, greasy carb sticks from the patron next to her wafted over. It was the kind of bar food that was only appealing when intoxicated, and it made the subsequent hangover a toxic mess on the toilet. Alize sniffed and her mouth watered. *Is that oil dip with it?*

Fil nodded. "Bloodmead for me and darkfruit cider for my associate."

After the bartender turned, Fil whispered in Human. "Sorry I ordered bloodmead. Don't want to appear weak or cheap for this to work." After a sigh, she added, "and this particular distillery kills the fish painlessly. You understand, right?"

Alize's hand threatened to leave its stowed position for a reassuring arm rub, but she remembered their place. She was sober enough to know she was impaired and was just as likely to grab Fil inappropriately by mistake.

The bartender returned with their drinks, and Alize responded to Fil in Arkouda. "Your kindness for lower life forms is accepted gratefully, Citizen."

Filenada eyed the bartender. "So how about that information?"

"What're ya asking for?"

Alize licked her lips but swallowed her words. *This guy isn't like Fil.*

Fil leaned in, a heavy elbow pressed against the bar, and shielded the side of her muzzle with her paw. "We need unofficial transport. Not exactly going to a population center."

The bartender cocked an eyebrow and curled his lip. "Something to hide?"

Alize nodded. *Good enough cover.*

"So what you need is someone who can get you onto a cargo vessel. What system?"

Fil pulled back. "Ah-ah. We need a name first."

"You're drunk. If you're serious, then I need more money." The bartender left and visited another patron further down the bar.

Behind them, an anglestick cracked against a table, and the Arkouda who'd been tricked growled loud enough to puncture the heavy music. Snapping her head over her shoulder, Alize's eyes widened, rivaling the disparate angleballs on the game table. The cheated Arkouda held the offending Lo-sat by the neck, pressed aloft against the wall.

The Arkouda roared, "Cheater!"

Every set of eyes in the room trained on the scene. Clattering from the kitchen even paused. The bartender stormed over, shouting "break it up!"

The pinned Lo-sat wrapped his long, thin tail around the Arkouda's wrist. This hold couldn't have done anything with how muscular Arkouda were. But Alize watched his unchanged expression. The Lo-sat spoke in flawless Arkouda with the cadence of someone who'd been in this position before.

"Now, now, fellas. How could I possibly cheat? Angleball doesn't have rules about what a tail can or cannot do, now does it? It's certainly not my fault this prejudicial game was made without Lo-sats in mind."

The Arkouda pressing him against the wall leaned in but didn't lower his voice. "How 'bout I rip your cheating tail off? Nothing in the rules about that, either."

"You played with someone else's money." The formality left the Lo-sat's tone, and a toothy grin curled up his long snout. "Hey barkeep, check the register."

The bartender stopped in his tracks, and a collective gasp echoed as eyes trained on him.

Alize glanced back to the Lo-sat against the wall, but he wasn't there. *Oldest trick in the book.* "Fil, did you see that?"

"Yeah, can't imagine when the bartender got robbed. Must've been before we arrived."

"No, the gray Lo-sat guy."

"The cheater?"

"He's gone."

Fil nodded and scratched behind her ear. "Huh. Win the fight without throwing a punch." Balling up wobbly paws into fists, she added, "Respectable, but not my style."

"No." Alize rose from the barstool, shaky on her feet. "That's our guy. If he can slip out of an angry Arkouda grip and disappear from a room in a matter of seconds, that's who can help us break into the tomb."

"And sneak us aboard the right cargo ship, I bet."

The bartender returned to the credit register and checked some flashing screens. He wheeled on the Arkouda patron who caused the ruckus. "Half the night's money is gone." Pointing an angry paw at him, the bartender shouted, "Clobber the thief!"

Drunken growls from Arkoudae, hisses from Lo-sats, and a few weak drunk Human shouts made a raucous chorus, and the patrons descended on the offending Arkouda.

Fil cracked her knuckles. "All right. Let's loosen some teeth—"

"Filenada. We're leaving. This is our cue to leave. You don't have your armor and I'd like you alive. Not like you can do the special electric force field without the armor. You promised you wouldn't get into any fights drunk tonight."

"I'm not drunk, I'm… alright fine. That's not how the force field works. Like I'd need it against these amateurs," Fil grumbled and they left, flanking the rising melee in the center of the bar floor.

Passing the dartboard, Alize's arm hairs rose. *I would clean house here. Oh well. Maybe I'll earn rent another night.*

Outside, under the dim streetlights, the grayish Lo-sat tapped his tail, staring at a timepiece on his wrist.

Alize pursed her lips and flattened her tongue. Speaking Lo-sat was a weak point, but it was her best option to get his attention. "Nice leave." That sounded wrong. "Good leaving."

The Lo-sat casually turned. He stood lithe and lanky, thinner than both women. He sniffed in a way which felt vaguely derogatory. Then he craned his head down to lock eyes with Alize before angling his head up to do the same with Fil. His scaled eyeridges furrowed in a way which removed all doubt to his discontent.

I probably sound like a drunk toddler.

The Lo-sat waved his claws dismissively and spoke in flawless Human. "Lady, if you were complimenting me, you failed."

Alize stuttered and responded in Human. "Um, sorry, I meant to say 'nice escape.' That was impressive." Fil's mead breath wafted over to Alize, and her eyes watered as she resisted the urge to wince at the stench of fermented fish blood.

He crossed thin arms over his chest, covering an odd set of traveler's gear with a diagonal chestpiece. His scales, in addition to their grayer tint, lacked the sheen of other Lo-sats she'd seen, but he didn't seem old. *Maybe he's overdue for a shedding?*

"I know what you tried to say, lady. It failed as a compliment because you didn't encapsulate my awesomeness enough. Marvelous escape. Daring escape. Or even better, the two of you furballs could escape while I wait for my autocab."

Jerk.

Filenada growled and spoke in Arkouda. "Watch who you call a furball. And we're not going anywhere."

The Lo-sat tsked. "No formality? How will the Collective military respond upon discovering your protocol breach?"

Fil wasn't quite sober enough to speak without slurring. "How'd you know I'm military?"

Sighing, the Lo-sat pointed all four claws on his left hand at the insignia on Fil's shirt.

Alize piped up. "We were impressed by what we saw."

"Rightly so. Now leave."

"We want you to—"

"I'm flattered, but no thank you. You both have a bit too much hair for a man of my refinement." He hissed, pushing his thin tongue between his serrated teeth. "I have standards."

Alize scoffed. "We want to hire you. We've got a job for someone like you."

"Not exactly a 'legitimate employee' type. And if you'll excuse me—" he indicated the smallish tear-shaped autocab idling on the curb. "My ride's here. Late."

As he stooped to fit in the cheaper Human autocab, Fil darted in front of the vehicle and knelt in front of it, paws on either end of the front bumper. "Come with us or I will tip this over."

That's why Fil's better buzzed. Sober us wouldn't think of this. Oh Earth, are we alcoholics?

The Lo-sat flared his neck frills slightly and exhaled sharply through his nostrils. "Fine, fine. You get ten minutes to pitch your job offer. But we can't stay here." He exited the cramped cab and dusted himself off. "Why do the ladies always think I like it rough? Probably the provocative way I dress." Standing to his full height, he waved a claw over his diagonal chest armor. "Now your friend can use her fancy Collective military pass to get us a nicer autocab to get to a decent part of town."

Fil lowered the autocab to its hovering position and grunted. Alize eyed him in between fiddling with her omni-tablet.

"So who are you?" she asked.

"Besides the sexiest man alive?"

Alize's jaw dropped along with her patience. "I'm Alize, and that's Filenada. Could you tell me your name, please?"

"Just call me 'Binh.' You might be surprised, but I'm not the most formal chap in the galaxy."

An Arkouda-sized autocab arrived seconds later. "Figures," Binh muttered.

Inside, Binh lounged across from Fil and Alize, stretching out his tail to cover the whole leather bench. "Much nicer than the cheap Human version."

Alize shrugged. "Like most things in the galaxy."

He clicked his tongue. "At least you accept it. Not like some other *ke-noks* I've met."

Fil nudged Alize. "What's a *ke-nok*?"

"I think it means idiot or moron or something," Alize responded.

Binh mockingly put two claws over his chest. "How dare you, Booze Breath. Calling someone a *ke-nok* is the highest compliment I can give."

Fil sunk her head to whisper in Alize's ear. The blood-mead stench followed her breath. "Is he lying?"

"Hey, fuzz lady. You're not as quiet as you think. Typical *ke-nok*." Binh rolled his eyes, the yellow and black of his irises a swirling marbled pattern.

Alize rubbed her temples. "Can we cut out the nicknames and discuss the job?"

Binh waved his three finger claws and thumb spike. "The Collective monitors all discussions in these auto-cabs. If you ladies want to hire me for something, this is a task meant to stay off the viewscreen, yeah?"

"Fine," Fil said. "Mind telling us how you gave everyone the slip at the bar?"

"Not everybody, apparently." He stuck his three-forked tongue from his snout, threading the space between serrated teeth.

Alize shrugged. "You're making us second-guess hiring you with that attitude."

"Nah." Binh pointed to Alize. "You're desperate." He indicated Fil with his tail. "And you're restless. Not the best combination for mental health, but good for someone who's in need of extra fluidity in the bank account." He took another derogatory sniff. "You're also both hammered, which's always a good sign."

"Extra fluidity in your bank account?" Alize asked. "But you just robbed that bar."

"I didn't rob them."

Fil snorted. "You're lying."

"No, I'm Binh." He tapped the autocab window with his thumb claw. "And I owed a gaggle of less salubrious characters some cash, and those funds were already rearranged. Oh, hey, it's getting brighter outside. Must be near where the rich live. The lights are on."

The autocab halted outside the museum at the edge of the university district. Alize opened the door for the others. "We're going to my apartment. No monitors there. And I doubt you'll think I'm rich when you see it."

"Hey, Fuzzy Frosty, I thought these fancy Arkouda autocabs came with snacks."

Fil growled.

"What? Are you upset I insinuated your people always require snacks? Or my rejections of your advances?"

"The bit's getting old, Binh." Alize said, some of her intoxication waning. "We're not into you."

"Why, because I have scales? That is so deeply racist. Are you one of those Earthquake fanatics? I wouldn't have guessed since it seems like you bathe at least bi-weekly, but you can never be too sure. Or maybe you're too drunk to appreciate how attractive I am? If that's the case, you might need to get your stomach pumped and checked for alcohol poisoning. I didn't think a Human could get blitzed enough to have judgment so completely clouded."

Alize opened the door to her apartment complex where other custodians and dusty mechanics in the university district lived. "Do you always talk this much?"

Smiling and strutting inside, he made grand sweeping motions with his tail like an arrogant pendulum. "I've been told I could wake the dead."

That might be problematic in the tombs.

Inside Alize's cramped apartment, the leftover stench of cheap noodles and regret never quite dissipated from the previous tenant. Binh sidestepped in front of Filenada to get the largest seat in the room, the raised cushionchair meant for Fil. Binh and Fil's height made the space feel even more compact.

Fil slumped her shoulders to get her head through the doorway and sighed. "Really, Binh?"

He laid sideways in the cushionchair, stretching legs and tail to maximize the amount of space he occupied. "Wow, this is comfy. Fit for a fuzzball indeed."

Filenada grumbled, then plopped on the stained carpet.

Alize ignored her couch and sat beside Fil. "Look, we need someone with your skills. You robbed a place and escaped without anyone noticing. We need to get to a specific moon far away from any settlements."

"Oh, fascinating." Binh scooted forward on the chair and propped his head in his claws, elbows on knees. Eyes widened, he said, "Please, tell me what kind of lucrative job could possibly be out there. Are we going to rob some rocks? That sounds exciting. Fantastic use of my time." He scoffed, slapped his tail on the floor, and stood. A little puff of dust rose.

Fil bared her teeth. "Sit down, scaly."

"What's the magic word?" He fluttered his eyeridges.

"Eviscerate."

Binh surrendered the chair to Fil. "Go on."

"There's a tomb. An archaeological find unlike anything else discovered. If you can get us to the moon, inside the crypt, and back home, you can take the majority of the treasure. I just need one specific artifact."

Binh stroked his chin scales. "Interesting. Why hasn't anyone else gotten to this place?"

Fil waved a paw. "You don't seem like the biggest fan of the Collective. You won't be surprised the university isn't interested in her research, even though she can prove it."

Binh lowered his eyeridges. "So this isn't a Lo-sat or Arkouda site, is it? Is it Makawe? We'd never fit inside the way they built stuff. You and I would have to crawl, and Fuzz Queen wouldn't fit at all. No offense." Covering the side of his snout with a claw, he added in a faux whisper, "You're huge. That's why."

"Don't talk to her that way." *Play it cool.* "Who cares what's in there?" Alize arched an eyebrow. "Someone like you knows who would buy those artifacts. If the Collective isn't interested in it, you could probably find a collector who'd pay a good price for what we find, especially with how exclusive they are. Even selling the location could be lucrative. And if the Collective does see how valuable this really is, maybe they'll expunge your record as a thank-you." Alize sat back and grinned. "And don't act like you don't have a record. You probably have a rap sheet longer than your tail. I know you want it cleaned. Anyone would."

Binh's neck frills extended a centimeter. "I don't know private collectors, but I would know where to find them. Still, this ain't worth my time."

Alize steadied her breath, but images of Pops in his hospital bed and the university board spun in her mind. Everything was slipping through her fingers.

"You're wrong, by the way." Binh stretched on the floor. "I simply don't have a record. I'm not a criminal."

"That's where you're wrong." Filenada smirked and tapped her shirt's insignia. "You admitted to an officer that you robbed that bartender. You want me to forget or report it?"

Binh stuck out his three-forked tongue. "I didn't admit to anything."

"Mind if I verify that? And who will they believe?"

Binh snorted and shot a piercing stare at Alize. "There's another reason you're doing this. Come clean."

"My dad's dying." Alize let out a long breath.

Binh took a slightly less derogatory sniff. "Let's talk specifics."

TWELVE

Hard copy of memo, left in a nondescript folder on the desk of Rick Crith

Found it. You were right. Pretty shocking. And yes, I now feel bad about my opinions. Some! - Amanda

From the desk of Prime Senator Obualla, Earth:

Senator Tecton,

The committee found your proposed education reform bill egregious and insulting. Introducing Human young to our neighbors in your proposed way is appalling. Why you thought any of this was qualifiable as educational is disturbing. Your inability to see this as racist says volumes about your character.

First, the Arkouda are cognitive and emotional, not cheap copies of extinct Earth fauna. Your section on them ignored the unique facets of their biology and their contributions to society. You called them wrongful conquerors. Have you forgotten the horrors of the Eleva War? And in case you haven't noticed, Earth survived its climate collapse and colonized the stars with their technology, not ours. Children need to understand the benefits Humans gained from cooperating with them, not racist drivel.

Second, calling the Lo-sats "walking iguanas?" Beyond the fact that Earth iguanas never had neck frills, it's not an iconic extinct animal most children could imagine. You described them as the "first race to submit to Arkouda harassment." Have you read any Collective history? The Lo-sat have been equal partners under Arkouda rule since before Humans forged steel. And what about their contributions to science, economics, philosophy? Frankly, Senator, this proposal seems little more than an attempt to reduce Humanity's standing.

After deriding the Citizen species, you belittle the Makawe. A Makawe's tattoos are etched into their carapaces and reflect deep personal symbolism. While their suffering has been long under the Arkouda, you conveniently omit their engagement in violent uprisings against the Collective. The only sentence in your entire document I can't take issue with is that they are near extinction. But what about their art, poetry, and music? Or their innovations in ship design? How do you expect to honestly educate a child without highlighting the wonderful aspects of these different cultures?

Officially, Blekk cannot be the subject of instruction without special permission from the Collective's Education Ministry. Comparing them to Earth squids isn't helpful for anyone.

Your entire proposal was disheartening. If your constituents had any idea what kind of radical hogwash you're pushing, your re-election would be jeopardized. You're expelled from

the Education Committee, effective
immediately. Take this opportunity as
an invitation for serious reflection.
Humans need leaders to work with the
Arkouda to become full members of the
Collective, or we can flounder and
return to prehistoric infighting. The
majority prefers the former.

For the pale blue dot,
-Prime Senator Obualla

THIRTEEN

Hen4 Moon, Balliol System, Collective space

EXITING HER APARTMENT, Alize zipped her jacket. After hurtling down the cold slate steps, she inventoried the tools in her duster. Goggles, scanners, brushes, and picks. Her first dig should've been a grand affair, with teams of excavators at her side ready to take instruction.

Under the nearest streetlight, Filenada approached, fastening a dark trenchcoat over her armor. The ensemble made her seem even more muscular than usual—Alize couldn't remember the last time she'd seen Fil armored outside of work. Probably never.

Alzie waved her over. "You can go anywhere in uniform, why hide it? You're practically untouchable. And with your force field—"

"Leeze, what is it with you and the force field? It doesn't even last that long." Her ears slumped. "Eh, I didn't want to draw attention. Or anyone to figure out where I am." Light from the streetlamp above reflected off an exposed piece of shoulderpads under her coat. \

Alize checked her timepiece, and a reassuring green pulse greeted her. *Always at my side. Thanks.* "Binh will show up, won't he?"

"It's been three days, and he's checked in regularly." Fil glanced over both shoulders. "I think he might be running or hiding from someone, and we gave him a good motivation to flee."

A midsize autocab hovered to the curb. The backseat window descended, revealing Binh's gray-green snout. "Ready to get in a car with a strange man? I have candy."

Alize scoffed and opened the door for Fil in case passersby had prying eyes.

When they entered, Binh tapped his diagonal chestpiece, then pointed at Fil with his tail. "You've been in space before—that a fair assumption?" After she nodded, he indicated Alize with his claws. "And you, Pinks?"

"Pinks?"

Fil chuckled. "I think he means your hair."

Binh's eyeridges danced. "Yeah, that bright pink dye is your best feature."

Alize pursed her cracked lips. "I thought you were grossed out by hair."

"Oh, I am. I love Humans with dyed hair. Kills it faster. Also on my hate list: dairy." He made fake retching noises.

"You're obnoxious," Alize said. "To answer your question about space travel, I've been on Hen4 my whole life."

Binh nodded slowly. "Not surprised. How's the adjustor on your grav harness working?"

Alize probed the gear on her neck. "I haven't calibrated it recently, but it's never given me problems. Why?"

"Alright, but prepare to puke if you don't adjust it fast enough. Almost no ship-wide gravity adjustment on cargo holds."

On the other side of the window, the lift dominated Hen4's city center, puncturing the atmosphere. She'd never set foot inside, but as a kid, she'd enjoyed watching its lift rise and fall with Pops on his lunch breaks. Even seeing it now, her olfactories recalled the nutrient paste sandwiches Pops ate. *Because they balance cheapness and nutrition.* She glanced at her pulsing green wristpiece and smiled.

Filenada grunted and pointed outside. "Why'd the cab pass the space elevator?" She slammed her paw against the window. "Where in the Nightmare are you taking us?"

"We didn't, Frostface. Not going to the passenger side. Notice how we're looping around? Maybe I could have found better accommodations for us if someone..." he leered at Alize and widened his neck frills, "had given me the specific coordinates of this mystery moon."

"We don't completely trust you." Alize narrowed her eyes. "You know enough. And you're sure this cargo has enough escape pods?"

"Plenty. Not as much jerky as I'd like, but beggars can't be choosers." He smiled and winked. "Come on, our luxury cargo awaits. Pinky, did you bring the food?"

Brow furrowed, she said, "Yes. Plant-based protein."

Inside the space elevator's cargo terminal, more Humans gathered in one place than Alize had seen in her life. And they didn't all appear destitute. Some even wore spacefaring suits without any patchwork or evidence of shortcuts like what Alize wore.

"I didn't expect this many Humans here," Alize said. "Where are the Arkoudae and Lo-sats?"

Binh tsked. "On the passenger side, genius. We're on the cargo side. These are unskilled technicians, engineers, groundskeepers—you know the type."

Alize examined the scene again—these weren't excited passengers with suitcases and plans for traveling or businesspeople on important errands, but more workers transporting cargo, grunting and haphazardly tossing crates and luggage onto lifts. Binh motioned them to follow toward a security checkpoint. When the women were close, he approached a bored and overweight Arkouda security guard.

"Say pal, my friends and I misplaced our ID badges. Would you mind letting us through?"

Binh flipped his credit chit between his claws and held his tail at a peculiar angle to obscure them. Alize followed the angle of his tail to the ceiling and saw the camera. Two omni-tablets clicked.

"Thanks, honored Citizen." Binh flashed an impish grin. "You make the Collective proud."

The guard stowed his omni-tablet. "Shaddup and get outta here."

"With manners to match." Binh tapped his tail on the floor.

When they passed him, Alize noticed a few furry fat rolls pouring out of the guard's armor.

I wonder if he has a peanut butter hookup like Fil does.

The loading terminal dockworkers barked orders at each other, and moving equipment beeped and groaned. This lacked the majesty she'd imagined. She stole a glance at her wrist. *Pops is okay, at least.*

They followed Binh through the expansive terminal, passing row after row of loading bays on either side. "There's a cold storage meat transporter nearby. Frosty, they have a freezer if you want it." Turning to Alize, he added, "And there's a fridge unit you can stay in."

A frown curled across Fil's snout. "What'll you do?"

"Well, staying in either of those units would be murder for my scales. They itch bad enough as is. And staying with either of you for any extended time is murder on my drive and attraction to the fairer sex. That would be criminal. I'm sure you understand. I don't make the rules, and—"

"By the Goddess' Dream," Fil moaned, "you have to stop."

"Fine. I recently returned to the crew's good graces, so I sit in the cockpit. Maybe I'll luck into a cabin. Either way, I'll use that leverage to check on you both."

They turned a corner, toward the export station. Alize sighed. "They'll let you in like that?"

"I'm always confident. Part of my charm." After a wink, he added, "Besides, I'm a professional. I'll get in.

You take care of watching what you're eating in those meat coolers."

"It had to be a meat transport to get us there?" Alize massaged her temples. "It couldn't have been anything else?"

"Nope. We could've left yesterday, but once I learned you're vegan, you forced my claws." He made an exaggerated wink.

Alize scoffed. "Excuse me if I don't think a sentient being should die so I can have one meal."

"Right, right." Binh waved his tail. "That's how nature works. But maybe you're just killing the wrong animals? What if the animals you ate were assholes? Like, they beat their children or committed tax fraud? No?"

"I will snap you in half if you don't stop," Fil said. "How much farther?"

"Just ahead. It won't be long until we can use their escape pods and go to this mystery moon." Binh pointed down the hall with his tail and motioned for them to wait behind two crates while he schmoozed the workers. He flashed more money, and two cap-wearing Human dockworkers approached the women.

"So ladies..." One raised his hat which matched his jumpsuit. "My friend tells me you need some accommodations?"

Alize licked her lips and nodded. One more glance at her wrist. Green pulse. *Thanks, Pops.* "Yes, we will. A bed would be preferable, but we can stow in crates, as long as we can eat and go to the bathroom."

The second Human wearing an identical jumpsuit harrumphed. "Tall list of demands. Best if you stay in the crate most of the time, what with that contraband you need to hide."

From behind the two men, Binh waved his claws and mouthed, "Go along with it."

Alize nodded and sighed, and the two dock-workers escorted them to different containers. While guiding Alize to the container, the dockworker whispered, "You'll be able to breathe fine in here. There's a radio inside for when you need the bathroom. You want a pillow?"

Alize cocked her head. "What's it cost?"

"Binh paid for it."

Blinking fast, Alize accepted the offering. When he handed it to her, a bit of his sleeve rolled up, revealing a small tattoo. Earth, with a diagonal line running through it. He adjusted his hat, high enough to expose a lopsided haircut.

Before Alize could thank him, the side of the crate came up, and she was boxed inside. A small portable light flickered near a pillow and a miniature refrigerator. The crate was at least large enough for her to stretch. Its steel lining wasn't enough to sterilize the blood stench from the hanging death.

Might as well get comfortable. I'm probably overreacting.

In the dim light, the green pulse from her wrist allowed her to relax. Reflecting on her final words to Pops, Alize retrieved the message on her omni-tablet.

Pops,

I followed your advice. Fil and I are
leaving to find the deserted moon. I
couldn't wait around for transport,
so we had to go with our first opportunity. But we witnessed quite the
bar fight that I know you would've
secretly loved to see. And no, Fil
didn't use her force field. Once we're
home, I'll beg her to activate it in
the hospital so you can see it.

Anyway, I want to respect your wish,
and I don't want to see you suffering,
but please know that I miss you, Pops.
You've always been my rock. You intro-
duced me to archaeology and showed me
how to love learning. I've met lots of
intellectuals with more degrees than I
have fingers, but they're all so stuffy,
and they don't care about the wonder
and majesty of discovery. With barely
a technician's certificate, you taught
me more taking me around the museum
than I learned in any of my classes,
which is quite the let-down in its
own way. I guess what I'm saying is …
thank you. Thanks for always believing
in me and encouraging me. And I love
you. I love you for being my Pops and
my first teacher, and always believing

me. When I reflect on my best memories, they're all with you. You always
said the museum was our special place.
I don't know if Dr. Dikaio will allow
a memorial for you, but if this discovery brings me any clout, I'll make
sure they honor you properly.

I hope I see you on the other side.

Love,
Alize

A light hum echoed. Alize's balance shifted as the sensation of rising overcame her. She pinged Filenada.

[Alize: Liftoff?]

Nothing. *Odd.* Alize shrugged. Fil was probably settling in for a nap. *Unless—*

After a few quick taps, she pinged Binh.

[Alize: Where's Fil?]

Nothing. Another one.

[Alize: ???]

While Alize prepared another message with much more colorful language, Binh responded.

[Binh: Cool your thrusters, Pinky. She's in a freezer. Probably early onset hibernation.]

Alize exhaled and gritted her teeth.

[Alize: The guy who put me in this crate is Earthquake. He had the tattoos and everything. You do business with them?]

[Binh: If the money's good. I don't have to share their politics if I can share their cash.]

Alize grit her teeth while typing.

[Alize: We are not doing business with them.]

[Binh: Too late. And you aren't, technically. Lady, you hired me. You get what you pay for.]

[Alize: Will they kill her?]

Alize's blood burned like acid. They'd realize Fil was military in a heartbeat.

Binh's response was slow to arrive.

[Binh: Of course not. That wasn't part of the deal. She'll live.]

[Alize: Let me out of this crate.]

[Binh: Just take a snooze. I'll get you when it's time to leave.]

Alize shut off the messenger. They weren't touching one hair on her friend. Not after Fil risked losing her job to come on this insane journey. The rising sensation ended, and Alize felt lighter.

We must be out of lunar orbit now and in the lowered gravity.

Her insides lurched before settling again. She glanced at her grav harness, clicking to signify a gravity adjustment. Settling, she examined the crate's corners with the portable light. Sealed tight.

Maybe she would use her archaeological digging tools, after all.

Heart racing, Alize withdrew the pick and handshovel. Shining the portable light on the crate's hinge, she set to work. The tools and hinge didn't cooperate, though. Her pick was meant for stone, and she couldn't dislodge the hinge, even when using the handshovel as a hammer to drive the pick.

After cursing the hinge's mother and imagining the hinge was on the university's dissertation acceptance board, she summoned enough fury and adrenaline to force a slight budge. Catching her breath, she considered what might happen to Fil, and rage facilitated the rest of the requisite energy flowing to her. The first hinge fell with a groan and creak.

The second and third hinges surrendered sooner. Alize kicked open the crate—dangling refrigerated meats greeted her. She cursed her decisions again. At least she didn't have to smell any of the death, only the coolant and chemicals used to preserve it—not much of an improvement.

Surrounded by waste. The money a few dozen people spend on this could feed thousands. Hand on the refrigerator door, she realized she couldn't fight Earthquake with an archaeologist's toolset. She'd have to sneak around. Maybe the crew here was big enough for her to blend in.

Deep breath, she attempted the doorknob.

Locked.

She let out a sigh and slumped her burning shoulders. Fil was doomed. *But someone will be in eventually, right?*

"Eventually" hung in her head like a sour echo. They'd kill Filenada. Binh would escape unpunished. And nobody would find the Chamayna's superweapon. Jaw clenched, she scanned the room for a meat-carving tool.

Something. Anything.

Her stomach and conscience averted her gaze from the ceiling. But she checked for Fil's sake. More dead animals hung around the crate, gently swaying from their hooks. She peered past the dead meat sacks and found her prize, nauseous as it made her.

Rows of meat hooks.

After a shaky exhale that fogged in front of her, she shoved the crate aside, assisted by the altered gravity. She climbed it and choked down vomit as a curing animal carcass swiveled millimeters from her face.

Do it for Fil, do it for Fil.

Wincing, she reached to the top and found the meat hook. Shaky hands disconnected the once-living creature from the torture implement. A slide and a click brought the hook out of the ceiling slider. Gagging, she maneuvered to the next hanging corpse, suspended in the lack of gravity, and did the same.

Under normal circumstances, she would've lingered on the animals and allowed herself a torrent of sadness and anger. But not when Fil was in trouble. Hooks in hand, she hopped off her crate and set to work on the lock.

Wedging the hook in between the door and the doorway, she pushed and pulled to no avail. She sliced the cooler door's spongy lining with her hook's tip. Smiling, she disconnected the strip, which peeled off, adhesive protesting with sickening snaps.

Collecting herself and ignoring the burning muscles throughout her upper body, Alize dug the hook into the new space she'd created and slid the thin end in between the door and wall. Heaving with the effort, she probed up the space between the door and doorway until she found the bolt. At least, she hoped she'd found it. Breaking into or escaping a locked room wasn't exactly her skill set. Left eye shut, she twisted the hook until she was confident it wrapped around the bolt.

Now what?

She grabbed the second hook and wedged it just above the bolt, sliding it down until she had the bolt on both sides with her hooks. She jostled the hooks until the door budged.

Alize allowed herself one victorious wipe to dry the sweat from her forehead. With another deep breath, she shimmied the hooks with renewed vigor.

Too much vigor.

Both hooks bent in the struggle. Teeth clenched, she grabbed her pick and hammer and gently nudged the hook handles back in place. More shimmying and more swearing, and she heard a click. Hand shaking, she tried the doorknob again.

It turned.

Under different circumstances, this would be an occasion for a happy dance, but Fil was minutes from freezing. Opening the door, she saw Binh on the other side, alone, eyeridges halfway up his forehead.

He scoffed. "Back to bed with you, young lady."

Without thinking, Alize punched him in the snout.

Binh recoiled and waved his tail in front of himself.

"Give me a second, will ya?" He rose and checked over each shoulder before whispering. "I was coming to get you out. We have a problem. Talk in the fridge."

"You go in first." Temptation to punch him again surfaced.

"Fine, fine—hey, you're learning." Binh whispered. He grinned like he hadn't done anything wrong.

Alize didn't like trusting him, but she had no clue where Fil was, and she at least had something sharp on her in case he tried anything.

One hook in front of his face and the other concealed behind her back, she whispered in the most intimidating voice she could summon. "Start talking or I start carving."

"Says the 'meat means murder' girl."

She curled her lip. "I can make an exception for pond scum."

Binh shook his head and stuck out his tongue. "Look, we have a problem."

"My problem is you."

"Pinky, listen. Once we get into space, they'll kill your friend. And probably me. That wasn't in the deal I made with them."

Alize advanced and placed the hook as close to his eye as she could. "What deal?"

"The deal was your friend's armor in exchange for free passage. Not a bad tradeoff, right?"

"We never agreed to that."

"Hence, I didn't ask." Binh pulled his shoulders back, tone suggesting Alize was the unreasonable one in this situation. "Look, Collective armor is expensive and hi-tech. Earthquake offers a nice little reward for it. Excuse me for finding a creative solution to this problem."

"Have they already killed her?"

Binh tsked. "If she dies on a settlement or space elevator, the armor's casualty alert sends instant feedback to The Collective fleet about where she died. Too close to anywhere official and they won't have enough time to get away. But once the ship's hyper-drive kicks in, the messaging system will have a tiny delay. That's their opportunity to kill her without the Collective knowing."

"So your plan was to kill her all along?"

"No, I told them to put her in a freezer unit, let her take a snooze, and snatch the armor. Less messy. When I finalized some details with the captain after you got loaded up, I realized they thought killing her was easier. So here I am to rescue you."

"So why didn't you go to her first?"

"She'd cause a big ruckus. Also, I wouldn't recover from her attacking me like you did. We're gonna have to be stealthy if we make it off this tin can before—" The floor shifted beneath them, and Binh's eyes widened.

The ship's shift lurched in Alize's guts.

Binh tapped his tail on the floor. "About get-ting off this tin can... potentially a tad more difficult than anticipated. Smugglers aren't usually known for punctuality."

"We left the elevator dock? You're positive?"

"Pinky, I've been on ships before. We're off the space elevator." He motioned for her to follow and ran.

FOURTEEN

On an unnamed asteroid in the Kuiper Belt, Human demilitarized zone

STUCK IN HIS office instead of the shooting range where he belonged, Rick squinted at the recruit before him. The Rymon kid. *Not technically a kid. Twenties. Still. So much he hasn't seen. Joined for the wrong reasons. I can smell it on him. Damn Tecton.*

If it were Rick's decision, he'd refuse punks like this. Rymon was the sort of riffraff who gave Earthquake a bad name, the kind of loser who made Rick want to quit. His gaze drifted to his stump for a moment, and he collected himself. They weren't in the strategic position to deny recruits, especially if the person in question had valuable information. At least valuable in Tecton's eyes.

"So." Rick flattened his tone and eyed the youth. "You claim to have hard evidence of an undisturbed tomb. What's in there?" He sipped the steaming stim-brew Amanda made him. Every time he insisted she had more important things than pouring him a stim-brew, her ubiquitous response was she'd rather make it than risk a recruit giving him any sugar on accident. She'd say her favorite line: "not after what happened with Mike."

The Rymon kid, who would definitely sully stim-brew with sugar, messed with his lopsided hair. Rymon looked the part, but he wouldn't survive any culling if Rick had full control. He'd need to be hardened, and fast.

The kid sat rigidly. "According to my source, it's a primitive tomb. Pre-Arkouda. But it has some kind of superweapon hiding in it. Should be worth a fortune." He licked his lips and stammered, "I bet it could be used against them. Put Humans in a dominant role." After a pause, he added, "Where we belong."

Rick held up his hand. "Let me stop you right there, Rymon." Rick sighed. "We don't fight for Human supremacy—" *...you dumbass...* "—only independence. The Arkouda can make us full citizens in the Collective or leave Humans alone as trade partners. Those are their options, and that's Earthquake's official stance. Nothing else. Always been this way. So comport your-self appropriately."

The kid winked. "That's what we have to say, right?"

Rick clenched his jaw tight enough to snap a rock and stuck a thin finger in the kid's face. "It's what we say because it's true. If you just want to kill people, you've joined the wrong organization."

Color drained from Rymon's face. "B-but Earthquake—"

"Moves the galaxy. We aren't the terrorists or extremists the Collective says. You can accept that, or I can put you on the first transport home."

The kid's gaze fell to the floor.

Rick's nostrils flared. "I'll kick your ass so hard your teeth will float back to wherever you came from. No racist garbage on my watch. We're better than that. Understand?"

The kid nodded slowly.

Of course, he doesn't understand.

"Now—" Rick's tone cooled, "how do you know for certain what's in this tomb?"

"I, uh, dated a girl. She told me."

Already hate where this is going.

The kid must've clocked the disappointment on Rick's face. "She's an archaeology student."

Whatever recruiter gave me this kid—

Eyebrows high and eyes wide, Ensign Rymon waved both hands defensively. "Oh, I get how this sounds, sir, but listen. She was super smart and found the moon where this tomb is, and the university refused to fund an expedition or research or whatever."

"Continue."

"She said they wouldn't accept it because the tomb wasn't an Arkouda one. Wasn't a Collective species— didn't think it was worth funding. She was pretty ticked."

Rick leaned forward, balancing his chin on his hand. "What species? Makawe? Blekk?"

"N-no. The ancient one. The Chamayna."

Rick closed his eyes, coaxing the name from memory. He'd seen a few passing mentions in books, but nothing explicit or helpful. "And you're positive this is why her theory was denied?"

The kid nodded, some hair falling into his eyes. "They kept warning her to change her topic, and she went and proved her theory. She figured out where the freaking tomb was."

"So after obtaining the information..." Rick opened his palm, beckoning the youth.

"Well, I talked to some of the guys on Hen4 I know who are sympathizers. They connected me with the recruiter, and they put me on the first transport here."

"But this woman. The student. Does she know what you've done with the information?"

"What?" Rymon fidgeted. "Oh? You see, I didn't tell her. I figured calling you all was best, so I didn't give it a second thought."

"So what you're saying is, another person has the information on the tomb's whereabouts and the desire to be the first one there to extract whatever valuables she can find."

Rymon scratched at the freshly shaved part of his head and a restless leg bounced. "Yes, sir. I don't think she can afford to travel, though."

"You abandoned a girlfriend without a word, huh? So now I have to wonder if you'll abandon Earthquake, too. Give the moon coordinates to my assistant. Amanda Martinez. We'll act on your information. If this turns out to be a waste of resources, we'll get what's owed to us. One way or another." Rick rose. "After you see her, report to the shooting range. Ever held a gun before?"

FIFTEEN

Aboard the light freighter *Kasoro*, Balliol System, Collective space

CONCERN FOR STEALTH flew out the airlock—Alize and Binh's footsteps echoed on the metal tile floor. Running alongside Binh wasn't feasible. Alize's lungs punished her, and her legs hadn't ached like this since quitting varsity hiveball. If nothing else, she'd burned off the cold from her stay in the meat cooler. Each thud of her boots reminded her that expeditionary archaeologists weren't runners.

With his long legs and impressive speed, Binh threatened to leave her in the dust. Doors to more refrigerator units lined the hallway, and Binh was three doors ahead of her now. Digging deep, she pushed herself to somewhat match pace with him. Fil wouldn't do any less for her.

At the hallway's end, two dockworkers brandished pistols that looked homemade.

She tsked. *Can't be surprised these terrorists aren't obeying the "no weapons for Provincials" law.*

One worker called out, "The slimeball let the chick free. They're coming for the Popsicle." Scowling, he advanced, pistol pointed at them. "Hands where I can see them."

Binh yanked open the nearest door with his tail and ducked behind it. Alize joined him.

"Don't fret," Binh whispered. "They aren't dumb enough to fire wild rounds inside a cargo ship."

Alize glared at him. "But they still have guns, and we don't. How long before the whole crew's on top of us?"

Binh tsked. "Small crew. Only ten." Under his breath he muttered, "I think. This ship's mostly bots and beef for rich Humans. Only a few crew members, and they're Earthquake sympathizers, so they can't be that smart. Not to mention they planned on killing me, so even more smart points deducted."

The gun-toting crewman was almost on them. "I repeat, slimeball, come out—claws where I can see them—or this won't end pretty."

"One, I'm not slimy." Binh strutted out of cover, claws on display. "Pretty dry skin, actually. I take medicine for it. And two, it'll never end pretty with your haircut." Binh winked at Alize. "I took the pink hair lady hostage. Toss me your gun, and you can have her."

Alize glowered, and Binh waved a dismissive claw.

The gunman tsked as he approached the door. "Like I can trust you, scale—"

Binh grabbed the gun with his tail. He yanked the gunman's wrist downward and he thudded to the floor.

"Pinky! Squeeze his grav harness."

He writhed under Binh's grip, grimacing. Alize froze. "Do it, hairball!"

Alize forgot how to move, and she had a furious compulsion to scratch her neck under her grav harness.

The gunman rolled over and wrestled with Binh's tail to free his arm. "Jake! Call for backup!" He bared his teeth at Binh, using his other hand to grab at his tail.

Binh dodged, jostling him with his tail. "Stop being so clingy." He grasped the gunman's hand and pried his fingers off one at a time. "Drop it or me start with the bitey-bitey." He rotated an eye to Alize. "Gonna help?"

Alize clenched her teeth, forcing Pops' mandatory self-defense class to memory and utilized a basic kick. She booted the gunman in the kneecap, and he dropped the weapon with a yelp.

The gunman's bottom jaw quivered. "P-please. D-don't kill me."

"Kill you? No, no, limpdick. I certainly get great joy out of seeing Humans defenseless and on their knees, but you're not dying today. At least not because of me. Now, hands." After the gunman raised his hands above his head, Binh glanced at Alize. "Pinky, got anything to tie him up among your archaeology tools?"

"Cut out the nicknames. I have a better idea." Alize knelt in front of their captive and reached for his neck. After she unfastened his anti-grav necklace, he cursed at her, then rose from the floor in the absence of a gravity field, flailing his limbs.

Binh smiled. "Huh. That was smart." He winked at Alize. "This is an old vessel, so no ship-wide gravity adjuster." Without moving his aim from the center of the goon's face, Binh used his tail and free hand to rotate him, suspended in midair. "Can't wait to see what you had for lunch when it comes out."

Binh examined his pockets until he produced a card key and a credit chit. "Why thank you, kindly. Now, enjoy the cold." He grabbed the crewman's boot and pushed him toward the refrigerator.

The hapless gunman flailed to escape the momentum of Binh's shove. "Let me down, you scaly b—"

Binh slammed the door shut and pulled out the card key. Before swiping the key to lock the guy inside, he stole a glance at Alize. "One down, Pinky." He snatched the dropped pistol from the ground, small in his claws. "Ever shoot before?"

Alize shook her head. "Never touched one, and I don't particularly want to."

"Ah. Hence the earlier paralysis. Suit yourself. I'll sell it somewhere."

"Can we get Filenada, now? The other guy took off."

Binh nodded. "Should be at the end of this hall. Those two must've been the firing squad." A ship-wide alarm blared. "Not good. Keep his grav harness. Might need it later."

Red lights flared from the ceilings, accompanied by a low-pitched buzz.

With heavy footsteps, Alize followed Binh to the end of the corridor where a neon sign blinked: "Frozen Storage."

Alize shouted over the alarm. "Any idea which room Fil's in?"

"My guess would be the third door on the left."

"How do you know?"

"Most Arkoudae are right-pawed, and they aren't as thorough as people give them credit for."

"Wait, really?"

"Of course not, genius. I've smuggled stuff on this ship before. That's the freezer they use. It's how I knew which refrigerator you'd be in." His tail curled tightly. "And it's why I'm so pissed they turned on me. Something's shaking up in Earthquake. They're prepping for something big."

"You sold us out to them."

"Semantics," Binh muttered.

At the freezer door, three more crew members greeted them with pistols.

"Nobody move," one said. "Binh, drop the gun."

"You first." Binh casually peered over his shoulder. Alize followed his gaze but didn't see anybody behind them.

The crewman who spoke advanced. "You're giving us that money you owe us."

"Gentlemen." Binh grinned wide. "I have no idea what you're talking about. You didn't check the fine print."

"Can it, slimeball. Nobody scams Earthquake."

Alize's eyes darted. If she bolted, they might kill Binh. With him a few steps in front of her, she had a clear view of his tail, which he moved around wildly behind him, almost as if he were probing for something with it.

Buying time?

One of the crewmen hit a button on an omni-tablet, silencing the alarm.

Binh's tail tapped the tip of Alize's fist, which still clutched the grav harness.

She murmured, "All right. Get him close, and I'll do it."

Binh's tail tapped her knuckle twice and slithered away, returning to the side of his body. "You know, Jake, we never did quite settle on any specific amount of cash. I didn't do anything wrong. I handed you a Collective soldier, practically gift-wrapped. Wearing armor. And told you the temperature to trigger hibernation. So really, I don't see what the issue is. I'd call that debt settled. Also, I'd call myself awesome. But in fairness, I do that anyway."

"Shut your damn snout!" The crewman was close enough for Alize to see his face. He didn't have the hardened appearance of a trained soldier as expected. In fact, he looked so casual it was unsettling. This guy could've been Garott or any other loser she'd dated.

With one more step, Binh whipped his tail at the crewman's ankles, and he stumbled.

Alize pounced, shoving the extra grav harness over his head. He collapsed to the floor under the added pressure and dropped his pistol. Grabbing it, Alize refused to shudder.

At least I know which way to point it.

Binh stomped on Jake's back and called to the others. "Now, it seems like we're in more of a bargaining position. We can still honor the original deal. You get the armor, and the ladies leave with me on an escape pod. Nobody needs to die. Sound good?" Switching to a mocking Earth accent, he added, "Well,

I sure do think it sounds just great dandy peachy-keen, Mr. Binh. You're quite the businessman."

"You're dead, scale tail," one of the remaining crewmen called.

Binh lowered his pistol and aimed at Jake's head. "I'm dead? You sure you want to clean up this blood stain I'm about to make? The way you *ke-noks* play fast and loose with the Health Ministry's guidelines on food safety, I highly doubt you have cleaning agents capable of handling blood and brain matter. Drop your guns, let them float over to us, and we'll get outta your nasty hair."

Beneath Binh's foot, Jake grunted. "Just do it." He writhed under the pressure of the increased gravity.

Alize inhaled and steadied her aim at the other two crewmen. She couldn't hit the broad side of a ship, but they didn't know that. "You heard him."

The two crewmen exchanged glances and tossed their pistols in front of them.

"Good," Binh said. "Now shove them over like good little rascals."

They complied, disdainful expressions clear from where Alize stood. Their pistols hung in midair, bobbing in the absence of gravity.

Once the guns passed the halfway point of the hallway, Binh grunted. "All righty, now scram." After they left, Binh stooped, meeting Jake's eye level. "And I didn't forget about you, Jakey." Binh wrapped his tail around Jake's wrist and pulled it behind the small of Jake's back.

Jake grunted again, deeper this time, as if his own wrist was a cinder block. Alize's eyes widened as Binh did the same to Jake's other wrist. "There, you got a little workout for yourself. Think of their faces after you beat triple gravity."

He started walking, motioning for Alize to follow. Jake's eyes bulged and ridged veins pulsed at the surface of his reddening skin. Chattering teeth prevented him from saying anything approaching comprehensible. Alize's choice was to save the killer from momentary suffering or save her best friend's life. She shook her head and mouthed "sorry" as she passed.

Binh glanced over his shoulder, increasing the pace. "Hey, don't shed any tears for that loser." He stuck out his tongue between his teeth. "Oh, don't gawk at me like that, Pinky. It was hurt him or get ourselves killed. You have to sacrifice if you want to survive to the next payday, and that's what I'm doing."

Alize nodded and caught a glimpse of her wrist. Green pulsing. She exhaled.

They opened up the freezer and found a huge crate that occupied the majority of the inside. As if alive, the crate shook, colliding with hanging cuts of frozen meat Alize could never afford. Alize gasped. "Fil? Can you hear us?" In her periphery, more frozen meat swayed in the absence of gravity.

A muffled roar returned the question.

Glaring at Binh, Alize said, "I thought you told them the temperature to let her hibernate? She must've been miserable in there."

Binh lowered his eyeridges. "I told them the wrong temperature, professor. That way, if they did try and lodge a blaster bolt between her eyes, they'd have an awake fuzzball to contend with instead of a sleeping one. In my experience, it's harder for individuals to defend themselves while they're dreaming."

Is that a dig at the Arkouda religion?

Alize gripped the crude pistol and found the lock on the crate. "Fil, take a giant step away from the sound of my voice. I'm going to shoot the locking mechanism." Alize approached the lock and steeled herself to fire her first weapon. She'd come too far and put too much at risk to get squeamish anymore. Alize and Filenada would be remembered as heroes of archaeology and ancient history. She fired, and the recoil almost made her drop the weapon. The blaster bolt snapped the locking mechanism in half. Alize's hands tingled with the gun's vibration, and it sickened her. Despite the rush of power she felt, she never wanted to operate one of these again—how Filenada could do this professionally and casually was a complete mystery to her.

But Binh wouldn't run this show. She clenched her teeth and took control.

Heart pounding, Alize dropped the pistol and withdrew her pick and hammer from her jacket—weapons she could wield with a clean conscience. Ordering Binh to step aside, she pried the front end of the massive crate open, and Filenada came into view, crouched in the fetal position, rocking back and forth. The pungent odor of Fil's nervous pheromones wafted out.

"Fil?"

"L—Leeze?"

"You're safe now."

Fil bared her teeth. "I need to hit something."

Alize entered the crate and grabbed Fil's giant paw. "I'm glad you're safe."

Binh shuddered, and his teeth chattered. "Hey fuzzball sisters, can we hurry it up? Your charming friend here wasn't cursed to wander the stars with natural insulation."

Misty breath forming, Alize nodded. She helped Fil stand, more for moral support than actual leverage. They left the freezer.

"Finally," Binh said. "The escape pods are down the next corridor on the right. We can—oh *nguc.*"

Five crewmen blocked the escape pods.

"Get on your knees, Binh," Jake barked from behind them.

Alize checked over her shoulder and saw another three crewmen, all with the same lopsided haircuts and Earth tattoos on their necks, Jake in the center.

Alize had left the pistol in the freezer. Fil's patience, too.

Binh sank to his knees. "You know it's customary in your culture to buy the other person a meal before making this request. That's really introductory level."

Jake snarled, "Shut up. Shoulda killed me, asshole."

Binh flicked his tail. "What can I say? I'm a softie. You sure recovered quick. Did one of your buddies help you up?"

One of the other crewmen at the opposite end shouted at Alize and Fil. "On your knees, too, ladies. This'll get ugly real quick."

Alize complied.

Binh contorted his claws in a gesture most cultures found offensive. "Get ugly? You're already ugly."

Fil snarled and removed her jacket, exposing her armor. The other crewmen staggered back and adjusted their stances. She tapped on the chestpiece twice, and a blue crackling energy field emanated from it. It created a rapidly expanding bubble of electricity, making Alize's hair stand on end and warming her skin.

I hope I can tell Pops about this later.

Filenada exhaled. "Maybe twenty seconds before the charge gives out. Binh, are you strong enough to hold an Arkouda sidearm?" She pressed a button on her shoulderpad, then her helmet and visor unfolded from the armor's back, folding around her head.

"Not without antigrav."

Filenada tapped the small of her back on her armor and withdrew a plastoid brick. It unfolded into a pistol bigger than Alize's head.

"Scatter," Fil barked. Alize darted left and Binh to the right. The energy field fell—Fil aimed at the bigger crowd of crewmen and shot one in the kneecap.

The crewmen shouted arguments among themselves about who to target and where to aim.

Blaster bolts flew at Fil. Some dented her armor, which she grunted off. Fil picked off another crewman, hitting him in the shoulder.

A bolt sizzled above Alize, missing her by millimeters, sending searing heat over her scalp. Amid the confusion and chaos, she ducked behind the open freezer door. More carcasses hung from hooks inside. Gritting her teeth, she lowered the settings on her grav harness and jumped high enough to grab two stray meat hooks dangling from the ceiling.

Gripping the hooks, she knew they could distract and slow even though she lacked the strength to kill. That was what she could do for Filenada. She couldn't shoot a gun, but she could throw a dart. At first, the hooks resisted her jostling and tugging, but eventually unscrewed.

She exited to find Fil trading gunfire with the crewmen on either side of her, and Binh sidled against an open door for cover. Fil ceased shooting and limped toward them.

Alize darted out from behind cover and threw the meat hooks in rapid succession. The first one sailed past her target's head, and the second harmlessly hit him in the chest. But that distraction was enough for Fil to align a shot and shatter his kneecap. Amalgamated blood and joint fluid sprayed on Alize's jacket, with several globules floating away in the absence of gravity.

One crewman remained standing, the others groaning on the floor, attending to wounds instead of their firearms while blood bubbled out, floating into the low-gravity hallway. The last crewman surveyed the chaos and dropped his weapon.

Filenada roared—guttural and horrible, making Alize's arm hairs straighten.

Groans of fallen crewmen muffled Binh's words as he said, "Damn. Can you teach me to shoot like that?"

Fil tapped a button on the gun, and it folded back onto itself. "Can we find escape pods first?"

"Next corridor on the left," Binh said. "One of these goons has something that belongs to me. I'll catch up."

Alize glared. "Are you going to kill them?"

Binh's eyes widened. "A little innocent Earth-lamb like me wouldn't do that. Turn around and keep walking. I'll catch up. One of these shitsniffers has the escape pod launch codes."

Flattening herself against the wall, Alize followed Fil down the metal patchwork hallway. Half of her expected to hear a gunshot and a hissing cackle, but she put the worry out of her mind.

Binh had plenty of opportunities to kill throughout this kerfuffle, and he hadn't pulled the trigger. But Alize had. The realization sent a shiver down her spine.

"Fil, this is a disaster. I'm sorry."

"Hey, you freed me outta that box and the bigger box that box was in." Fil smiled at her. "This'll be a Nightmare of a story for the bar."

"You really think we'll make it there and back home in one piece?" Alize asked. "After all this—"

"Don't finish that sentence, Leeze. We'll knock back drinks while sleazy guys tell us we're hot before you know it." Peering ahead, Fil pointed to a neon sign in Human. "What's that say?"

"Escape hatch. Emergency only."

"Why don't we toss these chumps in the escape pods and keep the ship?"

Alize shook her head. "Neither of us could reroute the pilot program. I don't know if Binh could, either. If this cargo's a front for an Earthquake smuggling oper-ation, I don't want them to figure out where we were or our intended destination."

A thud-thud-whoosh approached from behind. Alize glanced behind her to see Binh running. "Ladies, this is a run, not a walk situation."

They jogged to catch him, Fil's limp slowing their pace. Binh pulled out a card key and stopped in front of a locked door. Swiping entry, the door creaked open. They passed through the doorway, and the airlock decontamination began automatically. Alize covered her arms at the sight of the descending spray tubes.

Fil placed her paw on Alize's shoulder. "First decontam? Yikes. I thought you were joking about never leaving Hen4."

Binh tapped his tail on the floor. "Hey, so, uh, the decontamination... it's going to ding that I'm sick." He cocked his head at them. "Oh, don't make that face. It's genetic, not contagious."

Fil removed her paw from Alize and squinted at Binh. "Is that why your scales have a grayer look? Do you have that shedding disease? I heard it constantly hurts."

"Or is that why you're an irredeemable asshole?" Alize asked.

"I heard I have a right to privacy, and being in the same space as either of you constantly hurts my nose." His forked tongue poked through his grimace.

The chilled mist of the decontamination spray ended, and Alize felt lightheaded. After the spray passed over Binh, a dull chime sounded, accompanied by an amber light overhead. Binh scoffed and muttered something in Lo-sat. It was too fast for Alize, but she caught the phrase "every time."

As the acrid vapors dissipated, the airlock lurched open to the hangar. No nasty surprises inside, no crewmen with guns in their faces this time. Binh indicated the largest pod on their right. The other pods in the hangar were much smaller, meant for only one or two Humans. The biggest one could accommodate an Arkouda and was likely only there to comply with Collective regulations, even though Arkoudae would never join this crew. They lumbered inside the pod, Binh's lanky height and Fil's bulk making a tight squeeze.

At the helmboard, Binh strained to turn his head toward Alize. "Now can you give me those coordinates?"

"The moon wasn't designated with an official name."

"Thanks for the helpful information. Would you like to write my will? I have a few things I want to make sure my sister takes care of once it's my time. And you use such beautifully specific language—"

"Will you let me finish? The planet's a gas giant called Dusoi and the star's a brown dwarf designated Xechas. The planet has three moons. Two are ice cubes, and the smallest is rock. That's what we want."

"Lovely." Binh tapped in something to the helmboard, the airlock where they entered sealed shut, and the hangar opened.

The pod lurched out into empty space.

Alize turned to Fil. "We're in here pretty tight. Will this mess with your claustrophobia?"

Fil huffed. "I'm not claustrophobic. It was … very dark in that box."

"And stinky," Binh said.

"You'll be the one who stinks when I rip you a new asshole. Over here, there's a great view of space and I can see everything."

Binh sidled away from the women and slumped against the pod's curved wall. "You know it's not a window, right? That's just a viewscreen showing us what's outside."

Fil tsked. "Do you think I'm a cub? Of course I know that."

"So what's your return plan, ladies?"

Filenada tapped the side of her helmet, and it folded into her armor. "None of your concern, Scales."

Binh waved a claw. "So you're going to send a distress signal from your armor and wait out your rescue, huh?"

Alize shook her head. "How long until we get there?"

"A few hours. We could've gotten closer if you told me where we're going in the first place."

"Do many ships pass through the Xechas system?"

Binh yawned. "No, but I could've found one going to a closer star cluster. Or something."

Fil bared her teeth. "Or you would've sold us out even more than you already did."

"Well, yes." Binh winked. "That's always a possibility."

"Maybe not everyone is a *ke-nok*, then?" Alize winked.

"So it's an insult," Fil said.

"The only insult is you sullying my beautiful language. And the only circumstance in which everyone's a *ke-nok* is in comparison to me."

Alize let out a long sigh. "This'll be a long trip."

"Not if you shut up," Binh said through a grin.

"Take your own advice," Fil grumbled.

SIXTEEN

**Aboard the designated civilian ship, *Dizhen*,
interstellar Collective space**

RICK EXAMINED THE makeshift barracks inside
the *Dizhen*. Not a single unmade bed or speck of dust.
About damn time. It even smelled fresh, a welcome
change from its usual sweat and angst stench.

Five new recruits stood at attention. Each came
from different settlements, one bearing the tan of a
native Earther.

Of the ten he'd received last week, only this
handful surpassed his rigorous standards. Fewer if
Tecton hadn't been on his ass about his strictness. Why
Tecton hadn't made the connection to Rick's success
compared to the other commanders was anybody's
guess. Earthquake functioned best like a military and
worst when its members functioned like militants—a
pattern so obvious it defied logic.

The runt Rymon would've been shipped home if it weren't for the promised information. If Rick discovered who informed the leader of the kid's intel, he'd thank the rat with his fist. Acting on a rumor wasn't sound military strategy. The recruiters should understand and so should Tecton—he claimed to understand they waged war, but Rick's so-called colleagues operated like gangsters and terrorists.

They'd see. Once Rick's recruits survived the culture shock of the patented Crith training methods, they'd be loyal to him and unflinching in a fight. But so much of this hinged on them passing muster in the first place, and this Rymon kid was not.

Rick paced the line of his squad, the new ones in front, twelve veterans behind. His backup squad on the other ship would be getting their mandatory rest right about now.

"Earthquake. That name means something. Don't tarnish it. It's your life. It's your identity. We can only survive against the Collective if we succeed in smart, surgical strikes. If there's a Collective presence on this moon, we cannot throw our lives away. Their armor's their greatest technological achievement, but it's useless compared to a force of nature. Get that in your head. Earthquake's a force of nature. Stealth matters against them. The only successful kills of Arkoudae were unarmored. So take your shot carefully. You usually don't get a second chance once their armor's operational."

Feet planted shoulder-width apart, hand behind his back, Rick continued. "We hope nobody's on this moon, but we can't gamble on it. We go in silently.

No crazy stunts in space, either. One show of force, and it blows our cover as a transport." He intentionally made eye contact with each member. "There's a script if we're intercepted. Stick to it. And another script if space traffic controllers flag us. Stick to it. We have compartments to hide the guns. Don't carry weapons in the open, especially if we're docked. Act smart, fight smarter, and we live another day. That's how we beat the Collective."

Rick turned to his second in command. "Moreno."

The young man stiffened and saluted, face bearing the ghost of a grimace.

Rick nodded. "Moreno, tell the new recruits why we hit the archaeological sites."

Alejandro Moreno nodded. "Thank you, sir." He wheeled on the rest of the group like a marionette.

Not too rigid, son.

"We have two reasons." He held up one finger. "Undermine Arkouda culture." He raised another. "Unlock hidden intelligence from the past."

Rick waved his hand. "Thanks, Moreno. Back on Earth, Monsieur Tecton collects samples of lost technology. He believes that may hold the key to turning the tide."

At the mention of Tecton's name, the older recruits took the cue. "Hail."

Rick's facial features obeyed orders and suppressed the cringe. These kids never got the chance to read Earth history. "So if we find some lost technology and it's useful, we'll be the team to rescue Humanity."

A few new recruits and older members broke protocol and grinned, exchanging glances and nods. A lesser leader than Rick would chastise them for informality, but occasional lapses of protocol were good for morale.

"That's right. But brace yourselves. We could be in for a fight or running into a dead end. This moon's uncharted. So we are going in blind."

"Let's go." Rick headed toward the training room.

He'd prepared by outfitting the target practice module with hit sensors in a few choice areas. It was too large to fit in most other rooms of the repurposed civilian ship designed for Humans. The machine was specially designed by Earthquake to be the size of an Arkouda and moved like one. Rick's input had been key in its original design, so he was able to procure one for his squad at a lower cost.

"All right, folks, this'll move toward you at the top clocked running speed of an Arkouda without armor. We will fight the Collective military wearing armor. That will slow them down, but at the rate their technology advances, we need to be ready for anything." Stepping into the cargo hold where they drilled, Rick heard the training dummy machine whir to life, and then it charged him.

A few new recruits gasped and exhaled sighs after the machine retracted, millimeters from Rick's face.

"Calm down. It won't hurt you. Today." Rick indicated the few target areas on the training dummy. "Arkoudae are as easy to shoot as it is to shoot your feet. But their armor more than makes up for the difference. We have tech teams at headquarters dreaming up a way to puncture their armor, but for now, assume your weapons are useless."

Rick reached for the omni-tablet attached to his hip, and the training machine's frame puffed out, resembling an Arkouda in full armor. "When their helmet is up like on the dummy, even less of their body is exposed. For whatever reason, most Collective soldiers will avoid wearing the headgear if they can. The helmet makes most of them a tad claustrophobic. But they won't hesitate come battle-time."

With his knuckles, he rapped the area on the dummy representing the neck. "All the more reason we need to get the drop on them in all situations. By the grace of the Great Mystery or God or whatever you're praying to, you have a two second delay—then the helmet covers the face. Your only shot's right here." He pointed at the neck again. "A good hit will puncture an artery and knock them out of battle. A great shot will hit their windpipe. A perfect shot will go through to the spine and paralyze them." Rick smiled at the new recruits' dumbfounded blinks. "If we can paralyze one, we can take its armor and analyze it. The Collective hides their secrets. No surprise, right?"

Nods and scoffs answered his question.

"Well..." Rick grimaced. "Their armor has a failsafe to keep anyone else from deconstructing their armor. When the wearer dies, the armor sends a report to the Fleet and shuts off. A patriotic suicide, like a captured spy. But if we can paralyze the wearer—" he appraised the recruits' expressions, checking for comprehension, "we can keep the soldier alive while HQ learns the armor's secrets." After a definitive exhale, he pointed to the neck area on the dummy again. "If you think you can score a shot to the chest or face after the helmet shows up, don't bother. Even on an unarmored Arkouda, a shot to the torso is wasted ammo. Their midsections are so thick, the odds you'll hit an organ are minimal. Go for the cripple shot over the kill shot. But remember—" his tone flattened, "the lives of your brothers and sisters-in-arms are more valuable than anything else. Protect each other and yourselves first. If killing an Arkouda is the only way you'll leave a fight alive, then that's what needs to happen."

He inhaled, puffing his chest. "Now, we'll score for this session based on where on the neck you hit. Who's first?"

SEVENTEEN

Aboard an escape pod, interstellar hyperspace lanes, Collective fringe

ALIZE STARED SLACK-JAWED at the viewscreen relaying the rippled artwork of bent stars and nebulae cascading around the pod. She'd seen videos of this phenomenon, of course, but watching it live was breathtaking. Alize sighed. It wasn't technically happening at this moment since the viewscreen wasn't actually a window. Still. The ease and speed of travel was something she only fantasized about growing up.

Fil browsed reports on her helmet feed, sifting celebrity gossip from the military reports, while Binh napped, sprawled out on his seat, tail patting the floor every few minutes.

Fil gasped, snapping Alize's travel-trance.

After a snort, Binh rubbed his eyes. "What's wrong?"

Fil's transparent visor display flashed warnings too small for Alize to read. "Company. Something's tugging on the pod."

Binh sat upright. "Gravitational or physical?" Concern instead of sarcasm slithered through his voice. He wedged between them to the helmboard, eyes darting across the viewscreen. "Magnetic?"

The pod's velocity shifted, and Alize's guts somersaulted. Breakfast threatened a resurgence. Yesterday's dinner, too.

Watching the viewscreen, the interstellar dance halted. Alize's grav harness vibrated and whirred. A newer model would've prevented any grav settling sickness, but this was what she could afford. Any desire to eat again left.

A low-pitched alarm chimed in Arkouda and repeated in Human. "Stop imminent."

"Sarcasm imminent," Binh muttered, wiping away sleep-drool from his chin. "Eyes peeled, mammals. That was a magnetic tug. Something knew we were inbound."

Alize squinted and caught a glimpse of oblong gray dots in the distance. "What are those?"

Fil leaned toward the screen. "Ships?" Adjusting her head angle, she nodded. "Yeah, metal scrapper ships. Who in the Nightmare has a magnet on a scrapper strong or fast enough to yank a pod from hyperspace?"

Binh waved off her questions. "Catching magnetic asteroids to harvest the metal." The pod lurched in the dots' direction. "*Nguc.* Or catching small ships for scrap. Or ransom."

"Nope! That's not happening with us," Fil said. "Can this dinky thing escape the pull?"

Alize rubbed her temples. "If they're scrappers scumming for a payday, won't they just let us go if the ship's occupied?"

"They're usually a reasonable bunch. But—" Binh's voice stopped cold.

Once their pod was close enough for the scrappers to rotate and open wide hulls, another ship had materialized.

Cloaked no longer.

This gargantuan structure looked nothing like any Collective or Human ship Alize had ever seen. It pierced space like a grand hateful icicle, rivaling the space elevator on Hen4 City in size.

Binh gulped. "It's the Blekk."

"Don't tell me you're scared of some small-time goons," Fil said, a ghost of a laugh in her voice.

Alize folded her arms. "Fil, is it normal for scrapper magnets to be strong enough to pull a pod out of hyperspace?"

"No, but—"

Binh snarled. "But nothing. These aren't traders. They're pirates, for *nguc's* sake. And not just any run-of-the-mill bootleggers. This is the Drowned Star. Look at the symbols on the hull, Frosty. There's a short list of parties I don't mess with." He raised two fingers in succession. "One: the Drowned Star. Two: the Earth lady who sells me hot sauce. That's it."

A booming voice overtook the comm, speaking in accented Human. "Hail unnamed Vessel, you're coming aboard the *Takel*. Resist and we'll drown you."

"I could barely understand that," Fil said. "That was Human, right?"

"The language," Binh said, "but not the speaker. One of my kinfolk in all likelihood. Frosty, you have breathers for us, right? We'll need them. Blekk fill their ships with salt water so they can breathe."

Fil handed them each a breather.

Binh affixed the longer one to his snout and unfolded the eye covers. "That's why that voice sounded muffled, too. Likely had his face covered by a breather." Binh shuddered. "Can't imagine what all that saltwater does to someone's scales."

Alize unfolded the eye flaps on her breather. They didn't obscure her vision as much as expected, but they certainly didn't give the environmental informa-tion any of Fil's gear did.

The pod alarm buzzed, chiming a message in Human and then Arkouda. "Unauthorized latch opening. Potential docking inbound."

Alize thumbed her grav harness. "I never met a Blekk before."

Binh waved his tail. "Can't say I'm surprised. They're not exactly the 'museum visiting' type. Have you ever eaten the Human food called calamari? You can get it on Earth."

"Huh? N-no. I don't think so."

"Good."

The pod unlatched with a faint hiss, and an overpowering bite of salted air assaulted her nos-trils. Adrenaline pumped and goaded her heart to beat faster.

With a whine and creak, the door descended, flooding the pod with artificial light from the Blekk ship, but no water followed. The engineers designed the hull to be metallic and bare, meant for vast amounts of mineral cargo.

In front of the pod loomed a thin robot on a single spherical wheel. The entire machine seemed little more than a rolling stand for a viewscreen at the top, the center a long, telescoping pole over the wheel. The screen displayed a male Lo-sat's face. The verdant sheen of his scales contrasted with Binh's gray pallor.

He eyed the three of them, nodded in Fil's direction, and spoke in flawless Arkouda. "Citizens, Provincial, welcome aboard the Scrapper *Takel* in service of the Drowned Star *Blodsed*, helmed by the Pirate Lord, His Eminence, Sjorover. Mind your manners and you can leave for your homes today." After a sideways glance at Alize, he repeated the message in Human, albeit thickly accented.

Alize frowned. *This guy... I swear I've seen his picture somewhere.* Something in the pattern of his scales and eyeridges tugged at the edge of her memory.

Binh approached the robot. He hissed in Lo-sat, and Alize only caught the words, "who," "working," and "ship." Binh's cadence in his native tongue wasn't the stiff academic dialect of Lo-sat, which Alize had picked up over the years. It carried a lyrical quality, in defiance of her ability to translate. She observed with a cocked eyebrow.

Fil's ears flattened. "I thought this was a Blekk ship. Who's this Lo-sat guy?"

The Lo-sat in the screen hissed something to Binh in their shared rhythmic dialect.

Smirking, Binh peered over his shoulder at the women. "The Blekk suck at other languages. Tentacles instead of tongues and no vocal cords. Obviously not their fault, but they're worse than the Makawe at interspecies conversation."

"So he's their interpreter?" Alize asked.

"Contracting out a translator is standard practice. Lo-sats can mimic their sign language with our tails. Besides…" He placed a claw over his diagonal chest-piece. "…as the master race, my people make phenomenal translators." He pushed his tongue between his teeth. "For the same reason we make phenomenal lovers."

Alize rolled her eyes. "What'd you say?"

"Just asked him his name."

"Why would pirates notice us? Not like we have anything valuable…" Alize's heart froze. *Fil's armor!*

Balanced on the spherical wheel, the robot angled away from Binh and rolled toward Alize. "You eluded Earthquake, madam." The Lo-sat's expression was soft, and hints of a frown showed at the edges of his snout. "The Drowned Star pirate king is entering diplomatic relations with the organization known as Earthquake. Your escape pod was on a bounty list, updated within the hour. Your apprehension and delivery to them will make positive strides." A light sigh escaped, followed by a whispered, "Sorry."

Fil stepped in front of the robot. "And why're we on this list?"

Addressing Fil in Arkouda, he said, "You stole this pod, Citizen. That is, unless these two kidnapped you and forced you in." Arching an eyeridge, he added, "Although I find that incredibly unlikely since your armor's online."

With a click, the telescoping pole collapsed. The spherical wheel rose to the screen, expanding into a drone propeller. The Lo-sat on the screen har-rumphed. "Proceed to decontamination and pressure change. The scrapper will dock with the *Blodsed*. Lord Sjorover, pirate king, will have an audience with you before you're detained."

Alize glared at him. "What happened to us going home today if we complied?"

"Ah," the translator closed his eyes, eyeridges flut-tering almost apologetically. "Force of habit. I'm sup-posed to say that to everybody."

Something in his scale pattern and downcast expression tugged at her memory. Alize had seen this man before. Somewhere. Maybe as a kid. Or in a pic-ture. She just couldn't place who or when.

The drone spun around, and the three travelers gaped at each other.

Eyes trained on the robot, Binh shouted, "You rec-ognize that guy? You should, since his dad started the Eleva War."

Alize's eyes widened.

"You've never been to Earth, Pinkster. Never learned the full story." Binh folded his arms. "Yeah, see, his dad made the initial contact with Humans under an Arkouda crime boss' employ. Isn't it funny how the official Collective story leaves out the others involved, even when it's for something bad? So this guy's dad is a peculiar mix of traitor, outlaw, hated, and yet still overlooked. A forgettable footnote."

The robot halted.

From Alize's periphery, she caught a grin sneak across Binh's snout. "Don't deny it, Cu-dan. I grew up on Earth." He scoffed. "So ... translating for pirates like your dad did for crime bosses. The Sourstem doesn't fall far from the Greenbark."

The robot spun on its bi-polar axis, the face in the screen glaring with wide yellow eyes. He said something in Lo-sat, so fast and angry Alize couldn't parse anything.

Pulling back far enough to engage Alize and Fil, he spoke in Arkouda, his flawless accent marred by annoyance. He glared at Filenada. "After the War, my dad couldn't find work." Acid seeped into his voice. "Even after he served his time in reformatory." He switched languages to Human and stared blasters at Alize. "And half the Humans hate me because of my daddy, too. All the ones who don't like the Collective. I've gotten more than a few death threats."

The robot swiveled to Binh, and more rapidfire hissing ensued. Alize only caught the word for "time," but it didn't feel like it fit in their tone.

An ex-soldier, a pacifist, and a thief with questionable loyalties against a tub full of hardened pirates? "There must be another way, Fil." Alize's gaze strayed to the continuing poetic argument of hisses exchanged between Binh and the translator.

"Hey," she called out. "How well are they paying you? And what are the odds they could get someone to do your job cheaper?"

The robot whirled around to face Alize. "Both of those things are none of your business. You'll make me late. Now come on."

Alize smirked and folded her arms. "So your bosses want to buddy up with Earthquake, huh? Well if you think half the Human race hates you because of what your dad did, do you want to guess which side of that divide Earthquake falls on? If your bosses want a bargaining chip, you're a pretty good one, I'd say."

Binh sidled beside Alize, tail wrapping around her shoulders, which she nudged off. He spoke in Arkouda. "The pink haired lady has a point, Cu-dan. Earthquake would kill you. And they'd publish it. Everyone would know, and trust me, they'd make it slow and painful. Retribution." He put a claw over his chest. "It's not fair, I know. Most humans think they're better off with the Collective, but Earthquake hearkens back to a time when Humans fought over resources on a dying planet." He shrugged and winked. "And who can blame them? So how about you ditch the Drowned Star before they sell you to a bunch of Human terrorists, huh?" He inclined his snout toward Alize's hair. "Is this the last image you want? Nasty hair falling on your scales as you take your last breath? You think the Earthquake fanatics care about what happens to your claws after they kill you?"

Cu-dan responded in Human. "I wish I could say you were crazy. But living on settlements is where I got the death threats. And this was safely in Collective space." He glanced around and leaned toward the screen, lowering his voice. "Look, I'll let you free, but you need to take me with you. I have nowhere to go. If you're running from Earthquake and have a head start, that's where I need to be."

"Deal," Binh said.

Fil growled. "We can't talk about this first?"

Alize glanced at the escape pod behind them. "How will you get us off this ship?"

Cu-dan smiled thinly with his lipless mouth. "When under the employ of pirates, one must be ready for quick departures."

Binh hissed a string of mostly unintelligible rhyming syllables, but Alize caught the words for "steal" and "gun."

After another private exchange, Cu-dan nodded and addressed Fil. "Citizen, can I have a Guarantee of Passage?"

Alize nudged her and Fil nodded.

Cu-dan's shoulders relaxed. "Give me ten minutes."

The screen on the robot blinked off, and the drone hovered gracefully to the floor.

Fil wheeled on Alize, ears perked and stiff. "How do we know we can trust this guy?"

Alize craned to make eye contact. "Did you have another idea that didn't involve dead bodies?"

Binh folded his arms. "I like the 'no dead bodies' idea because that means I survive. It's not a horrible plan. And this guy isn't thrilled about his employers. He's scamming for a buck any way he can but isn't going to risk his tail more than he has to. You must've scared him good, Professor Pinkles."

"Being judged over something your father did isn't unique to Lo-sats," Alize huffed. "I've been harassed and belittled, too. I can't imagine getting a death threat, let alone several."

Binh raised an eyeridge. "Hmpf. In the meantime, Frosty, be ready in case any tentacle heads come through that airlock."

Fil tensed. "Did they hear us from the scrapper's cabin?"

Binh shrugged. "Definitely. But not many Blekk bother learning Arkouda. They're not even considered Provincials like Stinky Pinky."

Alize squinted and pushed the tip of Binh's tail away from her face. "You're trying to distract me. What did you say to him, Binh?"

Binh waved his tail. "Don't worry about it. We can trust this guy."

Fil bared her teeth. "We barely trust you."

Pacing in front of them, Binh said, "Then this will be a phenomenal exercise in overturning preconceived notions, won't it?"

Minutes passed as slowly as standard years while they deliberated a plan.

With a loud click, a light over the airlock door flared crimson. A hiss and draining noise followed. The airlock door descended, revealing Cu-dan. His spacefaring gear seemed more like a wetsuit with a full-head breather. Two Blekk flanked him, wielding rifles beneath unreadable expressions. The two pirates also wore full-headed breathing apparatuses, but their heads were conical and lithe.

Alize had never seen any Blekk outside of Collective war propaganda. An unblinking eye adorned either side of their faces. The rest of their bodies were a mess of tentacles, three of which held modified assault rifles. Their remaining appendages supported their elongated heads. Their height matched Alize's; their white-pink skin clashed with Cu-dan's bright green scales. The fluid-filled breathers covering their heads looked more like an underwater version of Fil's helmet than Alize and Binh's simple coverings. These Blekk felt alien in a way Lo-sat and Arkouda didn't.

Stop staring.

Cu-dan stepped forward and about-faced to the two Blekk. With his tail, he made a series of complicated contortions, all while alternating between crisscrossing and zig-zagging his arms.

Rotating his head toward Fil, he said in Arkouda, "I explained to them how you can't join us until you're officially greeted in person, as according to Lo-sat custom. Since they wish for your full cooperation, they agreed to comply. You all should be honored."

The dense stench of oily solvents and lubricants stung—somebody had done a repair job here recently. Alize whispered to Binh. "Is that true?"

Cu-dan hissed something to Binh while gesticulating to the Blekk behind him.

Binh leaned against the cold metal wall. "Of course not. Frosty, they want you to drop your rifle. That's the only way they'll go in with you. Stink-Pink, you stay next to me. Mr. Personality will walk behind us all and take care of the rest. Ready for the daring escape?"

Scowling, Fil unhooked her ammunition belt. "Cut the stupid nicknames. You didn't say I'd have to do it without my gun."

Binh shrugged. "You didn't ask."

After more exchanged hisses between the Lo-sats, Cu-dan motioned for them to follow. The two Blekk shifted on their slithering mass of tentacles as the trio walked up. The Blekk on the left nudged Alize with his rifle.

What's that mean? She shoved it from her mind and focused on the plan.

Once Fil reached the front, the Blekk on the right stiffly pointed his gun at a sharp angle at Fil's head. Not that he could realistically do any damage to her unless he scored a precise shot or had a hyper-advanced weapon.

Alize filed into the airlock, side by side with Cu-dan. Although Binh stood taller, Cu-dan's tail was longer. It hung over a series of switches at the back end of the airlock. His tail swung like a tight pendulum, ready to input any number of commands. As the airlock back door closed, decontamination spray arms descended from the ceiling. Cu-dan smashed a series of buttons on the control board, and water seeped in like a warm downpour. Even through the breather, a new wave of pungent salt stung Alize's nostrils.

The Blekk on the left fidgeted and made a series of motions with his tentacles in the direction of his comrade.

With a wet buzz, decontam arms began their spray motions. Binh jumped and grabbed a decontam arm, spraying the chemicals at one of the Blekk.

Fil activated her force field, lighting the airlock blue as it expanded. The Blekk dropped their weapons. Their wet slaps seemed more confused than pained. An alarm overhead buzzed, and both sides of the airlock opened, unleashing a flood of water. Alize clasped her grav harness, and adjusted it, increasing her mass enough to keep her standing in the onrushing wave.

The pressure on her chest squeezed her ribs, but her breather provided oxygen she needed—building adrenaline allowed her to stay sharp. Each inhale was exercise for her chest muscles.

The bursting torrent carried the two Blekk, Binh, and Fil toward the cargo hull, back where the escape pod was, while Cu-dan and Alize marched against the water toward the small scrapper's cabin. After a minute of the flowing water, the torrent stopped. Because the cabin was so much smaller than the hull, the water spread throughout the whole ship didn't rise past Alize's ankles. Inside the cabin, Cu-dan got the signal from Binh and prepared to open the hull. Fil grabbed the dazed Blekks, unable to swim or stand in the shallow water, and stuffed them into the sealed pod.

With the pod sealed, Fil shouted, "Time to make tracks." She and Binh rushed toward the airlock and Cu-dan hit the switch, opening the airlock.

He sent a message to the *Blodsed*. Alize asked what he said, and Cu-dan cleared his throat and stared ahead. "Prisoners attempting escape. Pursue escape pod."

When the airlock closed behind Binh and Fil, Cu-dan opened up the hull and entered the coordinates Alize gave him into the scrapper's command board.

They managed to engage hyperspace flight as they watched their former escape pod float behind them toward the *Blodsed*.

As the stars contorted and swirled about them, Alize's stomach lurched. *Now we're fleeing two criminal gangs who have it out for us.* She cast a glance at her wrist piece, patiently flashing green. *Sorry if I scared you, Pops.*

EIGHTEEN

Encrypted message, translated from Blekk using motion capture software: Free version beta

```
Sender: Tispe, secretary of His
Eminence Lord Sjorover
Recipient: Rick Crith
Subject: Found your quarry
```

Reck,

From boss Sjorover. I secretary and second translattor. Found the coordenates where the escapers swem off to. Moon. Not settled. No actevety en the whole star system. Good place to hide. First translattor send us coordenates. He's on board weth your escapees; they took scrapper boat, not escape pod stolen from yer other boat. They think

```
our old translattor is a traitor to
us. No no. He followeng our plan. You
can get them. We want translattor back.
Then alliance maybe.
```

———

Rick pinched the bridge of his nose. "Amanda, how much of that did you understand?"

She shifted in her seat across from Rick. "Less than you, I'm guessing. Do you see why I suggested we pay for the full version of that translator software?"

Rick sighed. "That financial decision came from command, unfortunately. Blekker is tough. Lots of subtleties that don't directly translate."

———

```
Sjorover wants to see your boss.
Only then alliance. We're respect-
able pirates. Except Avskum, Smultass,
Kilegjelle and they crews. No honor.

The escapees no kell Blekk. You told
our boss to expect losses. You may have
mesjudged them, ya?

You catch up, but don't act like our
old translattor es emportant. He dies—
you're en trouble. Enstead of alliance,
Sjorover will hunt you. Notheng per-
sonal about et, Reck.
```

Lots of ways to kell a Human slow, Reck. We know a lot and can learn more.

You get to that moon. We show up and take translattor back plus cut of fin-dengs. Lord Sjorover likes you because you're not like that from what we hear. You make sure your podmates follow yer example. Shed blood don't make for blood brothers and big trust. You're smart for a Human, Reck. Don't go be'ng a betrayer.

Signed,
Tispe
Kell count: 25
The ocean's depth eats the light.
<end message>

———

Rick groaned at the end of the transmission. On his next inhale, he whiffed the beautiful stimbrew Amanda brought, which almost covered the hint of her perfume. If this were a military ship, her perfume would break regulation. Rick had a short list of reasons why he was glad Earthquake wasn't an official military, and the occasional whiff of Amanda's perfume was one of them.

Amanda pushed a rogue twist of hair away from her eye. "Rick, that message was not subtle at all. Did you at least get the gist of it?"

Rick nodded and drummed his fingers against the desk. "It corroborates what Ensign Rymon told the recruiter, which is good. Them moving in a scrapper is useful. Slows them down. And if they have a mole from the Drowned Star traveling with them, they're even more vulnerable."

Amanda's face brightened, and three curls bounced down her forehead. "So we'll catch the trio on the moon?"

"Catch them? We might even get there first."

Smiling, Amanda slouched in her seat. "And you're sure that's the translator on the bounty list? Lo-sat translators are a dime a dozen."

Rick sighed. "Yeah, it's Zhen-trann's kid. Cu-dan. The poor kid probably gets harassed by any Human who recognizes him. Rumor is he's the spitting image of his father."

"Serves him right."

"Amanda."

"I'm sorry, Rick. I know you think meeting the Arkouda was good for Humanity, but—"

Rick held up his hand. "Enough. We're not arguing about history. Don't breathe a word of this guy's identity, understood? We'll take him into protective custody."

Amanda straightened in her chair and furrowed her eyebrows. "There's an active bounty on him. Not a small one, either. Harboring him'll get you in deep water."

After a sip of stimbrew, Rick nodded pensively. "We need the Blekk's help more than we need a dead innocent person, no matter how unpopular his daddy is."

NINETEEN

Aboard the scrapper *Takel*, Dusoi orbit, Xechas system, Collective fringe

AN ALARM BUZZED over the scrapper's dull loudspeaker, nudging Alize to rub the sleep from her eyes. This ship's accommodations didn't have bipeds in mind, so she'd slept on the cold metal floor of an empty cell. Even after they drained the last bit of water into the hull, Alize knew she'd reek of salt forever. On the bright side, her wrist flashed a reassuring green, gleaming in the scrapper's dim interior lighting.

Hi, Pops.

The viewscreen projected the planet Dusoi, a gas giant rivaling the Xechas star, giving Alize goosebumps. She'd seen pictures of planets like any student, but actually seeing another planet with a smattering of moons was jarring, mystifying, and—

"Quit droolin', Pinks. Seen one planet, seen 'em all."

Fil snorted. "That couldn't be farther from the truth. Each planet's unique."

"If they're all unique, none of them are. What dumb self-help drivel did you swipe that from?"

Cu-dan curled and uncurled his tail and cast a lazy glance at Alize. "Are these two always bickering?"

Alize slowly closed her eyes and nodded. "You can't get used to it."

Fil shook her head and flattened her ears. The scrapper's loudspeaker chimed, and a flash of flickering symbols displayed over the viewscreen.

Alize indicated the symbols. "Can you read whatever that says, Cu-dan?"

He pointed up. "But of course. Those symbols on the top line read, 'descent to rocky form imminent.' And the second line says, 'adjust coordinates or begin manual control.'" Lowering his tone, he added, "Blekker is much easier to read than to sign or speak."

The scrapper plodded toward the planet, which soon encapsulated most of the viewscreen. The other two icy moons faded in the periphery. Alize's heart thudded.

This was her moon, where her life achievement had lain dormant for eons. Her wristpiece flashed. Brighter. Faster.

We found it, Pops.

The Chamayna were a scant mystery to the Collective databanks, but Alize would rectify that. Maybe her achievements would earn Humans some clout in the Collective standing. Only one way to find out.

"Best fiddle with your grav harnesses, all you hang-ers-on," Binh said. "This could get a bit bumpy."

A light lurch in Alize's stomach indicated the grav harness had readjusted to Dusoi's pull and the gentler pull of the petrified moon.

Fil rubbed her back. "Scrappers don't spend much time in atmospheric flight. Not exactly aerodynamic, so this'll be bumpy—" The ship lurched and groaned. "I'm sorry."

"Is there any atmosphere on this ball?" Binh asked. "Or is that on the list of things I need to wait to learn about until it's too late?"

"Enough that we won't fry or freeze, if that's what you're asking," Alize said. "But none of us could breathe comfortably. Not for an extended time, anyway."

Fil whistled. "I packed a Lo-sat and a Human breathing apparatus in my armor. I'll be fine with my helmet." She winced. "Cu-dan, I'm sorry... I don't have another breather that could fit you."

Cu-dan waved a dismissive claw and pointed to his head. "Did you forget I came aboard with one? A breather was my only option for years. I slept in it. Honestly, it feels strange now without it on."

"Feel lighter? Or is that strange sensation just from smelling these two hairballs?" Binh hissed and blinked hard. "Well, Furryfrost, I guess it's a good thing we didn't sell your armor to Earthquake, after all. Very fortunate, indeed."

Fil glared and spoke in the flattest tone yet. "Yeah. What good luck."

"Generally, it's not considered a best practice to sell people's things to terrorists without their permission," Alize said.

A grin slithered across Binh's snout. "It's best practice for me to get money, though."

"The lot of you are impossible," Cu-dan said.

The scrapper lurched again, accelerating toward the green-tinted lunar surface.

Fil nudged Alize. "Any idea where the specific location of this tomb is?"

"N-n-not entirely."

Binh slapped his forehead. "So what, you want us to walk around this rock until we trip over it? No thanks."

"We'll know." Alize glared at him. "The Chamayna tended to build statues near the entrances to their underground dwellings."

Fil raised an eyebrow. "You said there wasn't a ton known about them."

"Well, when I say tended ... that's only based off two reported discoveries." She broke eye contact and straightened her jacket. "So those may be anomalies."

Fil and Binh groaned in unison.

Alize's smile was likely unconvincing. "But maybe not?"

They're bonding over something.

Alize winced. "It should be near the magnetic northern pole. Yes, it's an educated guess."

Cu-dan punched in the coordinates into the helmboard's nav-computer.

Somewhere to start, at least. Their descent curved downward to hover over the rocky surface, various shades of green obscuring shadows from Dusoi and Xechas.

"Not a ton of magnetism on moons," Binh said, voice drained of sarcasm. "This one doesn't seem big enough for its own field. Cu-dan and Fuzzbutt, can either of you feel the pull?"

Cu-dan shook his head. "My magnetic sense dulled over the years of spacefaring, I fear. We enjoyed little shore leave, and I haven't been close to many gravity wells while employed. Pirates prefer deep space, away from defended settlements."

Binh groaned. "Remind me not to ask you a yes or no question in the future."

"I barely feel the pull," Fil said. "But this moon definitely has a magnetosphere. Leeze, could the Chamayna sense magnetic fields?"

Through a shrug, Alize responded, "Humans are the only sentient species that can't as far as anyone knows, so ... probably? They didn't have a permanent settlement here, according to the inscriptions."

A green-tinted mountain loomed over the horizon, pointing to the hanging gas giant above. "We don't know where they had any permanent settlements. We've only found artifacts and evidence of them in their tombs. What's interesting is—"

"Literally anything else?" Binh asked.

Cu-dan shrugged. "I found it quite fascinating."

"Get your tails to the viewscreen and help search for statues." Fil's growling got Cu-dan moving.

After casting a wary eye at Binh, Alize crossed her arms. "This would go faster if you helped us."

"I can see from back here, milk-drinkers. Want me to tell you what I'm seeing? Rock, rock, rock, rock—"

Alize sighed. "That's not necessary."

"Well, I may have seen another crater just now, but you'll never know. Or maybe another gigantic mesa popping out of the surface like a nasty Human pimple."

Cu-dan tapped the side of the viewscreen. "Nothing appears different for kilometers around in all directions. Anything hiding here is deep within these mountains."

Fil folded her round ears back. "Any idea what these statues might look like?"

Alize scratched her chin. "The partially intact statues found at the other dig sites were most likely designed to replicate what the Chamayna actually looked like. Shorter than a Human, segmented carapace, taloned lower and upper appendages, danaid wings, short mandibles, and hardened antennae like horns. The number of appendages and mandibles varies between four and six."

"What the heck are danaid wings?" Fil asked.

"Remember the museum's silkwing flies that escaped a few months ago?" Alize asked. "That type of wing, except big enough for a Chamayna."

Crossing his arms, Binh said, "Hey, outside! More rocks!"

Alize didn't want to concede she shared Binh's bleak topographical assessment. They hadn't been searching for long, but the landscape was so unassuming. Mountains jutted from the surface sharply, as if the moon were made of stalagmites.

"We're never going to find anything at this rate," Fil huffed.

Binh scoffed. "What'd you expect, a giant neon arrow?"

Alize hated herself, dragging Fil through a near-death experience with nothing to show for it. And now add the guilt of pulling Cu-dan away from a safe job. But she didn't feel a tug of guilt over Binh joining and risking his life. She wished they'd had more time to find someone else.

The moon was big enough that they could spend the rest of the month trekking it. They didn't have enough supplies to last long before they'd need to give up, especially with Cu-dan aboard. Supplies in the *Takel* didn't add much to their provisions. At least all the food was fish the others could eat. She hoped.

Drawing her gaze to the pod's floor, a green light pulsed in her periphery. *No. Pops believes in me. So does Fil. Maybe with the money we get, Cu-dan could go and disappear somewhere away from prejudicial Humans. I owe it to them to try.*

"Do any of us know how to adjust the scrapper's specific coordinates on the fly?" Alize asked. "I want to try that mountain on the right."

Binh offered semi-sarcastic instructions, and Cu-dan guided the scrapper. The mountain stood taller than Hen4's space elevator and stretched wider than Hen4's metropolis—constituting a decent percentage of the moon's mass on its own. It punctured the thin atmosphere enough so someone standing at the base might not see planet Dusoi looming above.

Steeling herself, Alize squinted at a rocky outcropping, smoother than what they'd seen thus far.

"Fil, see that weird shape?"

Binh snorted. "Two weird shapes in front of me."

"Can it, Scales," Fil said. "Yeah, I think so. Why? What is it?"

The scrapper loomed closer, and the odd rock gained more definition. Alize licked her lips. "I... I recognize that from a textbook. It's a statue. Can we get closer?"

"Nice! Oh yeah, that's definitely a statue." Fil slapped Alize's shoulder. Meant as a friendly tap, it would hurt for a few hours, but Fil didn't need to know. "There's my girl."

They hovered close enough for the statue to sit in plain sight. A few degrees larger than she would have guessed, closer to Binh or Cu-dan's height than the anticipated sub-Human size, but it was unmistakably a Chamayna, facing the mountain.

"We're close," Alize said. "Cu-dan, how do we get this scrapper to stop?"

Binh snorted. "Did you try crashing it?"

Fil snarled at him. "I'll crash your face into the helmboard and see if that helps."

Cu-dan sighed. "I need to learn to speak up if I'm going to get a word in edgewise between you three." He rose from the floor and shooed the women away from the helmboard with the tip of his tail. He mused over the panel for a moment and hit three keys in rapid succession.

Binh tsked. "Why do the ladies always assume I like it rough? It's really perplexing. I'm such a delicate flower." In a normal tone, he asked, "Got those breathers ready for us, Frostbite?"

The pod slowed and descended, hovering gently over the ground. Alize took a deep breath. "Fil, you're probably the first Arkouda to set paw on this moon. It's uncharted and unnamed by the Collective. Will you name it?"

"Yes, but only because you legally can't." After a somber nod, she added, "When the university accepts your find, I'll see if I can transfer naming rights to you. In the meantime, let's call this place 'I told you so.' Has a nice ring to it, don't you think?"

Alize shook her head and accepted the small breather from Fil's armor. "I haven't given it any thought. The academics will probably want a stuffy name. But I like your idea." She inhaled deeply. "Let's go."

This garnered a chuckle from Cu-dan. "Regretfully, I won't join you in this endeavor. The cabin was designed to have a pool of saltwater inside. With the amount of time it's been dry, some instruments may have suffered damage in our transit. I'll remain behind to inspect the scrapper and make any needed repairs."

Binh raised an eyeridge and hissed a sentence at him.

Cu-dan waved his tail dismissively and responded in Arkouda. "Someone has to stay with the ship. Protect the escape. I'm sure our military representative agrees."

Casting a smug look at Binh, Fil nodded.

Binh snarled before responding in Arkouda. "Tell them the real reason."

Cu-dan's neck frills opened and immediately collapsed. With a sigh, Cu-dan looked at the women. "I want to spend more time outside a breathing mask. It's been such a long time. I need a break. Please understand."

Fil's fur stood on end, and she hummed a low growl.

Alize reached for the supply cabinet. "Fil, grab the food and store it in your armor." She cast a glance between her companions. "Cu-dan, I'm doing this so they'll get off your back. We're still learning to trust you."

Fil nodded and opened a container unit in her armor.

Cu-dan sighed and held the tip of his tail in his claws. "This is entirely unnecessary, I assure you."

"Maybe it is," Fil said, "but we won't risk it."

"All right, then," Alize said, "we'll still make sure to give you some credit for the discovery and treasure, if you'd like. If our search takes longer than anticipated, we'll come back and give you some food."

Cu-dan placed his tail over his chest. "Extraordinarily kind of you, madam Alize. You have my deepest gratitude."

Fil, Binh, and Alize approached the back of the cramped cabin. The airlock chimed, and an automatic decontamination spray followed. Another warning chimed, and the airlock door opened onto the moon, copper light reflecting from the gas giant above. Alize adjusted her grav harness and ventured the first step.

Her heart leapt the way prehistoric astronauts did when first exploring Earth's moon.

Boot connecting to the jade rock, she exhaled and drank in the sight of planet Dusoi domineering the sky. They'd made moonfall. *Finally.*

Fil and Binh followed her outside. Binh whistled. "That's a mighty fine looking planet in the sky. Don't usually get too close to the gassy ones." His tail hovered, suspended mid-air in the lowered gravity. Alize remembered learning about the prehistoric Humans jumping around Earth's moons like extinct Earth-rabbits. A small part of her was tempted to turn off her grav harness and repeat history, but she clenched her teeth. They had a mission, and they'd come too far to play around now.

Alize's breather apparatus smooshed her face. It would be suffocating without the steady stream of breathable air. Still, it wasn't much of an improvement from when she nearly drowned commandeering the *Takel.* The memory of the saltwater contrasted with this parched and silent lunar surface, the only sign of life being the statue.

Each step reverent, Alize approached the statue facing the mountain. Carved from the green lunar rock, it held a two-handed weapon in its upper appendages, gripped by talons. The weapon had a long shaft and a scalloped, crescent blade. She opened the camera function on her omni-tablet and snapped the first picture on "I Told You So" moon.

A light chuckle escaped. *We need a better name.*

The statue's compound eyes stared lifelessly at the mountain, stonily ignoring Alize. Traditional garb was carved into it as well—diagonal cloth, looping around the torso from shoulder to hip, extending down toward the knees on the standing appendages.

"First evidence of Chamayna clothing." If her jaw dropped any lower, she'd break the seal on her breather, and her chin would smack her grav harness.

She crept closer, inspecting the carved clothing further. What the statue wore was nothing advanced— not space-ready at all.

Rather, the carved clothing reminded her of what she'd seen in prehistory Earth books. It looked like something an ancient Human would've worn thousands of years before the Eleva War. "Fascinating," she muttered. "How old is this?"

Binh broke her reverie, idly twirling his tail. "You're the archaeologist. You tell us. Or I could get Cu-dan out here, and he could take twice as long to ask the same question. With bigger words, too, as if that impresses anybody."

Alize scratched the back of her head, accidentally dislodging the breather for a moment. "Well, it's facing the mountain, so I guess the entrance should be behind this statue somewhere. It's a welcome-guardian, I think. A decoration meant to welcome or intimidate visitors. Going off Human and other Collective species' archaeology, that's usually what statues like this do. These symbolically keep bad things out. Maybe scare the occasional animal or dimwit. But this doesn't seem like a moon that could have naturally supported life."

Binh cocked his head at an angle, eyes drifting lightyears away. "Well, it's not exactly doing its job since neither of you is scared. You know, Earth had some cool entrance statues on some of its older buildings." He sighed and shook his head. "Damn *ke-noks.*"

Fil and Binh began the search by overturning suspicious rocks. Alize snapped a few more pictures of the statue before joining the search. Opposite the statue on the right, she found evidence of a matching pedestal missing its guardian. A nearby crater with pulverized rocks inside solved the mystery.

"Too bad that second guardian didn't survive the impact. But where's the entrance?" Alize asked.

Waving her wide paw, Fil called, "Hey Leeze, any idea what this entrance would look like? A door?"

"Yeah," Binh said. "Does the door look like a door? You know what I'm talking about, right? You walk in them? Some have knobs? Others have handles? I saw a rotating one on Earth once and I thought it was a broken windmill. You're not getting it. You know what, I'll grab Cu-dan. He can do a better translation."

Fil scowled at him. "Will you shut up? It wouldn't take much to throw you into orbit. Just one setting on your grav harness, you know."

"Again with the rough-housing. Please, I need things to be gentle. Skin condition and all. I have a prescription."

"Well..." Alize's confidence faded. "I thought it'd be a standard opening without a door. But maybe it's hidden?" She stopped. "But that doesn't make sense. If they wanted to hide the location, they wouldn't have built a pair of statues here."

Alize knelt and grabbed a stone, smoother and greener than the others. It didn't look crafted or carved, but it had a natural arrow shape to it. And the way she held it, it pointed toward the mountain.

Scanning as she walked, Alize approached the mountain, toward the statue's backside. Its wings were partially damaged, likely victims of smaller meteors and gentle gusts of solar winds over the millennia. She snapped another twenty pictures for good measure.

Squinting at the mountain's base as she passed the statue, a dark crevice caught her eye. Coming closer, it wasn't a crevice at all. A deliberate line divided the rock.

"Door!" Alize shouted. "We searched on the wrong side of the statue. Fil, Binh, come here. I found it." Alize clasped her hands over her breathing unit.

The undiscovered tomb.

Discovered.

She glanced at her wrist, the green light pulsing quickly across the wristband. *Did Pops feel my excitement? Is he excited for me, too? Of course, he is. Thanks for believing in me, Pops.*

TWENTY

Intercepted dictation draft of message, recorded two weeks prior

Sender: Provincial Alize Oze. Hen4
Recipient: Citizen Dr. Hupomone Dikaio
Subject: Found evidence this time

Is this thing recording? Yeah? OK, good. Reminder: delete preceding lines of checking.

<audible inhale.> Good morning, Dr. Dikaio. I wanted to thank you for the colossal display of assholery yesterday. You're a prick, and I hate you. I hope your fur gets matted in a place you can't reach in the shower. Reminder: delete preceding five seconds.

<audible inhale.> I wanted to thank you for your feedback on my last theory. I know your time is valuable, and you're a giant snob who wouldn't know a good idea if it bit your tail off and shoved it up your furry ass. It would probably come out a diamond since you're such a tightwad. Reminder: delete preceding five seconds.

<audible drumming of fingers.> I know your time is valuable, so the time spent critiquing was well-appreciated. There is one more piece I'd like for you to consider, though, which is the potential for a windfall of Chamayna artifacts. I vividly remember you telling me to drop the theory and focus on cleaning the robots. And your prediction was correct: the university passed on my latest dissertation proposal. But what I want to suggest is that not only am I certain of the location of this moon and tomb, but I'm also certain this tomb has been undisturbed since before Collective recorded history. When a research and excavation team unearth and exhume the tomb, we'll find a trove of Chamayna artifacts unlike any other found to this date.

<audible exhale> What the hell's it matter, anyway… not like you're even going to review this. "Talk to me once you get a doctorate, bluudy-bluudy-bluu"

<audible throat-clearing> Reminder: delete preceding ten seconds.

<audible inhale> I certainly remember your suggestion to earn my doctoral degree before we open communication about this any further, but please understand that with nobody to back this research, I cannot prove it and thus earn my degree. Surely, you understand this dilemma. Even the funds for a simple exploratory probe of the moon could demonstrate that something's beneath the lunar surface. We can discuss this in-person if you'd like. And Doctor Dikaio, I grew up in the museum. I've studied all our Chamayna artifacts intensely, and I've worked on this for years. It was my favorite exhibit as a child, and I'd spend hours there.

<audible scoff> Reminder: delete preceding fifteen seconds. Not like she cares about my childhood. That'll probably weaken my case, knowing her. This is a waste.

With the recent advance in linguistic
sciences, a research team on Vee developed an updated lexicon for Chamayna.
With that in hand, I was able to
piece together more of the unreadable inscription we have on display.
The Chamayna may have been capable of
interplanetary and interlunar travel
without spaceflight as we know and
understand it today. If we could deduce
their methods, we'd revolutionize
travel and the galactic economy for
the better. And as the museum director,
you would have naming rights to whatever my expedition would find.

Thank you for your time and consideration.

All for the Collective.
-Alize Oze

Response:

Re: Found evidence this time
Sender: Citizen Dr. Hupomone Dikaio
Recipient: Provincial Alize Oze. Hen4

For tomorrow's stimbrew, I want an extra-large, double milk. Get a drum of their original brew. If you forget sweeteners again, you can find yourself a new place of employment. And get halfberry juice for Dr. Klania.

Intercepted dictation draft of message, dated one week, six days prior

Subject: I'm buying tonight

Sender: Provincial Alize Oze. Hen4 Recipient: Citizen Filenada Kaluteros. Military. Guardcorps

<audible inhale> Hi Fil, this was too much for a ping. So, I was wrong. That fithar player? Yeah, him. His singleness and ready-to-mingleness are confirmed. He was definitely checking you out. Anyway, thanks for that intel from the Vee research team. My student restrictions to the less flashy research is disgusting. And as you can see, it's not just limited to Human research teams, either. I mean, it's Vee, for Earth's sake. Lo-sat homeworld—not exactly a secret research facility. Anyway, I looked over that new lexicon. Based on what that team found, the Chamayna had somehow figured

out how to travel between planets. Big whoop, right? Get ready for your mind to be blown. Reminder: delete preceding two seconds. That expression probably doesn't sound right in other languages. Get ready for the craziest theory you've ever heard. Based on the existing inscriptions and the verified locations of Chamayna activity, they could travel between planets—

<audible inhale> without spaceships. I think they could teleport. Wow, that sounds so incredibly dumb when I say it out loud. Part of me feels like I'm probably wrong. Anyway. There's even better news. That updated lexicon definitely confirms what I've said all along. That inscription in the museum is talking about a weapon. I'm positive the inscription is describing "a weapon of unspeakable power." But this makes an even bigger mystery. Like, if they could teleport. Did they die out or just, you know, leave? Like, they could be living in some quiet corner of the galaxy, bouncing away from The Collective's prying eyes. The possibilities and the questions… so awesome. There was also a bizarre line on the inscription about "the light of the forest." Which is super weird,

since the Chamayna sites are on rocky moons, not green worlds. What do you think that means?

<audible exhale> All right, fine, I know you're probably getting bored with this stuff. You're such a patient precious gemstone. I don't deserve a buddy like you. So anyway, before I forget, I got that musician's ping address for you. I'll buy the drinks tonight, and maybe he'll buy yours tomorrow. Or maybe your breakfast. HEY-OH!

Gruntsisters!
-Leeze

TWENTY-ONE

Aboard the designated civilian ship, *Dizhen*, interstellar Collective space

IN A CHAIR matching his personal rigidity, Rick glanced from the omni-tablet to the mug on his metal desk. His stimbrew chilled an hour ago, but its souring roasted aroma lingered. "The hell's a 'gruntsister,' Rymon? Some kind of code?"

Garott Rymon fidgeted in the metal chair.

Weakling. "A nickname, or something?"

The ensign winced. "Look, her best friend is a popsicle."

Rick pointed a long finger directly under Rymon's nose. "No hate speech. Last warning."

"Sorry, sir." The kid straightened. "Her best friend was an Arkouda. A guard at the museum. They had dumb names for each other. Half their conversations were inside jokes."

Rick stiffened in his straight-backed chair. "You also failed to mention she was the stimbrew gopher for the museum. You made it sound like she was close to a PhD."

"Gopher?"

"Earth slang." Rick shook his head. "Never mind. Look, Monsieur Tecton greenlighted this mission personally. He's expecting results. We're hitting that moon in a matter of hours. Do you have any more of her passwords?"

A weaker man than Rick would've grinned at the prospect of this information. But this woman was a student, not a soldier. Treating her like an enemy to reconnoiter twisted his guts like Blekk tentacles, but war necessitated sacrifice. His time with the Collective taught him that much. Too bad his tour of duty in their ranks earned him a host of nightmares and screams he couldn't unhear. Hearing her voice, her struggle with an Arkouda superior, he saw the symmetry between them.

"I, uh," Rymon stuttered. "I don't know her other passwords."

Rick rose. "Then suit up for moonfall. Lose your gun, and it comes out of your paycheck. If anyone in the Collective finds it, then we never knew you and never hired you."

He straightened. "Understood, sir."

Rick leered at him, arcing his spine, letting the ensign feel small under him. "You don't leave until I say dismissed. One more question for you."

The kid gulped and leaned back, razor straight, neck craned to meet Rick's glare.

"Did you love this woman?"

"Sir?"

Rick's eyebrows furrowed and nostrils flared. "Don't make me repeat myself, ensign."

"No, sir. I just needed a girl for some release, if you catch my drift—but she wasn't into it. Total prude. You know the type."

I know your type. "So no emotional attachment?"

"None." Bastard dared to smirk as if this were an accomplishment.

"And what about her? Any declarations of love?"

The kid tsked. "Naw. Bitch didn't like me. Just dated so she wouldn't feel like a loser. But didn't even have the decency to put out."

I'll put you out of an airlock. See how you like that. "Understood. Dismissed."

Rymon's lips parted, but he snapped them shut again.

It'll be hard to shed a tear when the kid gets tossed around like a ragdoll.

With the door still open, Rick made eye contact with Moreno on the other side and inclined his head.

Moreno nodded with a dour expression and entered, squinting at Rymon as they passed each other.

"Close the door, please. At ease."

Moreno split the age and height gap between Rick and most of the other recruits well. Hailing from good Earth stock, he shared Rick's vision for organizing Earthquake into a real military. His clothing reflected his attitude. Except to sleep, Moreno was one of the few crew members who opted for staying in armor all day. The emerald and sapphire colors on the plates and flexweave made for poor camouflage, but they conveyed Earthquake's symbolism fine enough. The armor added some bulk to Moreno's already muscular frame, and the stitching from repairs was barely noticeable, in accordance with Tecton's aesthetic standards.

Rick could've gone without Moreno carrying his homemade shotgun and grenades at his side all day, but he had the discipline to show instead of use. If Rick had been in a unit run by a Human when he was in his twenties, he might've acted the same way back then.

Rick sat and gestured for Moreno to do the same. "What'd the science wing say?"

"That you're wrong. They can reverse-engineer Collective armor from a corpse."

"Hmpf. How many of them are on the take from the smugglers? They want to drive up the bounty on dead Arkoudae."

Moreno narrowed his eyes, accentuating his angular nose and chin. "The Leader agrees with them."

"Sergeant, I've seen Collective soldiers die in battle. I lost two commanding officers. One to some nasty Galsan worms—" Rick paused as Moreno cringed, "and another at the tentacles of a Blekk pirate who got the drop on him. Strangulation."

"You 'lost' them?" Moreno scowled.

"Yes, lost." Phantom pains in Rick's missing hand hinted at the urge to clench a fist. "They were good leaders. They treated me well. Doesn't change the fact that their armor decommissions when the wearer dies. I've watched it happen."

"But that doesn't mean a scientist can't reverse engineer it." Moreno leaned forward. "Do you want to hold back humanity?"

"Watch your tone. I watched the Lo-sat engineer in our corps try and open one. The guns and helmet locked inside of it, and we wanted to use it—stuck waiting for close air support." *Which never came. Nope. Don't go back to that hole, Rick.* He cleared his throat. "Once it sends a casualty report to the Fleet, it's useless. Still weighs enough to give you a hernia, though. For inert armor to be of any use to us, we'd have to slice it up and repurpose it like scrap metal. But cutting through it will be tough. Maybe impossible."

"Permission to speak frankly, sir?"

"You always have it."

Moreno's gaze flickered for a moment, and he inhaled deeply before speaking. "Your philosophy isn't sitting well with most of the crew. Most of us are worried your ... opinions will keep us from advancing."

"And?" Rick searched his dark eyes.

"And if you weren't a celebrity, you wouldn't have been accepted into Earthquake."

"Celebrity?" Rick shook his head. "Not a movie star. I hated doing public interviews when I first joined. I refused the damn book deal."

Moreno glanced at Rick's shoulder stump. "Sir, you don't live up to many of their expectations. Because you disagree with the Leader. And you're soft on aliens. Every time you censor someone, you deepen the divide."

Rick exhaled through his nostrils. "Expect the unexpected. That's one of the oldest rules of war in the book. The information is appreciated and will be considered under advisement. We need to discuss mission parameters."

No reaction from Moreno.

"Fine," Rick said, "what'll it take to get the squad to fall in line?"

"Show them you're the top dog." A hunger flashed in his eyes. "Before someone else does."

After a terse nod, Rick tapped his omni-tablet and brought up the intercom. "Amanda, please call the crew into the training area. We're about to have a demonstration. Fifteen minutes." Rick released the button and fixed his gaze on Moreno. "Follow me."

———

Stripped out of their armor, the difference between Rick's lithe and lean figure and Moreno's gymrat body was even more clear.

Moreno flashed a cocky grin as Lamont taped up his knuckles. "Are you sure you're up for this, old man?"

Smirks spread throughout the squad like dry fires in an old forest. Wellsford audibly whispered to Cheng, "This oughtta be good. Ten credits on Alejandro."

Not that Rick minded. "Need a refresher on the rules?"

"No injuries medspray can't fix."

Amanda cleared her throat from the side of the chalked-out ring. "Knuckles once you're ready."

Rick and Moreno nodded in unison. Rick offered his fist, which Moreno tapped with his own. After a second of hesitation, Moreno tapped Rick's knuckles with his other fist.

Cheng and Nkosi belted out the "Woot-doot," a crass barking from their otherwise feminine voices. The men in the squad responded with a baritone "Earth-quake!"

Adopting a left stance, Moreno lunged with a left hook, which Rick dodged. A right jab, and Rick blocked with the back of his wrist.

The damn hothead tried the same combination again. In parrying the right jab, Rick snapped his wrist to pull on Moreno's neck, bringing the second-in-command's face down to the business end of Rick's opposite shoulder.

This garnered a few "oofs" from the recruits and one "boo."

Moreno uttered something that sounded like a curse in an unofficial Human dialect and stumbled backward.

"Had enough?" Rick asked, offering his knuckles for a tap.

Two boos.

Moreno composed himself and stretched out two fists to tap Rick's knuckles. In the last instant before they tapped, Moreno grabbed Rick's wrist, his grip like a vice. "Gotcha, old man."

Like hell he did. Rick whispered, "Did your elbow ever heal after the Yaltz mission?"

Moreno's gaze snapped down to his arm. "I'm fine."

Liar. If Rick used the standard forearm-over-elbow escape from his grip, he might shatter the kid's ulna. Rick played out the rest of the fight in his head. He could yank his wrist hard enough to pull Moreno toward him, stomp on his insole and knee him in the gut with his other leg, all while giving him a good-natured headbutt in the same motion.

Jeers melted into cheers. Amid the crowd, Rick didn't catch Amanda's voice participating.

If Rick broke the hold and won the fight, he risked concussing or incapacitating his number two before a mission.

Rick slackened and used his diaphragm for maximum volume to silence the squad. "If we were in a combat situation, Corporal Moreno has left himself open for several counterattacks. I'm not going to cripple him, though." The crowd quieted enough for Rick to use his standard volume. "Moreno, before I tap out, tell the crew what I could do to you in this position."

After a long glance at their postures, Moreno winced. "Since you're taller, you could land a kick on your opposite leg."

"Good," Rick said. "And most opponents will have a second arm to contend with. You won the game." Rick unclenched his fist and wiggled his fingers. "You also won toilet duty."

TWENTY-TWO

Moon designated "I Told You So." Dusoi orbit, Xechas system, Collective fringe

JAGGED, FORGOTTEN ROCKS bunched together like abandoned ice in the back of a freezer. Hewn into the chartreuse minerals, a faint outline taunted Alize. A windless chill made her pull her jacket tighter.

Fil placed a gentle paw on Alize's shoulder. "Are you certain this tiny thing is a door? It's barely your size. Maybe it's a natural formation."

Binh rolled his eyes. "Hate to be contrarian, Miss Fuzzy, but your opinion of what's small may be biased."

"You love to be contrarian." Alize jerked her shoulder free from Fil's paw, forceful and grateful in equal measure.

She approached the phlegm-green stone and ventured a single gloved finger to trace along the crevice, searching for a pattern—some semblance of meaning. Cool to the touch, undisturbed for eons.

"This was cut. Intentionally." Alize retreated a step and absorbed the crude outline. It was just under her full height, which aligned with assumptions about Chamayna anatomy. "But what I'm not seeing is a hinge or an opening mechanism. Maybe they meant for this to be a hidden door."

Binh approached her side. "Doesn't make sense. Hiding a door? Sure. But statues in front? Cheapens the secrecy."

"Well," Fil said, scratching behind her ears, "it could still be hidden, right? I mean, the statues pointed the other way, so we searched in the wrong direction."

Alize opened her jacket, retrieved her pick and turned to Binh. "Now here's the other half of your job. Break inside."

With the tip of his tail, Binh grabbed and examined it. He reached into his gear and withdrew a thin piece of bony material. "My default is to see if I can use my trusty lockpick first. Then I'll try your toys."

"We'll try to find some other hinge or mechanism while you work," Alize said. Fil at her side, they scanned the craggy landscape for anything out of place. Fil searched the upper rock face with her helmet's visor scanner, and Alize kept to the ground with her omni-tablet, while Binh muttered occasional colorful curses, most of which centered around the door's imaginary mother.

After combing every rock in the vicinity, Alize returned to the statues, searching for any attached mechanism or out-of-the-ordinary fixture. Because so little was known about the Chamayna, everything seemed out of the ordinary.

After another hour of thorough inspection, Alize grunted and dusted off her hands. She returned to the door where Fil was perched on a rocky outcropping two meters off the ground, searching for anything peculiar. Binh abandoned his lockpick in favor of Alize's tools.

Alize recalled the inscription in the museum she'd pored over for more hours than any sane person would. *Is there a clue in there? Weapon of unspeakable power? Don't have that... and light of the forest? But what could that possibly mean?*

This moon bore no evidence of ever harboring natural life, let alone trees. The other two dig sites were also on uninhabitable moons without vegetation. So how could this possibly be activated or locked with forest light? If nothing else, this led credence to Alize's teleporting theory: the Chamayna could've originated on a planet or moon with forests and then traveled to rocky moons like this one. Yet neither tree nor fossil evidence corroborated her hunch.

Did those Lo-sat linguists screw up? Does Cu-dan keep up with Lo-sat language research? He wouldn't know anything, would he?

Maybe her companions were right. She nudged Binh out of the way and examined the crevice again, noticing little flecks of rock missing from Binh's latest opening attempts. With both of her hands near the top, she caught a glimpse of her wrist piece. Pulsing green.

Sweet, verdant, leafy green.

As a shy smile parted her lips, Alize removed the wristband and waved it near the crevice. She strafed her wrist piece around the circumference of the entire crevice.

Nothing.

She'd come too far to give up, so she ran to the standing statue. Hoisting the device, gentle green light danced and spread across the statue's stony face. Her heart thumped like a drummer when she saw tiny etchings on the mandibles. These weren't cuts from falling debris. The etchings were intentional. Meaningful.

A message.

Alize moved directly under the mandibles and craned her head, pulsing light from her wrist providing some clarity.

"Fil!" Alize shouted. "I need a boost." She hadn't known elation like this since Pops' diagnosis.

Fil bounded over, her armor reflecting planet Dusoi's orange light. Binh followed at a leisurely pace.

Without bothering to ask, she hoisted Alize onto her broad shoulders. From the sturdiness of Fil's pauldron, Alize could touch the mandibles if she dared. The green glow revealed symbols, but the flash's speed meant she could only read one glyph at a time.

Half a galaxy away, and you're still coming through for me. Thanks, Pops.

"What's up there, Leeze?"

"An inscription. The problem is, I'm not sure where to start reading. I could be wrong about the word order."

Fil chuckled. "Who cares? Read it and upend history! Now we can definitely call this place 'I Told You So.' A secret message. So awesome."

Studying the four mandibles, she considered what message might be on the broken statue, anxiety tingling. *I might start in the wrong place, the wrong statue, or the wrong mandible. Hopefully, they say the same thing.*

"Alright, the message will come slowly. Is your armor recording?"

"Assume always," Binh interrupted, joining them.

"So I think I'm starting in the right spot... I see the glyphs for 'power' and 'source.' Move forward a step, Fil. Okay, now I see 'lie within,' and 'unspeakable,' and ... 'weapon.'"

"Ready to move, Leeze?"

"Yeah." A giddy shiver ran through her spine, exacerbated by the dry, lifeless air around them. She recognized these. "This next one says 'open' and 'violence.' Good. Take a step to the right. 'Lie within' again, 'material,' and 'send?' No, 'transmit.' That's all four."

Fil set her on the ground. "So how do we get inside?"

"Better shine a light on the broken statue over yonder, too," Binh said.

They jogged to the broken statue, Alize's adrenaline and excitement in overdrive. "So the head wasn't intact when I first checked. The mandibles resemble small cones. Hopefully in one piece."

Alize found the first mandible, still attached to the head's dislocated jaw, hiding under a stray rock. Squinting, she read it out loud. "I see the glyphs for 'peace' and 'seal.' I wonder if this goes with the other side that said 'open' and 'violence.'"

Binh found a second and brought it over. "Can we get Cu-dan out here to help?"

Overturning a rock, Fil called over her shoulder, "You looked like you were about to attack the guy because you're worried he might ditch us."

"It's harder to backstab me if I'm watching you." With a hiss, he turned to Alize. "Here's the mandible, Pinks."

"Thanks. This has 'cage,' 'open,' and 'not' on it. I wonder if cage could mean tomb. Huh. Maybe this isn't even a tomb. Like, this could be a palace. Or a prison."

"A temple?" Fil asked as she crouched, overturning rocks.

Binh tsked. "A waste of time?"

After an hour of searching, Alize slouched on the edge of the crater. From her new vantage point, she caught a glimpse of another mandible, this one shattered into three pieces. 'Asleep' and 'god' were etched on this one.

"God, you say?" Binh asked, acid in his voice. "No wonder they disappeared. That's what you get for believing in imaginary friends."

Fil snarled. "Don't joke. The Goddess always listens."

He waved his tail in front of her face. "Guess how much I care? I thought your Goddess was in the middle of a nap, anyway?"

"Whatever, Scale Ass." Filenada sauntered over. "I think I found one, Leeze, but it's thrashed."

Alize examined the mandible, rotating it in her hands. One glyph was unreadable, and the other said 'death.'

Lovely.

Cross-referencing the recording, they compiled Alize's best guess at the message on the mandibles.

Source of power. Unspeakable power lies within. Opened by violence. Matter transmission lies within. Sealed by peace. Do not open the cage. Sleeping god. Death.

"Well this is about as helpful as a Makawe toothbrush," Binh said.

"Huh?" Fil asked. "They just have beaks."

Alize wedged herself between them. "How about we redirect this energy? Fil, remember what I said about them maybe teleporting? 'Matter transmission' is pretty suggestive."

Binh brought his tail toward his face. "If you think that's suggestive, get a load of—"

Alize cut him off. "One line says 'opened by violence.' Attacking or destroying part of the tomb—or whatever this is—is a bothersome thought. This is such an important find..."

"Hey, it's not a find unless the promised loot's inside." Binh curled and uncurled his tail before slapping it against the ground.

"Leeze, did the Chamayna have any ceremonial weapons? Maybe they have a weapon which works like a key? That would fit the whole 'opened by violence' thing, right?"

Alize's eyes widened. "Fil, you're a beautiful intelligent treasure, and every guy who never pinged you back is trash." Alize hugged her and returned to the statue. The weapon in its hands matched the pictures of statues from the other dig sites. Those led her to believe all Chamayna statues held polearm weapons, but these were part of the carving, not detachable. "The only problem is that there's not exactly a Chamayna arms dealer lurking around here peddling wares."

"Beat me to the joke," Binh said. "Frostfur over here packs real heat. She'll need to shoot at the wall, unless," his gaze rose to Filenada, "you've got some explosives on you. Those are fun and practical." Holding up a single claw, he added, "And a great toy for kids."

Fil shook her head. "Nightmare—I wish I had incendiaries. I'm Guard Corps. We don't get the fun stuff."

"You do get assault rifles," Binh muttered. "'Overkill' models, right? Or 'Excessive Force, Mark 1?'"

Alize paced before the crevice. "Don't engage, Fil. Maybe we can be a tad gentler with the door? Like, if we just hit it, maybe that will work. It doesn't say how much violence Is required—or what kind." Alize tapped the wall with her finger and shrank away.

Binh whooshed his tail in front of her face. "Ah, yes, the old break and enter. Break your fist and enter the hospital. Do you hear yourself, Pinks? This is solid rock, much like Sergeant Fuzzball's head. A little love tap won't do *nguc*."

Fil grunted and scooped Binh in her massive arms. Against his physical and colorful verbal protest, she maneuvered Binh to a horizontal position, his head poking past her stomach and his tail floating limply by her boots.

"How about a battering ram? If it shuts you up—double win." Fil swayed Binh in her grasp.

"Stop playing around," Alize groaned.

Filenada dropped him with a snort. "Just going with your idea..."

"Sure, Frosty. Sure." Dusting himself, he turned to Alize. "Look, you can't get the funds to dig out here. You'd need a huge team with heavy machinery to do any real excavation. You know that'll never happen, even though you found something. Blasting this door is our only option if you're convinced you must perform an act of violence against this door."

"Without a geological survey," Alize said, "we don't know if there's anything in this rock which would make it volatile, explosive, or otherwise more unstable than we think. I won't let my discovery be destroyed by a rockslide. Fil, do you have a low setting on the rifle? Maybe just one shot near the crevice?"

Fil tapped her armor and withdrew an amorphous block, which expanded into her assault rifle. She adjusted the power and aimed. Her helmet unfurled its focusing lens, and Alize gulped.

Fil lowered her rifle and stepped back. "We're not alone."

Alize's gasped. "What'd you see?"

Fil gestured in the distance to the right of the mountain. A trio of ships—cargos and civilian transport, most likely—all lowering to the lunar surface. She whispered one word. "Earthquake."

Alize glanced at her wrist, breath quickening. *Pops' heart is accelerating. He knows I'm nervous.* "What're the odds they've spotted us already?"

Moving flat against the crevice, Binh pointed at the ships, already hovering above the spot where they'd landed. Directly over the *Takel*—too big to hide.

One of the cargo ships rotated, opening its hull door.

Fil clasped her paw over her snout.

Alize's jaw dropped, nervous sweat beading from every pore. "Cu-dan. We have to save him—"

Binh blocked her with his tail and slowly shook his head. With his claw, he pointed at the biggest ship.

From the hull, a turret emerged, fashioned from salvage and scraps, but imposing nonetheless.

Fil stammered. "That—that's illegal. Cargo ships can't have weaponry."

Binh groaned. "Give them a citation, then. I'm sure they'll correct the issue, officer. They must've made it by accident."

Despite the moon's frigid atmosphere, Alize's stomach tightened as the turret glowed red, adjusted its aim, and fired at their scrapper. Plasma ejected in a bright blast, incinerating the small ship. The low gravity allowed for the shrapnel and dust to rocket in all directions.

"Duck!" Alize shouted.

Her breather whirred, signifying the extra work to filter the particulates. Alize plunged to her knees and her stomach contorted into knots. "What—Cu-dan! He—he—they killed him. And our ship! Oh, Earth..."

Fil slid to the ground and wrapped Alize in an embrace. "Maybe he stepped outside the scrapper first. Or took cover. Scrappers have decent armor."

"Those smugglers followed us," Alize whispered. "They must have."

Binh tsked. "I think we would've noticed a big-ass cannon in a refrigerator when we escaped, Pinky. This is a different group. You didn't tell anyone else about this moon, right?"

"No." Alize blinked hard. "Only my idiot ex-boyf—"

Fil gripped her rifle again. "That punk ghosted you over these clowns?"

"I—I mean, I knew he was kind of prejudicial, but I never thought he'd..."

Neck frills extended, Binh hissed. Saliva flecks landed on Alize's neck. "Look, Pinky, you can watch rom-coms and cry into some nasty ice cream about this guy later. We can even shed a tear over Cu-dan if you're feeling squishy. Alternatively, we can break into this tomb and seal it behind us. Because if we don't, these goons will. After they kill us, of course. Maybe they'll be in an extra horrific mood and the two non-Humans will get tortured first."

A second cloud of dust and shredded titanium from the scrapper explosion wafted over and Alize shielded her eyes. From behind, a chorus of grinding clanks made her swivel around.

Eyes rounder than moons, she gasped. "Those noises came from the rock." The crevice widened and the rock around it slid downward, rolling into the surface. *Opened by violence. Earthquake fired a weapon.* Alize exhaled sharply. "We're going inside. If we can seal it, great. If it closes behind us, great. If not, we'll have the cover of darkness to hide."

Fil tugged on the collar of her armor. "Are you sure we won't get stuck in there?"

Alize flashed Fil her "trust me" eyes. "The alternative is taking our chances with Earthquake." Despite the chill rattling her spine, Alize dared her first step into the enveloping darkness of the structure carved into the rock. The inside felt a single degree warmer than the moon's surface, and sour air from eons of stagnation slithered into her breather.

Fil and Binh hustled with mismatched footsteps onto the rocky tiled floor.

"Fil, lights? Come on, hurry!" Alize asked.

"*Skata,* right." Fil slammed a series of plates on her armor. It emanated a wide, blue light, more suitable for Arkoudae eyes, but bright enough Alize could detect some fine details of their surroundings. A glance from her periphery showed Fil's smaller "late for work" yellow light flashed, too.

Alize would normally crack a joke about Fil's no-call, no-show. There'd be an inevitable ping from her unhappy supervisor, and the low-hanging "I told you so" joke about Fil requesting the proper amount of days off. Rather, Alize drank in the sight of the tomb. Surrounding her was artwork and a novel's worth of glyphs. She wished she could forget for a moment that Earthquake was behind her and absorb the full display. The smudged and faded art depicted geometric shapes, suggesting some lost symbolism or warning.

"Think those Earthquake *ke-noks* will fly over here and hunt us?" Binh came dangerously close to leaning against a wall, which would obscure the art and induce nerd-rage like he couldn't imagine. "Can we close this stupid door? The mammals with guns will find us if we don't hustle."

Fil grunted and retreated to the entranceway, dimming the beacon on her armor. "I don't see any switches."

"Well," Alize said, "we were right about the whole 'opened by violence' thing, so maybe it's closed by peace?"

Binh waved his tail like a metronome. "Stupendous. And what's the opposite of shooting a stolen Blekk metal scrapper? Should we build one? Pardon me while I pull some supplies outta my ass."

Fil retracted her assault rifle and stowed it in her suit, then wrapped her arms around Binh from behind. "How's this for peace? How about a smooch, too?"

Binh hissed, "I'll give you warts you'll need a doctor to get rid of. With surgery."

"Fil, I love you, but please put him down." Alize put a hand up. "Gently."

Growling, Fil delicately lowered Binh to the floor, feet first. The door shook again.

All three turned to the entranceway, watching with dropped jaws as the rocky door rose with a gravelly rumble.

"Oh come on," Fil said. "That's what it means to seal it by peace? I had to hug his scaly ass?"

Alize let out a tight sigh. "Maybe, but we need to get away from the door. Earthquake's on our trail."

After a few meters, the last natural light petered. Fil crossed her arms, blocking some of her armor's soft blue beacon light. "At least those goons can't follow."

"They don't need an archaeologist or a universal translator to tell them to shoot something," Binh said.

A translator—*Cu-dan*. "If there's some seismic activity sensor which triggers the door mechanism, enough ships moving or people walking could trigger the door, too." Some indentations on the wall caught her eye. "Fil, can you run a scan with your armor? Am I safe to de-glove?"

After tapping her helmet, Fil said, "Just be careful, Leeze. This place is holy." She had a point. The whole place exuded a vague sacred aura, but not in some spiritual sense, more of a taboo or a restriction, as if something imperceptibly aware hid among the rocks. And they'd trespassed.

Must be nerves. Dopamine rush from all this artwork.

Alize steeled herself and inhaled sharply, the moon's musty odor slipping past her breather's filter.

She removed her glove with the same reverence she'd seen Fil use in handling her apartment's altar. That was all Alize had as a reference. Pops' religion was all cerebral and emotional, not tactile like Fil's. This called for the Oze brand of wonder and awe with the Filenada brand of delicate handling. Her glove detached with a little hiss of depressurizing air. Observing her naked hand in the blue beacon light, the flimsy shadow obscured the wall etching. An archaeology professor would scream at her for potential specimen contamination with her bare hand, but she'd come all this way; she deserved to touch history herself.

Fil tilted her torso toward the ceiling; the light stretched into the yawning empty space. Rather, all the light displayed on the ceiling was that this wasn't designed with Arkouda in mind.

Hands over her mouth, Alize spun in a slow, tight circle. Each mural was a distinct etching of what appeared to be Chamayna hunters moving toward unrecognizable creatures from a forgotten past; some strode upon five legs, while others glided with fins. If it weren't for the telltale polearm weapons, she wouldn't have known which were the Chamayna and which were the prey. She stepped toward the left wall, daring to touch an etching of a hunter with a weapon raised toward what reminded her of a colossal fish creature.

A squiggle occupied the center of each individual Chamayna eye. These didn't recall any Chamayna symbology she remembered, yet they didn't seem like pupils or random graffiti.

"Look at the angle of the feet." Alize gasped. "See how they aren't parallel to the ground or perpendicular to the legs, like in the other etchings? Two arms for holding a weapon, four extended in different directions, wings up. They flew! Amazing."

"The winged creatures flew, huh?" Binh asked. "This doesn't look like any treasure I can haul back to a dealer. You promised me loot, not stick figures."

Alize tutted while caressing the painting with two careful fingers. As she traced the outline, the rock surface cooled her fingertips. It depicted a Chamayna hunter, posed like a fierce hunter-warrior, conveying more emotion than some of the museum's most elaborate paintings. She touched the wings as if they were a live specimen. With how little the Chamayna left behind, this may be the closest she'd ever get to seeing remains, raising her elation and devastation.

"These societies," Alize said, more to herself than her companions, "they felt connected to nature, and their artwork reflected that." She glanced over her shoulder. "Humans, Lo-sat, and Makawe societies all did this at one point in their prehistory. That was how all early religions developed. The Chamayna had a religion—"

Binh forcefully yawned.

Alize's eye twitched. "You're impossible." She faced Fil. "For the official recording, we'll call this the entryway."

"Leeze, didja notice the art's facing the wrong way?"

"I'm not an art critic, but how can you tell? You slinging stick-figure paintings in between your shifts saving lives at the museum?"

Alize examined the other etchings in the room. The Chamayna's back wings all pointed toward the door, instead of the front carapace and faces. "Odd … just like those statues. They really do seem to point the wrong direction." Her breather fogged on her exhale. "All the findings at the other dig sites have statues pointing in the other direction, as if they're greeting the visitors. These don't."

"So we're not welcome?" Fil asked.

"Grave robbers generally aren't," Binh replied.

"We're not grave—" Alize pointed a thin finger near Binh's snout. "We're here to respect and learn from them." Alize gently pulled out her omni-tablet. On the home screen, the camera button blinked. When she tapped it, an error message appeared instead of the photography mode.

Must be too dark.

"Right, right. Conserve things by taking them away. Makes total sense. I guess that's why prehistoric Earth was peaceful, with so many resources to go around."

Fil slid her paw between them. "Maybe we used the back way? What're the chances, Alize?"

Binh half-crouched, angling his torso toward the ceiling, and gesturing at an imaginary sign. "I can see it now. 'Human chick finds a rear entrance.'"

"Grow up, will you?" Alize scratched her chin below her breather. "But that is a possibility, Fil. We have no way of knowing for sure right now, though." She cleared her throat and pointed ahead where the stones smoothed into an arched hallway. "Sorry, but the two of you will have to crouch."

Filenada harrumphed.

"Nobody wants to hear it, Frostbite. The whole stinking galaxy caters to your colossal asses. You think anyone likes opening those gigantic doors made for your clumsy paws? Most Makawe can't even reach them. Which is hilarious, so it gets a pass from me. But still."

"What made you such a racist, Binh?" Fil asked. "You'll have to duck, too."

Binh clicked his tongue. "I grew up on Earth. Great place to raise a kid and learn to hate everyone who's different from you. Pinky knows."

"I don't. My dad wasn't—" Alize checked the pulsing green light. "—isn't an Earther. His parents were refugees, and he grew up on a space station."

Binh walked in front of her, slouching his neck. "I'm sorry, but I hope you didn't confuse me with someone who cares about your depressing backstory."

"Wait." Fil joined him, back hunched. "Stay close to me so you don't lose the light. It weirdly feels dimmer."

Alize's eyes darted around the arched ceiling and searched for more glyphs. As Binh snorted and said something unrepeatable, Alize gasped—the floor around her foot sank a few centimeters.

"Fil," she squeaked. "Stop." A low, gravelly rumble followed.

Filenada and Binh angled their shoulders, and Alize froze. She followed their gaze to the loose tile under her foot. A sickening series of snaps echoed from above and behind them, and Fil's blue beacon light illuminated a net on the ceiling.

The net contained a series of polearm weapons with sharp curved blades at the end, affixed to each other like a fence. The net fell, the line of weapons swooping from the ceiling toward them. Alize unstuck herself from her fear paralysis and ran forward, straight into Fil.

Her massive friend caught her and spun her around. Gasping, they watched the weapons swing harmlessly a few meters behind them.

"What'd you *ke-noks* do?" Binh asked mirthlessly.

Alize caught her breath. "I... I triggered a trap?"

"But it went the wrong way," Fil said, approaching the dangling weapons. "So, that means we really entered through the back door?"

"Or we're supposed to think we did," Binh said.

"Please be careful, Fil."

"Hey..." She winked at Alize. "That hole where the net was is the only spot where I didn't rub my head against these stupid low arches. Now we'll know for the next one." After a deep breath, she reached for one of the polearms, and gingerly dislodged it from the trap. "Besides, we promised Binh some treasure. Here you go, Scale Snout, a priceless artifact and a self-defense weapon, all in one."

Alize sighed. *Cu-dan could've taken one and sold it, too. And maybe earned enough to buy some peace of mind.*

"Oh joy. This'll be so easy to sneak through security on space elevators. I'm elated. And what happened to not disturbing anything in the 'holy place,' O wise and exalted one?"

"Anything that tries to kill me is not holy." Fil dislodged the weapon. In her paws, it looked like a garden tool. Alize would've needed both hands to actually use it like the Chamayna.

Alize covered her bare hand. "It doesn't make sense at all. The other Chamayna sites weren't booby-trapped."

Binh accepted the weapon, examining the heft. Taking a few practice swings threatened his balance, and he nearly missed Fil's snout, earning a grumble from her.

Hands trembling, Alize examined the trap. It seemed like a simple series of ropes and springs. *That's it? Why am I expecting something super hi-tech?* The polearms' shafts ended with a hooked blade large enough to wrap around Alize's neck. Each polearm alternated the hooked ends facing opposite directions.

"I bet the convex side could slash through an appendage." Alize squinted in the blue light, reverently afraid to touch the blade itself. "And the concave side could pull an opponent downward. This mechanism would have tripped whoever triggered it and slashed the prone body."

Binh whistled. "These things got a name? I'd call them 'hookshafts,' but that's a bit reminiscent of my sister's ex."

Alize licked her lips. "They're called *O-ep R'oA*."

Filenada dislodged another. "Just take one, Leeze. We're probably going to run into more traps. And you won't be defenseless if Earthquake shows up again." She glared at Binh. "Maybe I could call this a de-scaler? Up for a shed?"

"Please, I wish I could shed my skin. It would save me a lot in pain meds—"

"Stop," Alize said, rubbing her temples. "*O-ep R'oA* translates to clawspear." She turned to her friend. Alize hoped Fil could see the memories running through Alize's head about her mom. "Fil, I'm not crazy about carrying a weapon."

Binh's tongue slipped between his teeth. "How about carrying a lethal walking stick? Very different from weapons."

Fil shook her head. "It's light. I'll carry it. We really might need it, though. As a tool. At least to test out more traps or use like a wedge or lever."

Alize inhaled deeply and glanced at her reassuring green light. "I can carry a tool. There are also terrorists outside." She accepted the clawspear and examined the shaft in more detail. Its sheen and resistance to her grip suggested it wasn't made from imported wood. A lack of green suggested it wasn't made from any minerals found on the moon, either.

Turning it again, she understood. It was chitin. This was a Chamayna's body, forged and reshaped into building material. The color matched the smudged artwork.

Her stomach and heart disagreed about the appropriate levels of nausea and excitement. She knew she'd be close to dead Chamayna in a tomb.

But holding this … crafted death feels wrong. They used the exoskeletons of their dead for their tools and art. Gripping it filled her with purpose.

TWENTY-THREE

Aboard the designated civilian ship, *Dizhen*, Dusoi orbit, Xechas system, Collective fringe

RICK HAD WARNED Monsieur Tecton about this mission, mentioning the glaring abnormality—the Collective never bothered naming Dusoi's moons. The damn imperialists claimed everything they laid their greedy paws on. But anonymity? Red flag. If the Arkouda didn't name it, they didn't want it. And if the Arkouda saw a piece of real estate without coveting it, something was deeply wrong.

This had all the markings of a no-win situation.

Not that Monsieur Tecton listened. "They took our culture, our history, Crith. We take theirs," he'd said. "Erase their history." Lesser men believed the ruse, but Rick knew the truth. Tecton and his inner-most circle believed the Arkouda had some hidden weakness lost to history's annals, possibly something mystical or cosmic in nature. So when ensign Rymon flapped his gums about the supposed superweapon, Rick's crew was shipped out before anyone could say, "Let's think this through."

Rick wished his mole in the Drowned Star didn't corroborate the story.

The *Dizhen* made moonfall as the atomized scrapper dust cleared. A chorus of grav harnesses chimed, signaling detection of a lunar gravity.

The assembled squad under his command, clad in homemade environment suit armor, stepped through the hissing decontamination spray. Their armor neither shined nor squeaked; they were patchwork and scrapwork, crude metal forged with utilitarian frugality.

Standing before their illegally crafted turret made from recycled ship parts, Rick addressed them. "We know they're here. The escape pod, which jettisoned from the *Kasoro*, held our targets, who then changed ships to the scrapper we destroyed. Our scan of the scrapper came back negative: no sentients aboard. The marks for our mission are a Human female, a Lo-sat male, and an Arkouda female. The Human, Alize Oze, must be captured—that order's from Tecton himself. She may possess information Monsieur Tecton wants."

Rick scanned their faces, and they took the cue to nod. "Good. The Lo-sat, Binh Ten-trom, stole from Earthquake. I'd like him to repay his debt, so capture is preferred. There's only so much money we can earn off a corpse. The Arkouda female is Filenada Kaluteros. Collective soldier armed and armored. The *Kasoro* team failed to take her armor. Approach with caution."

Moreno bristled.

Rick narrowed his eyes. "Got something to add?" More than a few grins appeared on the other recruits and Rick suppressed a shudder. *Damn. A year ago, I thought Moreno was one of the good ones.* "The tech wing wants intact armor with a living host for examination. Incapacitate or cripple, but don't kill her. That's an order."

"From you or the Leader?" Moreno's lip remained stiff.

Rick moved directly in front of Moreno, establishing the height and generational differential between them. Rick's nostrils flared. "It's an order. That's all that matters." Rick's expression was a glare Moreno should've known well by this point, the "if we survive, you're on toilet duty, and I'm not saying it out loud, so you don't get embarrassed" face.

Stepping away from Moreno toward the center, Rick addressed the squad. "The official primary objective from command is seizure of any artifacts for Earthquake to liquidate. If intel's correct—" he glared at Rymon, "and it better be—something worth a fortune's down here. This could mean a turning point in the struggle for Human independence. Secondary objective is the apprehension of these three people. No other sentients were found on the preliminary scans, but keep your eyes and ears sharp. Computers aren't perfect." Rick faced the open hull, gazing into the emerald-tinted rocky moonscape. "Earthquake, move out."

A few of the recruits fidgeted, and a deep crease formed in Rick's brow.

Moreno stiffened. "You heard him, grunts. Let's move."

The reluctant ones nodded assent, and Rick narrowed his eyes at Moreno. With this trigger-happy rabble, Tecton was sending Rick's crew into a slaughter. They'd ignore orders and kill on sight if he wasn't careful.

TWENTY-FOUR

**Automated ping to the armor of
Filenada Kaluteros**

```
Copied: Dr. Hupomone Dikaio

All glory to the Collective. May Her
Dream be pleasant and eternal.

Notification: Docked pay.
Cause 1: Unexcused tardiness.
Cause 2: Unexcused missed shift
Frequency: Cause 1, _SEVEN_
Frequency: Cause 2, _FOUR_
Rectification: UNAVAILABLE

For supervisors:

-Possible explanation 1: Cause 1, Cause
2 _INEBRIATION_
```

--Based on: history, conversations, vital signs, demotion from active deployment to museum guard

-Possible explanation 2: Cause 1, Cause 2 _ENDED EMPLOYMENT: SELF-TERMINATION

--Based on: conversations, repeated phrase "I can't wait to quit this bitch." -Appeal status: _NOT RECOMMENDED_

All glory to the Collective

May the Goddess's Great Slumber remain undisturbed.

TWENTY-FIVE

**LOCATION ERROR. CONTACT
COMMANDING OFFICER. DOCKED
PAY FOR TAMPERING.**

FIL'S ARMOR BEACON light blinked. "Sorry about that. Weird error message on my display." She tapped it with her finger a few times and tsked.

Binh held his clawspear aloft with his tail. "Because you're following a Human? Or is it that we stopped walking again so the Human can gawk at artwork a hatchling could make? All while actual Citizens are forced to squat and slouch? Those would definitely register as errors."

"Sniff my tail, scaleface. No, it can't read my location anymore."

Alize glanced over her shoulder at Fil. "Are you too far away from your base?"

Binh gesticulated with his claws. "What, you think she's using some prehistoric Human tech that can't work inside buildings? Gimme a break."

Fil's voice trembled. "This should work everywhere. *Skata*."

Shifting her grip on the clawspear, Alize cocked her head and glanced at the armor, as if she could possibly figure out the issue. "Did you take too much damage when Earthquake shot you?"

"Nah," Fil said. "Auto-diagnostics said I was fine—no repair recommended. It also would've given me an error message earlier—much more forceful than this."

Binh's grin unrolled through his snout. "How could anything disrupt Arkouda tech?"

Alize stepped back and scratched her chin. "Maybe it's not tech. Maybe something else is interfering. Something local?"

Fil balanced against a wall etching—it resembled a bludgeoning weapon. "If you're talking about cosmic radiation or anything, that wouldn't mess with the armor, either."

Alize shrugged. "The location signal functioned normally near the surface. We won't need it again until we return."

"But if I die—" Fil's voice flickered, "the Fleet won't find my body."

"Have you considered not dying?" Binh raised his clawspear. "It's part of my daily routine. Highly recommended. Most doctors agree about its value. And the ones who don't... well, suffice it to say—"

Fil cracked the knuckles on her paws. "Keep talking and your daily routine ends today."

Alize advanced, eyes still on the ground, and heard a light splash. Shifting focus on her feet, she noticed a dark, shallow puddle around her boot.

A moon this parched and devoid of life shouldn't have any liquid.

"Uh, guys..." She pointed to her boot with the butt of her clawspear. "You seeing this?"

Binh slinked toward her and took a few rapid sniffs. "Something faint. On the floor."

"Do you see the liquid down here?" Alize asked, petrified to the spot.

"Not really," Binh said. "This blue light is not doing much for the old peepers. But the scent is strong, I'll give you that. Chemical." He flicked his tongue and sniffed. His voice steadied, and his painted-on smirk disappeared. "Smells flammable. Must be a trigger around here somewhere."

"What, the clawspears weren't enough of a trap?" Fil grumbled.

Alize shook her head tightly, afraid to move any more than she already had. "This would have come before the clawspears. That trap was meant to finish off whoever or whatever survived this one."

Advancing, Fil lowered her torso. "I can definitely see the liquid now. And it does kind of stink."

Alize took some desperate sniffs. "Nothing. Is it faint?"

"Everything smells faint compared to Miss Fuzzy over here."

Ignoring Binh, Alize inhaled deeply. "Well, this is probably flammable liquid, and we're likely at the end of the trap. So, wherever this pool begins is where the trigger should be." After another few deep breaths, she added, "And the mechanism to ignite the fire should be close to where we're standing right now, right?"

Fil nodded and rotated in place, letting the armor beacon illuminate the surrounding cramped area.

Binh pointed to the ceiling with his clawspear. "Something smells out of place up there. I caught a slight breeze between a crack in the stone."

Another light splash. Fil gasped. Alize glanced at Fil's armored boots and saw the same liquid around them.

A whiff of the chemical scent registered. It reminded her of the cheaper ammonia-based lubricants used on the older bots she repaired. "This chemical pool is growing," Alize said. "Why's this expanding on us? Is there some other trap we triggered and didn't realize?"

Three light splashes followed, hitting Binh's boots and tail.

"Nasty," Binh hissed. "This was my good pair, too." He whirled in the liquid. "And I was moving away from the source. It's dripping from the ceiling."

A series of clicks echoed above them, and a piece of the arched ceiling recessed. A small, oblong device lowered. Made of stone, it resembled the animals in the etchings. It opened its stony maw, and inside the new opening, little glints reflected in the light from Fil's beacon.

Metal shavings.

Bits of metal shavings and small, rough rocks cascaded down toward the liquid.

Alize clutched her clawspear tight. "Fil!"

The metal shavings and rocks collided into each other, renegade sparks rebelling against the blue light of Fil's armor and the faint green light from Pops' heart monitor. Those tiny orange harbingers ignited over the chemical pool. A blazing inferno rose.

Alize sprinted, heart in her throat, flames licking her heels. The instantaneous heat altered the pressure inside the hallway and pushed her in a raging whoosh. Fil and Binh joined her dead sprint, racing toward the exit where they made their entry, toward safety, toward sanity.

Toward Earthquake. Alize gulped. It wasn't as if they had any choice in the matter. Terrorists could be avoided, or maybe even reasoned with, but a chemical fire in a hallway couldn't.

The gaseous flames encroached. The tread under her gave way to liquid, slowing her limp as the melting cheap material clung to the floor. She brought up her left foot, hopping on the right, and undid the boot, letting it fall behind her. It was that or her life. And these boots were her only pair. The stench of singed hair and fur snuck through the burning chemicals.

Sorry, Fil. Sorry, Pops. I'm botching this whole thing.

Reaching the sprung clawspear trap, the cloud of flame finally dissipated. Binh turned first, and the ladies followed. Catching their collective breaths, Alize broke the silence. "I-I...I'm so sorry."

"I should've noticed it," Fil said, massaging beneath her ears. "I guess I was too preoccupied with the armor malfunction."

Binh frowned. "Yeah, malfunctioning so bad you couldn't toss up a force field again?"

Fil snarled. "Do you want to gamble on malfunctioning armor? That hopefully works, but my legs definitely work. And the force fields were meant to stop plasma bullets, not literal fire."

Scorched air stung Alize's nostrils. "Binh, will you be able to tell when it's safe to go back there again?"

Binh nodded. "When you get someone else to do this instead of me, yes. Then, it'll be perfectly safe."

Time for a new tactic with this jerk. "How bad are the fumes?"

"Well, I haven't passed out yet—always a good sign. Neither of you mammals did either, which is a neutral sign."

"How is that neutral?" Fil asked.

"Because I don't particularly like either of you. Unfortunately, you two still need to pay me, which requires you both alive."

Alize rubbed her temples. "Binh, if I walk back there now, will I die or pass out?"

Binh lowered an eyeridge. "With only one shoe, Professor Pinky?"

Fil folded her arms. "She'll smack you with the other one if you don't start giving clear answers."

Binh stuck his tongue between his teeth. "Yeah, you'll live, Pinkster. Just don't walk too slow or breathe in too much of that gas. You might feel lightheaded, or you might even say funny things. That's when you know you're in trouble. Breathers can only filter so much, especially since the Arkouda engineer who made the Human version probably wasn't thinking too hard about keeping Provincials alive."

Cold stone chilled her left foot and reverberated through her body now that the fire and fumes had dissipated. Her guilt laden toes on her right foot curled in her boot, as if in apology to their homeless cousins.

Fil gasped. "Leeze, will you be okay?"

Alize huffed. "What, you don't approve of my new look? You're a better dresser than me, but I think I pull off budget chic."

Binh swished his tail. "You're always going to be ugly since you don't look like me, so you may as well get used to the idea. The bigger irony is the potential for hypothermia, even though you're a hairy heat monster."

Alize shifted with her lopsided balance, still sweating from the fire and fumes that the breather only half-blocked. "The breather should protect me, right? And this place isn't cold enough for hypothermia to be a concern."

Some composure left Fil's voice. "Leeze, I don't know much about Human biology—and I never had medic training."

"Probably wouldn't need medic training to guard old-ass paintings and rocks," Binh muttered.

Alize shook her head at them and went toward the fumes. *If I feel loopy, I leave. Easy as that.* Missing a shoe offered a spiritual connection to the Chamayna. In their artwork and statues, they all lacked footwear. Whether that was reflective of their actual culture or an artistic standard was impossible to know. Uncertainty aside, she imagined herself as one of the

Chamayna, flimsy wings, extra arms, compound eyes and all. *Experiencing the same cold stone the way they did.*

She approached the section of the hallway where the stones and shavings dropped, with little puffs of smoke waving around. Heavier footsteps from her companions padded behind her.

Alize squinted at the unburnt etchings—a pattern emerged. For every three hunting scenes, there was another type. Instead of a Chamayna hunter brandishing a clawspear in front of an animal, this would be a group of Chamayna standing in a circle around various other objects which seemed more like abstract shapes than anything discernable.

"A ritual..." she whispered.

Binh snorted. "Bah. Isn't that the default answer of stumped archaeologists? You can't understand so you say it was for something religious. Oldest Human trick in the book."

Alize huffed. "Fine. What do you see, if not a ritual?"

"Something I can't take off the wall and sell, despite what I was promised. So, white-hot rage?"

Fil pushed him aside and examined the etching in question. "Reminds me of one of the Goddess Dream Dances."

"Is that the one where you burn the incense to coerce the Goddess' dream to improve?" Alize asked.

Fil nodded. "We can't coerce the Goddess. Or her Dream. Only implore. But basically, yeah. The better the dream, the less likely she wakes up."

Alize touched the ritual etching. "Something's off."

Alize retreated to the previous iteration of the ritual etching. Same circle, but she counted the characters more carefully this time. One more Chamayna partaking in the ritual than the previous etching. The shape in the center of their circle was slightly different, too. Although it consisted of simple lines and curves, the center shape had less definition than the etching closer to the exit. She retraced her steps toward the exit. The next image displayed one more Chamayna, and less definition in the shape, more oblong and bulbous.

"Wow…"

"Did those fumes affect you?" A modicum of concern bled into Binh's sarcasm.

"No, something better…" Alize darted past them. "Fil, I need some more light."

Fil clapped. "That's my girl—what'd you find over there? I'm coming over."

"I don't know… There's definitely a message in these etchings. Do you see it?"

Binh followed, grumbling, "Is the message, 'hey, let's sprint through an unfamiliar dungeon filled with traps?' That would be worth carving."

Alize stopped short of the next etching. This had one fewer Chamayna in the ritual, and even more definition to the center shape. It was some kind of sprawled-out body, but it didn't match the profiles of any of the animals she'd seen on the hunting etches. It wasn't Chamayna, either. Even among these alien ruins, this seemed foreign. Wrong, somehow. It didn't match the artistic aesthetic at all: jagged, broken lines among smooth curves.

"Fil, are you positive the Arkouda never had any direct contact with the Chamayna?"

Filenada crossed her arms and pored over the next etching, an outline of the disturbing shape suggesting some kind of growth. "Well, it's not documented anywhere."

Alize winced. "But, like, maybe off-the-record interactions? Like covered up stuff?"

"You're asking the wrong person," Binh said. "If it happened off the official record, Madam Armored Asshole wouldn't know."

"Leeze, he has a point. Even though he's a bucket of shit with a tail. I'm sorry, but I don't know what else to tell you."

After a huff, Binh squinted toward the etching. "Some extinct Earth insects had queens. The Chamayna look buggy enough to me. Any chance you're looking at royalty?"

"Hm. Well, there's no conclusive evidence as to how they bred, so it's possible. But by that same token, it could be something else entirely. Judging by the relative size, it seems like it would stand at eye level to an Arkouda."

"That blob isn't an Arkouda," Fil grumbled.

"But Frosty—" Binh pointed at it with his tail, "look how full of itself it is."

"Do you think this ritual is somehow a resurrection ceremony?" Alize asked. "Or a summoning?"

"Leeze..." Fil scratched the exposed bit of her neck beneath her helmet. "This sounds far-fetched."

"Each iteration gives more detail to the shape, and it's appearing more clear and defined as a creature.

Maybe a sentient one. So if the number of Chamayna decreases while this gets more defined, maybe there's some ritualistic sacrifice happening. Or exchange. Like, a life for a life." Alize paced to another ritual etching, passing three more hunting scenes. "And see here, one less Chamayna again, and more definition to the shape. It clearly has legs and a few sets of arms. Right there, that's a head."

Binh slapped his tail against the floor. "Seems like they have to trade a lot of lives for this ... thing to come alive."

Fil clicked her tongue. "But we're going backward through this place. Maybe they're stealing life from this to procreate."

"Should we give it a name?" Alize tugged at a loose curl of hair. "I don't like calling it a 'thing.' Binh, I'm sure you can think of something creative."

"Weird blob with limbs. Inconsequential."

"You're impossible," Fil said. "I can't think of a name, either. But what do you think of my backward idea?"

Alize backed into the wall. The hallway was too cramped for her to see everything—some of the etchings were out of her periphery. "You might be onto something, Fil. But there's a civilization's worth of cultural context we don't have, so we can't be certain." Curling and uncurling her exposed toes and missing her boot, she added, "And there's another possibility. They want to get rid of or kill whatever this monstrosity is, and it can't be done alone." Alize rubbed her temples. "Let's move on. We haven't sprung a trap in a while, so be vigilant."

Fil shushed her. "Don't put that out there."

Alize faltered on the following step. "We're on a decline. Fil, can you run some armor diagnostics and check? We're definitely on a gentle slope."

A whirr-click sounded from Fil's helmet. She pressed the side of it a few times before the clicking stopped. "Sorry. More error messages. Yeah, we're going farther down underground."

The thought of penetrating deeper underground brought a new wave of goosebumps as Alize glanced at the next ritual etching. Only five Chamayna, but the center creature had six distinct arms, two jutting legs, and twisted protrusions leaving the top of the head. The subtle detail from the simplistic lines and curves was astounding. In some primal way which Alize felt more than she understood, these etchings conveyed more meaning and emotion than the most realistic portraits and landscapes ever produced by Human artists. Yet as the creature they couldn't name gained definition, she grew increasingly uneasy, her guts twisting with each development.

Alize glanced away from the etching and her jaw dropped. The blue light from Fil's armor beacon washed over a grand room. The ceiling catapulted from barely over Alize's head to accommodate Fil several times over.

Binh gasped, while Filenada gaped up at the ceiling, the majority of the light following Fil's gaze. The ceilings had etchings, too, but they stood too far from them to understand what they depicted.

"They didn't only fly for hunting," Alize said, beaming. "They flew for their art. That's huge. They must have had some biological organisms to make their flying require little stamina and keep them stabilized."

Sauntering around the room's oval perimeter, Binh said, "Or flying was normal for them. Imagine—having wings, and actually using them for everyday tasks. What a crazy concept."

Alize crept to the opposite side. In front of them yawned a wide wall-to-wall staircase, so gentle and long that it could've been mistaken for a ramp. Halfway down the stairs, Alize ran her hand against the wall and found an indentation.

"Fil, could you shine some light my way, please?"

With blue light cascading over Alize's wall, the indentation revealed a series of shelves. Small glass jars, carved stone tools, and what looked like cooking implements lined each shelf. Then, her attention was stolen by a snap from the other side of the room.

Binh leapt backward with a yelp. *"Ngucl"* Breathing rapidly, he added, "I hit some tripwire—harder to smell than other traps."

"Don't worry about it, Scales—looks like nothing happened," Fil said, paws on her hips. "Remember this humbling moment next time you have something snarky to say."

"The next time, of course."

Alize scanned the grand room. A waft of dust changed the scent in her breather. Faintly, a series of creaks echoed from above—the etchings descended. Or rather, the ceiling itself.

Collapsing above them.

Before Alize registered what was happening, the indentation beside her hissed, and thin smoke spiraled out.

A series of shrill electric bells squealed in Fil's helmet.

Fil grunted. "Poison?"

"Run!" As the ceiling creaked, Alize sprinted down the staircase. The poison gas billowed out from the walls, coiling around their limbs.

Tempting fate, Alize looked up mid-stride. The ceiling continued its descent. Quickly. Ahead was a branching hallway. "Can you tell which goes up, Fil?"

"My malfunction commands are getting louder and more frequent. I'm worried it'll be wrong."

The ceiling dropped close enough that it no longer echoed. Only grinding. Accelerating.

Binh and Fil's long strides drove them ahead of Alize. Even worse, Fil's beacon light steadily weakened with the increasing distance, threatening to leave Alize alone in the gloom.

The end of the room drew closer as the temperature dropped a few degrees. Either branch of the hallway beckoned, but it didn't matter which they took. Alize stole a glance at her wristpiece. Still blinking, but to an off-beat pulse. It had a rhythm, as if Pops were somehow communicating.

"I believe in you." It's that or I'm giving him a heart attack with my stress.

Loose rubble dug into her bare foot. Clawspear and teeth clenched, she pushed herself and nearly caught up to Fil. Alize's lungs tightened to the point of suffocation.

The stony grinding was so close, Alize didn't need to see the ceiling.

A dry noise cracked as the ceiling ground against the top of Fil's helmet.

"Fil!" Flashes of their friendship streaked through her mind. Fil's first day on the job when Alize found her sobbing in the bathroom. Alize's graduation where Fil got nasty looks for helping Pops get up the stairs. She couldn't lose Fil. She—

The grinding sputtered to a stop.

Fil and Binh halted, too. Rising on the balls of her feet, Fil reached up, and grazed the lowered ceiling. "It definitely stopped."

Gasping for breath, Alize put her hands on her knees. "It must be the staircase. The ceiling stopped when it hit the top of the ramp."

"Heh." Binh flicked his tongue between his teeth. "Smart. Going toward the exit means going splat."

Fil made a particularly offensive gesture at the slab. "I've got to admit, I'm surprised you triggered the trap, Scaleface. I would've expected the thief to be a little more cautious around security."

"Well, I expected tripwire around my feet." His snout curled into a grin. "Just not around this jewelry. And give me a break. I'm used to bypassing modern security, not scary rocks." He pulled out a smooth brooch in the shape of a Chamayna mandible. "Can't be worth much, but it's something."

With a gulp of air, Alize stood upright and put her wrists on her hips. "Binh..."

"What? You don't think this is your supposed superweapon, do you? The agreement was I can keep anything except that."

"No." Alize's breathing returned to normal. "I remember our deal. You taking that bauble could've killed us."

"Ah," he said, tail spinning around his face. "But guess what? We didn't die, and as a bonus, we got some healthy exercise. So, I may have saved us all."

"Yeah, yeah, laugh it up, Scale-ball. How are we going to escape now? That was the path to the exit."

"One exit." Alize grabbed Fil's paw. "There must be another."

"Professor Pinky's got a point. These fancy Collective breathers would start acting *nguc-nguc* crazy if we didn't have an influx of air from somewhere. There is fresh air coming in. Somehow. And there could be a mechanism to lift that ceiling back up. Why don't we try that power of friendship stuff?"

Alize shook her head and took advantage of the ceiling's proximity. The etchings were glyphs. A message. Her jaw dropped and she ran to the wall. "I can't be sure where the message starts, but there's something here."

She read each glyph aloud, trekking the diameter of the room. "*Knock for each arm. Raise. Remove object table*—no—shelf? *Shelf. Lower.*" She'd reached the opposite wall.

"Lower, huh?" Fil scratched behind her ears. "That's a nice and gentle way of saying squash like a bug."

"Hold on…" She squinted and reversed her orientation. "This says something else when I read the other way."

"What do you mean?" Fil asked.

"Chamayna glyphs. The few linguists who study them think that their glyphs are reversible. There's a whole subalphabet for reading backward. The theory is their compound eyes allowed for several layers of meaning for each glyph, so they could process more information and meaning from each phrase."

"So what's it say when you read it backward?" Fil asked.

Alize limped to the opposite wall. "Unspeakable weapons—below? No, underside? No. Oh. *Dormant.*" Alize tsked. "Smudge, damn. This next part says *Asleep. Awaken for matter transmit. Impart payment.*"

Fil's voice trembled. "You know, that doesn't make a ton of sense, Leeze. Maybe only the first way you read it is the right way."

Alize scanned the glyphs again. "That was harder to translate. There's also a theory that reading the glyphs in different directions follows different grammar rules, so I could've made a mistake."

"Or five," Binh hissed.

Alize folded her arms and sighed. "Look, that wasn't entirely clear, but there's no mistake: the superweapon is below us. We need to figure out which hallway goes lower, and we'll find it." She shifted her balance off her bare foot.

"That better be where the treasure room is," Binh said. "I didn't come all this way for nothing."

"You got two hugs from me, Scales. Most guys would kill for that."

"I think you mean get killed from that."

Fil brushed past him and straddled the fork in the hallway, letting her light beacon fill the space between them.

Glancing from side to side, Alize shrugged. "They seem equal, honestly. Maybe they both go down?"

Binh swung the clawspear in front of his snout like it was a prehistoric microphone. "Or we're stuck in a maze, mammals."

Fil clicked her chalky tongue. "Bad news. Scan says they're flat, at least for the first few meters. No more gentle decline. And we must've snagged something—my armor's data feedback is throwing up warning signs that I'm getting faulty and unreliable readings. More of the stupid 'contact the admin' *skata*."

"Fil," Alize asked, "is it possible you're fired, and that's why your armor's having issues?"

Binh snorted. "Gotta love Collective military. They're shutting down your system, Frosty. Dishonorably discharged for disgraceful behavior."

"I—I, no that can't be it. And it would be an all-at-once shut-down, not piecemeal like this."

"You're absolutely positive?" Alize asked.

Fil scratched behind her ears. "Well, sure. Probably."

"Wonderful. I'm going to die with two unemployed mammals. I have a doctor's appointment next week, you know. She'll miss me."

Alize approached the left branch, hand gliding against the wall. "We'll go this way."

"Horrible idea," Binh said.

"The right side doesn't have etchings as far as I can see. This side continues the hunting and ritual scene pattern. This has to be the way. Come on."

As they walked, Alize kept an eye on the etchings. The animals in the hunting scenes alternated between abstract wispy lines and grotesque stumps with mismatched limbs. The Chamayna artists had an uncanny ability to draw intense emotion from simplicity. Simple lines and curves, faded by time—still pregnant with forgotten symbolism and lore.

With each slight change in the etching, Alize's stomach turned tighter. They were approaching something, and they were close.

After a few minutes, the ritual etching only had one Chamayna standing in front of the center creature they couldn't name. But the solitary figure wasn't what caught Alize's attention. The creature in the center stood upright, six arms spread, carrying something in both center arms. One object resembled a mace and the other a staff. The head protrusions clarified into horns circling around from the top of the head to where the chin mandibles should've been. Faded and smudged lines prevented her from being certain, but the ovals Alize assumed were eyes had been painted with a different material—a faded purple wine that may have dazzled like fire eons ago. She hoped it was a representation of some shamanic figure wearing a symbolic headdress, and not something else, alien even to the Chamanya. Her heart rate accelerated at the mere sight of the eldritch depiction.

She stopped to gawk; she wanted to catch Fil and Binh's attention and invite them to look, but seeing it, she felt utterly speechless.

Not one word came.

Only dread.

Emptiness.

Somehow, seeing her own hands in front of her, she reflected on her own existence and felt utterly insignificant. Whatever it was she beheld, it was something of cosmic scope. She had no business to be here and no right to disturb this tomb.

She pushed it from her mind and pressed forward.

Fil broke Alize's trance. "Coming up on a corner."

The soft blue light stopped at a wall, a shadow suggesting a sharp turn. When the trio rounded the corner, Fil's beacon shone down the new section of hallway, revealing a descending staircase. Alize took a cautious step and held out her arm to block Fil from advancing.

"Fil, wait. There's a trap at the top of these steps. Bound to be. We haven't activated one in a while, and this would be a good spot for one."

Fil stepped away. The blue light from the beacon didn't reach the bottom of the staircase, even though it didn't seem to be that much of a descent. Alize glanced around the tight corner—a glyph the size of her head adorned the wall behind her.

"Stop."

"Huh?" Fil asked.

Alize cleared her throat. "That's what this glyph says. And backward... also stop? Huh. It's an upside-down palindrome." Pointing above, she indicated a faint outline cut into the wall. "Is that a panel?"

Binh scoffed. "Definitely a false wall. Step back." He shooed them with his tail and widened his stance. "We'll pry this open. Something nasty will fall out. Guaranteed. The trigger's probably at the bottom or halfway up the steps." Holding his clawspear with his tail, standing perpendicular to the false two-meter-high panel, he wedged the blade in the outline. "Okay, Frosty, time to put those big military muscles to use. Pry this open and don't get too close."

Fil grunted. "Don't want to take the brunt of the trap yourself?"

"Of course not. Also, you're markedly stronger than me."

In between heaves, Fil said, "Nice of you to admit it."

"Yeah, whatever."

Alize leaned her clawspear against the wall. "Fil, do you need help?"

The stone mechanism groaned, and Fil stepped back. The panel fell forward, creating a ramp to the top step from the panel, revealing a shiny dark sphere, nearly as wide as the stairway.

Fil gasped. "A boulder?"

Alize stole a quick glance at her clawspear. "The ball isn't made of rock. It's Chamayna chitin, like the clawspears." The mass of forged chitin lurched forward, as if from a coiled spring, and cascaded down the steps, with a heavy bounce.

How many Chamayna exoskeletons were harvested to make this? The number of dead... inconceivable.

And the thought of death brought a sting of guilt as Cu-dan's face flashed in her mind. Hopefully, the vaporization was immediate and painless.

From her periphery, she caught a reassuring pulsing green flicker.

Binh whistled. "That'll cause some damage for sure, whether it's a rock or a giant ball of crushed bugs."

The chitin boulder echoed down the steps, shaking loose debris from the ceiling on each thudding bounce. After a few moments of its vicious descent, a booming crash echoed from the bottom, and the foundations of the floor shook. The tomb shuddered through Alize's bare foot, making her wince and tense.

Catching her breath, Fil said, "Well, if there was a door down there, it's probably open."

Alize stole another glance at her green light. It slowed from her last check. Definitely shouldn't have opened the panel. The Chamayna took quite a few measures to protect whatever was down there from people like them.

Am I disrespecting the dead, just for the sake of my own hubris? Cu-dan's already a casualty. Who's next?

Alize sighed. "Let's go. Hopefully, that chitin boulder shattered, and we can step over or around it. Otherwise, we're stuck again."

Fil led the descent. The walls along the side of the stone staircase broke the pattern of the etchings, only showing hunting scenes. But with the way the animals were depicted, the distinction between predator and prey blurred. One depicted Chamayna even had the appearance of fleeing. The next was even more obvious; the hunter had dropped the clawspear.

Slowing her descent, Fil looked over her shoulder at the other two. "Hey, be careful, my armor is losing power."

"That makes sense with what's been happening," Alize said.

Binh sniffed. "I wasn't paying much attention to it before, but the light is definitely dimmer. Sergeant Frosty, I thought those things had generators ready to operate for days?"

"You didn't get an error message, Fil?"

Fil shrugged. "It should warn me when power's low, but Binh's right; the power generators in the armor can go for almost a cycle before a recharge. And the light wouldn't dim to save power; it would just shut off."

Alize felt the stairs with her bare foot, noticing the angle of her ankle and calf. "The stairs are definitely getting steeper. I think this is where the boulder bounced the first time. Does that have anything to do with it?"

"I don't think so," Fil said. "It's just not shining more than a few meters in front of us. Like the darkness is thick or something."

Or something is eating the light. Alize's blood ran cold.

No, that's ridiculous.

Binh scoffed. "Can you admit one of those Earthquake *ke-noks* got a lucky shot back in that meat ship? Part of your armor's circuitry is fried."

"Earthquake is incompetent," Fil said in a clipped tone, "and they can't stand up to The Collective. Even one of us with a tied paw is worth a whole contingent of those losers."

Alize raised an eyebrow behind Fil's back. *That sounded partially rehearsed. Does she think that about all Humans?* Sighing, she shook her head. *Of course not. She's my best friend.* As Alize prepared a mediating response, they all stopped. A thick boom followed by a series of sharp cracks like prehistoric gunshots echoed from behind them.

"*Skata!* What in the Nightmare was that?" Fil asked.

"Language," Binh said in a mocking tone. "You wouldn't want to upset your imaginary friend. But that came from the exit-entrance. Seems like Professor Pinky needs to share her discovery with Earthquake."

Sweat beaded on the back of Alize's neck. "How could those goons figure out how to open that gate? Do you think they have a Chamayna scholar with them?" Her heart fluttered. Could the so-called bad guys have some actual insight or interest in archaeology? Would they have dismissed her outright like the university's dissertation board?

But then her heart sank into her stomach. Earthquake was gaining on them. "They didn't have to figure anything out. They could've seen us walk in, found our bootprints, found the statues, or followed the tracks to the entrance. We've disabled all of the traps, too. There's nothing to slow them down."

Alize inhaled, failing to inject calm into her voice. "We need to get the hell out of here. The path down here was linear except for one fork."

"Did you forget about the collapsed ceiling?" Binh raised his eyeridges. "That's a bit of an obstacle keeping them from going anywhere."

Alize took off at a jog, pulling Fil by the paw. "If Earthquake is close, that's even more reason to press forward. Hopefully we can get what we need and escape. And then hijack or stowaway on their ship before they notice." *Which sounds impossible.*

"We're better off calling the Collective fleet with Frosty's armor. We can tell them Earthquake took us hostage. But if you really want to get what we need, stop staring at the etchings every ten seconds. I'll go ahead and tell you how the rest will be: more of the same while also creepy and unsettling. Oh, and incomprehensible. Can't forget that."

Alize sighed. "Fine. I'll stop taking pictures." They continued their descent, Fil's beacon dimming slightly with each step. It boggled the mind since Fil reported no drop in her power supply. The armor itself remained bright as ever, but the light emanating from it couldn't penetrate much farther than a meter in front of them.

Moments later, the brightness field dimmed to a half-meter radius, and they reached the stairs' landing. Shards and shrapnel from the chitin boulder littered the floor, bits of exoskeleton reflecting the dim glint from Fil's beacon. The shattered sphere's main portion was split in half on either side of the doorway.

Alize gawked at the scattered shrapnel representing uncountable dead Chamayna. "It looked so big and imposing at the top of the stairs..."

Binh sniffed. "Yeah, and it did our job for us. There's a new room on the other side."

"Quit lying," Fil said. "You can't smell a new room."

"Sure I can. In fairness, it's difficult over your body odor, but there's a different room in there. I swear on my dad's bones." He sniffed. "There are various metals inside it—if I were a gambling man. And I am."

Alize felt the doorway's outline. Double-reinforced. It was supposed to take the brunt of the chitin boulder. If it hadn't split in half, the sphere of dead bodies would've plugged the doorway. The boulder must not have followed the intended trajectory. Past the entrance, an ornately carved and thick stone slab lay on the floor.

"This must've blocked the doorway." Alize shook her head. "There's no hinge. This was a plug. Not a door. Deliberately not a door." She curled her bare toes on the floor in front of the broken slab, and a sharp pinch of shattered chitin threatened to puncture her skin. "We broke a seal on something."

Feelings of wrongness and violation flooded. It was a metaphysical variety of the "I don't belong here" mentality she had every time she set foot in her classes or ate dinner with Fil's family. But this wasn't the same as being the sole Human. This was something older, bigger, and somehow more significant than that. *Is it because I'm not a real PhD yet? Because I'm not a real archaeologist? Didn't I earn this? Or is it because I'm doing this over Cu-dan's dead body?*

Ominous nausea and tightness stirred inside, signaling she wasn't suffering impostor syndrome, but something more sinister tugged at her. It was reminiscent of the feeling she had earlier, gaping at the completed image of the dread creature they couldn't name.

"Um, stay close."

"Right," Fil said.

Desperate to lighten the mood, Alize glanced sideways at Binh. "What, no snarky comment?"

Binh responded with closed eyes and a slow shake of the head.

Are they feeling the same thing? She parted her lips, but no words followed.

When Fil stepped past the chilled stone slab, the light around her armor's beacon shrank, visibly this time. The darkness was so enveloping, Fil disappeared under the thick shadow. Her glowing armor created an illusion that it floated. Binh was invisible, and Alize couldn't see her hand in front of her face. It was as if the photons themselves fled.

Binh sniffed. "Stay sharp. There's a musty smell I don't recognize."

With a deep breath, Alize focused on her surroundings. Binh and Fil's cautious footsteps patted in the gloom. Another similar sound came through. *Breathing?* After a quick glance at her wrist, she caught the reassuring green pulse from Pops.

"Fil, does your armor make noise?"

"Little whirrs, yeah. I'm trying to mess with the settings. I'll see if I can divert more power to the beacon."

Binh hissed. "Frosty, stand up straight. Listen to the echo. We're in another big room."

So that was either an echo or Fil's armor. Alize unclenched her fist and loosened her grip on her clawspear.

The glowing armor rose. "Thanks, Scales."

"Anything for you, Sergeant Stinkfur."

They're joking. We're safe. The tension in her shoulders relaxed. Nothing in here could possibly "eat" Fil's light. Nothing could do that to photons. There must be some dense concentration of dust particles or—

A slight resistance on her bare foot. Alize peered down, for all the good it did. She curled and uncurled her toes, shifting the sole of her foot. A sticky, silken substance tugged at her toes. Another step increased the resistance. Risking a crouch, Alize brought her wristpiece down by her foot. Squinting, she could only identify faint details in the dim, pulsing green light.

Threads?

Her eyes widened, even without any light to take in.

Breathing labored, she yell-whispered. "Web!"

A tingling sensation snaked from her foot through her spine.

TWENTY-SIX

Lunar surface, unnamed moon, Dusoi orbit, Xechas system, Collective fringe

RICK GLARED AT the corpse-sized hole in the rust-green mountainside. It would've been barren otherwise—a forgettable cluster of rocks amid the craggy surface. Destroying another culture's architecture on top of a natural formation was despicable, but he had orders—no matter how much they twisted his gut. Lazy pillars of smoke and dust rose from the shattered remains of the false door.

Why the hell'd the Chamayna put these statues there, facing the wrong way? If it hadn't been for those tracks, we would've searched in the wrong direction for hours. Wish I could kibosh this whole damn operation.

A ping arrived on his omni-tablet from Amanda. "Sir. We performed a secondary scan of that scrapper's remains. You're right. No signs of life. Hell of a risky gamble. You could've killed all of them, even that translator. Our preliminary scans have been wrong before."

If by kill you mean put out of their misery and save them from exploitation, yeah. He prepared to tell her he didn't like her tone but decided against it. "Thanks for checking."

Rick double-tapped the shoulder on his modified armor and faced his squad. They were in various stages of suiting up. "Troops, we don't know what's in there. We have our targets and our orders. It looks like we're going underground. This civilization most likely died off before they could harness electricity, so odds are we won't have any light to guide us. We'll need light beams on at all times. Wellsford," Rick inclined his head toward a recruit, "radio the transports and tell them to get haul-teams ready to go behind us. Our squad doesn't loot." He cast a steely glare at Rymon. "We respect the dignity of these people. We're allegedly going into some sacred place. Act like it."

Lamont scoffed.

Rick glared at him. "Something to add?" Eyes narrowed all around the group, and a tense silence passed. "Didn't think so."

Moreno furrowed his brow, further darkened by his breathing helmet's visor. Other recruits made similar dour expressions with scowls and scrunched noses behind their helmets.

"There's an extraction team following us. They will assess the value of what we find—not us. We don't touch anything or take any souvenirs. Questions?" Rick scanned the crowd. "Didn't think so. Let's move."

Rick activated his pistol's light attachment and ventured inside the crypt, bunker, or whatever this damn structure was. His breather sputtered against the pulverized dust cloud; a stray whiff of the dissipated plasma grenade snuck through.

Phantom pains in his missing arm reminded him to exercise caution. The missing limb also served as glaring proof that Humans lacked independence and respect. If desecrating this place brought Earthquake's goal of Human sovereignty closer to reality, even one iota, the Chamayna would have to forgive him from whatever afterlife they had.

Prehistoric Earth mythology gossiped about tombs like this bearing treasures and curses for any who dared fate by trespassing. Gramps once told him about prehistoric movies that featured adventurers doing just that. Hopefully, the curse would be for the three who escaped the *Kasoro.* And the treasure for Earthquake, in the form of a promotion affording him the opportunity to shape Earthquake's direction. He could bring in more qualified and intelligent recruits who wanted more from Earthquake membership than slaughtering aliens. It would be tough with Tecton in power, but once he was replaced, that wouldn't even be a question.

Rick motioned for his squad members to follow while he strafed the walls and ceiling with his flashlight. A bunker, no doubt about it. Bizarre artwork, if it could be called that, lined the walls. This was undisciplined art—what people who wanted to be seen as trendy and cultured would gab about for hours, but regular people just saw as stick figures and blobs. Would come with a nice price tag, though. If Rick were younger, he would've considered the value in more precise terms, but that wasn't the mission.

Since they were etched into the wall, and of no use to the evac team, Rick addressed his troops. "Nothing in this entryway. Let's press forward down this hall. Stay close and keep those beams up. Eyes peeled for signs of our targets."

It broke his heart to walk past all the potential artifacts. Ceramic bowls and stone tools. Pretentious types would ignore these in favor of pointless art. Sale from these tangible artifacts could expand Earthquake's coffers enough to fund the charity work he envisioned. He wished he could have a team of professional excavators with him, yet wildcat miners waited behind to extract whatever looked shiny.

Some of the grunts whispered about how much money they would make, and Rick shushed them, only to be met with scoffs. Lamont whispered about how much a pleasure mech would cost.

The hallway ceiling pinched in, forcing Rick to crouch. Definitely not Arkouda or Lo-sat design, which was new. While more than a bit claustrophobic, the fact that this structure wasn't tailor-made for Arkouda was uplifting in a way Rick hadn't expected. This was how prehistoric Earth must've felt. Appropriately sized. Like people could walk around in homes, public buildings, spaceports, and places of business without being made to feel small. He was tall by Human standards, but standing this close to the ceiling in something crafted by non-Humans was a first.

Light beams punctured the hallway's thick darkness, illuminating more stick-figured artwork. Probably a pattern, a message, or some symbolism to the art. But his mission wasn't to stand around appraising etchings and watercolors. A few etchings twisted his stomach, maybe every third or fourth one, but he couldn't figure out why.

Reports of the Chamayna were scant, anyway. Not much in The Collective archives beyond "they lived, they aren't here, and they aren't Arkouda, so who cares?" *Prehistoric Humans were probably one war or plague away from being relegated to the same category.* It was hard to tell with the Arkouda narrating history.

Some recruits whispered in the dark. Rick glanced over his shoulder at Lamont and spoke a mere decibel over a whisper, letting his tone do the heavy lifting. "Not. One. Word."

A few nods. One grumble.

They continued until some light beams crossed over an artifact, gently swinging from an opening in the ceiling. Long-handled hooks.

Rick held his hand aloft in a halt motion. Continuing his not quite a whisper, he said, "Targets triggered a trap."

Lamont responded, "So they're dead?"

"See any bodies?" Moreno asked.

Rick clenched his jaw. "No blood or signs of struggle." He leaned in close, and some light reflected off the hooked blades, gently swaying. "Check the footprints in the dust. They removed some weapons."

Double shit. Rick sighed and turned to face the troops. "Update parameters. The targets are assumed to carry melee weapons. Likely they aren't trained in proper use, but exercise caution. Odds are a fight will be in close quarters. Only kill to save your life or a comrade's." *Didn't seem like they took four weapons. Translator not with them? Did they split up?*

A few nods. Two grumbles. Rick leered at the group, but they likely couldn't see his face. "Leave this for the evac teams. Move out."

A smile creased Rick's face as they marched down the corridor. The Arkouda among the targets, Filenada Kaluteros, knowingly committed a crime by looting this place. Those missing weapons proved it. *Watch her and the Lo-sats get excused or reprimanded while the Human girl gets incarcerated.* His smile contorted into a grimace. *That's why I'm here.*

After a few more minutes of silence, a whiff of charred hair caught his nose. The horrors of battle taught two odors—burnt Arkouda fur and Human hair. Without a decade of therapy, the damned stench would've sent him to a dark place, back to his days on the other side, fighting Blekk pirates. Raiding the *Vatter* ship—seconds from drowning.

Rick closed his eyes and sniffed again. "Spread out your beams. Watch for hairs, bones, or ash."

"S-sir?" Rymon asked, before retching.

Rick smelled it, too. A pile of half melted flexleather. *A cheap boot?* Human-sized. *Damn.*

Rick grabbed the destroyed footwear, the boot flaking off in his grasp.

Moreno joined him. "They sacrificed the Human woman to escape the trap."

"Calm down, soldier. Whatever flames were here weren't powerful or hot enough to incinerate this completely, so we'd see another boot, clothes, or some bones if she died. All we know is that the Human woman lost a boot."

Of course the Human had to lose some equipment, not the Lo-sat thief, the Lo-sat pirate, or the disgraced Collective soldier. She couldn't move as fast as the others and couldn't afford quality gear.

Poor kid deserves better. Rick released a sigh too quiet for his recruits to detect. *Maybe this tomb will reveal some atrocity deep in the Collective's past. Maybe they exterminated these Chamayna people, whomever they were.* The realization lightened his spirits a notch. *More disgusted Humans join—there'd be more sympathetic voices higher up in the Collective. Maybe I'm overly optimistic, and we'll find some useless trinkets or some damn forgotten horror.* Rick tightened his jaw. *But we better find something, or this Rymon guy will get me demoted.* He was too close to running a bigger squad for some punk to derail him.

The burnt hair and chemical stench passed, and the lights dimmed. In his forceful whisper, Rick asked, "Who lowered their beam intensity? We need all at full strength. What're you thinking?" Silence. Rick about-faced. Silhouettes of shaking heads and shrugs greeted him. He glanced at his own pistol and honed in on the flashlight setting. Full brightness. He let out a tight exhale. "Probably some molecular disturbance or a gas dimming our lights. Stay close and move forward."

Odd. Maybe he should've been honest. He had no clue what could possibly happen for all their flashlights to weaken in harmony. The Chamayna didn't appear to have any technology beyond stoneworking, but maybe they had something to obfuscate light, or it could be a natural property of this moon's rock. Not entirely out-side the realm of possibility. But damn if it wasn't unset-tling. After a few minutes, they approached a doorway, and by this time, the lights were noticeably dimmer.

Again. Shit. Don't want to do this mission blindly.

Edging through the doorway, a series of echoes told him he'd entered a cavernous room. He pointed his pistol upward, but the beam couldn't penetrate to the top. Advancing, he noticed the sound following his feet altered. Shining the light below revealed the floor material changed. Rick motioned for a halt.

"Shine your lights on the floor. Something's off."

Following the searching flashlights, Rick found a crease. The material closer to the doorway matched the faded malachite rock. But what he'd stepped on was a slab of a different color, a slate gray reminiscent of Earth stone. Staring at the crease, he thought this gray slab rested on the floor as opposed to appearing attached or connected to it.

Moreno whistled. "Sir, behind you. There's a pillar."

Rick followed Moreno's faded light beam. Jutting from the slab a few meters behind him stood a large column. On examination, it resembled a moving mech-anism. Observing the way the pillar was attached to the slab, Rick furrowed his brow.

"This was a dropped ceiling."

"Collapsed, sir?" Moreno asked, jerking his light between the room's corners.

"Lowered. I suppose it could be an elevator, too, but it's a bit wide for that."

Rymon spoke. Out of turn. "So this fell from the ceiling? This crushed them?" The detached coldness in his voice deserved a smack. Twenty years ago, Rick would've delivered.

"Only one way to find out." Rick holstered his pistol. "Everyone, huddle by the doorway. "Ensign Cheng, grenade. Reduce to one-third power—don't want a cave-in."

This earned a few nodding heads and grins. *These damn kids. They shouldn't be happy I'm destroying any of this. But the mission is more important than any bleeding heart sympathies.*

Rick lobbed the grenade in the opposite direction from the entryway and stepped back. The explosion had the right sound and shook his legs, threatening his balance. But it wasn't as bright as he anticipated, even with the reduced potency. *So it's not only the flashlights on our guns. Something else is messing with lightwaves. Maybe the evac team can figure out what. Or we can bring in some eggheads later. If there's tech able to obfuscate light waves, and The Collective doesn't have it, we could use that to turn the tide in our favor. Or at least toward the right direction.*

His breather registered increased dust particles. The vibrations in his boots and the sounds of falling rocks below told him everything he needed to know. "Move out, Earthquake. Watch for cracks in the slate. Keep the beams trained on the floor in front of us. We should be approaching our hole."

TWENTY-SEVEN

zzt-ERROR-zzt- ARMOR CODE: zzt-713516

FIL AND BINH trudged to Alize through sticky threads. The beacon from Fil's armor shrunk to a sputtering candle's flame, illuminating a small portion of the chamber. The revealed floor was a thick net of webbing with several stone pillars rising to the ceiling, each covered with web. When Fil reached Alize, her armor dimly illuminated Alize's bare foot and the surrounding floor, blanketed by the fibers.

Seeing her own foot in the soft blue light was equally horrifying and reassuring. Her foot was intact and nothing crawled on it, despite being enmeshed in the sticky threads. The musty air increased the workload on her breather.

"Keep. Breathing. Steady," Binh said a few decibels over a whisper. With his tail, he removed the claw-spear from his hand. Weapon aloft, he asked, "How about I cut you free?"

Ears flattened, Fil snarled, "Are you insane?"

"No, I'm Binh. What d'you think I'm going to do? Amputate her foot? I'm using something smaller." Binh withdrew his lockpick from his chestpiece. Alize hadn't gotten a good peek at it before, but it had a serrated edge. "This was meant for cutting Collective handcuffs, but it should do the trick."

Alize winced. "Is that made of bone?"

"This? Keratin. Made from my Dad's claws. Funeral ritual." With more care and precision than she'd expected, Binh crouched before her and sliced through the threads around her foot. But a few remained, dangling alongside.

Alize raised her eyebrows. "I'm sorry for your loss. You don't seem like the type who'd take funeral rituals seriously."

Binh lowered his eyeridges. "Thanks."

As the last thread snapped, Binh helped Alize stand and balance on her boot. He whistled at Fil. "Fuzzy, you'll need to carry her until we can get out of this room."

Filenada grabbed Alize and deftly put her on her shoulders. "Hey Leeze, this is like that one time—"

"We agreed we'd never discuss that night in front of other people."

"Fine." Fil harrumphed and sidestepped to avoid a web pillar.

Alize sighed. "But yes, it is."

The Arkouda smiled. "Told ya." The gentle rise and fall atop Filenada was somehow more relaxing than humiliating.

Binh sniffed. "So Pinky, got any ideas as to what web we stepped in?"

"No, I wish I did." Alize ducked, avoiding a dangling web. "It reminded me of the octopedes we get in the museum sometimes, but those need constant live prey."

Fil shivered, rattling Alize. "I'm not exactly a fan of your suggestion."

Alize adjusted her balance. "Sorry. But if a living creature in this room made this web, it definitely knows we're here. Another pillar of webs on your left, Binh."

Binh lowered his voice an octave. "You should be a doctor with that kind of bedside manner. And if we can get enough light, we should get a picture of the two of you. Sell it to Earthquake. Can you imagine what they'd pay for an unaltered photo of a Human riding an Arkouda? I could buy my own asteroid, a deluxe heating unit, and live out my days sipping fermented drinks."

"I feel like you'd get bored with that life." A ghost of a smile parted her lips as her bare toes bounced off Fil's cold armor.

"Think you've figured me out?"

"You're kind of one-note, Binh. Not much to you beyond the insults." Fil weaved around a web pillar.

Binh halted and motioned for them to stop while he sniffed several times in rapid succession. He cleared his throat and let out a shaky exhale. "Ladies, we're in the presence of a corpse."

A slight chill slithered through Alize's spine, so she forced a chuckle. "Well, this is a tomb..."

Retreating a step, Binh's one word came out shaky. "Fresh."

As Fil approached, Alize smelled it, too. Rancid death, carrying a putrid sting, like maggots that hadn't quite finished a carcass. It lacked the odor of rotting and decay she whiffed whenever handling skeletons in the museum before cleaning. This was fresher somehow, if that was the right word. Inhalation made Alize tremble, even more so when Fil shuddered underneath her. Even in the dim light, Fil's armor beacon outlined something breaking the room's pattern. Boots still squishing in the web, Fil crouched so Alize could get a better view.

The silhouette was an oblong corpse—reminiscent of the aforementioned octopedes, yet dwarfing Fil in size.

This monstrosity had coarse hairs, the type which would never be on a mammal. More like feelers. Its body looked twice Fil's size. Four spiny hairy legs sprawled out from a massive ellipsoid thorax. Its cracked carapace bore dents and scrapes suggesting it had turned clawspear blades eons ago. As Fil's light panned the body, Alize's heart skipped a beat when she saw the rows of eyes.

This was one of the animals depicted in the hunting etchings. It reminded her of one of the last ones she saw, where hunter and hunted were indistinguishable. *What would a predator eat down here?*

An echoing crunch came from behind her.

"What the Nightmare?" Fil whisper-shouted.

The crunch had come from a chipped exoskeleton, the same chitinous material as the clawspear shafts and the boulder. Whatever this thing was, it had survived off of Chamayna. What Alize would give to have a biologist with her to share the joy of finding Chamayna DNA. If only she could experience joy instead of dread.

But how long could it survive between feedings, and how'd it have any supply at all?

"Fil, lower me a tad more, I think I see—!"

Fabric. Bits of clothing on the floor. The precise material she couldn't guess, but the bits before her had implied sleeves and necklines, which could've fit the statues outside. She had real evidence of Chamayna culture in front of her. It resembled the hairs from the dead beast beside them, woven together.

Since her omni-tablet wasn't working, she had no way to show anybody.

Wincing, Alize said, "Binh, help yourself to the clothes. I need to save my carrying space for whatever the unspeakable weapon is."

"Assuming it's something we can carry." Fil rose to her full height again, which made Alize light-headed. "But how'd it die? Recently, you said?"

Binh's whisper was stone, devoid of any emotion. "Not dead. Killed. Not old age. Not starvation. Killed. I can smell the wound. And I doubt I could get a reasonable profit from these tattered fabrics."

Alize rubbed her temples. "But the Chamayna. How were they getting here? Does this mean they're still alive and never disappeared? This changes everything. And it might prove my teleportation theory."

"Alize," Fil whispered. "Calm down. I'm going to let you down again, and you need to stand with me, back-to-back." She tapped a plate on her armor near her abdomen, and a little drawer popped out. Fil crouched and snagged some of the tattered clothing, placing it in her drawer. "It'll stay safe in the armor. But Leeze, if this was killed, that means Earthquake got ahead of us somehow."

Binh leaned forward, taking a sniff. And two more. "I don't smell any plasma vapor, so no shots fired." Another two sniffs. "I don't know exactly how long Human scents can linger in a place like this, but I can say confidently Pinkster is the first Human in here."

When her bare foot touched the floor again, she immediately shrank back from the cold stone. Grabbing the clawspear from Fil, she used it as a crutch to keep her foot aloft. As Fil shifted to hand Alize the weapon, the armor light revealed something new.

The beast's dimly lit corpse sprawled in front of them, and details of the wound became visible. The segmented thorax, large enough Fil could fit inside, sported a sizable dent. A bludgeoning wound. Something must have fallen from the ceiling and killed it.

Alize sighed, and the tension in her shoulders relaxed. "Fil, Binh. When the ceiling came down on us or when Earthquake shot the scrapper…" A flash of Cu-dan's face and what it must have looked like in his last moment pierced her mind. "…that probably shook a chunk of the ceiling off in here. That's what killed this thing. Blunt force trauma. Guns don't make those wounds."

Binh grunted. "And this supposed chunk of ceiling is where?"

"It's so dark in here," Alize said. "It probably rolled away. Or crumbled and the bits are stuck in the web nearby or wedged against one of the pillars. We can panic-search or breathe easy. Take your pick."

"Whatever that was," Binh said, "it released a bunch of pheromones before it died. And not the sexy kind."

Alize shivered. *How'd the Chamayna get here?* She collected herself and sighed. All the more reason to come back with a professional team. *We need to find the superweapon, and it's not in this webbed room. But I bet I'm right about teleportation. Wouldn't mind a bit of that right now.*

"Let's find the exit, guys," Alize said. "Anything useful in this room would be covered in that web gunk."

"You know, 'web gunk' is what the ladies called me back in the day."

Alize rolled her eyes. "Charming. Can you smell a difference in the air quality from one direction to another?" After a quick wince, she added, "Without referencing our body odor?"

"Not quite but seems like everything so far in this complex has been a series of straight lines. Except that one fork earlier."

They passed the corpse of the thorax beast, Fil's light passing over seven mismatched black eyes. Alize squinted at its silhouette, guessing at the creature's final sight. "Do you think the web was something it made or something to keep it in here?"

"You're the expert." Even though Alize couldn't see her face, she imagined Fil said it with a wide smile.

"Thanks. Not on xenobiology, though. I only recognized this because of the etchings."

"Oh right," Binh said. "This must have been the scary oval. At first, I thought it was the scary line with dots on it, or maybe that creepy square. You should be an art critic."

An idea struck. "So," Alize said, "I feel dumb for not thinking of this before, but maybe we should try our omni-tablets instead of Fil's armor for our light. I've been so preoccupied with taking each step and not triggering a trap I forgot about them. If they're working, we'll know it's only Fil's armor acting up."

Tap-tap. Binh hissed. "Nothing. It was charged when we left the scrapper unless Cu-dan sabotaged it."

Thud-thud.

"Leeze," Fil said, "mine's not working, either. But it's synced to my armor."

Alize withdrew her own from her jacket pocket. *Tap tap.* Nothing. "And that makes three."

The sour stench of the beast's corpse assaulted her nostrils. She couldn't imagine the kind of agonizing sensory overload Binh must experience so close to it; it was probably worse than the time a classmate "accidentally" spilled embalming fluids on her. They continued in a tight huddle, Fil leading. They approached another doorway, this one arched high above Fil's head.

The light went out. Alize couldn't tell if her eyes were open.

"Nightmare in a nightmare," Fil cursed.

"No error message, I'm guessing?" Alize asked, chest tightening.

"Nothing, nothing, nothing." Fil's footsteps turned to stomps.

"Get a grip, Frosty."

"Shut up, Binh—"

"Never. And I'm serious. Grab my tail. I can smell past the corpse. I know where we're going." Under his breath, he added, "The direction, at least. Don't grab too hard. We haven't agreed to a safe word."

Binh rubbed his dry tail against Alize's arm, and she gently grabbed hold.

Alize attempted a reassuring nudge to Fil, whose breaths grew shallow. "Deep and through the nose, just like we practiced. We'll be fine. You don't need the armor to be tough."

Fil let out a shaky breath. "I know, it's—this armor's supposed to be cutting-edge technology. The best The Collective scientists and engineers have to offer. Supposed to make me invincible. If it doesn't work here, what in the Nightmare have we walked into?"

"If you're only confident wearing protection," Binh said, "you were never confident in the first place. Just misguided and cocky."

"Quit being an ass. Fil, there's just something different in the atmosphere here."

If Alize weren't leaning on the clawspear shaft as a crutch, she wouldn't have noticed the floor's slight tremble. "Did you feel that?" she whispered.

Binh sniffed sharply. "Nothing here but the three of us. Nothing alive, at least. Plenty of rocks."

Another tremble, slightly more forceful this time. *A footstep? Tectonic shift in the moon? Can that even happen?* "No, I felt something. In the ground. A shake."

Fil stiffened. "Maybe Earthquake did something. Maybe they're close."

Alize glanced at her wrist; even the green light had dimmed. *I'm still here, Pops. I'll be fine.* Though dimmer, the green light pulsed rapidly.

The floor trembled a third time. And a fourth. More forceful than the others—the floor shook beneath their feet.

Binh's tail stiffened in Alize's grip. "I felt that one. *Nguc.* Not good."

Alize shuddered. "Binh, you'd smell it if something else were here, wouldn't you?"

"Of course. Everything's got a scent."

Fifth tremble. It wasn't from outside but under her feet.

Fil's teeth chattered. "Um, Leeze? How much work's your breather doing?"

"Huh?"

"My armor's running out of power and starting to shut down. Oh no—" She hurriedly tapped a plate on her armor and withdrew a cube, which unfolded into her rifle. "I-I'm going to have to turn the filter on my breather down."

Binh hissed a whisper. "You sure that's smart?"

How much power did her beacon light use? And what about this technology running almost forever? There must be an explanation.

"I just got an error message saying there's not enough power for another force field."

A sixth tremble.

"Binh, you're sure you can't smell anything coming?"

The next tremor stood out from the others as quicker. More forceful. Angrier.

"Wish I could say so," Binh muttered as the three of them huddled together.

Alize blinked hard, although the abyss before her lids equaled the darkness behind. All light vanished like a depleted resource. Another blink, and the floor shook an eighth time. With it echoed another sound. A guttural trill. Clacking. And moist, as if it were—

Shaking mandibles.

Colossal. Salivating. Wholly unlike the corpse from before.

A Chamayna wouldn't make this much noise.

Alize approached the sound, gripping the claw-spear tight, and letting her bare foot fall to the floor. None of the gooey web stuck to her toes. Alize inclined her head. Two blood-red gemstones hovered above.

Approaching them.

The dim pulsing green light wasn't illuminating them, though. These gemstones had a luster to them, as if they shined faintly.

"Are you two seeing those glowing stones?" she whispered.

"Yeah," Fil breathed.

"I do," Binh whispered, "but those don't smell like gemstones or any other mineral." He took another cautious sniff. "They don't smell like anything. Something's wrong. Ev—everything has a smell."

"Those aren't rocks." Alize gulped. "They're eyes."

From behind, Fil cocked her rifle and took a shaky step forward. "Whatever you are, you need to stand down." Her confident words didn't match her shaking tone.

The clacking repeated, and the gemstone-eyes neared. Alize attempted the geometry in the dark, judging by Fil's height and the relative distance of the floating shining eyes. As they neared, Alize caught faint lines running through the eyes in various directions like cracks and fissures, adding to their mineral appearance.

Alize stepped back and held out her arms in front of Binh and Fil, for all the good it did. Her heart sank— it was the creature from the ritual etchings. Every sign had been a warning to turn and run from this insectoid mass of walking nightmare.

"We need to leave!"

Fil pressed her fur against Alize's arm.

Shoom. A shot from Fil's plasma rifle briefly illuminated the surroundings. The microsecond to absorb the scene was insufficient. Whatever towered over them resembled the Chamayna but was significantly taller. Taller than Filenada. Orange mandibles drooped from its chitinous maw. Above its head, a series of ridged horns protruded at impossible angles, but the light was suffocated so quickly that Alize couldn't count the horns.

The plasma bullet sailed over the creature's head, hitting the ceiling and loosening bits of rock.

The creature roared, clacking mandibles together. This wasn't an animal or anything sentient. This was something else entirely.

Fury.

And they'd trespassed. Alize couldn't collect herself. "Run!"

Binh took off at a sprint, pulling Alize by his tail. Filenada fired another round at the creature, this time making contact.

In the instant of illumination from Fil's gunshot, the creature extended all six arms. It lunged toward them, clacking its mandibles in a guttural percussion.

Alize followed Binh's lead; she'd become so turned around she didn't even know if it was the correct way. Only escape mattered. "Fil!" she yelled. Fil retreated a few steps, lighting up the room with each successive rifle shot.

Enveloped in shadow, the creature didn't flinch or make any yelp of pain. It absorbed plasma shots with the casual indifference Alize would absorb drizzle on her skin. But in its lunging and the bursts of light from Fil's rifle, Alize saw what the creature carried.

On its left side, it wielded a massive bludgeon. The spiked ball was bigger than Alize. And on its right side, it held a staff the length of Alize's body in one of its hands. The staff had the wings of a Chamayna sculpted onto either end—it reminded her of scepters from pictures of prehistoric Earth royalty, yet it bore an eldritch series of curves and swirls. Both the mace and scepter seemed fashioned from chitin, like this entire place and all its adornments were built on sacrificed Chamayna corpses.

But in the brief half-seconds of light, Alize noticed this creature lacked the trademark wings of a Chamayna. Alize's scientific curiosity wondered what this actually was. She'd first assumed the ritual etchings were symbolic. Yet adrenaline and survival instinct took over, and she fled from the unspeakable monstrosity before her.

Filenada roared, but the sound lacked the confidence of the earlier fight with Earthquake. "Keep running, Leeze!" Fil shouted. "I'll fight this thing."

"Like hell you will!" Alize spun on her booted heel and grabbed at Fil's wrist with both arms. "You saw how big it is—"

The floor shook behind them. *Clack clack,* like bone on rock.

Alize tugged on her wrist again. "If we can get to the—"

Tremble. Rumble. Clack.

Clack-clacka-clack.

"—last room and hallway, it won't fit."

Clack-clacka-clacka-clack.

Fil fired again, and in the brief half-second of illumination, Alize's eyes grew to moons. The ritual creature they couldn't name was directly ahead of them, mace raised, swinging back, crimson eyes glittering. The bullet sailed into the beast's pectoral region, which was covered in loose wrappings, like a burial shawl come undone after eons underground.

All Filenada could mutter was "Yeah." She gripped her rifle with one paw and scooped Alize into the other. They sprinted away, the squish of webs soon softening Fil's heavy armored steps.

Tremble. Clacka-clack. Tremble.

Fil's grip tightened on each rumble, and her panting intensified.

In between the monster's dread mandibles clacking together, rubble and dust dislodged from above them. Stepping with such force, it threatened the foundations of the tomb itself. The gemstone compound eyes dimmed, and Alize glimpsed her wristpiece, pulsing a slightly less dim green than a few moments ago, as if the light dared not shine in the monster's presence.

"We're almost there, Fil," she whispered.

Fil huffed, slowing to a jog.

"I'm getting off you. I'll run."

Fil increased her pace. "Like Nightmare you will." In between gasping breaths, she added, "If I know I'm saving you, I can go faster than if I'm just saving myself."

Binh snarled. "Quit wasting breath, mammals."

Fil's armor clicked underneath Alize. The pale blue light resurfaced. "You'll waste your armor's energy for the light. We don't need the beacon now. Seriously."

"It." Huff. "Came." Huff-puff. "Back." Huff-huff. "On its own."

With each step, the light grew incrementally, and the trembles behind them weakened. After a few more steps, the beacon brightened enough to reveal Binh's tail ahead. Squinting, she saw the hallway's lower ceiling.

Alize's fingers dug into the gaps in Fil's armored pauldrons. "We're almost there, Fil. You got it."

A positive grunt was the only response.

Five seconds passed without a tremble, but more pieces of dust and small pebble-sized debris cascaded from above.

When they reached the hallway to the stairs, Binh bent over, tail curled, catching his breath. Fil's armor beacon light had grown bright enough to show his panic.

She helped Alize stand and slumped against the wall, wheezing. No trembles.

"Binh," Alize said. "Did you get a read on that thing's scent? Can you tell if it stopped chasing us?"

Binh laced his claws behind his head as he caught his breath. "That—that thing. It didn't have a scent. I don't know what to tell you, Pink Lady. I can smell the difference between the rocks here. Whatever that was, it didn't give off any scent at all. The only reason I'm convinced something was even there was that you two saw and heard it, too." He leaned toward Alize, tongue slipping out of his grimace, pointing his tail in her face. "The bigger question for you: what was that?"

"The creature from those ritual etchings."

Gasps slowing, Fil waved a dismissive paw. "I don't know what it's called, but that's what killed the other Nightmare in the web room."

Alize nodded. "Yeah, remember the indentation on its thorax? The beast must've killed it with that mace."

Binh's eyes widened. "The tall monstrosity didn't try and eat the thorax-thing?" He tsked. "I told you so. Those pheromones I got off the thorax beast. It knew it was hunted."

Fil stood, grazing the ceiling. "But why kill it now? You said it was a fresh kill, and I smelled the blood, too. They've been living close together for how long?"

Alize closed her eyes and exhaled. "The monster from the ritual, the one we can't think of a name for, it had been in some kind of stasis." She glanced at the other two before hanging her head and licking her lips. "We awakened it. It was the last trap guarding the superweapon. It's gotta be."

Climbing the first steps, Binh flicked his tail. "If your ritual monster killed but didn't eat the thorax thing, it's sentient. It also doesn't like us. Not going anywhere near it. I'll take my chances with Earthquake. You two do what you want."

The rocky floor shook twice in succession, threatening their balance.

Fil grabbed her rifle and pointed it to the darkness. "Leeze, we gotta go up these stairs."

"Binh, if there's a way around it, or a way for us to capture it, the payoff could be even bigger. If you're right and we found a new sentient species or living Chamayna, you'd be famous. Paid interviews for the rest of your life."

More trembles. Debris fell.

Alize and Fil followed Binh, and a distant clack echoed behind them. Stepping over the last shrapnel of the shattered chitin boulder trap from the top of the stairs, Alize's blood ran cold.

No, that unnamable monster wasn't the last trap. All of these traps triggered already, the clawspears, the fire, the chitin boulder, probably even the thorax creature and its web—they weren't all facing the wrong way. *We've gone backwards through this tomb.*

Those traps weren't meant to stop or impede intruders; they were meant to stop this abomination from escaping.

And we disabled all of them.

Alize's breathing shallowed and heart accelerated, the mixture of climbing stairs and dread boiling her adrenaline. Her mind went to the inscription outside and on the walls and ceilings. How many messages had she mistranslated? All her bravado and inflated opinion of her language skills brought her to the wrong conclusions about the tomb at every turn. Maybe the weapon of unspeakable power was a metaphor. Or a mistranslation.

But what else could "weapon" possibly mean?

Alize gritted her teeth.

At least they had found this place. The Collective military could come out with a team of archaeologists. She only needed to escape with Fil, and they'd get home and tell their story. *Maybe tell Cu-dan's story, too.* She'd get her dissertation approved, and—she glanced at her wristpiece. Up to now, Pops' pulse had matched hers. He was calm when she was, and excited when she was scared witless each time she checked. But now, her heart was running faster than a hoofbeast, but Pops' pulse flashed at a glacial pace. *He said expect a delay. Please be okay, Pops. Please.*

Midway up the stairs, Fil's armor beacon shined at a quarter of its restored brightness, enough to see more than her companions' silhouettes. The emotional part of Alize's mind believed it was like a portable star. And the light's strength grew with each step.

"Hm," Fil said, "my armor power storage reads acceptable. Not great, but nothing critical like I was getting before. Leeze, do you think that creature caused the light situation?"

"Maybe. If it can mess with its biology enough so it doesn't produce an odor, maybe it produces some other kind of pheromone that messes with electrical components?"

Binh took a few sniffs.

Alize opened her mouth to respond, but an image flashed in her head of the message. *Sleeping god.* She wished a linguist was with them to offer another interpretation or confirm her own.

Could that be referring to the ritual monster? Did the Chamayna worship it as a god? What would Cu-dan have said? Alize shook her head. She had to get the dead man out of her head. He wouldn't have known Chamayna, anyway.

At the top of the stairs, they returned to the cramped hallway, and Binh and Fil squatted to fit. "Well, if it could manage to squeeze up those steps," Alize said absently, "at least it can't fit in here at all. Way too narrow." She paused. "Hey, we should check our omni-tablets again." She checked hers, which hummed an error message: low power, disconnected to network.

Binh tsked. "I have enough juice to play a round of Block Bash or peek at some racy pictures, but that's it."

Fil huffed. "It's working, but all it says is 'contact administrator.' Same garbage my helmet's head's-up display fed me."

Turning the corner, a slew of lights from the other side threatened to blind her. Instinctively, Alize raised her arm, shielding her eyes, then opened them. Faces scrutinized them from the other side of the beams of light.

Earthquake.

A stern-faced man with one arm approached, pistol in hand, held sideways, fingers demonstrably absent from the trigger. "Surrender, and we won't fire." He had the distinct clipped Earther accent. In the dim light, Alize saw his armor, modified to accommodate a missing arm. Green and blue metal plates contrasted against his dark skin.

As Alize gulped, she spied Binh in her periphery. *He would've smelled them coming. He didn't warn us.*

TWENTY-EIGHT

Subsurface structure, unnamed moon, Dusoi orbit, Xechas system, Collective fringe

RICK'S QUARRIES LOOMED before him. The primary objective, Alize Oze, clutched an ancient polearm, eyebrows twitching like someone afraid to show terror. Her dossier didn't mention anything about a nervous tic. Beside her, the secondary objective, the Lo-sat thief named Binh Ten-trom, also brandished a polearm with a curved cutting edge. *Looks like he could do some damage. Has the sneer of a guy who's survived a few scrapes.*

But Rick's official tertiary objective—his personal primary objective—dominated his view. Collective soldier Filenada Kaluteros. And then Rick spotted it: A little downward arrow beside the Collective military insignia. *Good. Why the hell isn't the other Lo-sat with them? He couldn't have been on that scrapper. Damn. Don't like loose threads.*

The Arkouda brandished her rifle like she wanted to intimidate them, but her constant readjustment suggested to Rick she was terrified shitless of Earthquake, or they had seen something horrific.

The Lo-sat should've smelled us coming a mile away. What's his angle? Without a response, Rick used the formal construction in Arkouda. "Citizens and Provincial, we mean you no harm. Surrender and we can leave together."

Oze clenched a dainty fist. "You destroyed our ship."

"Exactly," Rick said. "You're stranded, so come along."

The Arkouda snarled, hairs on her face rising, illuminated by the dim beacon on her armor. "I'll call the Fleet."

Rick shifted his grip on his pistol to the firing position. "The blinking yellow light on your armor says otherwise. You're not supposed to be here. Your armor is also compromised. We know this place messes with tech."

Her jaw dropped, along with her rifle. A lesser man would relish her expression. A few satisfied chuckles sounded from behind him. Rick clenched his jaw.

The Lo-sat thief spoke in flawless Human. "You guys must be from Earthquake. We'd be happy to join you." No accent at all, not a single unnecessary H sound. He spoke the language better than most colonial and spacer Humans. "Or at least I would."

The two women glared at the Lo-sat.

Attempting a double-cross?

Ten-trom advanced. "Make your offer, Mr. Earthquake."

"Already did." Rick wanted to give the squad some form of reassurance. "You're outnumbered. Drop your weapons."

A light reverberation shook the walls. Seismic activity, probably. But the Arkouda's eyes widened. Rick cast a glance down—Oze only had one boot. *Solves the melted shoe mystery.* The bare foot added to her haggard look.

The thief tapped his tail on the floor. "We'll need more than that. You see, we're privy to the new bounties on dead Arkouda and Lo-sat bodies in your little organization. Your word's worthless."

Damn. This is what I've been telling everybody.

Moreno whispered, "Let's just kill them."

"That was them," Rick said. "I'm me. As long as you cooperate, we won't harm a scale on you."

"I wish you would harm some of my scales. Really nasty itches, you see, and my medicine's running low."

Making jokes as a distraction, huh?

Rick affixed his gaze on the woman and switched to Human. "Earthquake can fund an expedition here. We'll dig, you'll lead, and you'll get published and noticed. Do you wanna be a cog in the Collective machine? Their academic world must be as convoluted and nepotistic as everything else in the government. Come with us. Your friends will go unharmed, and we'll give them safe passage. You don't exactly have another way home."

Unless they call the damn fleet.

The three of them fidgeted. Another tremble sounded in the distance, vibrating the soles of his boots.

No mistaking that time.

Rick tightened his jaw. "No requirement to take any of you alive. Last warning."

Oze licked her lips, and glared past Rick, eyebrows slanted. "Garott? That's why you haven't returned my pings? You sold me out to Earthquake?"

The Arkouda roared. Hairs on end, she raised her rifle—pointed at Rymon. "You don't ping someone because you joined a gang? Who does that?"

Rick sneered. "Come with us, and he'll stay a deck apart from you at all times. I can even put him on a different ship."

Oze scrunched her face. "I'm not going with you. We'll call the Fleet."

Another tremble shuddered the floor slightly, and some of the squad murmured behind Rick. He distinctly heard one say, "Shit's getting nowhere fast."

Moreno advanced.

Breaking ranks?

Moreno's makeshift rifle pointed at Alize's head. "You! Oze. Come with us or pick which of your friends dies first."

"Stand down, Moreno," Rick hissed through his teeth.

Moreno must've heard him. But the kid sure wasn't acting like he had. He quickly aimed his rifle at the floor in front of Oze and fired. Some debris kicked up.

Why can't I threaten with a court martial? Rick raised his voice. "Stand down or I'm tossing you out an airlock."

Moreno glared at Rick and lowered his rifle.

The floor rumbled as everyone struggled to maintain their balance. Nervous sweat beaded on Rick's upper lip. *What the hell did they do down there?*

Oze spoke with forced confidence. "There's a creature down there guarding the treasure we found. If you can get past it, you'll have more access to the chamber than I could've possibly gotten. Leave us alone, and we won't report you to the Collective."

Another tremble came, but this one was accompanied by another noise, a low sticky beating, like a clacking. And the clacking increased in intensity and reverberated in the hallway behind the trio.

Is that sound the alleged creature? Must be some undiscovered species that didn't know well enough to go extinct on this barren moon.

Rick checked the beam from his flashlight. Darkened. Undeniably. The armor beacon on the Kaluteros woman had dimmed, too.

"I've got a better idea," Rick said. "You come with us willingly. You," he indicated Kaluteros and switched to speaking Arkouda, "You could kill all of us. Don't think we don't know it. But you can't do it fast enough. Both of your friends would die. And the three of you don't seem too fond of whatever's behind you. So Citizen, how about you lay down your rifle and sidearm and come with us?"

The thief stepped forward, claws in the air. "Look, I surrender. These two just gave me money for this break-in job." The women glared at him with arched eyebrows and flattened ears.

They don't know if he's playing a game, either. Shifty bastard. No wonder he conned those smugglers.

Rick nodded. "Put down that weapon and you can join."

Another tremble. The flashlight beams and the armor beacon dimmed noticeably again.

More wet clacking.

The trembles increased in frequency and intensity. Bits of debris dislodged from the ceiling. A few stammers of "what the—" and the like sounded.

Before the lights dimmed entirely, Rick noticed a little flash of green on Oze's wrist. *Curious.*

Rick caught something in his periphery, rounding the corner behind the trio.

A foot.

Three times the size of the biggest Arkouda hindpaw. Its claws scraped the chilled stone floor as it flattened, ready to run or dive or pounce.

The cavern blackened, leaving Rick with only a horrifying memory of the thing in front of him.

Rick's mouth dried as his gut twisted into a knot, and he stepped backward. This was the foot of a monster from Earth's deep past—the razor-sharp clawed toes of a goddamn dinosaur and yet mixed with some bastardized tarantula-cockroach.

He swallowed, inching another step. Childhood nightmares of hairy spiders laying eggs in his ears nudged into his mind, only now those arachnids had become the size of Earth's most colossal beasts.

Clack-clack-clack-clack.

Rick whipped around to face his squad. Before him lingered an impenetrable blackness. No faces to be found—only the scraping of dozens of boots as they took shuffling backward steps.

Damn.

Clack-clack-clack-clack. The floating garnet orbs descended and advanced. A little green flicker approached also.

Shit. They're running into us.

"Hold your ground, Earthquake," Rick shouted.

Rick aimed at the amber orbs. *Must be that creature's eyes. How the hell can eyes produce light?*

He pulled the trigger and a plasma bullet shoomed out. The brief light flash confirmed several things.

First, the trio ran toward his squad.

Second, those were definitely eyes. Compound eyes, judging by the crisscrossed lines and curves.

Third, whatever the holy hell this abomination was, he'd never felt so small and insignificant. His imagination, horror, depression, shame, all wrapped into one beast, so intimidating light itself couldn't stand in its presence.

The plasma bullet connected with a mandible.

It had as much effect as the dust landing on Rick's shoulder.

Shit.

Rick gave the order, the worst word in Earthquake's dictionary. "R-r-retreat!"

He turned.

Moreno's voice broke through. "Negative. Open fire!"

Rick's eyes widened enough to take in the extra light from a dozen plasma bullets exiting homemade pistols and rifles. "Damn it all, retreat! That's an order!"

While the useless lights from the guns erupted around them, in between flashes, Rick glimpsed Moreno shaking his head.

As he turned his defiant gaze forward, Moreno continued, "Kill the popsicle and the slime ball. Catch the girl if you can."

Clack-clack-clack tremble tremble.

Over his shoulder, Rick counted six arms on this nameless monstrosity from the depths of hell. The bullet stream from the defectors lowered, darting all around in the dark, briefly lighting the trio's location, still charging them. Squinting against the brief flashes, the dropped ceiling made him pause. The rampaging creature couldn't fit through, so whether they could kill it was irrelevant. Lingering halos and starbursts from the intense light flashes polluted Rick's vision.

His squad had made their decision. And it was the wrong one.

"Earthquake, the ships won't take off without me. Quit firing and move out."

Moreno's damn traitor voice cut through. "No. You're relieved of duty."

Rick aimed at Moreno. "You sonofa—"

A force like a rogue ship wing collided against Rick's side, and his feet left the floor. A whooshing sensation. An odd, metallic chill. A gentle glow.

So, one of those traitors shot me, huh? This is what death feels like.

And then came the odor, penetrating his breather. Fur.

Rick squinted at the dim glow and made out the insignia of the Collective military, Guard Corps.

Damn.

TWENTY-NINE

ERROR MESSAGE, RETURN TO CITIZEN SENDER:

AUTOMATED MESSAGE, CODE 092088

Dream's Greetings, Citizen.

The Provincial this ping was sent to
lacks a valid address. Before con-
tacting an administrator, certify that
the Provincial is not a con artist.
Afterward, ensure the Provincial's
name was typed correctly in Arkouda.
Do not use native spellings. If problems persist, inform the Provincial
in-person to contact an administrator
to rectify the issue.

Glory to The Collective.

May the Slumber remain undisturbed.

Original message:

Sender: Citizen Dr. Hupomone Dikaio.
Recipient: Provincial Alize Oze. Hen4
Subject: Where in the Nightmare are you?

Oze—you ran out of vacation days. Get your skinny ass back in the museum. I've got stimbrew orders that need to be bought and distributed. If your disappearance is somehow connected to that Guard who pals around with you, suffice to say you are both in deeper tangles than you can handle.

If you left to pursue your theories, you're even dumber than your greasehead father. This ridiculous notion in your tiny head must come from the excessive drinking you're famous for.

Or have you accepted you'll never amount to being a professional archae-ologist? Quit school? If you're quit-ting your job, you need to submit a formal letter so you don't get arrested, too. Your damned omni-tablet's always on you, so you're never too far from

the Collective network. You'll spend
the rest of your life in prison for an
unauthorized quitting, and Provincial
prisons are not glamorous. From what
I hear, you'll share a cell with a
Makawe rebel or another dirty Human.

I don't know how you put your omni-
tablet in an incognito mode and baffled
the auto-tracker, but rest assured, the
second you're back on the grid, you'll
be found, and the arrest warrant I'll
prepare will be active by then.

And after all I've done for you, too.
Despicable.

If you arrive in person to quit, please
be sure to bring stimbrew with you. I
want extra cream and sugar, get decaf
for my husband, and extra sourberry
juice for the visiting professor.

All glory to the Collective.

May the Goddess' Dream remain benevolent.

THIRTY

LOCATION ERROR. CONTACT COMMANDING OFFICER. DOCKED PAY FOR TAMPER—zzt-zzt-ERROR

ALIZE TIGHTENED HER grip on the clawspear's chitinous shaft, which kicked back as it connected to an abdomen.

A man "oofed" and a rogue gunshot flashed, raining debris from the ceiling.

Alize hated wondering if she'd tripped Garott but had no time to verify.

Binh's tail coiled around her polearm, her hands on either side, and he guided her behind Fil. He had similar success tripping Earthquake goons on Alize's other side. The trio wedged between the crowd of the Earthquake gunners, using Fil's wide armor as cover.

Tremors echoed behind them. Two thuds followed. *What was that? Nope. Looking back is a bad idea.*

The pattern of thuds increased from two to six.

That unnamable monster must be crawling, holding those two weapons aloft. Being taller than Fil wouldn't matter in the cramped hallway anymore.

They tripped maybe a quarter of the gang of Earthquake members. They'd die painfully. Garott, too, in all likelihood.

Heart and stomach twisted. *But it's us or them. And they still have a chance to escape. This is our only one.*

The Earthquake members hadn't given chase. Instead, they concentrated fire on the unspeakable horror, plasma bullets bouncing off its jet-black carapace. She clenched her teeth and continued.

Dead ahead, Binh sniffed. "Left up here."

Fil shifted left, light from her armor beacon following her. *We must be back in the dropped ceiling room where we saw the stairs going up.*

They bounded toward the stairs, and Fil called for a halt. "Binh, did those guys follow us?"

"Can't smell them, except for the one-armed goon you're holding."

Fil dropped the leader she'd grabbed. He smacked the steps unceremoniously, grunting and cursing. Fil withdrew her rifle, and after warning with a nod, shot behind them at the archway.

The plasma bullet sailed over their heads, hitting the keystone over the entrance. A few rocks from the ceiling fell, obscuring the stairway entrance.

Fil swirled around, the light from her armor brightening again, and aimed the rifle at the one-armed man writhing on the steps. "Not so tough now, huh? Where are your other weapons?"

The man spat and coughed, and with some difficulty, propped himself to sit on a step, peering up at Fil. His furrowed brow and curled lip made the surrounding stones seem warm. "My pistol fell. It's by the Lo-sat's feet. I've got a blade in my boot. Take them." He inclined his head toward his belt. "I've got grenades here."

Binh grabbed the pistol and climbed two steps to meet the man's eyeline. "So what's your name, Lefty?" Using the tip of his tail, Binh undid the grenade pouch on his belt and passed it to Fil.

Alize's first inclination was to scold Binh, but this guy was Earthquake. He didn't deserve her sympathy.

"Rick Crith. Earther. Former Collective Provincial Corps, currently Earthquake." His downward inflection was a cruel inversion of Pops'. "Although it seems my current employment's in question." His voice carried the weight of age, and she couldn't imagine the horror story behind his missing limb.

"Where's your arm?" Binh asked. Even though Alize couldn't see him, she knew he was grinning.

This guy's unbelievable. Total ass.

Brow furrowed, Rick glared at Binh. "Binh Ten-trom. Earthquake has a bounty on your head."

Binh opened his snout, but Fil cut him off.

"Shut it," Fil said. "Crith. Tell us what you're doing here."

Rick shook his head. "You know why we're here. Earthquake wants artifacts. This is an untapped resource."

Alize approached him and took a shaky breath. "Did you mean what you said earlier? That Earthquake would fund an expedition here?"

Rick sneered. "Oze, I mean every damn thing I say."

In the dim light of Fil's armor beacon, Alize studied his face. Pops earned his wrinkles from decades of smiling, laughter, and endurance. But Rick's scars and weathering were of a different sort. They didn't have joy behind evidence of hard work but rather a sadness mixed with resolve. Anger and acceptance combined with the unmistakable aura of a plotter. Her heart plummeted into her stomach.

"Well," Alize said, "if you really mean everything you say, then you'll take us to your ship. You can call for a pickup for those other guys, right?"

"I don't know how deep the mutiny goes." Rick lowered his eyes at the three of them. "I also don't know if you left them for dead."

"Us or them, soldier." Binh hissed the last word and lowered his eyeridges. "And if you would've just accepted my surrender, we all could've gotten out of there before the six-armed … thing … came up the steps."

Binh still can't conjure a nickname for that monster?

Rick waved his hand dismissively. "Not sure how trustworthy you are."

Fil scoffed. "So if your whole crew mutinied, you're as stuck as us. Too bad some assholes blew up our ride."

Rick's expression was blank. "There are sacrifices in war. I'd rather destroy a ship to set an example than take a life."

"But you took a life." Alize sneered. "Our friend was there when you blew it up."

Binh snorted. "Acquaintance. We'd only met the guy."

"Negative." Rick arched his brow. "We scanned after. No remains." His eyes darted between the three of them.

He's gauging our reaction. Crap.

Perhaps satisfied with whatever he gleaned from reading their expressions, Rick deadpanned, "So you traveled with the Lo-sat translator, Cu-dan. My assumption was he was with you. Low likelihood he was aboard when we destroyed it."

Fil got in his face. "How can we trust you?"

Rick wiped away the flecks of Fil's spit from his cheek. "Earthquake put a bounty on him. They want him alive, or at least his body intact. It would be a symbolic victory to kill him since his father died. No reason for me to lie about it. If I had him alive, I could use that as leverage with you."

"But where is he, then?" Alize asked.

Binh groaned. "Lefty doesn't know, or he won't tell us. Maybe Cu-dan's alive, maybe he's not. That doesn't change that we need to leave."

Rick straightened himself. "So I assume you've already explored the upper portions of this bunker. What's upstairs? I only ask..." he pointed to the rubble covering the entrance to the stairway, "since you blocked off our escape."

Alize sighed. "We haven't. But we can clear those rocks later if we need to."

"What's going to happen if that nightm—" Rick glanced at Fil and quickly shook his head. "Excuse me.

What's going to happen if that monstrosity escapes this bunker?"

Binh held up a claw and nodded. "Probably visit the grocery store." He shrugged after the other three shared a sigh. "What? Poor thing probably ran out of hot sauce."

Fil nudged him and chuckled. "Now that's worse than being trapped since the prehistoric eras."

Did they just share a dumb joke? Maybe the brush with death wasn't such a bad thing. Maybe this means they'll stop bickering. "So we'll explore the top, then. But we gotta return to the ritual monster's lair." Alize stopped herself. *This guy can't know about the super-weapon.* But if Garott told him about her and her journey, what's to say Garott didn't spill the details on the superweapon, too?

Rick squinted at her. "That's where the big prize is, huh? No material object is worth a life."

Binh grumbled. "Says the killer."

"Hey," Rick said, acid in his voice, "Every life I've taken was self-defense or for a greater cause. Not for trinkets or money."

"Oh," Binh said. "I guess that makes a difference somehow." Brandishing Rick's pistol, he added, "You'll forgive me if I hold onto this, though."

Rick nodded, slow and deliberate.

That's the face of someone who doesn't need a gun to kill. Suppressing a shudder, Alize said, "Like it or not, you're coming with us. You help us, and maybe my friend here can get you some clemency." She offered her hand.

Rick shook his head and rose on his own. "No clemency for me. Not from the Collective. I know what they'd do. Lead the way."

Fil's armor dimmed.

Tremble-tremble.

More loose bits shook from the ceiling.

"Yeah, we need to go," Alize said.

The ascending staircase broke the pattern of what they'd seen so far. No etchings, no artwork. The steps themselves were jagged, and each one threatened to trip Alize. Fil and Binh took to climbing on all fours, Binh holding his clawspear by his tail.

Binh sniffed. "We're coming up on an intersection."

"Not a new room?" Alize asked.

"I can smell the air passage coming from multiple directions ahead. A room wouldn't do that to my tender nostrils, Pinky. Unless it had fans or an exhaust system. But something tells me your bug friends weren't overly concerned with air circulation."

Dull clattering echoed up the steps, which shook significant debris from the ceiling.

Alize gasped, shielding her face from the detritus with her forearm. "What was that?"

"A grenade." Rick grunted as loose debris hit him on his shoulder. "Damn mutineers pursuing."

Alize's heart raced. *Sorry if I'm scaring you, Pops.* "Hey, if we hit an intersection and they're following us, are they more likely to split up or stay in a unit?"

Rick dusted himself. "If it were me, I'd split my team into two. But if my second-in-command is calling the shots, he would keep the unit together. Keep in mind, they may have suffered casualties. We don't know their numbers now."

Fil peered over her shoulder at Alize, pleading with her bloodshot eyes. "We don't know if we can trust him."

"He's our best chance of getting home, Fil. Binh, can you tell how many paths there are, or how close we are?"

Binh grunted. "We're close. At least four." Another sniff. "Maybe more. Can't be sure."

Speeding her pace up the steps, Fil saw her armor beacon increasing in intensity as she climbed. "I see a fork ahead. Maybe five branches off the main one."

"Right." Alize increased her pace as much as possible without scraping her bare foot on the stone steps. The stairway leveled off into a landing, with other hallways branching, and one continuing straight. She bit her lip and shot quick glances down each hallway. "Binh, can you shine the flashlight on Rick's gun down these paths?"

As he shined the light, Fil asked, "What? Nothing snarky to say?"

Binh shrugged, shining the light down the second hallway, which spiraled sharply downward. Three of the paths off the intersection went downward, and two others went up, but the center path flattened into a straight hallway. Rick's flashlight couldn't penetrate far.

Alize turned to Rick. "Where do you think they'd go?"

Rick scratched his chin. "Impossible to say without a casualty report. Knowing your objective, I would've stayed the course. Whoever is leading now is an unknown."

Binh snorted. "No wonder they mutinied. I want to mutiny from listening to you, and I don't even work for you."

Footsteps and voices echoed from behind them. Alize shot quick glances at the downward stairs in front of them. One of them had an etching on the side. She couldn't tell what it was in the darkness, but its presence was enough for her. "This way," she said, leading.

"Because...?" Binh's voice trailed off.

"Because she said so, Scales. You—" Fil aimed her rifle at Rick, "walk in front so I can point a gun at your back if you try anything."

Rick passed them, lips tight.

What's this guy going to do? Is he setting us up for a trap? Alize licked her lips at the thought. Whatever Earthquake's plan was, it couldn't involve that unspeakable horror and it definitely didn't account for Fil kidnapping this Crith guy after a mutiny. *What'll happen if they catch us?*

THIRTY-ONE

Subsurface structure, unnamed moon, Dusoi orbit, Xechas system, Collective fringe

DESPITE THE DIM light obscuring his vision, Rick clocked the signs of an Arkouda under duress: raised fur, lowered ears, and exposed teeth. This Filenada Kaluteros didn't approve of Oze's plan, and her playful banter with the thief wasn't enough to lose the edge. Cu-dan's unknown status likely added to their uncertainty.

Rick joined in his squad's mutiny by drifting from the objective at hand. How many members of Earthquake mutinied? His fire team, sure. But what about the reserves?

Galsan worms bore into his heart.

What about Amanda? *No. Not her.*

The whole mission could've been a ruse by Tecton to kill Rick off in secret. Sick of hearing the voice of reason, no doubt. Shaking his head, Rick knew he couldn't jump the gun. He'd get out and return to base. He could count on Amanda. Moreno and the mutineers were working out their daddy issues on him. The engineers and other brains at base wouldn't join the fire team.

Rick tapped the part of his belt which concealed a compartment the others hadn't searched. His comm device was still attached. He shot a quick glance at his omni-tablet in between the downward steps. *Offline. Weird error message, too. Hm. Must be related to the armor and light malfunctions. What's the deal with this damn moon? Everything worked fine on the surface. Could that ... thing play a part in this?* Rick shook his head and focused on the steps—that damn thing couldn't possibly mess with their tech.

In front of him, Oze nearly tripped. Had to admire her resolve. She carried the innocence Rick lost decades ago. In another life, with that skin and those eyes, she could've been his daughter. But he and Amanda wouldn't have a kid who resembled either one individually. And that was assuming Amanda ever reciprocated. Even in his imagination, they were just— *DAMMIT, CRITH. Focus. Focus.*

With more ceiling height in this downward spiral, the thief and the Collective soldier resumed their upright walk, although the tip of her helmet grazed the ceiling occasionally.

"Oze," Rick said.

"Huh?"

"The Chamayna. They could fly."

Without glancing back at him, she nodded, pink frizzy hair obscuring her movement. "Based on their art, I think they could."

"Why'd they build stairs?"

"What?" Oze asked.

The Lo-sat chuckled. "Uh-oh. Captain Haircut got you there, Pinky."

Captain Haircut? Better than Lefty.

"That's not something we can worry about now," Oze said.

Rick bit the inside of his cheek. *Damn. Shouldn't've said anything. Echoes can carry.*

Ten-trom sniffed. "Shh."

Some debris cascaded from the ceiling. Footsteps above. Hard to tell how many. More than one. At least five. The squad roster spun through his head. Who would've survived? Moreno and Lamont, for sure. Not Rymon or Neena unless they got lucky. Or someone took a bullet for them. Or a mandible, in that thing's case. *Doesn't matter, though. All dirty traitors. Giving Earthquake a worse name than it already has.*

"No more whispers." Nods met Kaluteros' words.

They continued descending and the footsteps dispersed.

After a few minutes, the Arkouda peeked over her shoulder and whispered, "We lost them."

Oze nodded. "But we don't know where these paths lead. They could reconnect. Or dead end and force them back to the center hallway, and then they could follow us down here."

Unbidden, a religious adage from his childhood spewed forth. "No paths are dead ends," Rick said. "Not truly."

"I have some walls I'd like to introduce you to." A grin curled up Ten-trom's snout.

The Collective soldier stifled a chuckle. But as she raised her paw to her muzzle, the beacon on her armor dimmed.

Shit.

Oze clocked it, too. "Let's move." Her hand slid across an etching on the wall. The artwork was simple and delicate. A collector would pay top dollar for it. At least that's guaranteed. A positive result from this mission. Rick's gaze settled on the Arkouda's still-functioning armor. *Potentially two positive results.*

The steps steepened as they descended. Keeping track of their location in relation to ground level was impossible. How far had they descended to awaken that creature before Rick caught them retreating? Hard to say. And they may not give him a straight answer, anyway.

Kaluteros called for a halt, and Rick's body obeyed without his input. *Damn. They conditioned me well. Would I outrank her if I stuck with the Collective? Wouldn't matter. Arkoudae always outrank Provincials.* Rick gritted his teeth and squinted past her armored paw.

The beacon illuminated the end of the spiral stairs, revealing a wide room. Between elongated shadows, more etchings greeted them.

Following a gasp from Oze, Rick gazed at the walls and saw what must've made the thief salivate. Stone shelves stretched across the walls, supporting various trinkets and artifacts. Most appeared useless, perhaps some sculpture art form he wasn't sophisticated enough to recognize. These artifacts could've fit in his hand, but he had no clue how he could've held them. They were small stone globes, riddled with holes. Whether the holes were by design or a result of decay, he couldn't tell.

Waving his tail, Binh muttered in Lo-sat, and Rick barely parsed it out. He could write a book in Arkouda and converse in Ma'ak or transliterated Blekker, but Lo-sat was never his forte. The only word he could suss out from whatever Binh whispered was "mine."

Typical thief. But Rick didn't say anything; his limited knowledge of the thief's language may prove a strategic advantage later.

Oze apparently forgot the order to whisper. "Look!" She pointed at an etching. It wasn't any clearer than the others, yet it didn't resemble them, either. It was like a smudged swirl going the wrong direction. The etching implied an unnatural movement, tugging something primal within. Maybe this was that "call of the void" Rick's first therapist blabbed about.

"No clue what that is," the thief hissed, "but that's nasty."

Kaluteros crossed her wide arms and nodded. "It does look kooky, Leeze."

Rick inched closer and remained silent.

Oze deciphered the incoherent symbolism. "I think the etching suggests my hunch. Teleporting."

"Teleporting?" Rick asked. They didn't need to know he'd intercepted some of their correspondence, as much as he'd like to see the thief tease them with that "gruntsisters" garbage. "That's a load of shit or a translation error."

The Lo-sat snorted. "Have to agree with Slick Rick on this one, here."

Oze shook her head. "Listen, they got here and two other locations on opposite ends of the galaxy. They lacked spacefaring tech. What other explanation is there?"

The Collective soldier's tone shifted to one of reverence. "Maybe the Goddess dreamed that gift for them."

Ten-trom slapped his tail on the floor. "Hey, the Goddess' dream. Got some questions. Does it ever get kinky? Or going to school without pants?"

Oze clicked her tongue. "Maybe teleport isn't the right word, but they traveled the stars, and there's no evidence they had spaceships."

"Say that again," the thief said, "slowly."

"Stop it. I know how it sounds, Binh."

Rick rubbed his chin. Sometimes the simplest answer was best. Thank prehistoric Earth philosophers for that lesson. But it was strange. "How are you getting that from this etching?"

If Earthquake acquired real teleportation tech, their war would end immediately, and they'd finally assert Humanity as an independent species, no longer delegated to the damned fringes of Arkouda and Lo-sat society. His pulse quickened. If this were real, he needed it.

"See here," Oze said, indicating a four-armed figure. "This Chamayna is pictured adjacent to the glyph we saw earlier for 'transmit.' And check out these movement lines. So it goes 'poof,' and teleports over here." She pointed to another figure beside similar lines and a second glyph, illuminated by a dim flashing green on her wrist. "It's where we have the same movement lines, the glyph for 'arrive,' and the same four-armed Chamayna."

Rick squinted at the art. "You sure those lines signify movement? Seems like a leap in logic." *If that Lo-sat translator were here, what would his take be?*

The Arkouda turned and glared at him, fur on end. "If she says it's movement, it's movement. Are you an expert on this—in addition to being a scumbag terrorist?"

Rick's nostrils flared and he craned his neck to make eye contact. *How dare you use that word?* "I'm fighting for Human independence. That requires sacrifices and occasional blood on my boots."

"Quit growling at each other." Oze rubbed her temples. "If it weren't for the glyphs, I wouldn't be confident. Rick, you didn't see the corpses downstairs. Exoskeletons. All Chamayna. And we believe they were fresh. Or at least some of them."

"Fresh corpses from an extinct species?" Rick asked.

Alize's face brightened. "Yes. There was another creature down there. It reminded me of Earth tarantulas, and its expression suggested sentience, if I understood it correctly."

An unbidden shiver rattled Rick's spine. He clenched his teeth. This was not the time for a breakdown. He refused to retreat into his dark place.

"And the other monster, that—that thing," Oze continued. "We think killed it. Today. You saw its weapon?"

Forcing childhood memories of spiders away, Rick nodded. "The bludgeon? Not exactly easy to miss."

"We saw an indent that size on the thorax of the first monster."

"No bite marks?" Rick's eyebrow cocked.

"None," Kaluteros said.

"Doesn't kill to eat." Rick stiffened. *So it's smart. And angry.*

A tremble shook in the distance above them, but Rick couldn't be sure if it were his own nerves or not, since none of the others reacted.

Phantom pinpricks like the footsteps of a spider rattled Rick's missing arm. "What's the connection to teleportation?"

"I think the Chamayna teleported here, as if in some sacrifice or punishment, feeding the tarantula nightmare, which was meant to safeguard against the … other one. But … it awoke."

Filenada crossed her arms and huffed. "Can we settle on a name for—for… for whatever that monstrosity is?"

"I'm getting sick of saying I've tried, Fuzzle Muzzle. And usually, names are my specialty." With a bastard's grin, he indicated Rick and Oze with his claws. "Ask Mister What's-his-face and Miss Forgettable over there."

Oze bit her lip. "Think there's a reason we can't name it?"

The damn thief curled and uncurled his tail. "What, you think that monstrosity has some kind of magic where we can't name it? That's about as believable as Sergeant Fuzzball's naptime religion."

Oze's eyes widened. "Unspeakable."

Rick arched an eyebrow. "Excuse me?"

Oze gulped before responding. "We can't say its name or give it one. It's unspeakable." Her tone softened and her shoulders slumped. "I was wrong."

"About what?" the Arkouda asked, ears raising.

"The superweapon—"

Kaluteros shushed her. "Don't say that around—" She pointed to Rick with a disdainful paw.

"He already knows, Fil. Garott told him the whole story, I bet."

And Cu-dan sold you out, but it seems like that's an unknown for you all.

The Collective soldier glared, and Rick nodded slowly. "You were saying? The superweapon?"

"I was wrong," Oze said. "What I translated as the 'weapon of unspeakable power' wasn't referring to an actual weapon."

The thief snarled. "What the hell was it, then? Or do you even know? Can't be a shit translator and expect good results."

"Well," Oze said, "the Unspeakable itself is what I assumed was the weapon. Those traps were meant to keep it in. I guess what I translated as weapon could also mean force or violence. I don't know." She sank to the floor, the wall's friction slowing her descent, exposed toes curling. "I'm sorry."

That monster is a weapon. Must be a way to harness it, if they imprisoned it. Built this whole structure knowing they'd use it, but weren't sure when. Cold admiration rose. This wouldn't have any difficulty bashing Collective armor.

Ten-trom slapped his tail against the floor. "Let's use some logic, you damn dirty mammals. You really think a living organism carries magic so we can't say its name—dumb power, by the way—and messes with light waves and sophisticated technology? A lifespan pushing immortality, I can almost buy. But this other stuff? Makes me wonder what you're smoking. And if you'll share it. My painkillers ran out, so I wouldn't mind taking the edge off."

Rick shook his head. "What you want to believe is moot. The fact is we have a hostile and obstacles. Who or what's producing them is irrelevant. We must overcome and survive."

"Unless it's not a creature at all." A tremor permeated Kaluteros' voice.

Oze stiffened. "That one inscription said 'sleeping god.' Maybe—"

Rick fidgeted. "You think you awoke a sleeping alien god?"

Eyes ablaze, Oze glared at him, fuming. "Or you did, Mr. Crith, when you shot our ship."

Another series of lurching trembles—four this time. Debris rained. Rick's eventual report wouldn't mention an awakened god. Maybe Oze thought this was a sleeping deity, but that's not what he'd write. Not concrete. Not in-line with Earthquake philosophy. And if he needed to kill it, it wouldn't make the fight any easier if he believed the Unspeakable divine. Hard enough without his squad for support. But then he wouldn't need to concern himself with giving the right orders. Move and fight on instinct alone, unconcerned about the welfare of others. He'd survived that before.

"We can't stay in this location," Rick said. "We need to advance."

Kaluteros snarled. "You don't call the shots here."

"Fil, we have to go." Oze tugged at the Arkouda's paw.

"Finally," Ten-trom muttered.

The Arkouda sauntered forward until they hit a wall. No other lateral or forward path.

The Lo-sat slapped his tail on the floor. "Wonderful. Really wonderful. A dead-end. Thank my Imaginary Friend we listened to the Humans."

Oze stepped in front of the wall. "There's a crack here. And a message. Reading it standard says, 'final barrier.'" She cocked her head. "Backwards it says, 'allow slumber.'"

The Collective soldier folded her arms. "That's not very helpful, Leeze."

"Perhaps we shouldn't have messed with the Unspeakable if you translated it correctly," the thief said. "Although we can't exactly trust you."

Oze waved a tiny finger in front of his chest. "You're one to talk."

Do they always bicker like this? No wonder Cu-dan didn't join them.

"Oze," Rick said, "what's the final barrier a reference to?"

Ten-trom stopped his banter for a moment and spoke in an even tone. Almost mature. "Well, since Pinkster's not an ace translator in this regard, maybe instead of exactly saying 'final barrier,' it means something close to that. Synonyms, maybe."

"Last wall," Rick offered.

Oze nodded. "That might be right. Last wall to what?"

Kaluteros tapped on the wall with her fist near a thin crack. "Any idea how far down we went that staircase? What level this is?"

Ten-trom sniffed. "We're below surface level." Three more sniffs. "And you all need a bath."

This is getting old. "How far down?"

Ten-trom shrugged. "Tough to say beyond we're below surface."

Two trembles shook the floor and walls. *Damn thing's close.*

Rick eyed his grenade pack, attached to Kaluteros' armor. Didn't have many left, but if they needed through this wall, this was a surefire way to accomplish it. "Give my grenades back. I'm going to blow a hole."

Another tremble. Closer.

Kaluteros growled. "Why is your solution to blow things up? Do you want to collapse this place on our heads?"

"Don't necessarily have the time for deliberation. I'll set it to low power. We cannot go back into the Unspeakable's path. Unless you think this is a false wall and there's a switch somewhere. Otherwise, stand clear."

Some glances exchanged between the other three, and the Collective soldier returned his pack. They all stepped back. Rick armed his grenade, placed it at the bottom of the crack, and joined the others several yards away. "Citizen Kaluteros, would you activate your force field to shield us from debris?"

"No," she said, solemn. "But you can all stand behind me."

Why? Conserving power? Is it compromised? Putting me in the line of shrapnel?

Oze made a small bow. "Thanks, Fil." As she did, the thief slid in front of her, Rick behind.

The grenade exploded, smashing and shattering a hole into the wall, and the tremor rumbled in his boots and armor. *Probably rattled Oze's whole skeleton with her bare foot.*

The soundwave's force alone was enough to wake the dead. Explosives conjured painful and tense memories of his last missions before defecting. Rick clenched his teeth, forcing the dark thoughts from his mind.

Even from the cover of Kaluteros' wide figure, shrapnel and shards of rock flew in all directions, a few scraping against Rick's own plated armor. The thief cursed, even though he had the most protection and likely felt the pain evaporate earlier. Oze surely had it the worst, but she bore it like a real warrior. She made a few glances toward her wristpiece, which flashed green at patterned intervals. *Repeating some kind of mantra? Nervous habit? Doesn't matter.* Whatever her reason, she apparently drew strength from it.

When the dust cleared, Rick peeked from Kaluteros' behind, checking the hole he made. More debris from the ceiling cascaded downward. Between his detonations and the Unspeakable's shaking, the whole damn mountain was liable to come crashing down on their heads. If he'd said that out loud in front of his squadmates, some dumbass would've said at least it would kill the popsicle and slime ball first. Bastards. Rick trudged ahead; the Arkouda and Lo-sat joined him, lights pointing forward.

Oze came in from behind and joined them. "I recounted the steps on the staircase, well I guessed them, but I think we're on the same level we were before we turned around. I think we're about to enter the chamber where we first saw the Unspeakable."

A pair of light trembles shook the ceiling, deepening the ceiling's crack again.

And as the reverberation from the trembles faded, Rick noticed in his periphery the two sources of light on either side of him. They brightened again. And with each consecutive step toward what Oze called the chamber, the lights intensified.

Rick licked his lips. "If the Unspeakable caused the malfunctioning tech, wouldn't going into its chamber weaken and dampen our power further?"

Oze's tone was somber, like a green soldier after killing for the first time. "It only does that when it's close. And it's not in its chamber because we unleashed it." She forced the kind of sigh meant to convince the audience some tension was released. "We're safe, I think."

A light vibration from Rick's omni-tablet chimed. "Check your tech. See if your armor's back online. I just got a notification."

THIRTY-TWO

Earthquake internal messenger

```
FORWARDED TO: Crith, Rodrick
FORWARDED BY: Martinez, Amanda
ORIGINAL SENDER: Moreno, Alejandro
ORIGINAL RECIPIENT: Tecton, Jacques
SUBJECT: Reporting Treason
Timestamp: Three hours ago
```

Exalted Leader,

Let's begin with acknowledging that
I shouldn't have access to your messaging account. I took it from my
supervisor, Commander Crith. I understand that is grounds for reprimand.
I will accept that when the time is
appropriate.

But Leader, please read this before informing Commander Crith. He's acting against Earthquake's best interests. He has known associates in the Drowned Star as well as various Makawe insurgent groups. Crith believes we will defeat the Collective scum only by joining forces with them.

Crith doesn't believe in Earthquake's values. He's attempted diplomatic negotiations with aliens. He's preached empathy for the Arkouda and reprimands degrading talk about the enemy. I have recordings of him saying not to kill a Collective soldier in battle if possible, which would deny our squad members a bounty.

Commander Crith is unfit to lead in your organization. His symbolic value served its purpose.

I've spoken to the other members of our squad. They're willing to follow my lead instead of Crith's. The only member I didn't approach is Commander Crith's staff manager. She's too close to him, and rumors abound of an inappropriate relationship between them.

I know what's at stake in this mission. I'll find the weapon of unspeakable power. It'll become a tool for Earthquake. If Crith gets it, he's liable to destroy it. Or he might even try and use it against you in a bid to replace you and steer Earthquake down a dangerous path. With your blessing, I'll lead this squad unflinchingly. I know Commander Crith argues against your decisions. It's disgusting.

Until now, I've been biding my time, waiting for a promotion the standard way, but that relic won't retire any time soon. I can't prove it, but I think he even has active Arkouda contacts, and he's not using them for Earthquake's greater good. My recommendation is a demotion from you. Barring that, I'll lead a bloodless mutiny against him. He's too proud to expect it.

Rodrick Crith is a threat to Earthquake and Human supremacy. He must be stopped.

Earthquake moves the galaxy.

-Alejandro Moreno.

THIRTY-THREE

Moon—zzt—— zzt. ERROR. Zzt— Dusoi
orb- zzt. ERR—

A HARSH HALF-CHUCKLE broke Alize's concentration. "What're you smiling about?" she asked Rick.

A gruff grin spread across the veteran's face. "Had a suspicion about my second-in-command. Left a little bait for him." After a sigh, he added, "Would've been nice if my staff manager had forwarded it to me sooner, but that can't be helped. She's busy."

Binh hissed. "Was your suspicion that he didn't like you? This was the friendly chap who mutinied? Seemed like a lovely fellow. Definitely not a hardass who thinks muscles and guns can substitute for personality."

Fil joined the teasing, but Alize couldn't pay them any mind. She studied the chamber, the holding cell for the Unspeakable, where it had lain dormant and undisturbed for eons.

Until she woke it up and pissed it off.

The realization's sting softened as she marveled at the chamber, finally lit well enough by Fil's beacon to appreciate its macabre glory. More glyphs lined the walls, as well as shelves with various tools whose purpose she could only guess at. With the tools' thin spikes, they could've been for embalming, eating, or building.

But at the room's center lay a gaping hole, resembling prehistoric wells from Earth.

"Binh," Alize said, "quit harassing Rick. Please shine the light down this pit."

"He's Earthquake. Practically asking for it. But since you said please, I'm legally obligated to comply."

The light penetrated to the bottom. Doing some mental geometry, Alize figured the well could hold Fil standing upright twice over, at least. Deep enough for her to break a bone or twenty if she jumped in, but not so much to kill her. More glyphs lined the well's inside.

Filenada whistled behind her. "Leeze, see anything down there? You should check out the ceiling etchings."

Alize leaned over the edge, following the beam of Binh's borrowed light. "Yeah, I think we found the holding cell." A crack in the foundation stole her attention, and she followed the snaking line to the well's top. Alize nudged Binh to approach it with her, and they found the crack was in the floor on the other side.

Binh deadpanned, "Looks like a fissure in the ground ruptured the floor."

Alize dared to run an exposed toe across the crack. The floor's texture and the lunar rock were nearly indistinguishable, but the floor was somehow mark-edly warmer than the exposed rock. "What do you make of it, Binh?"

"Fresh crack. Few hours old." He swirled the light beam around until it landed on a wide stone oval, almost a meter from the well, unceremoniously tossed on the ground.

"That was the seal." Alize glanced at the well's opening and walked to the stone oval. "We can mea-sure it if you don't believe me, but this was a lid for the well. The Unspeakable was kept down there. Like … some kind of prison. Whatever caused this crack weak-ened or broke the seal and woke the Unspeakable."

Rick scoffed. "Or it wasn't sleeping. If it's a higher life form like the glyphs say, it may have been in there, fully conscious, for hundreds of years. Or longer."

"Divinities sleep, too," Fil whispered.

Binh folded his arms. "Care to share any other platitudes from Make-Believe-Land? If that mon-strosity was stuck in there for as long as you think, that's plenty of time to snap. No wonder it came out angry and swinging."

Filenada peered into the yawning well. "But it had weapons with it. Or at least one. I don't know if that scepter thingy was a weapon or not. But if the Chamayna wanted it imprisoned, why in the Nightmare would they leave a bludgeon and that scepter with it? I know I wouldn't let a prisoner have a weapon."

Alize rubbed her chin. "Maybe to fight it?"

"In case something like this happened, you mean?" Binh hissed. "Thank my imaginary friends this didn't immediately grab them."

Alize's eyes widened. "The chitin boulder. What if the bludgeon on the Unspeakable's mace…" She bit her lip and gulped. "…maybe that was the core of the boulder, and the chitin was patched around it. And when it crashed, all the chitin plating fell off." She exhaled shakily. "And that's what it used to kill the thorax creature."

Rick nodded. "That doesn't do much to explain its scepter, though, or how it attached a polearm to the bludgeon."

Alize shrugged. "I can't think of a better explanation."

"Maybe it had two scepters and used one as the handle," Fil said.

Binh's mocking tone returned. "It probably had a bunch of ultra-glue in here for all its arts and crafts, too. That or hyper tape."

"Quit being a dick." Pacing around the well's perimeter, Alize approached Fil. "Any chance you could lift that lid? Maybe whatever's underneath will give us a hint?"

Light from Fil's beacon scattered and caught a glint.

"Wait—" Alize stooped in front of what caught her attention, and once it was washed in the light, she realized it was a shiny carapace fragment. More Chamayna chitin. "Fil, mind sitting on the well's edge? I want to check again with your beacon shining. Hey Rick, put up your hands against—shit, sorry—hand on the wall. Binh, keep him at gunpoint."

Grim-faced, Rick nodded and complied.

A quick glance at the pulsing green on her wrist reminded her of why she was here. *We'll figure this out, Pops.*

Sick grin on his snout, Binh followed orders.

Alize whispered to Fil, "I didn't want him to push you in."

Fil cocked an eyebrow. "Like to see him try."

"I don't want anyone to try." Alize put her hand on Fil's paw. "Not when I owe you so many beers."

Filenada perched on the well, and the blue light from her beacon scattered, reaching places Binh's standard light beam hadn't. Alize squinted at the bottom. More glinting reflections. Her mouth dried. More chitin. More Chamayna corpses.

"Fil..." A tremor ran through Alize's voice. "There's broken exoskeletons below. Hundreds. I bet they lined the walls." Alize shifted her gaze toward the glyphs, and they all read the same thing. "Adhere."

"Huh?" Fil asked. "Leeze, mind if I move? A bit off-putting up here."

"Yeah." Alize glanced over her shoulder at Binh, who was pointing the pistol at Rick and sizing him up with the light beam. Rick remained statuesque, despite the taunts Binh threw at him ranging from juvenile to unrepeatable.

Alize had heard stories about the "one-armed war hero" who defected from the Collective military, but they never registered to her as interesting or important enough to divert from her studies. Unless of course when her classmates would harangue her about the latest Earthquake activity.

"Don't torture him, Binh," Alize called.

"Was gonna force him to smell himself, but I guess I'll save that torture for me."

This garnered a light chuckle from Fil as she heaved the well's stone lid. As she lifted, another glyph caught the beacon light.

Alize cocked an eyebrow. "'Adhere.' Again? Hey, Fil... weird question, but would you mind poking the glyph to see if it's sticky?" Alize felt six eyes train on her. "I have a dumb idea."

"I'm not taking my glove off, Leeze, but my armor's not sticking to the glyph."

She nodded tightly. "Yeah, I didn't think so." Mid-sigh, another idea flickered. She crouched and grabbed the broken chitin on the floor, then walked over to the stone lid. Gently, she placed the shrapnel in front of the glyph. Despite Fil's concerned humming behind her, Alize heard a tiny click.

Grimacing, she released her grip, and the chitin remained in place for three seconds masquerading as three years. It slid off the stone instead of falling, like a weakened magnet.

Fil gasped. "What in the—"

Alize bit her lower lip. "The glyph said 'adhere,' and the chitin plate stuck to it. At least for a bit."

"How?"

"I don't know." She stood and called out, "Binh, you and Rick can come over here. Check this out."

She repeated the procedure, and the chitin stuck again for three long seconds before gently slipping to the floor.

Rick grunted. "And you think it's because of what the glyph says?"

"Could be a coincidence, Professor Pink. We also can't rule out grubby hands."

Fil growled at him.

"What?" Binh said. "She's touched half the stuff in this creepy bug bunker. Try putting it on somewhere else and see if it sticks?"

They repeated the experiment on different parts of the stone lid, and the chitin fell off each time. She moved to a different glyph on the wall: 'transmit.' Same results. Nothing stuck.

Alize stole a glance at her wrist, pulsing slower. *I figured something out, Pops. This is huge.* "The glyph for 'adhere' could make chitin stick to it. Do you realize how huge this is? Their glyphs had extra functions."

Rick squinted at her. "So why didn't that chitin move anywhere when you put it over the 'transmit' glyph? Shouldn't it have sent it somewhere, by your logic?"

"What he lacks in symmetry, he makes up for in good points. Rebuttal?"

Alize scratched her chin and adjusted her breather before turning to the others. "Maybe there's something else..."

Fil tapped the stone oval. "Think they slapped some special glue on those glyphs? My scan said 'inconclusive,' but it's still acting up."

Alize's eyes were on the glyph as she tapped the area nearby. "Hold on. In reverse, it says 'skin.' Maybe—" She gently nudged Fil out of the way and motioned for her to lower the stone seal to the ground. Alize extended her arm, which Fil instinctively grabbed, placed her booted foot on the lid, and hovered her bare foot over the glyph.

"Oh come on," Binh said.

Alize brushed her toe across the area directly around the glyph. Cold, rough, no resistance. After an exhale, she gently tapped the glyph with her big toe. Cold, rough, and a slight tug.

Impossible.

She tried again, applying more pressure.

And she was met with another tug on the pad of her toe, less gentle.

In her periphery, Pops' heart rate accelerated. *I'm excited, too, Pops. Thanks. And a little nervous.* "Fil, I'm going to put my whole foot down."

"Right."

With a shaky breath, Alize rested her whole bare foot on the glyph. The etched symbol snagged her foot, and she immediately felt the bond, as if hundreds of tiny claws latched on. "Uh-oh."

This wasn't right. Horrible idea. "Fil," Alize struggled, but her foot wouldn't budge. "I'm stuck."

Binh chortled. "To the adhesive? Wow. Didn't see that coming."

Rick stepped in front of him and walked over to the lid, squatting in front of it. He squinted at Alize's foot while Fil attempted to lift her.

"I don't want to hurt you." Fil nudged Rick out of the way and grabbed Alize's exposed foot. Alize rested her arm on Fil's back and planted her booted foot on the floor.

And the room shook. Lights dimmed. Every pore on Alize's body oozed sweat.

Fil heaved, and Alize's skin resisted, drawn to the glyph like a stubborn magnet. She'd doomed them all.

More shaking. Stronger this time. "Nightmare," Fil cursed. "Leeze, I don't want to hurt you."

Binh hissed. "Can we hurry this up? It's adorable—" Loose bits of stone fell from the ceiling. "Yank her damn foot off!"

Why'd the chitin slide off after a few seconds but not my foot? Cold metallic armor plates dug into Alize's ankle and calf. Fil's grip tightened; Alize winced. "Fil, we have to try something else."

The next series of tremors were violent enough to make Rick stumble. Binh had to brace himself with his tail and Fil's legs threatened to buckle.

The beacon dimmed again, almost to nothingness. "We're running out of—" the floor shook, attacking everyone's balance, "—*skata*! What do we do?" Larger chunks of the ceiling fell.

Alize puffed a shaky exhale. "We have to smash this damn rock."

Trembles. Much more forceful. Alize shielded her eyes from the descending debris. The room's shaking grew so loud she couldn't hear herself think.

"Right," Fil shouted. "You. Rick. Grab her other arm. Scales. Come here and grab this arm."

Rick snaked his arm around Alize's. Binh looped his tail around her elbow and tricep. Fil hoisted the stone oval in both paws, lifting Alize's foot also.

"This'll hurt, Leeze."

A fissure in the floor snaked toward them with the next set of rumbles. Fil's features were enveloped in darkness, beacon reduced to a faint glow.

"Smash it against the well," Alize begged.

Fil grunted. "Lift her a little, boys."

Alize floated, aloft by hands, claws, and a tail she couldn't see. "Do it!"

Rumbles pulsed, shaking the limbs holding her.

More debris loosed from the ceiling as dust cascaded over her breather.

Like a pendulum of flesh, bone, and stone, Alize's leg swung back, and the stone connected to the raised well wall behind her. A few stony bits drizzled to the ground, but her foot remained glued. The stone bounced forward, swinging back toward Fil. A grunt and the change in pressure were the only signals to Alize that Fil caught it. Alize looked to her side. She couldn't even see her wrist piece. The force alone could've dislocated her femur from her hips, and even then, Alize knew Fil wasn't using the full extent of her strength.

Tremble-tremble-tremble.

"Do it again, Fil." Alize clenched her teeth. "Harder."

"Hurry up, damn it!" Rick shouted.

"Right," Fil said. Another heave. The shove was harder, the kickback was faster, and the vibration from the stone connecting to the well wall ran up through her spine. A crack snaked through the back of the lid, coming to her heel's edge. Her whole body ached.

The room shook. *Clack-clacka-clack.*

Nononono. "One more time, Fil. As hard as you can."

Binh flared out his neck frills. "Do it!"

"I'm sorry, Leeze—" Fil grunted and shoved.

Alize had never broken a bone, but the wet crack in her hip and the blinding pain told her everything. Filenada pushed with so much force, it dislocated

Alize's hip. The lid connected to the well wall snapped, and the crack webbed through the rest of the lid, under Alize's foot, splitting in half.

Wincing, Alize managed to squeak, "It worked." Sharp searing agony bolted through her foot and up her entire leg before rattling her spine. Bits of skin from the pad of her foot ripped off onto each side of the split stone, and her ankle shattered near the source of the impact. Alize bit her tongue to prevent herself from screaming—she tasted blood.

They could've escaped, but saving her doomed them.

Splotches arose in her vision as the blood drained from her eyes. The room spun.

Clack-clack. Tremble. Clack clack.

Breathing heavily, she assessed the damage. Attempting to rotate her foot, curl a toe, or move her knee was met with stabbing pain she'd never known before. Her body issued a warning—try again, and vomit follows. Hot, anguished tears streaked her cheeks, and she clenched her teeth to keep from wailing.

One of Binh's claws left her arm. A thin whoosh sound followed. And then a gunshot's crack illuminated the room. In the moment of light, amid hazy splotches and stars orbiting her vision, Binh and Rick stood slack-jawed, staring at whatever was behind her. Directly in front, Filenada's eyes were fixated on Alize's limp and dangling leg.

Fil's eyes watered and she winced, which turned into a whimper.

"It's here." Binh's tail lazily unlatched from Alize's arm. "We're dead."

Rick grunted and repositioned his grip. With a heave, he hoisted her over his shoulder in one fluid motion. So much burning and stabbing pain circulated through Alize, she couldn't tell if she were going blind or if the darkness had simply enveloped them.

Clackclackclack.

Groggy, Alize heard Filenada move, but the ringing in her own ears intensified so much that all else muffled.

Rick lumbered away from the Unspeakable, each step sending shooting pain up Alize's lower body as her useless leg collided with his torso. The utter blackness made leaving her eyes open irrelevant. Only one sound reverberated through the piercing cacophony in her ears.

Clack. Clack-clack.

A flash ignited the room again, the shoom of a plasma bullet leaving Fil's rifle. Limply, she raised her wrist to her face. *Are you there, Pops?*

Blackness.

Clack-clackaclackaclack.

Alize brought her face so close to her wrist that it brushed her cheek. It would flash directly in her eye.

Complete darkness.

No... Pops...

Everything faded.

Clack-clack tremble.

Thud.

THIRTY-FOUR

Somewhere beneath the surface of this damn moon and millimeters from walking death

DAMN. DAMN.

Rick huffed under Oze's limp weight. He couldn't confront the walking nightmare behind him. He needed an evac but had nowhere to go; the realization made him shudder. The damn mandibles' horrendous wet clacking shattered any chance of coherent thoughts, let alone tactical ones.

Instead, memories surfaced: sitting in the worship center as a kid, hearing about a positive afterlife for the righteous and a negative one for evildoers. The good one boasted a paradise of comfort, images he understood literally as a child and relegated to symbolism in adulthood. Conversely, the negative alternative warned of fire, monsters, and agony. More symbols and metaphors. Nominal observance of Abrahamist holidays lasted until his mother died, but

Rick never gave much credence to any of the beliefs beyond "think about others first." Years later, an old veteran told Rick "no atheists in foxholes." Expressions with extinct animals didn't do much for him. Not that any all-powerful being ever gave a damn about Rick.

Until now.

Kaluteros believed this was a sleeping alien god. But in the flashes Rick saw this creature, the vibrations in the whole complex shook him with each step. His subconscious understood why they couldn't say this name, why they resorted to calling it "the Unspeakable." His parents' religion had the answer. Goosebumps covered his skin at the realization.

It was the fucking devil.

Straight from the chittering depths of the blackest insectoid hell.

With a whoosh of air, the dread beast swung its mace, narrowly missing their heads. Elongated shadows made it impossible to tell anything's relative size or shape.

"Ten-trom," Rick called after the Unspeakable swung again. "On its next swipe, grab the mace's shaft with your tail. Try to pull it down."

"Fat chance!" The Lo-sat fired another wild shot with Rick's pistol.

Kaluteros fired more rounds at the Unspeakable. Whether they connected was irrelevant. It marched forward, swinging its dread mace as if destroying the walls was equally preferable to squashing them.

The thief wasn't trained in fighting with a weapon. "Do it or come here and take her."

Between light bursts from the Arkouda's plasma bullets, Ten-trom complied, arms open to receive Oze. The cocky bastard even appeared scared.

Rick hefted the limp woman off his shoulders, and the men ducked, avoiding the mace.

Whoosh. A gust pushed his hair aside.

Clacka-clack clack clacka-clack.

This time, the mace connected with a wall, shaking significant amounts of the ceiling down. *This whole damn place will collapse.*

"Ten-trom, take Oze and run. Kaluteros—fire toward the ceiling."

The Arkouda snarled. "You don't give me orders."

Binh lumbered away, Oze dangling over his shoulder. Rick watched the pattern in between plasma bursts and the angle the Unspeakable swung the mace. *Only getting one chance.*

Whoosh.

Rick jumped and grabbed the mace shaft as it sailed centimeters over his head.

Clack clacka-clack clack.

Hm. It doesn't like this. Can't say I do, either. Rick gritted his teeth, latched his fingers around the massive polearm, and swung his body weight down.

It wasn't enough—the damn abomination resisted his force. The Unspeakable didn't come crashing down with its momentum like it was supposed to. It was stronger.

Of course it is.

Rick was left swinging—dangling—from the nightmarish beast's bludgeon. Kaluteros continued firing at the creature, for all the good it did. The connecting bullets had no discernible effect other than to make Rick wonder if the Collective soldier aimed at him. She could kill him here while Oze was knocked out, unable to act as her moral compass.

Clacka-clack. Clackclackclackclack.

Not good.

Rick pushed himself and swung until he finagled a toehold on the polearm. His boot tip was all he needed. He had to kick a few of the Unspeakable's six arms away as he leveraged balance.

Kaluteros shot again, this one narrowly sailing over Rick's head—a centimeter closer and it would've singed hairs. This provided ample light for him to see his grav harness for a brief second. Straddling the handle with his legs on either side, he clenched his jaw and thumbed the setting.

This'll hurt me a lot more than you. But I'm not sorry.

Jaw clenched, Rick cranked his grav harness as high as possible, increasing his mass and threatening half his organs and bones.

Clacka-clack clack clackclack.

The unholy beast careened toward the floor, weapon first. Every bone and joint in Rick's body pressed down. He was ready to vomit, and his heart struggled to beat.

Damn it. Two more seconds. And—

Rick gulped and reversed the grav harness in the opposite direction. His insides lurched, and he slid off the weapon as the Unspeakable crashed into the floor.

Calling what the walking nightmare did a "roar" would be an understatement. Human ears weren't built or meant to experience the guttural howl emanating from the beast: malice manifested into a sound wave.

It fell longer than it should have; Rick's heart froze. *The well. Damn it.*

Another wild shot from Kaluteros flashed the area, allowing Rick to confirm the beast falling into the well. The dark cylindrical walls threatened some darker claustrophobic memories, but Rick blinked them away.

He adjusted his grav harness to the opposite extreme, and his organs and bile lifted. Pushing off against the mace, he forced himself into a leap, and in a parabolic arc, floated to the well's rim.

A thud reverberated from the bottom of the well, and the Unspeakable's clacking softened to an equally unsettling series of chitters. Knowing the distance between himself and the damn thing was impossible. Couldn't see the bottom for shit. Shivers threatening his grip on the wall, a cascade of vomit sprang forth, splattering and filling his breather.

Damn. Drowning on vomit isn't how I die.

Cold metal clutched his wrist, enveloping his entire hand. Collective armor.

Kaluteros' spoke, voice steady. "You saved my friend. You get one." She lifted him and promptly shoved him on the floor.

After nodding thanks, Rick remembered his surroundings. More vomit and bile punished his mouth, and he had no choice but to hold it along with his breath. With trepidation, Rick unsealed his breather, letting his vomit spill in a dull trickle.

Through heaves, Rick adjusted his grav harness to the proper setting. He alternated between sucking in tainted oxygen from his dirty breather and pushing the apparatus aside to vomit. After the contents of his mouth emptied, the acidic body fluids settled back in his stomach—hardly an improvement.

Wiping bitter saliva from his mouth, Rick managed a meek "thank-you" to the Arkouda. Each inhale threatened more nausea with the stench of his first puke lingering in his breather.

"Ready?" Kaluteros asked.

More chittering and rustling from below. Of course it survived. "Yeah."

An Arkouda grabbing him by the wrist threatened a flashback. *Shit. Not a hostile. Not a hostile.* He kept the nightmarish memory at bay, but his arm and neck hairs refused to stand down.

Ten years old. Beach. Sand. Sun. Ocean.

Twenty years old. Graduation. Family. Mom alive.

Rick exhaled and his pulse slowed. Teeth clenched, he accepted the Arkouda's help.

THIRTY-FIVE

Moon designated "I Told You So." zzt. ERR— Dusoi orbit zzt. ERROR

A ROUGH VIBRATION from beneath her spine jolted Alize from her hazy stupor into awareness. Her skin felt like a thin bag stretching against shattered bones poking in unnatural directions. Loose bits of debris from the ceiling drizzled on her, obscuring her breather.

Every breath flooded fresh agony, lungs groaning.

A gloved claw tapped her face. Alize forced her eyelids open, and she glimpsed Binh, scales lit a luminous blue. Emotions she couldn't read burned beneath Binh's lowered eyeridges.

Her breather pressed against her face. Muffled noises around her slowly clarified.

Alize blinked. Binh's scales glowed because Fil's armor was near. But not Fil.

"Where…" She heaved a breath. "…the hell…" She huffed air out. "…is Fil?" Her cement tongue fought against loose teeth.

"I'm here, Leeze," Fil said from above. "You're in bad shape. You need this."

Binh growled. "You awake enough, Pinky?"

She nodded and he helped her sit upright, supporting herself by wobbly arms.

"Listen…" Binh's eyeridges flattened and snout leveled. "That little trick to get unstuck might kill you. We ain't doctors, but you've probably shattered half the bones in your leg, disconnected all your major joints, and have some nasty internal bleeding. Our options were remove Sergeant Stinkfur's armor and connect you to its life support or leave you here." A grin crept across his snout and he winked. "An option which wasn't fully explored in committee—"

"Wrap your tail around your snout." Fil knelt beside Alize and placed a fuzzy paw on her shoulder. "I'll keep my helmet to breathe. I can lower the gravity on the armor itself so it rests almost weightless. It still won't fit, but at least it won't be heavy."

"Fil, your armor's your life."

Rick sauntered over. "You were unconscious. We acted. Not for you to decide. We can't treat you, but that can sustain you until we get out of here. We're leaving. Mission failure. We need to move on. You have proof and those clawspears to take home and sell, display, or whatever you want. Officer Kaluteros got the adventure she craved. And don't think the thief hasn't snuck a few items in while he thought none of us watched. We didn't kill the Unspeakable.

Not even sure I hurt it. But you all achieved what you wanted. Time to evac."

Binh hissed. "You were watching? Pervert."

More alert now, Alize absorbed the surroundings. They were near the staircase outside of the room with the webbing and the thorax monster. "Why's your light so bright, Fil? It's almost like when we entered."

It wasn't of course, but the brightness was a marked improvement from the cloying dark around the Unspeakable.

Fil helped her stand. "Not as bright as it could or should be, I promise. I fired a few shots at the passageway to the chamber behind us until a bunch of stones caved in. It'll have to come quite a long way to catch us."

"Odds are it escaped the well and moved in another direction," Rick said, eyes adrift.

Binh muttered, "What's fun is that when it inevitably finds us, we won't have anywhere to run to. Really lovely thought."

Alize drew in a deep breath. "Are your omni-tablets working?"

Rick nodded, Fil gave an emphatic yes, and Binh waved his claws dismissively.

Exhaling sharply, Alize glared at her wrist piece.

No flash.

No.

She waited longer than a reasonable person should.

No flash. Her eyes widened and she forgot how to breathe.

No!

She removed her wristpiece and examined the bottom. The battery indicator was over eighty percent. Signal strength: average.

No… Pops said there's a delay.

A marathon runner having the best sleep of her life wouldn't survive this long between heartbeats.

Pops. He's … dead. Alize bit her lip and shuddered. She winced on her exhale. He wouldn't see her diploma. Join the ranks of the few Humans in the Collective to earn a PhD. Take Dr. Dikaio's job. She couldn't even hold his hand when he died.

Goodbye, Pops. I love you. I'll be home for your funeral. I'm sorry I worried you. I'll make you proud.

A tear welled. Pops' response would've been something supportive, like "you do every day." Would he be proud, knowing how much she'd lost? Knowing her research and loud-mouthing led to the Unspeakable? She blinked hard. There wasn't time to mourn him.

"Leeze," Fil whispered, "we need to affix the armor to you."

Alize cleared her throat and avoided eye contact. "Fil, did my wristpiece flash while I was unconscious?"

Fil rubbed her shoulder. "I'm sorry. I'm so sorry, Leeze. I watched, too. He… he was a good man. I'm glad I knew him. Didja know he sent my sister a card when she miscarried?"

Binh flared out his neck frills. "Ain't exactly an appropriate forum for mourning, hairballs. Strap on that armor and leave. The Unspeakable's skittering around and Tricky Ricky's haircut terrorists are snooping nearby." He took a breath and his tone softened. "…Alize. When we get home, after you get treatment, we can all have a round of bloodmead. I'll listen all night to stories about your Pops with limited interruptions. We gotta go."

Rick grunted. "He's right. We need to leave."

Binh folded his arms. "You're not invited. But thank you for saying we need to leave. How about some more obvious things? Mammals smell. Earthquake's fashion sense sucks. Galsan worms are—"

Fil arose, letting her lengthening shadow pour over Binh. "Her dad was a good man. Nothing like you."

Binh frowned. "We'll all be like him if we stay here."

Though not aimed at Alize, his words twisted a knife in her heart.

Pops is dead. Cu-dan's dead. And Binh is right. The four of them would die in this Earth-forsaken place.

Her fault.

Shouldn't have told Garott about the moon. Should've stayed with Pops. Shouldn't have hired a lowlife like Binh. Worst of all, she shouldn't have mentioned anything to Fil. She was too good a friend to let Alize come alone, and here's what she had to show for it. Fil was right. This suicide mission proved the obvious.

Exhaling, Alize attempted standing and immediately fell. Burning pain from her lower body reminded her of why she had to lie down. Another burden on the others.

"Easy there…" Fil knelt again, supporting Alize's head and neck in the crook of her armored elbow.

Stars and splotches clouded Alize's vision, and Binh hissed. "How in the *nguc* can we get this on her?

It's gigantic. Put two of these together and she could build an escape pod."

Fil relayed instructions. Rick's shadow loomed and the world spun. Alize bit her lip, hoping new pain would snap her focus back.

Binh hoisted the armor over her, while Fil eased her into it. Both Alize's arms fit inside the torso, and the massive sleeves of the armor hung to the side, simultaneously limp and sturdy. She had enough room to cradle into the fetal position.

"Binh, Rick, look away. Alize, take off your jacket." A quiver snuck into her voice. "I'll remove the life support until we get this on top of you."

Alize felt a pinch in her wrist, noticing a thin wire snaking from the armor for the first time. "The life support systems won't work through your jacket. They'll likely rip it apart. You can keep your underclothes on, though. Expect some holes."

Fil tapped a few plates of the armor on Alize's side, and gentle tendrils extended from the inside of the armor until they caressed her weak body like an exploring vine. A little series of tiny stings and pinches peppered her torso and arms, immediately replaced by a fuzzy warmth.

Fil nudged Alize. "This won't fix your leg, but it'll keep you alive. I'll hit the form-fit button, but it won't shrink quite enough to fit you."

Some whirring followed, and the armor's internal tendrils pulled closer to her. The agony in her lower body melted to a dull ache. Fil helped Alize stand, and Rick knelt beside her, clawspear in hand. Without peeking through the gap between the armor and her exposed skin, Rick maneuvered the handle end of a clawspear up her side until it stopped under Alize's shoulder.

"This'll act like a crutch," he said. "Drag your bad leg."

Alize eyed him and her attention fell to his right shoulder where an arm used to be.

Maybe it was the influence of the painkillers, but between his missing arm and her destroyed leg, she noticed a disturbing symmetry. She shuddered, despite the armor's warmth.

She glanced over her covered shoulder—Fil was only partially clothed now. An undertunic pulled tight against her furry, muscled frame. It nearly hid the slight paunch Fil earned in her time guarding the museum, supplied by Alize's occasional peanut butter contraband.

"Will you be okay, Fil?"

A smile weaved up her muzzle. "Men who aren't good enough for me have seen me in less clothing than this. There's a draft, but I'll be fine as long as I have my helmet. We can't run into Earthquake goons."

Rick eyed Fil, but not in the way creepy guys at the bar did. The armor's blue light obscured his eye color.

Rick's gaze shifted to Alize. "If you haven't eaten recently, you could adjust your personal grav harness. You'll feel nauseous, but it might ease some of the pressure on your joints."

Alize nodded and thumbed the setting. Flashbacks of messing with her harness on drunken dares from Fil and the Earthquake goon losing his lunch on the meat freighter stayed her hand.

They climbed the stairs, Fil and Rick assisting her. Each step burned but inched her toward freedom. So much of the tomb remained unexplored and would have to remain that way with the Unspeakable still alive.

Maybe guns can't kill it. "Opened by violence."

They reached the step where the chitin boulder hit and bounced earlier. Glancing down, Alize could see bits of shattered chitin reflecting the beacon's light. For as deadly as the Unspeakable's mace was, the Chamayna chose to cover it in chitin.

Like the well. And the clawspears. Maybe they had a bigger reason beyond the macabre for using their own exoskeletons to defend against The Unspeakable. Maybe that was the only way to kill it. Or at least hurt or weaken it. That's why they needed the seal to be lined with chitin. The Unspeakable had a weakness. *But the fire?*

"Binh," she asked weakly, "the Chamayna chitin we keep finding, does it have a distinct smell?"

Binh lowered an eyeridge. "Your ability to focus on immediate priorities is astounding. I bet you'll survive a long time."

A dagger twisted in Alize's heart. Pops hadn't survived the stress of knowing she was in danger.

Filenada snarled.

Waving a dismissive claw at her, Binh rolled his eyes. "Whatever. Humans aren't sniffers. You know how every object has a distinct visual? That's how it is for Lo-sats."

From behind them, Fil said, "Thus, the Unspeakable freaks you out."

"It's a murder monster who doesn't appear fond of me," Binh said. "That's a bit more freaky than not having a scent."

Alize moved her arms to rub her temples, but the armor prevented her. "Focus, please. How's the chitin's scent?"

"Each one's a bit different, but musty overall."

"Does it have a chemical kind of smell?"

"Yeah. Oily, too. I'd complain about it if I didn't have you three hogging all my insult-focusing powers. I mean, I wish I could spread the love, but you fuzz-heads could really use a shower and—"

Rick sneered. "Answer her damn question."

Alize bit her cracking lip. "Did it smell anything like the liquid we stepped in? The stuff that caught fire?"

"Huh. Yeah, actually. Much more intense." The sarcasm drained from Binh's voice. "Why? Think there's a connection?"

"I'm close to figuring out the Unspeakable's weakness." Alize's painkillers slowed her speech, but not her thoughts. "I wonder if that liquid was Chamayna blood. Maybe they had flammable blood. Or urine."

"Why?" Rick asked. "Some kind of ritual?"

Alize couldn't turn her head far back enough to spot Rick. "I think the Unspeakable has a weakness to Chamayna bodies. All the traps and the sealing well were lined with their chitin. Even our clawspears. If their blood ignited the fire trap, it would fit."

"You're a genius, Leeze." Fil tapped the shoulder area of the armor, almost a half meter from where her actual shoulder sat.

Rick made an affirmative grunt. "Maybe. Or perhaps their chitin hid some kind of great power."

"Gotta submit my dissent," Binh said. "You might be making a few leaps in logic. Now cue the big best friend growling at me and getting defensive for daring to disagree with you."

"Oh, I don't get... Shut up, Binh."

"Maybe I'm missing something in the glyphs." Impossible to say. What Alize would give in that moment to confer with another archaeologist or another linguist. The idea dragged her thoughts back to Cu-dan before they spiraled down into Pops. She squeezed back a tear.

I don't know what kind of guy Cu-dan really was, but I know Pops. "Win first; cry later." Or "keep your wits in the moment; cry when it's safe. You can always cry with me, Little Leezey." Jaw stiff, she swallowed hard. *Damn, I'll have a good cry when we get off this rock. But Pops is right.* Habit drove her to check her wrist, but it was covered by Fil's armor. Wouldn't pulse, anyway. *But Pops is still helping me. Wherever you are, Pops, thanks. I love you.*

Alize averted her eyes to conceal her tears; the shift in movement let her catch a glimpse of one of the etchings on the staircase wall. Perhaps it was the third time checking this one in particular or perhaps it was the painkillers' influence, but she noticed a new, curious detail in the depicted Chamayna hunter.

A glyph etched onto its eye—too small for legibility, but it had the proper shape. Continuing toward the next, Alize stared at the new hunter's eye, noticing more small lines suggesting another glyph. It curiously resembled the glyph for "eat," but she wasn't positive.

As they climbed, Alize noticed each depicted hunter sported a miniature eye-glyph. Some were incomprehensible, but more than a few formed simple words or phrases. Even the shifting number of Chamayna in the ritual etchings had them, too.

Was this how they communicated? Could the Chamayna project a glyph onto their eye as a means of talking? Maybe they lacked vocal cords like the Blekk. The possibility sent the excited research-tingle up her spine, although that was possibly another wave of painkillers taking effect.

Reaching the top of the steps, the revisited hall-ways seemed different, now more properly illuminated. Forgotten artifacts the size of Alize's feet once obscured by the darkness poked around the corners. Larger chunks of fallen debris and shrapnel from the ceiling littered the walkway. Dimly lit ahead of them lay the spot where Earthquake confronted them. With each step, the armor's beacon light illuminated more until they came to a Human corpse. It lacked the smell Alize would've expected but turned her stomach none-theless. The armor's stabilizing medical technology must be the only factor preventing her from fainting. She'd never seen a dead body before, and this corpse, this former member of Earthquake, was sprawled out in such apparent agony. He had a massive dent in his ribcage, collapsing the homemade armor.

"Must've been the bludgeon," Binh mused.

Fil's ears pressed back against her head. "You probably smelled the dead body a few minutes ago. Why didn't you say anything?"

Binh inclined his eyeridges toward Alize. "I had hoped the body was buried under something and Pinks wouldn't have to see it. Didn't know what shape she'd be in."

"I'm not some delicate flower, Binh. I can handle this," Alize grumbled.

Binh glared at her. "Sorry for extending a mercy."

Rick stooped over the corpse. "Darius Lamont." He closed his eyes and shook his head. In a soft tone, he switched languages to Human and intoned, "Great Mystery, may he find an answer in the next life."

Fil's ears drooped. "That sounded beautiful. Is that your religion?"

Rick closed his eyes and rose slowly. "No. His. There are a few different Human religions."

"And they're all full of garbage." Binh folded his arms. "But you're in good company. The Lo-sat one is trash, too."

Alize shook her head. "Rick, I'm sorry for your loss."

Binh scowled. "Yes, I'm deeply sorry the person who pointed a gun at us was brutally killed by a walking freakshow with a mace. It's so tragic when bad people get killed."

"He wasn't a bad man." Acid surged in Rick's voice. "He had a family... father and brother. Colonists. I'll need to prepare a letter after we disembark. Don't know when I'll be able to make it out there..."

Fil scoffed. "You think that's your place to deliver bad news, still? After they mutinied?"

Rick gritted his teeth and glared at her. Speaking Arkouda again, he said, "That's still part of my job. I led them into this, and I need to tell his family. Whether I'm Earthquake or not. That's how it's done. His family deserves his story. Even if it's one you don't like."

Alize turned from their argument, scanning for more miniature glyphs, squinting and craning her neck.

Binh sniffed loud enough to snap her attention. "Earthquake. The living variety."

Alize shuddered. "You sure?"

"How many? Where?" Fil asked.

Notably, Rick remained silent.

Binh sniffed again. "Can't be sure. A group."

Fil jabbed the back of the armor, nudging Alize. She heard some whirrs behind her. Fil put a paw closer to her actual shoulder this time. "Just need my rifle, Leeze. Don't worry. The bits of clothing are safe."

Rick tapped something on his side, checked his hip, and nodded.

Wheeling his head around in different directions and taking another sniff, Binh said, "Approaching from the other set of stairs and near the entrance. This is problematic."

"Both sides?" Alize asked.

Fil snarled and cocked her rifle. "We have a third side, though."

"Which dead-ends," Rick said. "We have to confront them."

Alize's heart dropped to her stomach. "Fil, you need your armor back."

"No way." Fil winked. "You keep it. I'll duck behind you and fire from there. Mobile cover. Pretty nice."

Rick darted in front of Darius Lamont's corpse. Staring icily at Fil, he said, "I'm taking his sidearm. The thief isn't a soldier, and Oze isn't in any shape to do much past cower in that armor. You're the only one besides me who can fight. You'll get overwhelmed. Two people in the squad are sub-par shots. The rest all had decent or better marksmanship and all of them would love a killshot on an Arkouda. The Unspeakable isn't dimming the lights this time. Without me, you'll die. Simple as that. I'll stand where you can see me."

Binh sniffed again. "Just let him, Fuzzle Muzzle. There's more than one Earthquake goon approaching."

"Take the pistol," Fil huffed. "But it's gone the second the fight ends."

Alize bit her lip. "Maybe we don't have to fight?"

Footsteps echoed. Heavy and booted.

The reverberating noises came from the ascending staircase on their right and from farther down the hallway in front of them. And lowering light suggested the Unspeakable approached.

Despite the armor's medical stabilizers, Alize's heart raced.

They're going to kill or capture us. I can't have more blood on my hands.

Rick sneered and inched toward her. "Ten-trom," he said. "Fall back. You're too obvious a target."

Binh shrugged. "I already surrendered to them. They can trust me."

"There's a bounty for killing Citizens and an additional one on your head." Rick stated the fact as plainly as if he were reading from a menu. "They'll show your face to High Command, execute you, and keep the money."

Binh faced him, and the echoing footsteps neared. "Is that what they'll do or what you'll do?"

No pause or hesitation. "Them. I'd have you work off your debt. I don't approve of the outright xenophobia."

"Well then." Binh slinked toward the other three, tail curled tightly behind him.

The two paths in front of them converged, and footsteps overtook the echoes. At least six people, but maybe as many as twelve. Alize wished for a moment to have Fil's helmet, Binh's senses, or Rick's tactical ability so she wasn't so much in the dark, so ignorant of what unfolded before her. The others all at least had some sense of how to anticipate and respond, but she was left to shiver in her friend's armor, barely holding on to her useless life, while everyone risked theirs to protect her. Wasn't fair.

Fil whispered, "It'll be alright, Leeze. You're safe in that armor. The only problem is if one of these punks walks over to you and points his gun down the head opening. I won't let any of them get close. I promise. Gruntsisters."

"Gruntsisters," Alize whispered.

Binh turned to Rick and mocked Fil's tone. "You're safe with me, Lefty. Safe from hair. Safe from dairy products. You are my precious treasure."

"Shut your damn snout," Rick grumbled. "Eyes ahead."

The heavy footsteps halted. Alize slumped, head poking out enough to see at least ten Earthquake members, all panting like they'd run through a near-brush with death. All the armed and armored terrorists trained guns on the four of them.

From the center of the formation, an Earthquake member, noticeably shorter and younger than Rick, but taller and older than the others, stepped forward. After a second, Alize recognized him as the one who led the mutiny against Rick.

Rick addressed him, "Moreno. Stand down. The objective was completed."

The other man's face remained stony. "Negative. You were abducted by the popsicle and slimeball. Mission parameters changed. We're taking that creature back with us."

"You outta your damn mind?"

"Negative. We harness that monster in battle, and we're unstoppable."

"Nothing like using a weapon you can't control," Binh muttered. "Historically, that works out as a winning strategy. Every time."

Alize bit her lip and dared to stand, calling out across the hall. "Hey, if we go peacefully, will you let my friends live?"

Moreno's gaze moved to her. Garott stood beside him, and that jerk leaned over, whispering to Moreno. After a moment, Moreno furrowed his brow, and his eyes met Alize's—a chill rattled her spine. "There's no peace with the Collective. You come peacefully, and they'll die peacefully. It'll be quick and painless. Best I can do."

Rick clenched the dead man's pistol and whispered, "Oze, stand down." He continued in his normal tone, "Moreno, we can go back to the way things were. I'll forgive your mutiny. We need to evac. We have material worth a fortune. We can sell this moon's location back to the Collective through a shell company and profit. They'll waste resources fighting that thing. That's a better victory. No more deaths."

"Negative. Stand down, and drop all your weapons. Don't make me kill you, sir."

Rick sighed, and a whisper escaped. "Alejandro Moreno. You'll be remembered."

Shoom.

A plasma bullet shot from Rick's pistol, and it illuminated the hallway enough to display Moreno's expression as the bullet punctured his throat. Sheer horror blended with an acceptance. A microsecond's worth of a sense of cosmic balance. Moreno's rifle clattered to the floor, metal on stone reverberating through the hallway. The remaining Earthquake gangsters adjusted their stances.

Rick held the pistol firm. "Anyone care to join him? Or would you prefer your mutiny forgiven? He didn't take Lamont's dog tags. Moreno didn't respect any of you. Let's get off this rock and sell the artifacts we nabbed. We don't have to see that monster again."

A tremble rattled the ceiling.

Oh no.

Tremble-tremble.

Bigger chunks of the ceiling rained down.

"Nguc," Binh muttered. "This whole place is going to collapse. I'm leaving."

Tremble. The beacon light dimmed.

Rick shouted over the cacophony of falling debris. "Do you really want to be stuck in here? With that thing?"

Garott stepped over Moreno's corpse, brandishing a too-big rifle. "Screw you, Crith. You're working with the damn popsicles. You're a traitor." He fired, but Rick anticipated, dodging before Garott pulled the trigger.

Fil growled. "Duck, Leeze."

Gunfire erupted.

In the cocoon of Fil's armor, Alize stretched her neck. She saw Fil's face overhead, as her best friend opened fire. The armor's gentle whirring muffled much of the surrounding carnage, but the gunfire exchange was clear. Each shot fired briefly lit Fil's brave face. Muffled curses from Rick and hissed taunts from Binh didn't fully reach Alize's ears. A few bullets thudded against Fil's armor, which all bounced off harmlessly. But as the gunfire exchange continued, more bullets sailed near Fil's face, brightening the space overhead in a different way. Alize's blood chilled. One shot connected with Fil's helmet before ricocheting into the wall.

Above, Filenada's bravery resembled an action hero, smirking in the face of oncoming bullets.

Until one bullet ripped through her exposed neck.

"Fil, no!" Alize shouted.

Fil's purple blood spewed forth, showering Alize, covering her breather and drenching her hair.

Fil growled and huffed. Snarling, she aimed her rifle again. Sucking on air, she braced herself on her armor, resting a paw on the shoulder.

"It'll be okay, Fil," Alize whimpered.

Flashes of their past streaked through her mind: crying with Fil's sister when she lost the baby, cry-laughing at their favorite dumb movie, crying into Fil's arms after her dissertation rejection.

Fil grunted, and another gunshot connected. This one in her paw which balanced on the armor's shoulder. Fil coughed, and Alize felt another spatter of blood. Fil's grip on the armor's shoulder slipped, and her massive body slumped with it.

Her howl dissolved into a choked whimper.

Fil's lifeless body descended, collapsing over the armor meant to protect her. The dead weight pushed the armor and Alize to the stone floor.

The armor became a tomb, sealed by Fil's corpse, trapping Alize inside.

Her breather made two shrill beeps under her ear.

THIRTY-SIX

Somewhere beneath the surface of this damn moon and surrounded by damn mutineers

A BULLET PUNCTURED Kaluteros' trachea.

The mutinous xenophobic scumbags Rick once called his squad made the mistake he knew they would.

Those sons of Galsan worms stopped firing and cheered, ignoring the most important lesson of combat: win first, celebrate later. *Moreno wouldn't have let them cheer.* With the mutineer's focus shifted to the dying Arkouda woman, Rick clenched his teeth and added a name to his list.

Shoom.

"Victoria Cheng. May God have mercy on you." Plasma bullet through her eye.

The Collective soldier slumped onto the armor protecting Oze and keeled over. And then those wastes of flesh cheered again.

Their funeral.

Rick added another name on his next shot. "Thomas Beyer. Great Mystery, may he find an answer in the next life."

Between the few Kaluteros killed, Ten-trom's one lucky shot, and Rick's new kills, only four mutineers remained.

Beyer collapsed.

Rymon shouted, "Focus on Crith. We've got their asses now."

Firing another shot, the thief shouted back. "You can't handle this ass!" The shot missed wildly, unless the ceiling was his target.

Trembles.

Damn.

Rick slid to the floor behind the overturned but still functioning Collective armor, Oze inside. From his cover, Rick rose and fired.

Missed. *It was suppressive fire, anyway.*

He ducked again and pushed against the overturned armor with his shoulder. He heaved and clenched his jaw until the armor rolled, and Kaluteros' corpse slid off. *There. Now your breather has something to work with, Oze. Don't say I never gave you anything.*

Tremble-tremble.

Earthquake rounds pinged against the rolling armor. May as well have tossed pebbles at it for all the good it did.

The armor works. Rick's heart rate increased. *Even though Kaluteros is definitely dead. As long as Oze survives, I have my functioning armor. Mission success, assuming I survive.*

Ten-trom wailed from a few feet away.

"*Nguc!*"

Rick stole a glance to his right—the thief cradled his arm. Rick's confiscated pistol slipped from the Lo-sat's claw and clattered to the ground.

Shit.

Rick clenched his teeth and left cover. Three of the damn mutineers, one of him. With their eyes focused on Ten-trom, Rick had an extra second to aim.

Direct hit to the throat. "Juliette Nkozi. Great Mystery, may she find an answer in the next life." *Too many Human names on his list. Despicable. But these were all self-defense. And they forfeited quite a few luxuries after mutinying. Still horrendous.*

Ducking behind the armor, Rick hissed at Ten-trom. "Flatten yourself against the wall or scamper across the floor."

Two more shots. One nicked the armor's collar and the other whizzed past Ten-trom's bad shoulder while Oze moaned from inside the armor. Straining his ears, he heard sobbing.

Damn.

Tremble tremble—Rick's knees buckled.

Double damn.

Tremble.

Closer. Cracks snaked through the ceiling like mineral lightning bolts.

The armor's beacon light neared nothingness.

Rick left cover as another damn mutineer fired. It missed wildly, flying into the blackness above. They weren't that good of marksmen to hit a target in the dark. But the flash of light from the homemade rifle afforded Rick an opportunity to aim.

Finger on the trigger, he whispered. "Otto Goldsman..." *Atheist. Right.* "...if I can't get your ashes to your family—" The bullet connected to his breather. "—I'll give them your story." Not the painless death Rick intended.

Tremble-tremble-tremble.

"I surrender!" Rymon. Of course.

Wouldn't be here if it weren't for this little shit. A lesser man would've pretended he hadn't heard and fired. "Drop your weapon," Rick shouted back. After the rifle smacked the floor, Rick rose to his full height.

The shaking floor threatened his balance.

"Hands up, Ensign."

The thief gasped and limped, supporting his weight with his tail. "Told you..." he huffed, "...you wouldn't ... get my ass."

As light extinguished, two blood-red eyes floated above Rymon, softly illuminating the insectoid face of malice.

Clack. Clack-clack clacka-clack.

A bloodcurdling scream. Man's voice. *Rymon.*

Rick activated Lamont's pistol flashlight, for all the good it would do. It shined enough to cast a silhouette of the Unspeakable, crouched somewhat in the cramped hallway. With free hands, it clenched Rymon by the mouth and lifted him midair. Rymon's legs flailed like stubborn beached fish. The dumb kid may as well have fought a cloud or a dura-crete slab. With more horrendous clacking mandibles, the

Unspeakable threw him to the floor. Rymon landed with a grunt, which morphed to a howl as he skidded.

Rick aimed at the creature's eye—the only body part he hadn't seen a bullet bounce off yet.

Defying Rick's aim, the Unspeakable's silhouette reared back its mace and collided with the floor with enough force to knock Rick and the Lo-sat off-balance. Steadying himself, Rick felt intense sympathetic pain, watching the Unspeakable's mace connect just below Rymon's stomach.

The ensign's armor crumpled, drowning out his final screams. The Unspeakable lifted the mace, Rymon's corpse clinging to it. And with a series of hideous, wet clacks, it slammed the mace against the wall to scrape Rymon's corpse off.

It smacked the wall with too much force. In the entire exchange, Rick couldn't line a single shot. He clenched his teeth. What a rookie mistake to get caught up and distracted by the freakshow.

Crack.

From above.

Rick shined the barely functioning flashlight overhead and vaguely perceived the fissure forming in the ceiling. Buckling.

Damn.

A hysterical dying woman in front of him and a helpless limping person to his right.

"Ten-trom, we need to fall back."

"It-it shouldn't fit in this hallway. It was too small. I-I barely fit standing."

Large chunks of debris fell, some the size of an Arkouda head.

Damn stuttering nincompoop. "Snap out of it, man. Back down the stairs."

"Yeah." Ten-trom's dim silhouette nodded and about-faced, clutching his damaged arm with his tail and limping, balanced on the clawspear.

"Oze," Rick said to the teetering armor in front of him. "I hope you don't get motion sickness. We're going for a ride."

Tremble tremble. Clack clack clack-a clack.

Shit.

Rick hopped over the armor with his back open to the Unspeakable. With his strong leg, he shoved the armor forward, rolling toward the stairs. Descending into the damn thorax monster's chambers.

Deeper into Hell. But if it snuck in front of us, there's still a way out. Gotta be.

More of the ceiling buckled and descended behind him, softening the noise of the sickening clacks. Rick clenched his teeth.

Whole operation's gone to shit. Squad's dead.

A flash of Blekk tentacles. *No.* Burnt flesh. *No.* Singed scales. *No!* Heart accelerating. *No. Dammit. Not again.* Rick exhaled and pushed the armor again, allowing it to gain momentum. He passed Ten-trom, still limping.

Between hissing heaves, Ten-trom asked, "How is she?"

"Breathing." More ceiling chunks fell.

The beacon flickered to a dim glow.

The thief nodded. "What about Filenada?"

"Killed in action. Died a hero." Rick stole a glance over his shoulder and had enough light to see the path behind had collapsed entirely.

"Do you think it died?" The Lo-sat's tone remained even, as if the gunshot had taken the last of his sarcasm.

After a glance at the dim beacon, Rick exhaled. "Negative." He stole a glance at his omni-tablet. Limited functionality. He gritted his teeth. "Ten-trom, you keep going down the steps. I'll catch up. I want to see if there's any more salvage from Lamont's corpse."

Binh hissed. "Whatever. Go back and feed the monster while you're at it."

When Binh descended far enough, Rick turned and typed a message.

THIRTY-SEVEN

Earthquake internal messenger

SENDER: Crith, Rodrick
RECIPIENT: Martinez, Amanda
SUBJECT: Send reinforcements

Amanda,

Thanks for the warning. Moreno is dead.
Like the other mutineers.

Bunker is weaponized. Patrolled by a
guardian of an unknown species.

I have Oze and Ten-trom with me. Both
need immediate medical attention. They
don't seem to know Cu-dan's location.
Unless you found him, drop the hunt.

The guardian may follow if we escape. How it'll function outside is unknown. It's vicious and kills without hesitation. I need the backup crew fanned at the entrance, ready to open fire. There's some forgotten mechanism in this bunker that allows the creature to interfere with certain technology. As I send this, I'm not even sure this will get to you in time. Or at all.

The forgotten technology in here gives the beast some kind of immunity to standard fire. If the backup squad can't gun it down, we'll need to evac and attempt using the turret against it. Otherwise, save who we can and leave.

Above all else, we take Oze alive. The Arkouda guard gave Oze her armor to save her life, and it bonded to her. A mutineer killed the guard while Oze was inside.

It's still working, at least to some degree. We have Collective armor, still functioning, ready for the taking. Oze belongs to Earthquake now. Everything else is secondary. Even our lives. Make no mistake. We need this.

Rick's eyes hovered over the letters on the typing display. If he died in this damn bunker, this message would be his only chance to tell Amanda what she meant. Rick clenched his teeth. *Outside mission parameters.* After a sharp exhale, he continued.

```
<message draft resumed>

I trust you. Let's save who we can, and
then save Humanity.

-Rick

Earthquake moves the galaxy.

<end message>
```

A trembling echoed in the distance. Rick was safe behind the fallen debris, which had smashed and mangled the remnants of Lamont's unhelpful corpse. After a sigh, Rick turned around and jogged to catch Ten-trom rolling Oze down the staircase.

THIRTY-EIGHT

Lost and dizzy in an armored coffin

DESPITE THE NAUSEA, the spinning, and the general disorientation, Alize knew one thing for sure—Fil was dead. Another name for her list.

Fil's armor bonding to Alize wasn't much consolation, either. The armor would've shut down if it had registered a casualty and sent a report to the Collective Fleet. Even if it meant incarceration for Alize, the Fleet would've brought salvation. But in keeping her alive, the armor denied her survival.

In other circumstances, she would've laughed at how she was rolling in Fil's armor like an old-timey cartoon character in a barrel. She cascaded down a staircase, farther away from the tomb's exit. She pushed the clawspear, which doubled as a crutch, out the head hole, so she wasn't stuck inside the armor with a spinning death-blade, guided by the feet of a terrorist and a thief. The armor's tendrils slithering into her skin, slowly numbing her pain, braced her from the impact and dulled the urge to vomit.

We're fleeing the only exit in a collapsing moun-tain. If there's an afterlife, what kind will greet me? This place feels more and more like the Abrahamist belief in the bad afterlife. An eternity of torment. Left alone for eons, haunted by images of the people who died because of Alize's ridiculous quest—the only thing to keep her company.

The rolling stopped. Alize craned her head to see Rick staring from the armor's head hole. "No other way to move you quickly. I'm sorry." He clenched his jaw and winced. "Kaluteros died. Bravely."

Someone else saying it gave the concept a fresh sting like when she'd open a new can of the muse-um's maintenance bot degreaser and it immediately watered her eyes. Alize bit back a tear and nodded. "I know."

"How're your injuries?" Rick asked. "Can you walk?"

Alize repositioned the clawspear, and with a heave and a wince, managed to stand. Fil's armor hung lightly, touching the floor like a gown. Its cool touch soothed her lightheadedness. Her damaged leg hung limply. Thank Earth Fil adjusted the armor's gravity before handing it off.

She sighed. *Good old Fil. I didn't deserve a friend like her.* Alize shook her head. *Can't go down that hole again. Fil, Pops, Cu-dan I guess, they all need me to stay strong, wherever and whatever they are now.* After a sharp exhale, Alize met Rick's gaze.

"What happened to the rest of Earthquake?"

"They died. That includes Rymon. I'm sorry if that's upsetting."

Binh snort-coughed. "Ricky-rick, was that the pompous kid who tried to kill you and then surrendered?"

Rick nodded. "Last of the mutineers standing. The Unspeakable killed him."

"Killed?" Binh asked. "That's putting it mildly. I'll have nightmares until I die."

Alize fidgeted after noticing a holstered pistol on Rick's hip. "He was only with you because of the information I gave him. Like all the others in your squad." The deaths of however many Earthquake members didn't compare to the pain of losing Fil, but it certainly stacked on to it.

Rick shook his head and waved his hand dismissively. "Rymon would've joined Earthquake eventually. For the wrong reasons, too. Probably hoped to earn some kind of prize or recognition by joining when he did." Rick paused, evaluating her. "I know that frown. You're blaming yourself. Don't."

Alize nodded—then, noticing Binh, her eyes widened. "You're bleeding. What happened?"

"One of those lunatics shot my arm." The mirth in his voice returned. "Being cold-blooded doesn't afford me a ton of chances to feel warm on this stupid rock, so a burning plasma wound is nice and toasty." He waved his tail in front of his diagonal chest piece. "This unit keeps my blood warm. I won't freeze. But hey, I might pass out from the pain, so there's that."

Alize shook her head. "So the ceiling collapsed behind us, didn't it? That was that horrible noise, right?"

"Affirmative." Rick indicated the walls of the room and the webs on the floor. "There's either another way out of this room or we'll have to clear away the plugged doorway we made earlier." Pointing to a web pillar, he added, "These seem to cover up some support beams. This ceiling won't come down as easy."

After a sigh, Alize crutched back to the wall. "We need to find more glyphs. They hold the key to our chances of escape." And then she muttered, "I hope."

"We're boxed in on both sides," Rick said.

"Pessimistic and obvious." Binh massaged his wound with his tail. "What a helpful contribution. Glad you're the one who survived that exchange. At least Silly Filly—"

Alize shot him an icy stare. "Too soon." She brushed past him and examined the wall, searching for any glyphs or artwork.

The edge left Binh's voice. "You're right. I'm sorry, Alize. She deserved better." He cleared his throat and pointed his tail at Rick. "Lefty, I don't suppose you have any of those fun grenades hidden in a pocket?"

"Negative."

Alize found a design on the wall, but webbing obscured it beyond legibility. "Either of you have a knife?"

Binh produced a thin piece of bone. "Lucky lockpick." He displayed the serrated edges. "I'd tell you to be careful and not to break it, but it looks like I'm cutting unless you planned on holding this with your teeth. In which case, gross. You'll get it germy. But it would be impressive to accomplish that through a breather."

Rick squinted. "That's carved from a Lo-sat claw, isn't it?"

"Yeah. You have a good eye for maimed bits of my people. It's quite exceptional," Binh said. "Pinky, where do I cut? Close to this squiggle or more by that gibberish? Ooh, or what about this nonsensical pattern likely influenced by drugs?"

Alize narrowed her eyes. "The squiggle."

Rick stepped behind them. "Whose claw is that pick made from, if you don't mind me asking?"

"I do mind, and it's incredibly offensive to ask."

"You don't have to tell me, but I know enough about your culture to know it's respectful to ask."

Binh pouted. "Humans aren't as fun when they do their homework."

"Would it be any consolation if I told you I researched your people's customs and etiquette in hopes of turning some against the Collective?"

"No. Your whole cause is idiotic. Sorry, I'm not saying anything against you, just everything you stand for and believe in. Going against the Collective is like clawfighting a star. Pointless."

Rick grimaced.

"My dad," Binh said, "whittled these with his claws before his funeral. Happy?"

Rick let out a slow sigh and holstered his pistol. "I'm sorry for your loss."

Binh loosed a swath of webbing, revealing more of the glyph. "Don't be. He wasn't much of a fan of my profession, so now he helps me on jobs. It's phenomenal bonding, really."

"You don't seem like the religious type, Binh." Alize stepped closer for a better view of the glyph as he continued cutting.

"I'm not. Intelligence and whatnot. Sister is. She wanted to harvest his claws for his funeral." After registering Alize's raised eyebrows, he added, "Old Lo-sat afterlife idea. It's a realm of peace, so our claws can't come. We remove them and make something useful. Sister wanted it but was too emotional to craft something. So she got what she wanted, and I netted a sturdy tool. Now can we please take some time to gawk at these nonsensical symbols while two of us slowly bleed to death? That feels like a more efficient use of everyone's time."

Alize wedged in front of him. "This glyph says 'communicate.' And below..." Her heart stopped. "That's the same image from the ritual etchings. That's the image for the Unspeakable. Identical."

Rick stooped. "You think this is suggesting we can communicate with it somehow?"

Alize stepped back, getting a wider scope of the glyphs around the cutting area. "Maybe the thorax creature could communicate with the Unspeakable."

"Oh, so naturally, you want to end up like it?" Binh asked, another section of web falling.

"I'd rather not," Alize said. "But I—wait. Stop." Alize leaned forward, indicating the partially uncovered section. "Same thing over here. This whole wall's lined with this message. To communicate with the Unspeakable."

"When plasma bullets didn't work, I guess that should've been our second attempt. Silly us for not discussing it. Think it wants to lounge around a stim-brew cafe to discuss things? You know, somewhere quiet, slow-paced."

Rick stepped backward. "Oze, even if we can communicate with it, it's clearly hostile."

"Here's an idea for what we can say," Binh said. "How about 'Ahh! Ahh! Please don't kill me!' or, ooh, how about this, 'Take the Humans, not me!' How do you say that in this language you think you can magically speak?"

Alize cocked an eyebrow. "I'm surprised you went that route instead of mentioning the irony of speaking to what we call the Unspeakable."

Binh shrugged. "Tough decision. Only so much time in the day."

Rick shook his head. "Speaking and communicating aren't the same thing. Maybe there's another way."

Smirking, Alize nodded toward the symbols on the wall. "The glyphs. With the clawspears and Binh's tail, we can make crude versions of different glyphs. Maybe we can slow it down and explain ourselves. It thinks we're intruders."

"Where'd it get that idea?" Binh asked. "When we intruded? No, probably something else."

Alize averted her eyes. "Fine, I guess I deserved that."

Rick unholstered his pistol and his voice hardened. "Even if we can lure it here, there's no guarantee it won't kill us. We need an option for fighting it."

Scanning the rest of the room with Fil's armor beacon, Alize counted the few pillars scattered throughout the chamber. Some still had bits of Chamayna chitin attached.

Alize let out a deep exhale. "I have an idea."

Over the next few minutes, Alize instructed and the men carried out her request. They organized chitin scraps onto the floor and web pillars amid Rick's grunts and Binh's complaints. She didn't tell them they made the glyphs for "help" and "peace." Alize also didn't tell them about the separate pile she made, kicking plates around with her good foot and the claw-spear's blade in moments of turned backs. She hoped it was inconspicuous enough to them but still legible for their expected guest. Maybe the Unspeakable was beyond reasoning, but she had to try.

Beyond her own sensibilities about violence, the Unspeakable wasn't something a soldier and thief could kill. If it even could be killed. Once satisfied with their work, she inventoried the remaining chitin scraps. From her periphery, she caught Binh removing his hand from the site of his supposed injury for a moment. In the darkness, she couldn't see any wound or dried blood.

"Now comes the gross part." She winced. "We have to use the webbing to stick the remaining chitin to ourselves."

Rick cocked an eyebrow. "Excuse me?"

"The Chamayna believed the Unspeakable had some kind of aversion or weakness to their chitin. Their chitin covered all of their traps, and the one they didn't utilize their blood—"

"—according to your hair-brained theories," Binh interrupted.

"Got a better idea?" Alize narrowed her eyes at him. "If we're covered in it, we're safe."

Rick pulled out a chitin scrap the size of his head embedded in a mess of webs. "Fine. There's natural adhesive in this room. We can use this to augment our armor. I don't have any capacity to make bullets out of their chitin, but I can use that clawspear weapon you're using to damage it. Cut at its legs. Give us a chance to evac."

"Or," Alize said, "we're safe while we communicate with it, and it doesn't harm us." If Fil were here, she'd support Alize. But she wasn't.

Binh pinched the bridge of his snout. "You want us to die. You're the galaxy's worst assassin, conjuring the dumbest ways for us to die. That's the only logical reason behind your plans, Pinky. Shove a blaster bolt between my eyes, for *nguc's* sake." Grumbling, he removed a chitin plate from a tangle of webs and grimaced as he slapped it to the outside of Fil's armor. The soothing tendrils inside absorbed the shock.

Rick clenched his jaw. "Then offer a better plan, Ten-trom." He yanked another chunk of the shiny carapace and affixed it across his chest.

Binh cleared his throat. "You two engage it, and then I leave."

"No," Alize said, smiling. "We need you, Binh. With your tail, we have some freedom to make more glyphs, if you can hold it in certain positions high enough."

"That still leaves the problem of how we get it here." Rick balanced a piece of chitin under his chin, sticking it to his arm.

Alize folded her arms under the armor, not that anyone could tell. "Simple. We summon it."

"Bad assassin and clinically insane?" Binh whistled. "Not a horrible combo. You should work for Lefty's goons. They like Humans a few bugs short of *gog-wa* salad." With a sick grin, he found the most tangled piece of carapace he could and stuck it to Alize's hair. Webs tugged her curly hair as he pushed down.

Jerk.

Rick attached a plate to his leg. "And how do you propose to summon the Unspeakable?"

"The tactician didn't see the pattern of when the Unspeakable shows up?" Alize smirked.

"Hurry up, Pinkster." Binh stuck another plate to the shoulderpad where Fil had rested her paw with her last breaths. "Time's at a premium. Two of us are dying, in case you forgot."

Rick cast a wary eye at Binh.

Alize smirked. "Fire your guns, gentlemen. You can shoot at the rocks you brought down earlier, blocking off the Unspeakable's chamber."

"You think it's that close to us? That it's on the other side of the wall? That doesn't fit the pattern since your armor hasn't dimmed yet." Rick cast a glance at his hip. "Plenty of light poking through the gaps in the chitin plates. My omni-tablet has some minor functionality, too. What's your game?"

Alize inclined her head toward their guns, freshly tangling the mesh of web and hair further. "Don't you see? It appeared whenever someone fired a weapon. You start shooting, and it'll show up. I guess you didn't have the chance to read or understand the statues outside the tomb. They said 'opened by vio-lence.' When you shot at the scrapper, the seismic disturbance opened the Unspeakable's chamber. It's attracted to violence."

Binh lowered his eyeridges and placed a strip of exoskeleton near the bottom of Fil's armor. "Or seismic activity and vibrations."

"Potentially." Rick affixed a final piece of chitin to his armor. "But walking around and talking doesn't seem to attract it, and those cause vibrations. It's the best plan we have. If nothing else, we follow its path. If these chitin plates give us an edge, we might slip by." After a sigh, he added, "Come here, Ten-trom. I'll help you get this on."

With his tail, Binh stuck a bit of carapace to the back of his neck, wincing the entire time. He sighed as if the effort hurt. "Nice sentiment, Ricky-Rick-Rick, but I don't want you touching me. And not for my usual sanitary reasons: I have Softscale, and my medicine's wearing off. So now..." He wiggled his eyeridges with a fake grin. "My scales itch to the point where they feel like they're on fire. It's worse if someone else touches me. And these webs aren't exactly doing much good to soothe the pain or make me feel any more comfortable in my scales."

Alize bit her lip and wondered if he needed Fil's armor for pain management more than she did. *Unless this is an act.* She watched as Binh winced through attaching chitin shards over his suit. The web's sharp, musty stench finally infiltrated her breather, and she choked back vomit. Every eyebrow or mouth movement further enmeshed her hair with the webbing.

"Rick, shoot those fallen rocks. Even if I'm wrong, if we can clear them, we'll at least have a way to leave this room."

He unholstered his pistol.

Shoom-shoom.

The room briefly lit brighter. Both shots connected to the green-tinted rock, fracturing different pieces of debris. Alize braced herself for the tell-tale trembling, but nothing happened. Rick fired off three more rounds, with much of the same effect. Bright flash here, little debris cloud there.

Binh tsked. "Some plan. Thanks for waiting until I finished covering myself, by the way."

Alize shook her head. Surely the Unspeakable pursued. She balked at her own thought of summoning this creature after desperately fleeing. "Keep shooting. You, too, Binh."

Binh grumbled and obliged. His first round missed, hitting the side of the doorway.

"Are you that bad of a shot?" Rick glanced over his shoulder.

Binh shrugged. "Some people are handsome and smart. Some play with guns. Not my fault I'm one and you're the other."

Alize strained for any advice which might be useful. "Are you checking where you're shooting?"

Waving his tail made a tapping sound from the attached plates. "No, I wasn't. Any more condescending advice you'd like to give? How about you coach Lefty on how to give a hug or clap?"

Rick fired another round into the debris. One rock shattered and another small one rolled away. "We're not exactly getting anywhere with this exercise, Oze."

Binh adjusted his stance, creating another tapping sound as the chitin met rock. "Why don't you try belly-bumping the pile with that armor?"

Lowering his gun, Rick cocked an eyebrow. "Oze, any explosives in that armor's storage? Like where Kaluteros stored her rifle? Or any other useful munitions?"

"If there were," Alize said, "I have no idea how to access them. But I don't think so. Fil's demotion meant they removed a lot of her supplies and privileges." As far as Alize knew, the only items in the armor's storage were the remains of clothes Fil found and the bits of food from the *Takel*.

"Ah yes, the privilege of carrying explosives into a crowded area." Binh's next shot actually connected. "The luxuries of power."

Rick eyed Alize, and it sent a shudder down her spine. His cold, calculating glare made Alize feel like a figurine in a strategy game.

He'll try and take Fil's armor somehow. Or kill me. She gulped. *Maybe these painkillers are making me paranoid. He's been more helpful than Binh.*

Alize steeled herself. "Rick." *Oh, man. Oh, man. This is a mistake.* "What'll you do if we escape?"

Rick closed his eyes for a moment. "If my ships are still outside, you and Ten-trom will receive medical attention."

"But then what?" Alize asked, refusing to let any emotion show.

Returning to the debris pile, Rick fired. "That depends on various factors."

"Incredibly specific." Binh shot. "You should be a lawyer with that level of linguistic precision."

Rick fired again. "Maybe I'm more concerned with getting out of here first than what happens long-term."

Alize limped forward. "You have a plan. And you're not telling us what it is because you don't like to lie."

He glared at her, and his icy gaze rattled her spine. "You'll be on one of my ships. You'll cooperate with our agenda. Depending on your level of cooperation, you'll go home in peace."

That didn't satisfy or calm her. "But what about Binh?"

"He has a debt to Earthquake, which he'll repay."

Binh hissed, lowering his pistol.

"You'll repay your debt with work, not your life." Rick furrowed his brow and flared his nostrils. "Satisfied?"

Sweat poured down Alize's neck. "You'll force me to join Earthquake, won't you?"

Rick pivoted from the debris, gun sliding toward his holster. "We'll figure out how to transfer the armor to another Human. You'll be offered a paying position in Earthquake. The Leader has an interest in archaeology and will find a research position for you."

Images of teaching a class or leading an actual dig swirled. Only Human students meant nobody would be the awkward outsider. If she led a dig, people would listen and they'd discover things beneficial to understanding history and cultural development. But then her imaginary students and expeditionary team crystallized. The haircuts. The tattoos. The poisonous rhetoric. The hate. The terrorism.

Alize furrowed her eyebrows. "And if I refuse?"

Rick aimed his pistol at her exposed head. "You won't."

Binh slinked toward her. "He'll put you in a medically induced coma. They'll study that armor while you're wearing it."

Mouth drying, she gaped at Binh. "How'd you know?"

Binh sidestepped toward her, as if to shield her and faced the wall of debris again. "Lefty here's not too complicated. Go ahead. Tell her I'm wrong."

Without lowering his weapon, Rick nodded. "You'll have the option to join again after we let you out of medically appropriate stasis. After we've studied and discovered everything we can about the armor, you'll be free to go. I'd fast track the project, but we don't know what we don't know, so the research could take months. Or longer."

Alize tensed. She'd be their slave. Forced to be an unwilling lab insect stuck in a cocoon meant to protect her friend. Their plans would advance over Fil's dead body. And it was Alize's fault. "You're not worried I'll tell everything to the Collective?"

"They won't listen to you. Kaluteros is dead, and they'll blame you. If you want to join her, you can resist. If you don't want to join her, then you'll cooperate."

Binh sighed. "He's got you, Pinky. No way out for us."

The armor's tendrils injected a fresh wave of serotonin to combat her accelerating heart rate and steaming adrenaline. "I'm not working for Earthquake."

Rick nodded slowly, pistol aimed at Alize's head. "The alternative is death."

"So you're threatening me?" She intoned it as statement and question.

"Yes."

Tremble tremble.

The beacon dimmed like a shriveling forgotten star. *Should I be happy this worked?*

Binh cleared his throat. "How about instead of making death threats, we kill these rocks? Can you pretend they're Collective military?"

Tremble tremble. Closer this time, and more forceful.

Fil's armor steadied her vitals, which didn't alleviate her chattering teeth and cold sweat.

Tremble tremble.

The beacon's blue light shrank to a faint glow, and the flashes of light from the gunshots quieted.

From behind them, a pair of heavy footsteps echoed through the stairwell.

THIRTY-NINE

Somewhere beneath the surface of this damn moon and millimeters from walking death

RICK'S ATTENTION LEFT the debris pile. "Oze, we can worry about what happens next later. For now, we need to deal with the monster heading our way."

"Don't shoot this time. Give it a minute to read the glyphs."

The thief's voice shook. "A minute's a long time, Not-Quite-Fuschia."

A familiar tremble rattled Rick's feet and the last light blinked out.

The Unspeakable neared.

Rick clenched his pistol and advanced. He knew where the damn abomination would be. His shot would be lined up the moment the damn creature stepped inside. The only variable was whatever double-cross Oze had planned. Rick assumed Oze thought herself pretty clever, using her feet and the blade of the clawspear to organize a separate pile of chitin away from where he and Binh worked.

She must want some separate communication with this beast. He wished he knew what all these symbols said, but nobody in his crew or back at headquarters would've been able to translate any of this. Not enough bookish types.

Another tremble. Nearby clacking echoed along. *Does the clacking have a pattern?* Prehistoric Earth had a code which was all a series of clicks and beeps, but he didn't know much else about it. It didn't seem out of the realm of possibility for the Unspeakable to attempt communication. *But what would this thing say after Earth-knows-how-long here? Is it conscious?*

Tremble.

Or have free will?

Tremble-tremble.

If the mutineers had caught it, could it be tamed?

Tremble-tremble clack clack.

Rick steeled himself.

Clack-clacka clack clack.

The two gemstone eyes floated into the pitch-black room. Ready to fire, Rick noticed something new on the eyes. In the faint glow, they had something over them, which he couldn't quite figure out. Hesitating to fire, he squinted instead. The eyes bore some kind of marking over top of them, or perhaps inside of them, which he hadn't noticed before. They didn't seem like wounds, but rather, letters or characters. If these were letters, they resembled nothing in any Collective species' alphabets.

Because it's not from those languages. Shit.

Rick adjusted his gaze and recognized the markings. The damn monstrosity had glyphs in its eyes. Whether they'd been there the entire time or appeared in response to Oze's message was inconsequential.

Shuffling from behind. "Oze?"

The clacking stopped, and the hovering eyes rose.

If he hadn't been watching intently, Rick wouldn't have believed the shift in the creature's eyes. They made another glyph, or at least something with that appearance.

She actually got a response from this thing. Shit.

And then her voice cut through the silence, more confident than she had a right to be. "Binh, I need you to rotate your tail. Push the back part toward me and the tip to the right. Try and move fast."

A few clacks followed.

"What'd you do, Oze?" Rick shouted.

She sighed. "Let me concentrate."

A thwip sound followed.

Silence.

Straining his ears, he caught his own breathing and the gentle hissing respiration from Ten-trom. The Unspeakable grew motionless. "Where's Oze?"

Binh took a series of sharp sniffs. "She's not here." Another sniff. "Or she figured out how to mask her scent and stop breathing."

The Unspeakable shifted its weight, and its gaze lowered to Rick.

What the hell did she do?

Clacka-clack clack-clacka.

The sound was wet. *Damn thing's salivating.*

Only one option left. He aimed at the eye with the damn glyph on it.

In the brief flash of illumination, he registered the thief's expression. Scared shitless.

"Gimme your spear!" Rick holstered Lamont's pistol and Ten-trom poked his chest with the weapon's butt. "Distract it. Shoot its eye while I cut."

The Lo-sat sniffed again. A sinister chill replaced his usual sarcasm. "No. It can't chase both of us." Hisses and thudding footsteps on stairs followed.

The Unspeakable's clacking reclaimed Rick's attention. *Amanda has permission to leave without me. Now I have to fight this thing in the dark, one-handed, no backup.*

His only metric to fight this thing was its eyes. At least those couldn't conceal themselves. Retreating three steps, Rick adjusted his grip to the clawspear shaft and balanced it in his armpit, freeing his hand. With a deep breath, he thumbed his grav harness. Ready for an onslaught of nausea, Rick adjusted the gravity until his insides lifted. Only so much time before the blood wouldn't circulate properly. Maybe more blood would flow to his head and he could think clearer.

Doubtful. More likely to get a clot.

Clack clacka-clack clack.

Jaw clenched, forcing vomit to retreat, he adjusted his grip on the clawspear shaft. *One big hop, slash at its eyes. Maybe it uses those to eat all the light.* Only needed one hit. *Hopefully.* The Unspeakable may not be visible, but its arms and weapons would cause a whoosh of air in motion, so he could account for that.

A wave of dizziness hit him. Not good. Rick forced a sturdy exhale. He braced himself for the biggest jump of his life, aided by his lowered gravity. Wincing, he leapt forward. Mid-air, he pulled the clawspear over his head.

He would slay the beast.

Finally the hero.

But an onrush of forced air cut the smirk from his face. Then an unimaginable blunt furious pain caught him in the stomach, forcing him backward.

Rick didn't need his vision to know it was the monster's damn mace that offed him. It stank like a corpse up close. Hell, flecks of Rymon's body could still be stuck to the mace for all Rick knew. Only one thing in his life had hurt as much as this, and the phantom pains in his missing arm tingled with this impact. The Unspeakable batted Rick away with enough force to send him backward toward the bunker's wall, still covered in webs. Slamming against the wall, the bits of chitin affixed to his back shattered. He descended the wall slower than he should have. The fact he was even alive was mind-boggling.

Except... He glanced at the part of his chestplate without a chitinous covering. If he had left the standard gravity on, either impact would've killed; he'd have plummeted, not floated. He groaned as the Unspeakable's heavy footsteps shook the floor.

Rick clenched his teeth. No. Not today. Not here, and not like this. Using the clawspear as leverage, he stood, and agonized breathing told him his ribcage was at least partially shattered.

Shit.

Breathing felt like inhaling lava. Rick rotated the shaft of the clawspear and choked up on it, wielding it more like a handaxe than a two-handed spear. Killing this thing with a headshot wasn't an option.

Crippling it was, though.

Rick charged. Each step reminded him of his desire to vomit and his broken ribs pressing into his organs. Internal bleeding would kill him soon, that much was certain, but he didn't have time to whine for a medic. Another whoosh of air from the same side. Mace again. Rick dodged to the right, dared another three steps, and slashed at the imagined wrist enveloped in darkness.

Creak-thunk.

And the blade stuck.

Direct hit to a joint. Likely the wrist holding the mace.

But the cut didn't sever it. In the five seconds Rick attempted to dislodge the axe from the Unspeakable's chitin, he realized he'd never sever anything or even penetrate the exoskeleton. He'd altered his mass to make himself as light as possible and had no chance of doing any damage now. His only solace was escape or use his last weapon.

Clack-clacka-clackclackclackclack.

This thing laughing or pissed? Damn. Rick unholstered Lamont's pistol. Two shots remaining. Walking toward the stairs, Rick wheeled around for his farewell. One shot at the Unspeakable's left eye.

Shoom.

It connected and bounced off.

One more bullet left. He wouldn't miss it if he turned it on himself.

Clack-clacka-clack.

No. Humanity needs Earthquake, and Earthquake needs me. Besides, that's outside mission parameters. Rick lowered his aim toward where the thing's damn mandibles were. One last shot.

Shoom.

No reaction from the damn beast.

Every breath was agony. Rick limped toward the stairs, sped by his lightened mass—weaponless, fleeing a monster.

FORTY

Where the hell is she?

THWIP.

A burst of magenta and azure lights which she didn't have words to describe or capacity to comprehend swirled around her. Her insides churned like her grav harness malfunctioned.

Thousands of eyes drilled through her. Not Human. Not Arkouda, Lo-sat, or Blekk. Alize had never met a Makawe in person, but those eyes couldn't belong to them, either. These eyes weren't those of an unthinking animal, either. Rather, they glowed cognizant, aware, thinking, alive. Disembodied, distant yet imminent. As the impossible orchestra of color drowned her senses, she felt the invisible beings around her, judging, evaluating.

By the slant and glare implied in their movement, she caught one other aspect. Rejection.

Thwip.

Alize's cheek collided with the mint-tinted rock, softly illuminated blue. Acidic bile fumes escaped her drooling mouth, breather unable to mask the stench. Back against the floor, arms stuck inside Fil's armor, Alize couldn't prop herself to sit or stand but craned her head around.

No webs. No eyes, either. Definitely no judgment.

More importantly, no men. Alize was alone in another room. She whistled a shaky exhale. *Either that worked or I'm dead.* She glanced around, absorbing more of the room, and recognized the entrance. The armor's soft blue light filled the whole room, unobstructed by the affixed chitin plates, which lay strewn around her.

Her smile faded. *Winning shouldn't come with a body count.* She only moved a few meters, not across the whole galaxy. Alize inhaled. *But the principle is there, and the Unspeakable is part of it.* Her blood ran cold—the Chamayna purposely kept it in stasis in this tomb. Somehow, it was a component of their teleportation. She glanced at the chitin strewn about her, broken from the impact. *All these dead Chamayna— they weren't eaten by the thorax creature. They molted when they teleported.*

Footsteps from behind.

Alize's chest tightened. *Only one.*

An angry snarl followed. "Pinky? Where in the *nguc* did you go?" Binh's voice echoed.

Alize couldn't gauge how he'd react. She had no way to hide from him and no reason to. With her good leg, she pushed off against the floor, but the clawspear's shaft shattered beneath her weight. She tumbled down.

She winced. The chitin couldn't handle the teleportation; most of it must have remained in the web chamber. Alize opened her eyes to see Binh's tail, coiled near his boots.

"Some disappearing act." Rage throttled through his voice. "You left me to die with Sergeant Sociopath." He grabbed the clawspear's blade and wedged it into a pocket on his armor.

Alize gritted her teeth. He probably still had a gun, but she didn't care anymore. "You would've done the same. You already did. You sold us out to Earthquake from the get-go. And you did it again here. This is me learning from you. And you never had a gunshot wound. You faked it."

Binh sank his claws into the armor's neckline and heaved her to stand. "Well, you caught me, Pink. Unless you want to wiggle out of that tin can and get us both killed."

Alize wobbled, wincing from the burning throughout her body. Either the armor was running out of resources to dull her agony, or it was too intense for the technology to keep up.

Binh coiled his tail around the waist of the armor. He pulled her toward the tomb's entrance despite her protests. All she could manage was painful hopping. She couldn't fight back, and she was delirious from the pain and the teleportation. "Binh, if you kill me, secrets of the Chamayna die with me."

Some of the rage had left his voice, but it still carried his sarcastic bite. "The universe survived fine without them."

"Expensive secrets."

"Nice try, professor. But Earthquake has money and a way off this green rock actually and immediately. You have those things hypothetically and distantly."

They approached the very first room. The entryway where she still had her best friend, her Pops, and full control over her body. "Binh, you know Rick was the only one in their organization who would let you live. And it seems like you left him for dead, too."

"He attacked that thing after you... whatever you did. That one-armed bastard wanted my help. And I certainly didn't give it." He hiss-sighed. "I'm a survivor, Pinky."

Binh rotated her to face the door remnants. Earthquake had blown a hole in it, probably through explosives or the turret they used on their scrapper. Natural light from Dusoi and Xechas poured into the tomb. One step away from escape and full admission of her failure.

"Binh, don't you want to know how I escaped?"

He shrugged. "You found a secret passage hinted at in the little scratches on the wall. How you covered your scent and snuck away without me or Skinny Rick noticing is impressive, but I don't care all that much at this point."

"I teleported. It worked, Binh." *How does he not care?* "The Unspeakable—it's a demigod. Or a god. Or a demon ... thing. I don't know, but it has a supernatural power."

"You're insane," Binh hissed, shaking his tongue between his teeth. "The medications are making you crazy. You're in mourning, in pain, in shock, and in denial." His neck frills retracted, and a note of compassion hung low in his eyeridges. "It's time to admit you're not right in the head, Alize. Grief makes people insane. Trust me, I know. If mourning didn't make people crazy, nobody would've conjured that religion garbage in the first place, anywhere."

"Binh, what we saw down there, what I saw while teleporting... I think I saw the afterlife. Or at least the Chamayna's version of it. This tomb is a waystation. They teleport here to progress to the afterlife. They shed their chitin and die. That's why the process spat me out. Either because I'm not Chamayna or because I'm not dead. It even explains why we've only found chitin and no other remains."

After a tsk, Binh shoved her into the light, onto the moon's rocky surface.

An unfamiliar female Human voice shouted, "Don't move!"

A fanned-out squad of Humans greeted them, rifles and pistols in hand, pointed at them from all directions. Unrecognizable faces, but she knew the haircut, green-blue armor, and overall demeanor well. More Earthquake, and no Rick to mediate.

FORTY-ONE

**Retreating, bleeding, vomiting.
Chased by the devil.**

IF OZE WANTED him dead, she wouldn't have allowed him a chance to put on the chitin plate. She either didn't have the heart of a killer or couldn't strategize well enough to escape and get him killed.

Pathetic.

Rick clenched his teeth and hoisted himself up the steps. Even with the lowered personal gravity, his ascent from this tomb was a damn war. However this creature operated, Oze had some correct intuition about the chitin. The Chamayna's exoskeleton affected the Unspeakable. If nothing else, the plate broke his fall and absorbed most of the impact of the mace hit.

But that protection lay shattered, and only a few token pieces of Chamayna carapace remained attached to his armor. No ammo, no blades. If the damn monster caught him again, game over.

And yet, no trembles. No clacking. Despite the bunker's cascading darkness, his omni-tablet glowed gently at his hip. On a whim, he tried the flashlight on Lamont's pistol. The light didn't have its full luster, but it shined bright enough to illuminate the wall etchings.

From his periphery, he dared to take his eyes off the front and examine a few between strides. It seemed like some depicted hunting scenes. Others, though, resembled some kind of council meeting around a grand table. But ascending farther, the hunted animals grew less fierce-looking, and more members of the council appeared also. Some art professor could waste a career staring at these, postulating blind, unhelpful inferences about the Chamayna culture from these etchings. If they wanted to deal with the Unspeakable, that is.

Rick smirked at the idea of a platoon of Arkouda soldiers mowed down by the beast. He couldn't blame Moreno for wanting to capture and harness the monster. Maybe some part of Rick wanted the same thing. Catch it, stun it, piss it off, and launch it at the enemy. But his smirk faded, knowing Tecton would eventually want to use it in population centers. Rick reminded himself he wasn't alone and shuddered.

This thing was close.

Why it stopped pursuit was impossible to guess, but it appeared it had. He couldn't be too far from Ten-trom. Despite his probably fake injury, Lo-sats' long legs gave them an edge on foot, so the thief would outpace him before too much longer.

But where the hell was Oze? She'd disappeared somehow. The strange "thwip" noise must've been a door closing. But the way she struggled to move—opening some secret door seemed improbable. Rick clenched his teeth and hoisted himself over the last step. He now found himself in the room with the fallen ceiling, the site of his second use of explosives in the bunker.

Realizing the vibrations and disruptions his violence had caused sent a shiver up his spine. The Unspeakable wouldn't have come to the surface if it hadn't been for him. If he could've said no to the damn mission in the first place, a whole squad would still be alive. Rick heaved himself up the hole in the stone slab, swinging his legs for the proper momentum.

But those damn traitors would've found another reason and opportunity to mutiny. And he wouldn't have had Kaluteros to save him. Damn if that wasn't embarrassing. A dark part of him was glad he wouldn't have to hear about that story later. But instead, he was doomed to survivor's guilt. Again.

At least Amanda knew about the mutiny. She'd understand and keep it quiet, too. Rick crossed the threshold into the next room, wondering if he'd ever tell her the whole story. Or if he'd even get the chance.

But if he ever earned the chance to debrief, he'd be hard-pressed not to wring some necks. Moreno's betrayal stung; Rick failed somewhere in his training.

Dedication to the cause wasn't enough. Rick needed soldiers more loyal to him than to Earthquake. He clenched his pistol tighter, and the light beam wavered. If he commanded the entire organization, this wouldn't be an issue. Considering how Monsieur Tecton's poisonous rhetoric hurt their cause as much as promoted it, he wanted to wring his neck. Choke the racism out. His trigger finger itched. Maybe keeping the Lo-sat alive wasn't worth the hassle. Asshole had a bad case of flapping gums. Nobody would bat an eye if he put a bullet through the thief's skull. Just like fighting damn pirates back in the day.

Tremble.

No. No, goddammit no.

Tremble.

He loosened his grip on the pistol, turned the safety back on, and winced as he quickened his pace. *Happy thoughts.* Rick forced seagulls' cawing and crashing waves into his mind. He grimaced and conjured the aroma of synthetic hops. *Damn—a beer sounded good.* And maybe he could share the beer with Amanda. *No. Shit. Unprofessional.* He remembered her face before the mandatory Earthquake haircut and tattoo. Flawless, vivacious. Smart, independent. But the haircut and tattoo, what should have bonded them, were the only things about her he didn't like. The things he was required to enforce in his staff. *Damn.*

Rick crept past the hallway where Oze had triggered the fire trap, and the mixed stench of charred boot and burnt hair lingered like an unwelcome guest. Almost at the exit. Vomit threatened again. Rick needed to adjust his grav harness, but increasing his mass would mean slowing. *Shit. Sacrifice joints or the last bit of fluids?*

After a half-heave, Rick positioned the pistol in the crook of his elbow and thumbed his grav harness. Halfway to normal. His insides lurched, but he had enough time to slide his breather away before unleashing his vomit. *Is this the kind of violence that attracts the Unspeakable, too?* In another circumstance, he would've laughed at himself. Maybe he could laugh with Amanda about it later.

Wiping the viscous line of drool and bile from his lips and reaffixing his breather, the flashlight briefly illuminated the puddle of body acids on the floor. If the thief were in this bunker, he'd smell Rick coming from a kilometer away. Rick clenched his jaw. Not much worse than smelling him a room away per normal. He couldn't get the drop on the thief and didn't have a sniper rifle. Letting out a sigh, he accepted entertaining a violent thought about Ten-trom was pointless. This wouldn't be the day he died, and Rick wouldn't be the one to kill him if it were. Tempted to stow his pistol entirely, Rick decided he wouldn't kill again today. Enough blood had been shed, Human and Arkouda. All that mattered now was getting outside before his ships departed.

Would Amanda wait for me? It's her decision, after all. But he'd sent an order, and she knew the importance of immediate obedience. *She'll leave. Because she's a damn good manager and chief of operations.* As his knees threatened to buckle, he grimaced and trudged forward.

It was the only direction he knew. He needed to survive, so Earthquake could learn this direction, too.

Tremble tremble.

What the hell? I didn't have a single damn violent thought—

Tremble tremble. His flashlight dimmed dramatically.

Tremble-tremble-tremble. Closer this time, louder.

He wasn't too far from the entrance. Chunks of ceiling debris ruptured, raining stone around him.

Tremble tremble. A jagged section of the ceiling fell next to him, and Rick was thankful for his missing arm.

Clack-clack-clack.

Shit. Rick glanced at his omni-tablet. Dark.

The Unspeakable's thudding footsteps shook the floor, which reverberated through Rick's spine. He wheeled around, assuming the most defensive stance he could for the situation. This thing couldn't be outrun, not in his condition. A worthy opponent to die fighting, though.

FORTY-TWO

The surface of "I Told You So" moon. Final resting place of Filenada Kaluteros.

Alize leaned into Binh and hissed, "Was this your doing?"

One of the Earthquake members in the semicircle's center stepped forward. "Ah-ah," she said. "No whispering."

A youngish male squad member steadied his rifle, aimed directly at Binh. "Where's Commander Crith? Didja kill him, slimeball?"

Binh harrumphed. "Skinny Rick? Nah, I didn't kill him. He's in there." He cocked a clawed thumb over his shoulder toward the tomb. "Leave us alone and go in there and see for yourselves. Don't let the door hit you on your way in. Or cave in and collapse on top of you, but you know what I mean."

"Talk—" the first woman's eyebrows furrowed, "— or we'll kill your friend."

Alize shook her head and stiffened her gaze. "You can't kill me. Check your mission log. You need both of us alive."

The Earthquake woman scoffed. "Not you. The slimeball's friend."

Binh raised his claws defensively. "Think you have the wrong guy, sister. My only friends are the people who give me money. Also, I'm not slimy—quite dry and flaky, in fact. Ask your mom." He drew a series of rapid sniffs and his tone darkened. "I know who you have. Bring him out, already."

She barked into a comm-link on her shoulder. "Bring out the other scalie."

From behind a boulder of granite, another Earthquake goon emerged, walking backward, gun pointed at whoever followed him. After a few steps, the follower emerged.

Alize gasped. "Cu-dan."

Binh flared out his neck frills and tapped the ground. "Well *nguc. Nguc* indeed. They roughed you up good."

Abrasions littered Cu-dan's body, and a crack webbed across his breather. He lowered his eyeridges as they brought him closer to Alize and Binh.

The woman apparently in charge snarled at Binh. "Tell us where our boss is, or we put a bullet through his leathery head."

Binh hissed. "You should've killed him. That would've been better than torture. Now I told you, Little Miss Haircut, your one-armed wonder is back in that cave. You want him? Go get him."

Another woman brandishing a pistol spoke. "And what about the rest of our squad?"

Alize kept her eyes on Binh. He was about to be honest, or say something else to upset them. She stepped in front of him before he had a chance. "There's a security system in the tomb. It's deadly. Killed almost everyone, including our teammate. Caught us, but Rick stayed behind to fight and let us escape."

"Satisfied, hairballs? Lefty also promised us medical attention and a hot meal. All meat."

Cu-dan spoke. Hearing how broken he was brought new remorse rushing back. "And thus we can see there's no need for violence. So if you'll unhand me—"

"Shut up!" The man who brought Cu-dan out elbowed him in the stomach.

"Hey!" Alize shouted. "Leave him alone. He wanted a better life. Away from a bunch of pirates."

Cu-dan collected himself from the impact. He glanced up at Alize, voice steadying. "The pirates weren't too bothersome, actually." Standing to his full height, he withdrew an omni-tablet and typed something. "In fact, they remain good employers."

Binh flared his neck frills. "What'd you do, you bastard?"

Alize shook her head at Binh. *What's he upset about?* Gazing skyward, a massive spaceship blinked out of cloaking technology. She'd seen it before.

The Drowned Star pirates.

Cu-dan stepped away from his captor. "Phenomenal employers. They retrieve me when I'm in a scuffle."

One of the Earthquake members growled. "Slimeball's working with the damn squids."

Another whined. "This punk told them we're here."

Two more shouted for blood.

"Tut-tut-tut," Cu-dan said, waving a finger. "Kill me, and Sjorover will be most upset. The Drowned Star have something of a score to settle with these two." He pointed at Alize and Binh. "And your commander owes them a ship. That was an act of—"

Shoom.

Alize's eyes bulged as Cu-dan collapsed to the green-tinted rocky ground, blue-tinted plasma smoke rising from the seared hole in the back of his head. The Earthquake woman had shot him.

They would kill her just the same.

Above, the Drowned Star flagship descended, puncturing the stratosphere, dominating the view of Dusoi above.

Alize bit her lip. Binh was right about Cu-dan—he'd sold them out from the beginning. She cursed herself for feeling any guilt over him. A hot tear escaped her eye. She'd be the next to die, accomplishing nothing with her stupid life except unwillingly aiding terrorists and bringing her best friend to her death.

From below and behind, the lunar surface trembled. Faint at first, but it intensified within seconds.

Alize tore her gaze from Cu-dan's collapsed body, his exposed scales matching the green rocks.

Wincing, she hopped to reposition her body, the armor's internal tendrils absorbing the physical shock but unable to stymie the emotional trauma of what unfolded before her eyes. Just another dead body as a result of her meddling. To think she could have amounted to anything except a failure.

Dr. Dikaio was right about her.

Her professors were right about her.

Tremble tremble.

And Pops was wrong about her.

Fil's armor didn't quell the sweat pouring from Alize's body.

Tremble.

"Nguc."

Tremble tremble.

A few of the Earthquake gangsters stumbled, glancing around like a swarm of invisible insects approached. They cursed and shouted over each other, and the shaking increased.

Binh hissed. "These *ke-noks* will get us all killed."

Alize steeled herself. "We need to get out of the way if it's coming through the opening."

"Smart." Binh called out to the Earthquake goons. "Hey, I'm moving my pink-haired associate a few feet to the right. We think that's Ricky-Rick-Rick coming up to the surface. We want you to have a clear view of him. We'll stay where you can shoot."

Tremble tremble. Closer, more intense.

With Binh's assistance, Alize hopped away from the entrance. *Will the Unspeakable act differently outside the tomb? Can it leave the tomb?* "Binh, when the Unspeakable emerges, we have to escape as fast as possible."

"Look at you with the good ideas." The trembling increased, so loud and intense Binh had to wrap his tail around her and brace himself against the sheer rock wall for balance.

"You'll have to roll me. Maybe we can still get on their ship. Or the Drowned Star pirates will take us. We have to get off this moon. Even if it means as prisoners."

Over Binh's shoulder, the Unspeakable's staff protruded from the tomb's opening. What it lacked in the mace's cold ferocity, it made up for in its elegant otherworldliness. A piece of Alize wished she could dedicate the rest of her career to studying the staff by itself, but dour realization overshadowed her initial excitement. The Unspeakable had reached the surface, not Rick. She'd left him to die, and so had Binh.

Rick had pointed a gun at Alize's head, so her remorse dried up.

Clack-clack-clack. Even without any walls to echo, the dread sound carried over.

Another tremble, and the mace protruded from the tomb. Seeing the bludgeon in full light sparked the same sense of awe and horror as seeing massive fossilized predators in the natural history wing of the museum. But where the fossilized animals developed natural weaponry as a result of evolution, the Unspeakable's weapons were malice given form.

Tremble clack-clacka-clack-clack.

A head emerged, sporting protrusions which blurred the line of antennae and horns, compound eyes and mandibles on display. Alize squinted at the eyes. Whatever glyphs lay on them at the moment were unreadable—probably for the best. Communicating with it before was a nightmare, and she shuddered to think what message the Unspeakable would have for Earthquake. The unobstructed light allowed her to see the intricacies of the other horns atop its head, and a carapace more purple than she'd expected. The deep yet vibrant color reminded her of the impossible purple she'd seen while teleporting.

Another series of trembles and clacks followed as it fully emerged from the tomb, rising to its full height. The Unspeakable flexed its six arms, which stretched the tattered bandages covering its torso and hips.

Alize gasped at the mesmerizing display of horror, and Binh wheeled around to gawk.

"How in the *nguc* did that thing fit inside some of those dinky hallways? Half the ceilings weren't at my head level."

Realization dawned in Alize. "It can grow and shrink, depending on its needs. Look—"

"Earthquake! Light it up! Don't worry about the pirates for now."

Shoom-shoom-shoom-shoom.

Plasma bullets flew from the fanned-out members of Earthquake, all of the shots sailing above Alize and Binh.

The attack had failed. The rounds of plasma may as well have been pebbles against a mountain. A series of wet snaps followed as the Unspeakable's carapace elongated. It grew until its appendages dwarfed its mace and staff.

"It doesn't make sense," Binh said. "It shouldn't be able to support its own weight. That-that's not how exoskeletons work."

"It's not an animal, Binh. It's something ... grander. We need to accept that. Now roll me out of here while these creeps are distracted. This is our only chance."

FORTY-THREE

Under the devil's shadow, ready to die.

ALL THE SCANT surrounding light dissipated. Rick planted his feet and clenched his jaw.

I'm ready for you. Only one of us leaves, and I'll make it as difficult for you as I possibly can.

The Unspeakable's glowing compound eyes sailed forward amid the damn floor trembling and its mandibles clacking, wet with hunger. The eyes lacked iris and pupil, only showing unintelligible symbols. He had no indication of where this thing gazed specifically. Or maybe it was blind and those glowing orbs weren't eyes at all. Maybe he did face some kind of dark god, and he'd picked a lovely time for a crisis of faith.

But as the Unspeakable approached and the remaining seconds of Rick's life stretched to eons, he couldn't shake the feeling of indifference and insignificance from the monster. Rick had no empirical way of knowing, but it seemed as if the dread creature's gaze, perception, whatever it had—wasn't affixed on him. Even though this thing had certainly registered Rick's presence, no intention came with it.

As the trembling threatened Rick's balance further, the air pressure altered as each colossal leg bore down. The darkness was so complete, Rick couldn't even see the silhouette or outline of the damn abomination's mace or staff. At least those weapons would swing with a momentary delay and push the air around to give Rick a chance at dodging. The trembling floor gave way to thudding foot claws. It hadn't slowed, and its head hadn't changed its angle. A whoosh over his head. But this wasn't left-right like when it had attacked him before.

This movement of air was parabolic.

Another thud and tremble followed. The vibration and direction of sound told Rick everything he had suspected. The Unspeakable wasn't chasing him but going the same direction for its own purpose, and Rick had been a small hurdle. If it even registered him at all. Rick had delivered this thing the fight of his life, and he wasn't even a microfly to swat away. The apathy weighed heavier than the earlier malice and hatred.

Rick about-faced toward the exit and the rumblings of the Unspeakable's gait. *I'll show you what happens when you ignore—*

As Rick's pride surged, he exhaled and unclenched his fist and jaw. *Couldn't win. At my best, I merely slowed it down. I don't even know if I pissed it off. Discretion's the better part of valor. But if this thing's going out into the open...* Rick shuddered. With a fresh dose of adrenaline, he hobbled through darkness toward the exit and toward the Unspeakable.

Is this all some kind of trap? Waiting to ambush me in some other room? If divine or supernatural, standard logic couldn't be applied to the creature. Perhaps it killed in certain areas of the bunker for its own cryptic reasons.

Or maybe it craved freedom—where his backup squad and Amanda waited for him.

Rick gritted his teeth and limped forward. He'd lost some blood, but pain rattled in too many places for him to be sure where from.

A tinge of light filtered toward him. It wasn't the flashlight of Lamont's pistol suddenly working, since he'd turned it off when he faced the Unspeakable. He unholstered the weapon.

And the flashlight worked. Normally.

Rick glanced at the omni-tablet on his hip. Full brightness.

His heart raced, demanding he either keep going or collapse into a coma. His iron will forced his nausea and exhaustion to the side. *This damn thing isn't taking another life today. But I might have to.*

The natural light from outside the bunker intensified with each step. It grew in clarity and luminosity. But the Unspeakable left no signs, and it didn't linger anywhere he passed.

The abomination escaped.

As Rick neared the exit, the light eclipsed. He stole one final peek before something swallowed the light. The Unspeakable was outside and had somehow grown after leaving. Rick was trapped in the bunker again; the Unspeakable's expanding leg blocked the exit.

Plasma bullets shrieked outside, though muffled by the Unspeakable's tree trunk, which was a leg one minute ago. Rick inched toward the carapace until close enough to reach out and touch it. Daring his luck, he removed his glove with his teeth and laid his hand on the thing's leg. It should've been smooth, like insects he'd seen on Earth, but it scratched roughly like exposed rock. The maroon chitin chilled his fingers more than any creature had a right to. *Because it's not alive. Never was. Shit. Oze was right.*

He rushed to replace the glove, lest the chitin freeze his hand or draw blood with its razor-jagged surface. He unholstered his omni-tablet and pinged Amanda: "Evac who you can. Get the hell off this moon."

As he assessed his next action, a ping returned.

Amanda. *So maybe there is a God or a Great Mystery or the damn dreaming Goddess of the Arkouda.* Her response:

[Amanda: No can do, sir. What're your coordinates?]

[Rick: Dead in a few hours. Or sooner. Call for evac. Full retreat.]

A muffled boom rocked outside, shaking the bunker. *And pissing off the Unspeakable.* It lurched forward.

Another ping.

[Amanda: We're not military. You can't order me around. I'm in charge. If you're stuck in the tomb, there's an opening now.]

The turret. Clanks advertised that she powered the turret and shot the damn thing in the chest or head or somewhere. Ambient light from the planet and starlight poured into the bunker, and Rick's first sight as his vision adjusted was the massive Unspeakable lumbering away from the tomb. Its colossal maroon appendages and overall demeanor seemed even more hostile than before. *The mace and staff grew, also.*

It could bat a ship out of the atmosphere if it continued growing. Rick clenched a fist and limped outside. Ahead of him, his backup squad hauled ass away from the Unspeakable. And above, menacingly hovering in the stratosphere, floated the *Blodsed*, pirate lord Sjorover's personal one-ship armada. *Deal's off, I guess. Double-shit.*

As Rick summoned his last reserves of energy to the surface, straining all his muscles to increase his limping speed, he glanced in all directions, desperate to find any signs of the thief or Oze. They gave him the slip. *If Ten-trom could shut his trap, he'd make a useful asset.*

At this point, only leaving mattered. Another party with better armaments and ammunition could deal with the Unspeakable. Maybe the Collective could waste resources fighting this abomination, pulling defense forces from spots his new squad could hit. The prospect of leaving without the two surviving targets wasn't ideal, but the Drowned Star's appearance had forced his hand. And he'd be damned if he let this monster take any more Human lives today.

Same as ever: only one forward progress mattered.

A familiar hiss cut through the cacophony, a little bit on his right, a few meters away. "*Nguc.*" Rick shifted his direction toward the thief, rolling Oze across the lunar surface like they'd rolled her on the stairs before.

"Gotcha." Rick sent another ping to Amanda:

[Rick: Ten-trom and Oze are on the surface. Don't leave without them.]

He hated all these shifting orders, but if he could come away with one thing from this damn moon, it would be that armor.

FORTY-FOUR

**The surface of "I Told You So" moon. Final
resting place of Filenada Kaluteros.**

ROLLING IN THE cradle of Fil's armor again, Alize
pulled her head into her shoulders. It insulated her
somewhat from the noise, and she didn't have much
choice since Binh wasn't too careful about avoiding
jagged rocks.

Screams from scared Humans ricocheted between
the moon's jutting rock formations. Each of the
Unspeakable's steps outside shook the armor more
than its shock absorbers could handle. Her nausea
overpowered the gentle tendrils in the armor, and
she retched inside her breather. She fidgeted with
her arms to detach it, but another violent tremor
shocked her hands away. The acidic stench invited
more heaves, along with the wet sensation of her bile
puddling around her lips and chin inside.

She couldn't stop herself from puking again. Whatever the armor operations sustained her life might prevent choking and drowning on her own bodily fluids. Another retch. Her mouth was submerged now, and each revolution in the rolling armor brought new drops of acid into her nostrils.

Clenching her teeth and wincing, she forced her arms back to her face and detached the breather, letting the vomit spill onto her jacket. What should've been a sweet inrush of fresh air was instead another expulsion of vomit. She gagged, taking in thin air on the inhale. But it wasn't enough. Each breath brought her closer to asphyxiation.

Nonono, come on... no

The gunshots and shouts outside dulled, along with Binh's hissing commentary. *I'm sorry, Pops.*

With each heavy blink, her blurry vision darkened around the edges.

Fil... this was all my fault...

The dizzy spinning stopped. A gloved claw on her face, blanching her mouth and nose.

Slap slap.

A hiss. "Alize!"

A rumble from the Unspeakable rocked her body to finality.

Darkness.

———

Adrenaline jolted Alize from the haze. Her lungs expanded. Eyes snapping open, she discovered her head sticking out. Binh knelt before her. He somehow brought the armor upright while she was unconscious. They sat under the cover of a rocky outcropping, a miniature cave. Light from the gas giant Dusoi poured in. The inside of her breather must've been wiped clean, but the sour old vomit stench lingered.

"You with me now?" Binh's eyeridges lowered, his gaze more sincere than she'd seen them before. "I thought you bit it. You've lost a lot of fluid."

Alize peered over his shoulder.

In the distance, the Unspeakable stood like a colossus, having grown to the size of a space elevator. The illegal turret on Earthquake's civilian ship boomed. Several Earthquake squad members shot at it from the ground, and fast-floating Blekk buzzed around its midsection, shooting from various angles to no effect. Swimming through the thin air and low gravity, they seemed much more graceful than the two she'd seen on the scrapper—practically a lifetime ago.

Alize fought the urge to lick her lips, unwilling for a fresh waft of vomit stench. She winced. "How long was I out?"

"Long enough to haul your hairy ass in here. That Arkouda armor was meant to keep something much bigger than you on life support, but we're probably stretching it." Bihn's shoulders slumped. "Bad news."

Alize squinted at him and cocked her head. "I don't see how much worse things could get."

Binh tapped his tail on the rocky ground in three quick beats and stood, hoisting Alize to stand with him. He averted his eyes, staring at the ground. "I, uh, asked for help."

"Meaning?"

From the front of their miniature cave, a gruff voice cut through, and Rick Crith stepped into view from the cave entrance. "He's trying to say he surrendered. You're coming with us." Rick's gait was haggard and labored. Eyes steel, heart stone. "It's over, Oze."

Another person stepped from the other side of the cave entrance. She was much shorter than Rick, near Alize's height. She had dark curly hair cut to the Earthquake fashion and a softer presence than the other gun-toting Earthquake members. She pulled out a hover-stretcher.

Rick moved to Alize's side and, with Binh, lifted her onto the hover-stretcher.

The curly-haired woman spoke in an accent more like Alize's than Rick's. "The ship's ready, Rick. Our last distraction will go on your mark."

Alize's vision blurred again, this time from tears. Delivered by scum into the hands of scummier scum, without Fil or Pops to comfort her. Alize exhaled; she was done needing the comfort of others. It was time to come up with a plan. There was no way she would let them win.

FORTY-FIVE

Lunar surface, unnamed moon, Dusoi orbit, Xechas system, Collective fringe

ALLISON PIERRE, GEORGE Arrow, Thomas Yezika, Sasha Round.

Rick updated his list. He didn't pull the trigger on any of them, but ordering them to stay and fight the Unspeakable was a death sentence. He'd compensate their families. Apologize in person if he could. Their names would be remembered well in the annals of Earthquake, unlike those other damn mutineers.

Beside him, Amanda gripped the hover-stretcher, pushing it toward the *Dizhen*. As long as Amanda's staffers hadn't raised a damn mutiny against her, the operation would be a success. Rick flitted his gaze between Ten-trom and the doomed battle against the Unspeakable in the distance.

Foolhardy Drowned Star pirates, for all their nimble fluidity in the low-gravity air, shot and occasionally dodged the chitinous titan. They must have been buying time for the *Blodsed* to charge its main cannons, which would obliterate much of the lunar surface. Pirate king Sjorover was smart enough to know they wouldn't get their intended revenge on Earthquake. Not with the Unspeakable swinging the dread mace before them. Or maybe this was a sign they'd accepted the alliance and arrived to help. Impossible to say. Cu-dan created more trouble than he was worth, anyway.

Rick couldn't be sure if he'd killed him in the initial strike on the targets' scrapper ship, if one of his backup squad found and killed him, or if he eluded them entirely. And for all Rick knew, the Unspeakable could've stomped on the poor bastard. He was at a loss if he should add the Lo-sat to his list of names. Cu-dan would be the first.

Followed closely by the thief, if the sarcastic asshole tried anything again.

The moon's surface rocked with each of the Unspeakable's strides. With its four free hands, it brutally swatted the Drowned Star Blekk like microflies. Amid the attacks, it slammed the mace down on another Earthquake squad member, reverberating the surface like a tectonic shift. For all the plasma bullets bombarding the damn thing, it never flinched or reacted.

Rapid growth as well as how it moved with agility defied all known science about biology. The thought threatened a shudder, but Rick maintained a stiff lip.

Beneath Amanda, Oze lay on the hover-stretcher, gazing at stars lightyears away. She bore the expression of a defeated person, one who had finally surrendered on more than the tactical level. He'd only seen the expression a few times before, and it never ended pretty.

But when Oze healed and Earthquake pried the armor off, she might be in better spirits. Maybe she'd join willingly. Earth knows Tecton would love a personal archaeologist to fill his head with tales of mystical power from the past. Oze would forgive Rick for what had happened today, and she'd fully understand his drastic measures.

And if she didn't, Rick had a guaranteed way to keep her mouth closed about Earthquake's findings. He'd add her name to his list, albeit reluctantly. Civilians usually didn't deserve a bullet between the eyes, but if Oze didn't join, Rick wouldn't have much choice. She was smart enough to understand, but not enough to obey.

Damn. Rick clenched his jaw, measuring the distance to the *Dizhen*. Only a few more meters. Maybe half a hiveball field away.

A scream from the battle carried over. *Damn.* Sahsa Round. Only three—

A thud scarred the surface. The Unspeakable dislodged its mace from the ground. Rick couldn't identify the attached body, but he now only had two backup troops alive. Not enough to keep guard over both Oze and Ten-trom at all times. Damn.

The Unspeakable rose, clacking mandibles so loudly as to garner a reaction from Oze. She lazily turned her head. At the gruesome sight, she half-sighed, half-shuddered before closing her eyes and turning her head back to center.

Amanda shuddered and peered over her shoulder to Rick. "Did you fight ... that?"

"A bit smaller earlier, but yeah." Rick's gaze remained on Ten-trom. He wanted to increase the pace but couldn't risk Oze falling off.

The thief had surrendered in his own way, making him potentially useful. Hiring thieves wasn't the most ethically pristine method Rick could use to further Earthquake's agenda, but if Ten-trom really was only in it for himself and the money, his allegiance and silence could be bought. He certainly had no love for the Collective. Having an alien in his crew might alleviate some of the xenophobia, too.

Without averting his gaze, Rick spoke. "Amanda, how're our stores of meat aboard the *Dizhen*?"

She balked. "Um, enough? It's hard to know without the full casualty report." Her voice sank. "But we'll have more than we need since so many ... died."

"And our medical supplies? Where's the general application kit? The kind that would work on non-Humans?"

Amanda angled the hover-stretcher around a rock. "Well, you insisted we keep some 'just in case,' so nobody wanted to touch it."

Rick faced the thief. "Ten-trom. Rations and treatment aboard my ship wait for you. You'll be treated well." A lesser man would've added "despite you leaving me for dead," but he couldn't let Amanda know about the thief's failed betrayal in the bunker.

Without meeting Rick's eyes, the Lo-sat hissed. "Feed and treat me before you kill me? Hoping to ease your conscience?" The sarcasm, the mischief, the snark, all evaporated. Only grim acceptance hung in his tone.

Thuds reverberated the surface. The Unspeakable was on the move.

Rick kept his expression cool, despite the shaking ground vibrating his voice. "You owe us. I could leave you on this rock with the monster."

Ten-trom sighed. "Join or die. I bet you're a blast at office parties."

Rick cast a glance at Oze. If it weren't for her blinking, she would've appeared dead.

The *Dizhen's* loading ramp stretched before them. Another death howl rang out. *George Arrow. Damn.*

Amanda stepped onto the ramp with the hover-stretcher.

Rick motioned for the Lo-sat to follow. "I wouldn't use those bleak terms, but if that's what it takes for you to come peacefully, so be it."

"Do you hear yourself sometimes, Lefty? If we're going to work together, you need to get the stick out of your ass."

Peering over her shoulder, Amanda said, "Careful, he's been known to dislodge the aforementioned stick and beat people for misbehaving." Amanda followed with a cocked eyebrow to Rick.

If death weren't hovering around him, he would've smiled.

Up the ramp and into the decontamination in the *Dizhen's* airlock, Ten-trom hissed. "Look, I have a medical condition. The decontam will put up an alert. It's not contagious."

Rick nodded and glanced at Amanda. "Softscale, sometimes called Greyscale. He can't shed."

The decontam arms lowered, and Binh tsked. "Any other private medical information you care to share? Hey, Curls, check this out, after visiting a woman of ill repute one night, I grew some persistent warts on—"

"That's enough," Rick said.

Amanda grimaced.

As Binh promised, the decontamination ended with a dull amber warning, confirming Binh's non-transferrable illness.

Rick held up his hand, halting anyone from exiting the airlock. "I want to check the scans. If we brought some foreign bacteria aboard, I want to know, even if the spray killed it."

"Nothing," Amanda said. "Not a single living organism down there besides the sentients and that... that... I don't even know what to call it."

Ten-trom crossed the threshold out of the airlock. "We've had that same problem. Ricky here wanted to call it Fluffy, but I preferred Mr. Huggles. But Coma Girl here called me gender-reductionist for assuming maleness. It was a whole thing."

Rick arched an eyebrow. "You named it. You couldn't in the bunker, but now you can." He closed his eyes and inhaled deeply. "Amanda, prepare for immediate takeoff. Get me on the line with the *Blodsed*. They need to attack the surface." Rick glared at Ten-trom. "Hand over your pistol and stay with Oze.

Anyone in this tub would be happy to kill you. I'm the reason you're alive now, copy?"

The thief made a mocking military salute and complied. They exited the airlock, and Amanda repeated Rick's order; Rick stormed toward the communications officer.

The first staffer Rick passed in the halls was the cook. Rick grabbed him by the collar. "Kowalski, there's a Lo-sat with a woman on a stretcher outside the airlock. I need you to watch them until I relieve you of duty."

The aging man stammered and dodged Rick's glare.

"I'll help you make dinner tonight," Rick said. "Thank you."

Hurrying past, adrenaline easing the pain in his joints, Rick arrived at the communications array. "Johnson, get me in contact with Lord Sjorover," Rick shouted for the navigator. "Harada, engage liftoff. We're evacuating now."

The remaining crew of the *Dizhen* stared at Rick, jaws agape. They all knew about the damn mutiny. But they neither joined nor warned Rick. Neutral. Smart. "Moreno is dead. He tried to kill me and failed. We leave now."

Officer Johnson cleared her throat. "Sir? I have Tispe from the *Blodsed* on the line. He says he's the translator for Lord Sa-so—"

"Sjorover," Rick said. "Good." He scanned the command center until he found the gunnery chief's eyes. "Simas. Don't fire at the creature. We don't need the attention." Rick leaned over Johnson and spoke into the communicator. "This is Rick Crith of the *Dizhen*."

On the other end of the screen, an unblinking Blekk face greeted him. Only a gentle floating suggested the image wasn't static. Tispe raised a few tentacles in front of his face and rapidly contorted them while a rough translation followed onscreen.

His tentacles moved in an elegant fashion, signing an entire sentence at once. "Reck. Theren's monster on the surface. Lord Sjorover asken ef that theng kelled old translattor. Dearen frenden he was to Lord Sjorover."

"Unsure," Rick replied, cursing the beta version of the software. "Assume yes."

A brief pause followed and Tispe signed again. "Too bad. We liked old translattor. Good guy. What we doeng about thess monster below. Gunshots not work. Those pirates down lookeng for old translattor. We telleng them to scatter."

Rick nodded. "Small weapons don't work."

Another pause. "You try begger weapons? Cannon on yer shep? We descendeng to atmosphere for closer strike."

Rick clenched his teeth. "Negative. Our turret wasn't powerful enough. If your cannon's ready, fire full power at the creature as close as possible."

The *Dizhen* rose from the surface.

"You no want catcheng monster? You no useng agennst Collecteve?"

Rick smirked. "If you think you can hold it, the creature is yours. Lord Sjorover can keep it as a pet for all I care. We're evacuating."

"We escapeng our pirates below ferst."

The *Dizhen* lurched like a pouncing hyena. Its transitional thrusters engaged. "You won't have enough time. If you're going to attack, attack now."

"Lord Sjorover sayeng you no help. Negotiateng over."

The screen clicked off. Rick stomped toward the viewscreen.

Outside, the Unspeakable swung its mace, likely connecting with another Blekk pirate. Above the surface, the massive *Blodsed* loomed over the Unspeakable, its lower cannons glowing. Rick made a cursory check to see the distance between the *Dizhen* and the surface. They'd be safe from any impact.

Faster than sound, the glowing cannons below the *Blodsed* fired a concentrated plasma blast at the Unspeakable. A direct hit followed by a massive explosion of light and dust which knocked the *Dizhen* off-balance.

The navigator whined. "Sorry, sir. We need another moment to recalibrate."

"That's all you have," Rick responded.

Onscreen, the dust and plasma cloud settled, and the Unspeakable stood, unaffected. But as the image onscreen clarified, the Unspeakable grew again.

And expanded.

More.

Rising, it rivaled the moon's sharp mountains. The *Blodsed's* guns glowed again, signifying the Drowned Star pirate king had learned nothing.

After another blast, pushing the *Dizhen* off-center again, Rick braced himself. When the cloud from the explosion dissipated, the *Blodsed* was still in view, but pointed downward.

Rick's jaw dropped. The Unspeakable had grown enough to grab the destroyer from orbit, yanking like a fruit picker. It raised its mace, now rivaling the ship itself in size.

Rick exhaled and turned to the navigator. "We need to leave. Now."

The Unspeakable slammed its mace onto the *Blodsed*, defying all gravity, biology, and reason, sending the huge ship hurtling toward the lunar surface. The ship careened into the ground, creating a grand fissuring canyon in the surface, fracturing mountains in its wake. Meanwhile, the Unspeakable rotated, facing the *Dizhen*, the entire ship now smaller than one of its eyes.

Rick steadied himself. "Get us the hell out of here."

The Unspeakable advanced, blocking out light from the gas giant above.

"Now!"

"Ready!"

The *Dizhen* left orbit, bound for the stars. A wave of applause and hoots erupted.

Rick allowed the crew their moment. When the cheers slowed, he waved his hand. "Johnson. In my last communique with Tispe, he rattled off the names of other Drowned Star pirate captains. Sjorover's rivals. Prepare a message to go to each of them from me. Tell them I killed Sjorover and have an offer for them."

Without waiting for confirmation, Rick turned toward the airlock and marched toward the thief and Oze.

FORTY-SIX

Aboard Earthquake's ship. Orbit of 'I Told You So.' Ready to die.

ALIZE STARED AT the overhead conical lights inside Earthquake's ship.

Rick had won.

Her discoveries would never get published, and her name would be forgotten. Alize would die slowly and painfully while Earthquake's engineers deciphered the Collective's technology grafted to her body. All for nothing. So many people lay dead because of her actions.

She remembered the promise to herself. Maybe she'd never get published, but she wouldn't let these scumbags win.

The ship rocked a few times, a gentle reminder of the carnage outside. Probably from firing at the Unspeakable. Ridiculous. They couldn't kill an angry god.

A scoff from Binh broke her trance. "Big explosion outside. I bet those Blekk fired their main cannons."

"Not us?"

"Ah, the depressed coma girl speaks? And here I thought you'd resigned. Nah, the ship would've rocked the other way if we'd done the firing. Good for you to say 'us.'" He hissed with slumping shoulders. "Guess you've accepted that we're stuck with Earthquake."

"Where are we going?"

Binh shrugged. "Probably a hospital for you. A real one or whatever Earthquake calls a real one. You heard Lefty and Curly say they've got basic stuff for me, but you need more intensive attention. At least you're back in Human gravity, right? Maybe that'll help."

Alize hadn't noticed but paused to examine and observe the pressure around her. With a shaky hand inside the armor, she thumbed her grav harness, which must've clicked off on its own. "This is natural Human gravity?"

"Well, yeah, Professor. This is an Earthquake ship built for their own purposes. The meat smugglers had to follow Collective regulations to keep up their front, but Ricky Rickster doesn't seem to share that concern here, so the default artificial gravity is Human normal."

Alize noticed her insides had settled, no longer floating higher than they ought to. "Binh, will they let me go?"

"Tricky Ricky is more honest than either of us, and that's what he said. Wouldn't cross him, though. We watched him kill his own troops."

A familiar voice cut off Alize's response. "Yeah, you did."

A vibration rattled the hover-stretcher. Alize tilted her head backward to see Rick Crith of Earthquake, standing over her.

Triumphant.

His gaze left Alize and turned toward the Lo-sat. "So don't give me a reason to pull the trigger."

"Mr. Huggles didn't give you any new murder ideas?"

Rick's lip curled halfway up his face. "I'm already regretting this, Ten-trom. Follow me to the med bay. Don't try anything."

Binh limply made a faux salute.

Alize rolled away inside the armor, doing what she could to assume the fetal position between the armor's tendrils. Bringing her destroyed leg up was impossible, so she cradled the other. The position reminded her of some stretches she'd done in her athletic days. A lifetime ago.

As they passed under an overhead light, a glint from above caught Alize's attention. In the chaos and distraction, neither Rick nor Binh had detached the chitin from their spacesuit armor. But away from the Unspeakable's power and the moon, doing anything meaningful with the chitin might be impossible. If nothing else, she had something to study.

Alize inhaled. "Will I be awake during these experiments?"

Rick did a double-take before responding. "We can put you to sleep if you'd be more comfortable."

"No, I want to be awake. If it's alright, I want to study the Chamayna chitin we have."

Rick blinked hard as if he'd expected a more loaded question. "Fine."

Alize injected more weakness into her voice. "Thank you. Please don't destroy the chitin when you remove it from your suits. Both of you."

For an instant, Rick arched an eyebrow, then snapped it back. "If you're planning on carving yourself up with one of the jagged pieces of chitin and ending things, the Collective fleet won't catch us since we're minutes away from hyperspace."

He suspects something. Tread carefully. Alize winced. "I'm more likely to die from pain overload than to kill myself."

The hover-stretcher swerved to the right as they rounded a corner. "Just remain calm," Rick said. "You'll get treatment soon."

"Yeah," Binh added, "and try to stay alive so they can conduct horrific experiments on you."

"The armor, not the body." Acid flecked Rick's voice. "Don't make me toss you out an airlock."

"Well, in my few hours since you said I was hired, you never provided me with a task."

"Then your first task is to shut up," Rick said, still pushing the hover-stretcher.

Alize tuned out their banter. Had Binh found a home with Earthquake? *Is Binh the perfect Lo-sat to teach these Humans about tolerating and accepting other cultures?* Steeling herself, Alize exhaled. If her plan worked, she could get away, but not Binh.

FORTY-SEVEN

Aboard the designated civilian ship, *Dizhen*, Dusoi orbit, Xechas system, Collective fringe

DAYS OF HYPERSPACE travel, and Oze's condition stabilized. The thief's minor and imaginary wounds healed as well.

For all Oze's bluster about staying awake and studying the Chamayna chitin, she waffled through consciousness for days. No signs of struggle. No attempted escape. No attempted suicide. Sleep, eat, bot-assisted trips to the bathroom, and occasional re-arranging of the chitin left in her infirmary cell.

The base's doctor approached Rick, hovering nurse-bot in tow. Oze hadn't been in the unit long, but Rick was glad for her presence and even more thankful she hadn't joined any mutineers.

"Sir?" Her accent was flatter than most spacers and colonists.

Rick acknowledged her with a nod. "Dr. Windsong? What's the update?"

She cleared her throat and averted her gaze. "Sir, she's going to lose that leg. We need to amputate."

"Not surprised. You must have expected this."

"May I proceed with grafting her a prosthetic?" The doctor's eyes strayed to Rick's stump. Typical.

Rick grunted, eyes fixed on the two-way mirror, watching Oze sleep in her armored cocoon, thousands of wires converging from all sides. A team of engineers buzzed around her, glaring at clipboards and omni-tablets. "Did the engineers give you the go-ahead?"

Dr. Windsong tapped her omni-tablet. "No. They said they need a few more days to monitor how the armor interacts with the healing body."

Rick nodded slowly. "Well, if we know how it heals Arkoudae in battle, we can find a way to reverse its effects. Or at least stop healing mid-fight." He turned to Dr. Windsong. "In your estimation, will Oze die if we leave that leg there?"

"Lots of ruptured blood vessels. Catastrophic internal bleeding, which still hasn't healed. The armor's doing a better job keeping her alive than most of our tech could. If I don't graft a prosthetic, I at least need to amputate. Her body's diverting lots of resources to numbing her pain and attempting to heal something that can't be healed."

Rick arched an eyebrow. "Do you think the armor could repair her leg entirely, given enough time?"

"It's a mechanical painkiller, not a doctor. Seems to lack the capability. Maybe that's because Oze's Human, but I don't think so based on what I've seen."

Phantom pain tingled in Rick's shoulder. "Understood. We can't let Oze die. Proceed with the amputation. Need more nurse-bots?"

Dr. Windsong withdrew her omni-tablet and typed something. "No, I have enough. Will you clear the engineers out?"

"No. They'll keep working."

She grimaced. "I need a sterile environment to perform a surgery, sir, especially one so delicate. Too many people inside spread germs."

"Do you doubt the station's decontam spray? Everyone who goes in or out is sterilized and masked."

"Sir, I can't work with that kind of an audience."

"How long's the surgery? I can't set this project too far behind."

"A few hours. I'm sure the Leader will understand."

A lesser man would've scoffed. "I'll leave in one senior engineer and her assistant."

The doctor blew out a tight exhale. "It's better than the ten in there. Thank you."

"One more thing before I kick the team out..."

She clutched her omni-tablet to her chest. "Yes?"

"Does Oze seem coherent to you? In your estimation, has she snapped? Given up on life?"

"I-I'm not a psychologist."

"Guess."

"Yes. She seems like a shell. I don't have anything to compare it to, but the slimeball—"

"Watch it."

"Habit, sorry. The Lo-sat says she isn't acting like she was. Like she's a million miles away."

Rick nodded and pounded on the one-way mirror. "Sanchez, Pai. Stay. The rest of you, get some rest. Oze's getting surgery."

Rick sauntered toward his office. Amanda, seated at her desk, typed furiously on her omni-tablet. A chipped pair of stimbrew mugs sat in front of her.

She glanced from her tablet to Rick. "How's Oze?"

Rick eyed the cartoon squirrel painted on his mug; Amanda used these whenever she added a shot of whiskey in them. "Thanks. Stable." After a sip, he added, "I need to contact Monsieur Tecton."

"Something new to report?" Her arched eyebrow implied how much she knew Rick detested these calls.

He nodded. "I know how to beat the Arkouda. It's time we earned that promotion."

Amanda smirked like someone sneaking a shot at work in an Earth rodent mug. "Don't tease me with a planet."

Rick couldn't resist a smile. "We'll see, but don't get your hopes up."

"Alright, I'll start the connection. Need a minute to get ready in your office first?"

"No. Initiate."

Rick entered his office, grabbing the chair as rigid as him. His screen buzzed, signifying the decoding and encrypting process.

After a moment, the grainy visage of Jacques Tecton clarified, Earth's sunrise behind him.

"Good morning, Monsieur," Rick said. "I hope I didn't wake you."

Tecton ran a hand through his full head of hair, which nobody else in Earthquake was allowed to have. "Well, I can make time for the best commander I have."

He was baiting him, but Rick didn't engage. "You honor me, sir."

Tecton waved a dismissive hand and a cold smile crept across his aging face. "What've you learned about the armor? Found a weakness yet?"

"Bludgeoning and puncturing. The armor was designed to repel plasma bullets. We don't need to make better bullets or guns. We need different weaponry entirely."

"Oh?"

"Sir, their armor is effectively bulletproof. Their ship hulls, too. But if we can utilize heavy or sharp enough objects as projectiles, we can collapse the armor in on itself."

On the other side of the screen, Tecton leaned back in his chair and rubbed his goatee. "And for their ships?"

"Sir, if we could upgrade the magnets on standard scrapper ships, they could launch ferrous asteroids through space."

Tecton leaned forward, eyes ravenous. "Asteroid catapults?"

"Sir, yes sir." Rick's turn to smile. "And barring that, Earth's history tells us what else we can do. In one of the bigger international wars in Earth's history, aircraft pilots would ram their planes into the enemy after running out of ammunition. If we can remotely pilot civilian ships, we can crash them into Collective fighting ships."

Tecton, practically salivating, nodded. "And how'd you discover this?"

Rick's smile faded, and his mouth dried. "Blunt force and bludgeoning have been on my mind recently."

"The creature?"

"Rather not discuss it, sir. No tactical bearing on my report."

Tecton waved a dismissive hand. "Be that way. So what is to become of this girl?"

"Sir, she's an archaeology student. Collective politics prevent her from a PhD, as far as I understand. I thought you'd want her on your team. She could find more archaeological sites. Maybe lead an expedition. But she might also be too damaged from what we experienced. She's refused the therapist I've sent. I requisitioned another."

"Don't bother. Put a bullet between her eyes or toss her out an airlock if she won't join."

Rick clenched his fists below the camera's view. "Sir?"

"You heard me, Crith. She knows too much. If she's unhinged, you're doing her a favor."

"Understood. I'll upload the engineers' latest report on their specific findings in the armor, and I'll take care of Oze."

Tecton's smirk returned. "And there is, of course, the matter of your promised promotion. Don't think I forgot. Have you selected a planet?"

Unclenching his fists, Rick nodded. "There's a planet on the frontier with an unusually high magnetic field. It's so overpowering that the Arkouda and Lo-sat never bothered to colonize it. Home to an impoverished human population. I want to set up a homeless shelter there, and use that as a base of operations."

"Done. Upload the coordinates and forward them to my assistant."

"Thank you, sir."

FORTY-EIGHT

In armor resting on a bed. On a space station, maybe on an asteroid. Earth knows where.

ALIZE ENJOYED A rare moment of privacy in the bathroom. She didn't have a plan for when the doctor discovered Fil's armor filtered Alize's bodily waste on its own—she imagined Fil cracking a joke about disconnecting the waste tube and spraying Binh. She hadn't needed to actually use the bathroom since the armor grafted itself to her. The armor was an extension of herself now, a reality both chilling and reassuring, as if Fil were somehow still with her.

Alize glanced at her lifeless leg. Jagged bones poked at the edge of the surface, a loose collection of tendons and flesh struggling to hold anything together. Surgery would be soon, and she'd get some kind of prosthetic. Losing a limb on its own didn't bother her as much as the prospect of having one more commonality with Rick Crith. The way the engineers treated her, Earthquake couldn't see her as valuable. She'd be discarded with the garbage once they'd figured out the armor's secrets. Once she was healthy enough to stand, they'd perform all manner of tests on her to see what could destroy the armor.

Whatever they came up with would eventually kill her. Only a matter of time. And without Fil's helmet or even the ability to reach outside of the armor, she couldn't call the fleet. She'd have to die. And if Rick's team knew what they were doing, they would've disabled that function already. So there was no way out except one, which might not work anyway.

Alize balanced against the wall with her hands and let the pieces of chitin she smuggled fall out of her armor, which she rearranged on the floor with her good foot, while her hands pressed against either side of the tiny bathroom wall. She'd soon have enough to write a glyph. Only one more trip to the bathroom with the chitin contraband.

A knock came at the door. "Alize?" Dr. Windsong was kind to Alize and cold to Binh, which was about as much as she could expect from Earthquake's rank-and-file. Only Amanda treated Binh with any kindness, but when pressed, she'd admit Arkoudae earned her primary hatred.

Dr. Windsong knocked again. Harder. "Are you alright?"

"I'm ready," Alize said. She righted herself and opened the door to find Binh and Rick, standing behind an apologetic Dr. Windsong.

Rick glared at her. "Care to share what's going on?"

"I-I went to the bathroom."

Binh lowered his eyeridges and shook his head. "Alize... I'm sorry. Lefty asked if I smelled anything off with you. I mentioned how I didn't think you really used the bathroom since I couldn't smell anything when I visited."

Rick glowered. "Do I need to repeat my question?"

Alize's gaze flitted between the three of them. Dr. Windsong stared at the floor, Binh's eyeridges drooped, and Rick's eyes held the beginnings of an apology. A lump formed in Alize's throat.

"It's my only time alone. I've lost everything except my sense of self. Can't I at least have some solitude?"

Rick's expression cooled. "I would've given it if you asked."

Dr. Windsong met Alize's gaze and nodded with a sheepish smile. Binh closed his eyes and shook his head slightly.

Alize stiffened. "I didn't know if you'd deliver on that promise. I've had no privacy."

"Fair enough," Rick said. "Prep her for surgery, Dr. Windsong." He kept a stern eye on Alize. "Do you want a prosthetic leg?"

"I'll take it."

———

Alize inhaled the anesthetics and slowly drifted into darkness. The one place she knew better now after her life had fallen to pieces.

———

When she emerged from her stupor, the armor still cocooned her, and her leg tingled. No numb burning. Glancing down, she took stock of her new limb. It would take some getting used to, but it felt sturdy and looked natural.

Alize poked her head out of the armor. Binh slumped in a too-small chair, snoring.

"Binh?" Alize barely recognized her own voice, scratchy as the buffpaper she cleaned bots with.

The sleeping Lo-sat harrumphed and lifted an eyelid.

"How long was I out?"

Binh straightened and stretched. "A while. Almost a full day. I kept an engineer from peeping at your nasty bits while you were unconscious."

"But I'm in the armor."

"I meant your face."

"Really? You sold me out and still mock me?"

"Look. Alize. I have to survive. That means watching out for me. I could've left you for dead. I could've lied to Lefty and you'd have wound up with a bullet between your teeth."

"Where did Rick put my chitin?"

"I didn't let anyone touch it." He lowered an eyeridge. "Why?"

"Can I ask a favor?" Alize asked weakly.

"What, you need water or something?"

Alize kept her tone flat. "Would you please bring in the scraps of chitin from the bathroom? I want to see them, and I can't move much."

He coiled his tail. "Why?"

She worked to keep her breathing even, deter-mined not to give off any nervous sweat that might clue off her scent to him. "Please? I'm afraid to go in the bathroom now. Can you let me study them?"

"So you'll work for Earthquake?"

Alize sighed. "Binh, please, just bring them in here."

"Fine, fine, fine," he groaned. "But I didn't hear a 'thanks for waiting for me to wake up, Binh.'"

"It evens out with your most recent betrayal."

"I accept the arithmetic." Binh returned from the bathroom, holding the various carapace plates in his claws and tail.

"That's all I ask. Thanks for bringing these out. Can you arrange them a certain way, if I tell you what goes where?"

His marbled yellow eye bore into her. "What's your game, Pinky?"

"Asking for a favor. You feel bad for me. Let me exploit your guilt."

"Heh. You don't stink as bad today."

"Thanks. That's the sweetest thing I've heard you say."

"Don't push it, hairball."

"Do you know if the engineers removed anything from the armor? Fil had some personal stuff in here I want to return to her family."

"No, these *ke-noks* won't admit it, but they're terrified of accidentally calling the Collective fleet. Lefty's ordered one evac drill each day, just in case. And if they mess with the armor's internal grav harness, you'll get smushed good."

"So that's why it's taken them so long?" Alize would've eaten a Galsan worm if it would open any compartments. She couldn't accomplish much with the stolen Blekk food from the *Takel* or Fil's rifle, but the remnants of clothing Fil found before she died were a different story. "And you're positive they haven't opened any of the compartments?"

"What, Frostbutt stash porn in there or something? If they did, nobody's bragged about it. And they would've opened them all, hoping to swipe Sergeant Hairy's rifle."

Alize resisted the urge to wink. "Thanks, now get to work."

Over the next few minutes, Binh dutifully followed Alize's directions to the letter, spreading out the chitin across the floor, crafting shapes. When his back turned, Alize stretched and swiveled her prosthetic leg, getting a feel for it. More effort was placed in getting the color correct than the cybernetics.

When she told him he'd finished, she instructed him to arrange the remaining scraps on the outside of her armor.

"What kind of freaky ritual is this?"

Alize smiled. "Doesn't matter. You're almost done. Can you help me sit up so I can see the whole thing?"

Binh hoisted her. "Oomph. Is this payback for the nicknames?"

"No. I honestly pity you. You're afraid to make friends, so you use childish insults to keep people away." Alize scanned the glyphs he'd made under her instruction. Only one chance to get this right. Alize shimmied to the edge of the infirmary bed and shot him a wink. "I forgive you. I hope you find a way to escape Earthquake, too."

"Huh?"

Pushing off the bed with her new leg, Alize belly-flopped onto the makeshift glyphs.

Thwip.

A warm swirl of impossible colors surrounded Alize, and the gaze of infinite eyes enveloped her. But Alize understood the process this time and exactly where she needed to go.

FORTY-NINE

Home.

THWIP.

Shattered glass rained around her, along with a thud near her feet. Alize's vision clarified, and her body's throbbing rattled her bones. Glass shards scraped her face, a few embedding in her cheek. Bloodied and panting, she rolled onto the armor's back and gazed up at the ceiling. Sweat beaded on her forehead. If she had made a mistake, Rick would kill her. Blinking twice, she confirmed what she really saw.

The museum's ceiling, directly over her favorite exhibit.

An alarm blared, penetrating the ringing in her ears. Alize had heard the alarm many times in testing but never for real. She was the first person to break into the museum in Hen4 city, the first person to disturb the Chamayna engraved tablet, protected by glass no longer. She rolled to her side and saw the crumbled tablet, cleft in half from her appearance. In between gasps for air, she allowed herself one chuckle. Her "superweapon" translation wasn't exactly correct, but she got the "transmit" glyph right.

"Oze?" one syllable.

It had to be her? Alize craned her neck. "Dr. Dikaio?"

"What in the Nightmare is going on?"

Alize chuckled and winced as the laugh rearranged the glass shrapnel in her face. "Get me a stimbrew, and I'll tell you on the way to the hospital."

One week later...

Alize emerged from an autocab into the bright street. Phantom pains in her prosthetic leg still throbbed, and the physical therapy left her incredibly sore, but the Collective's new mechanized leg implants allowed her to walk to the condominium, encased in a thin layer of decorative ice. Through a shiver, she sent a ping to the door mech.

Within seconds, the door opened, revealing an aging Arkouda woman.

Glancing upward and holding her elbow, Alize stammered a greeting to Fil's mother.

The woman lowered her monocle, revealing matted fur in long streaks from her eyes. "We talked about this, Alize. You can call me 'Mom,' and nothing else." She pulled in Alize for a tight hug, enveloping her in darkness from the all-encompassing fur.

After the longest hug she'd had since Pops' diagnosis, Alize followed Mrs. Kaluteros through their frozen condo. She tossed Alize a hanging sweater— one of Fil's from when she was a cub.

"You remembered..." Alize pulled the sweater over her, and the chill dissipated. They passed pictures hanging over Alize's head of younger versions of Fil and her sister: Fil in her armor for the first time, her sister's graduation, and the sisters in the hospital together.

In the sitting room, Fil's sister, Cilla, sat on a wide couch, bouncing a cub on her knee, bearing a tired smile. "Good to see you, Leeze. How's your dad?"

Mrs. Kaluteros waved a paw in front of her throat and shook her head vigorously.

"Oh, sorry," Cilla said. "Hey, Gno, say hi to Auntie Fil's friend."

The cub, only a few hairs shorter than Alize, waved heartily. "Look at Granny's new toy!"

"It's not a toy," Cilla hissed. "Mom, I swear I didn't let him touch it."

A wide grin creased Mrs. Kaluteros' snout. "It's alright. He can play with it." She went to the wall and grabbed a hanging decoration. It was a badge meant for adorning a jumpsuit: a black pawprint with a white heart in the center. "It's not like I'll wear it anywhere. I don't want strangers congratulating me on my dead daughter."

Alize's eyes widened. "Does that mean the Collective military recognized Fil's death?"

"Yes," Mrs. Kaluteros sighed, handing the badge to Gno. "I have the 'honor' of giving a child to the Collective military brave enough to lay down her life in the line of duty."

Alize stared at it, while Gno pretended it was an eyepatch. "So, the Collective accepted my testimony?"

Cilla harrumphed. "They left out the Chamayna demigod monster who ate your ex-boyfriend."

Not this again.

Mrs. Kaluteros bared her teeth at Cilla. "She's grieving, too. We aren't the only ones who lost someone." Her tone softened. "Alize, dear. There are some strange things locked away in this galaxy. I don't know what you saw down there, and I'm honestly scared to. Fil died protecting you. On an adventure. She wanted to see the stars. And I'm sure she kicked some tail in the process."

"Mom!" Cilla pulled Gno close to her and covered his ears. "Language."

Alize scratched the back of her head. "I know the story does sound incredible... I'm surprised the Collective accepted it."

"Officially?" Mrs. Kaluteros said. "No. Officially, it never happened. Officially, she died because of a cave-in. They kept the part where she died saving you, at least. That makes her a hero."

Cilla nodded. "They let us hear her armor's recording. We had to sign a mountain of paperwork. If we discuss it with anyone else, we're looking at prison."

Gno eyed his mother. "Why would you look at a prison?"

Alize nodded. "That's gentler than the threat I got."

Mrs. Kaluteros placed a paw on Alize's shoulder. "Fil was part of a breakthrough archaeological expedition, and the moon's location is classified until the Collective government can fully explore and document it. She died saving a Prov—" she cleared her throat, "—friend. Any mom would be proud."

Cilla sighed. "They won't decommission her armor, though. After they let us hear the last records, they confiscated it. They refused a military cremation-alternative but gave us money to have a private one."

"I'm so—"

Mrs. Kaluteros put a finger in front of Alize's lips. "Fil believed in you. If your places had been switched, you would've done the same. Don't you dare apologize. She died with purpose. I can't hug a memory, but I can be proud of my daughter."

Alize wrapped Mrs. Kaluteros in a hug, and the four of them hailed an autocab to take some of Fil's possessions to the crematorium. Fil wouldn't get the memorial she was legally owed, but she'd get one she deserved.

One month later...

Sitting in the university library, Alize received a notification on her omni-tablet. The dissertation approval board had sent her a message. Eyes wide, she read a message she hadn't seen before.

Acceptance.

The clothing Filenada found was confirmed, and the armor's recordings were verified as authentic. Alize remained the only Human in her classes, but professors called on her. Her classmates listened to her, and most of them asked her questions about archaeology, not if she'd turned anyone in from Earthquake. All for the best since Alize remained blissfully ignorant about the conflict. Alize returned her humble gratitude to the board's message and scanned the library.

A pair of Lo-sats lounged at a nearby table, books open and eyes lightyears away. Certainly too much of an audience for Alize's happy dance. Fil would've done the happy dance with her. Pops too, despite his limited mobility before he died. Fil would also have recommended dancing in the middle of the library, regardless of the audience. Instead, Alize plastered a giant smile and strolled past the library patrons. She could happy-dance after arriving home. She had to go to her new job at the museum, anyway. No jumpsuit or stimbrew required for entry.

Three years later...

A Human father and young daughter sat on the new bench in the museum, facing the newest exhibit. Alize spied them and walked over, heels clicking as she moved. She knelt in front of a little girl, wonder and hope pouring from her.

"Welcome to the Chamayna exhibit, young explorer," Dr. Alize Oze said. "What'd you come to learn about today?"

The girl, sporting pigtails and mismatched adult and baby teeth smiled up at her. "My daddy told me these Chamayna looked like bugs. And that there's a dossint—"

"Docent, honey..." The kind encouragement in his smile resembled Pops'.

"Right," the girl said, "docent. Well, daddy said a lady here saw a Chamayna monster."

Alize extended her hand. "I don't know about a monster. Would you like to see what the Chamayna drew and colored in their buildings? They made pictures of all kinds of animals."

The girl glanced over her shoulder at her father, who nodded. When father and daughter stood to follow Alize to the Chamayna artwork, they revealed a plaque on the bench, obscured since they sat.

Smile glued to her face, Alize stole a glance at the bench's plaque.

In loving memory of Chet Oze, the museum's unofficial tour guide. A man of unspeakable love and character.

THE END

Alize may have gotten her happily ever after, but there's a big galaxy out there and Rick is just getting started. Look for the second book in the series in Fall of 2023.

—Several professional scientists offered guidance. Any scientific mistakes are the author's, not theirs.

BOOK CLUB QUESTIONS:

_____

1. There are several themes in *Mummified Moon*, such as prejudice, loss, inadequacy, and friend-ship. Which were you most drawn to and why?

2. Both Alize and Rick have a "list" of people whose deaths they hold themselves accountable for. Where do you see the differences between their rationale for keeping these lists?

3. Rick's backstory behind his injury is hinted at. What's your theory about what happened?

4. How would the story have changed if Fil and Alize's roles were switched?

5. Why do you think Rick spared Binh instead of killing him?

6. Do you think the Chamayna still exist somewhere, hidden? Explain why or why not.

7. Where do you see the symmetry and dissonance in Alize's father and Rick regarding other species and Humans' place in the galaxy?

8. Would you have given the book a different title? Explain your reasoning.

9. Will the Unspeakable continue to seek more violence or will it remain confined to the moon? Explain your reasoning.

10. Which character felt the most real to you and why?

ΛUTHOR BIO

PC IS A science fiction and fantasy author from the Great Lakes region of the USA. Sci fi has been a deep love for PC, growing up on Star Wars movies and reading the Animorphs series. The Star Wars novels along with classic sci fi greats like Asimov and Le Guin are constant sources of inspiration and wonder. PC loves taking his daughters to the zoo and the occasional sushi or taco date with his wife. With the help of friendly scientists and science documentaries, PC tries to blend what is just on the technological horizon with the impossible in his stories. PC is a NaNoWriMo winner and an active critiquer in the Scribophile community.

Be sure to follow PC on Twitter for updates. @ nottingham_pc

Visit PC's website at authorpcnottingham.com and sign up for the newsletter.

MORE BOOKS FROM
4 HORSEMEN PUBLICATIONS

SCIFI

BRANDON HILL &
TERENCE PEGASUS
Between the Devil and the Dark
Wrath & Redemption

C.K. WESTBROOK
The Shooting
The Collision

KYLE SORRELL
Munderworld

NICK SAVAGE
Us of Legendary Gods

PC NOTTINGHAM
Mummified Moon

T.S. SIMONS
Antipodes
The Liminal Space
Ouroboros
Caim
Sessrúmnir
The 45th Parallel

TY CARLSON
The Bench
The Favorite
The Shadowless

DISCOVER MORE AT
4HORSEMENPUBLICATIONS.COM

Lightning Source UK Ltd.
Milton Keynes UK
UKHW011956030123
414791UK00007B/159

9 798823 200622